Serendipity's
Claw

By
Annie White

Front cover by Shiv Grewal

For Olivia Rose and Eloise Jasmin

CONTENTS

PROLOGUE

One magical claw. Four friends.
One adventure of a lifetime.

1

The Black Box

"What is all the commotion?" Professor Inchenstein's bright white lab coat flapped out like a cape as he whizzed past the science benches. His sparkling eyes that were protected behind thick plastic goggles peered down at the class inquisitively.

"She said that the dinosaurs did not exist and that they were made up by the Devil!" Raj was outraged and flushed red in the face as he pointed towards Amber.

"Ooooh a theological debate! I love a good debate! They don't usually happen in the junior classes, but I welcome all debates. Yes, yes nothing like a good debate!" The Professor responded cheerily.

He then bounded towards Amber and crouched down in front of the bench where she sat, so she couldn't help but look him straight in the eye. Amber glanced at the Professor and thought that he was by far the strangest looking man she had ever seen. His head was surrounded by a fluffy white cloud of hair, so big that it bounced up and down as he leapt about the classroom. He had kind pale blue eyes, whose vision was often obscured by wiry eyebrows that curled forward like a row of spiders' legs performing the can-can. He was always dressed very smart, with a tweed jacket, white shirt and a brightly coloured bow tie. He held Amber's gaze through his smudged plastic goggles, which pressed down around his head, causing his unruly mop to resemble an overgrown mushroom. A heavy silence fell across the science lab; no one had ever questioned the existence of the dinosaurs before.

Professor Inchenstein tilted his head to the left and looked harder at the freckled faced girl. He then removed his goggles stood up and said at last, "We have not met! There is a new face among us. What is the name of this fine young lady who has brought such an intriguing debate to my science lab on the first day of school?" He beamed at her with pleasure.

"My name is Amber sir, and I am from Texas." She replied in her heavy, mid-western accent.

Professor Inchenstein continued to beam at the new girl encouragingly.

"My father told me that the dinosaurs were invented by the devil." Amber glanced around the classroom apologetically. "I did not mean to cause a disturbance."

"Oh, how marvellous! An amber haired Amber, who does not believe in the dinosaurs!"

Professor Inchenstein swung round theatrically to face the rest of the class. His cheerful expression had suddenly faded, and he dropped his voice to a whisper. "Children," he said slowly, showing his yellow stained teeth "should we show her the black box?"

An electric silence filled the room. The children all sat bolt upright with excitement. Amber shuffled nervously on her stool. "Well, Amber," continued the Professor, "can you keep a secret?"

Amber found herself nodding despite the butterflies flapping around in her stomach.

ΔΔΔ

It was indeed, as Professor Inchenstein mentioned, the first day of school. The summer holidays had ended, and new adventures were about to take place. Pembridge Hall was bursting with excited chatter as year six eagerly caught up with one another. The privileged children compared their different apps on their iPads, new ponies and yachting holidays, for this was indeed Pembridge Hall; an exclusive, private school situated in the trendy location of Notting Hill, London. The school used to pride itself on recruiting the most intelligent pupils for miles around, but since the recession, money spoke louder than brains, and the school was slowly filling with more and more spoilt, dim, offspring from the local elite. The energy in the room concentrated around one particular desk belonging to a girl who had bright orange, frizzy hair and milky white skin the colour of the moon.

"So, you are the new girl?" Alison, the most popular girl in the year demanded.

"Yes, my name is Amber."

"How many yachts does your dad have?" Alison enquired flicking her long blond hair.

"Oh, err, none. I am from Waco, Texas. You don't really need yachts there."

Some of the pupils looked confused so Amber explained, "I am from America."

"Nobody needs yachts, it is just something we all have." Alison said and rolled her eyes at Amber.

"Wow, Texas, is your dad a cowboy?" Arthur interrupted.

Arthur was the class' mischief maker; he was constantly getting into trouble, but his angelic appearance often rescued him from any severe punishment. His accomplice, Rocky, on the other hand was less of a charmer and more the class bully.

"Of course, her dad is not a cowboy!" Rocky smirked at Amber unkindly, "You would have to be cool to have a dad as a cowboy and you are clearly not cool!"

Amber blushed uncontrollably and stared down at her desk, hoping that the children would leave her alone.

Arthur pushed his blond floppy hair out of his eyes and asked again, "So what does your dad actually do?"

"He is a preacher." Amber replied quietly.

Someone snorted loudly in the group.

"What like a priest?" Arthur asked.

"Yes, kind of." Amber replied, finally starting to feel more confident. "We are Evangelists from the Columbus Mega Church. My father had a parish of ten thousand worshippers."

"My dad plays cricket for England; do you play cricket in Texas?" Arthur enquired, but before Amber could answer Arthur, Rocky fired another question.

"Does that mean you are religious or something?"

"We are all the children of God." Amber responded, smiling nervously at her interrogators.

This religious dogma did not go down well with her new classmates as they quickly lost interest and began to move away from the desk, sniggering nastily amongst themselves.

Before the crowd fully dispersed, Alison said loudly, "I suppose I should name you."

Confused, Amber replied, "But I have a"

Alison lifted her hand to silence Amber as she looked her up and down thinking of an appropriate name. "I've got it" and she turned to her friends triumphantly.

Everyone was waiting to know what Alison would come up with. Even Amber was curious to know her new name.

"Chubby cheeks!" Alison shouted so as to make sure everyone heard her.

Rocky roared with laughter and slapped Arthur on the back.

Amber tried to ignore the giggles around her and she sub-consciously placed her hands over her cheeks and wondered if they were in fact, chubby. She quickly moved her hands from her cheeks to her ears and tried to block out the tormenting cries of "chubby cheeks" when all of a sudden, as if her prayers were answered, silence crushed the wicked taunts; Bunny Bristlepott had entered the room. Amber turned towards the door to see what was going on and gasped out-loud in horror. Bunny Bristlepott, the class' teacher was so notoriously terrifying that she was classified as scary teacher number one. She was an incredibly tall woman and her towering appearance was accentuated by her ginormous bosoms that heaved up and down with her every breath. Her face was always screwed up in some sort of bitter rage as if she was constantly munching on a peeled lemon. She wore the same long brown pinafore, day after day, which made her look like a paralyzed log bobbing upright in a forgotten swamp. Bunny's hair was an abundant mass of brown curls and her large dark eyes were so big they were the size of golf balls. Her wooden like appearance gave her the nickname Log Head, but Bunny did not care; she had a heart of steel. Bunny stood glaring at her new class with disdain. Without saying a single word, she slithered to the front of the classroom and read the register in a monotonous tone.

Amber looked around the room in fright, even the two boys that were so mean and naughty to her a minute ago were sitting quietly at the back of the room as good as gold.

"BRADSHAW!"

Amber jumped and faced the front of the room like a scared rabbit.

"Yes!" she replied quickly.

The class gasped, but before Amber could work out what she had done wrong a shadow the colour of death loomed over her desk.

"I imagine from your modern accent that you are not from around here, but I would like to entreat you, Miss Bradshaw, that manners and respect are the most basic of requirements that all pupils at this prestigious school are expected to maintain."

Amber stared dumbfounded at her teacher who was scolding her so vehemently.

"I imagine in the new world that colloquial responses to the register are widespread, but I can assure you young lady, that in the old world, the world of heritage and wisdom, colloquialism will not triumph!"

Amber was completely lost and close to tears; she had no idea what she had done wrong or how to rectify it. She looked around for help, but all eyes were firmly fixed to the floor. Amber felt her throat close up with fear and she glanced upwards, wondering what was going to happened next.

"A HUNDRED LINES!" Bunny hollered at her prey.

Another unified gasp scuttled around the room. Bunny glared ferociously at the frightened pupils until silence filled the room again. She then slowly left Amber, who at this point was a nervous wreck and continued to read out the register, to which the pupils of year six replied, in an extremely clear and respectful manner, "Yes Mrs Bristlepott." With the register finally over, year six obediently got in line ready for assembly. Alison and her gang pushed their way to the front of the queue whilst Amber, head down walked to the back. Amber clasped her hands together to stop them shaking and wondered how she was going to get through the day. She longed for her hometown.

Just as she closed her eyes and began to pray she heard a voice in front of her, "Hi, I am Serendipity." A girl with long, brown hair and green eyes smiled broadly at Amber, flashing her metal covered teeth.

"I, I," Amber stuttered, not sure what name she was supposed to call herself.

"You are Amber, yes I heard" Serendipity continued to smile.

Amber nodded and felt the weight on her chest lighten slightly.

"Don't take any notice of Alison and her snooty crowd, they always pick on the new kids."

"Did she give you a name too?"

"Oh, sure I was easy!" Serendipity gave Amber a big grin and said, "I am Metal Mouth!"

"Doesn't it bother you?"

Serendipity shrugged. The two girls followed the rest of the class down the long, echoing corridors until they reached the main hall where the entire school gathered for the morning assembly. Year six shuffled in at the back of the grand hall and sat down on the wooden floor, waiting for the Head Teacher, Mrs. Bromelow to appear.

"Are you really called Serendipity?" Amber asked shyly, not wanting to offend her new friend.

"I know, crazy name! My brother is called Flo, F-L-O!"

"Yikes!"

"The media says my parents were high when they named us."

"What does that mean, being high, and who is the media?"

"When I asked my mum, she told me it means that they were very happy."

"But who said it?"

"You know The Sun, The Mirror, all the tabloids." Amber looked back confused. "The newspapers! Der."

"Why do they write about your parents?" Amber asked bemused.

"SHHH! Bunny Bristlepott hissed a glare towards the new girl and her companion chatting.

Serendipity lowered her voice and replied cautiously, "Oh, you don't know, I forgot you are not from here! My dad used to be in the rock band, The Smoking Nettles." Serendipity waited for the usual reaction of "Wow, how cool!" but Amber had never heard of The Smoking Nettles and to Serendipity's dismay the usual, impressed response never appeared.

"You don't know who The Smoking Nettles are?" Serendipity asked in despair, rolling her eyes at Amber.

"Shhhhhh!" Another Log Head glare attacked them.

"I am from Texas, and I have been brought up in a very religious house, the only rocks I know are the ones in the cliffs and the only nettles I know are the ones in the ground!" Amber whispered.

"You are kidding?"

Amber shook her head.

"OK but tell me you have heard of The Sequins?"

Amber shook her head.

"Chloé Davine? Oh, what about Stardust?"

Amber, her cheeks growing redder shook her head again.

Serendipity, seeing her new friend was feeling embarrassed decided to stop the questions and said instead, "Don't worry, you can come back to my place and we will watch YouTube and listen to music, every kind of music there is!" Serendipity flashed Amber her braces once again and they finally started to pay attention to Mrs. Bromelow, who was talking with great gusto about the importance of sharing.

Mrs. Bromelow was a rather unusual looking woman; she had long, thick, auburn hair that was swirled and curled in an elaborate twist. Keeping the flaming keratin coated locks in place was a mixture of flamboyant jewelled clips, and to finish the effect was a pink polyester Dahlia Mary's Jomanda, positioned right on the top of her head. Her fingers were weighed down with sparkling glass, which would often shed prisms of light across the pupils' expectant faces as they reflected the sun's rays beaming through the four-meter giant windows. Amber looked at Mrs. Bromelow with fascination as she walked confidently back and forth like a proud lioness, her silk, paisley printed dress floating harmoniously around her limbs: Amber had never seen anyone like her. Amber listened to the head teacher attentively forcing the faces of Alison, Rocky, Arthur and Mrs Bristlepott to the back of her mind.

ΔΔΔ

Later in the afternoon year six sat themselves behind the big wooden benches in Pembridge Hall's finest science lab. The school had a fantastic reputation when it came to the sciences, especially earth sciences. The science teacher, Professor Inchenstein, was notorious for his experimental teaching methods, but he achieved remarkable results and was utterly adored by all the pupils. He was old, crazy and loved the dinosaurs with a raging passion that earned him the nickname Doctor Dino.

"You are going to love Doctor Dino" Serendipity said smiling at Amber as she perched herself on the wooden stool.

"Oh gee, I don't know much about science – my father says it is the devil's work."

"How can science be the work of the devil?" Serendipity replied in surprise.

"I am not sure exactly, but my father definitely thinks the devil is involved.

"How very strange! Have you asked him why?"

Amber thought for a moment and then replied, "He is not a fan of questions."

Serendipity raised her eyebrow sceptically.

"I guess it is a little odd but back in Texas I was not allowed to attend science lessons."

"But why?"

"To stay away from the Devil's work of course."

"Then why did your dad choose this school? It is renowned for science."

"Well, we came to London because my grandma Rose is sick. You see my mother is English and her mother lives here in Notting Hill, just down the road. We came here so my mother could look after her."

"Oh, I am sorry to hear about your granny."

"It's OK, it is her time to be close to God." Amber paused looking down at her hands, "Anyway this is the nearest school to grandma Rose's house and it is the most religious. My father said just to concentrate on my religious studies and not pay any attention during science lessons!"

"That seems very strange."

Amber shrugged her shoulders in response, she'd never questioned her father before, nobody did. The girls' conversation was brought to a halt by one of the boys shouting from the back of the classroom.

"Oi Raj!" Rocky shouted. "Oi, lend us your tea-towel mate! Arthur spilled some water!"

The class roared with laughter. Raj blushed a strong crimson and touched his turban uncomfortably. He tried to ignore them, but it got to him, every time.

Amber asked Serendipity who Raj was and why everyone was laughing at him. Serendipity pointed towards an Indian boy at the front of the classroom who was wearing a turban.

"But what is so funny?" Amber asked again.

"What do you need it for anyway?" Rocky shouted.

"Maybe he is cold!" Arthur suggested, and the class laughed some more.

The jibes continued and so did the laughter. Raj stared down at the scratches on the wooden desk and tried to block out the noise behind him. Luckily for Raj the torment did not last too long as in waltzed the famous Doctor Dino. "Good morning fine specimens!" roared Professor Inchenstein as he slid into the classroom.

"Good morning Professor!" the children chanted with delight at seeing their favourite teacher.

The teasing had stopped. The lesson had begun.

"How were the summer holidays? Full of adventures and discoveries? Full of pimples and pulling of pony tails?" The Professor did not give his class any time to answer, but raced down the middle of the classroom with the wooden benches on either side, skidded to a halt, raised his arms dramatically in the air then swooped them down to cover his eyes and asked, "Who saw a dinosaur fossil over the summer holidays?" He paused and said, "Please, please, for there was once water on Mars, please let there be some hands raised!" He slowly took his hands away from his face and cautiously opened one eye, peering hesitantly around the classroom. "One, two, three four! Only four! Well I suppose four is better than three and two and one and none!"

The class was oozing with excitement and giggles. "Raj, tell the class what fine specimen of a fossil you laid your lucky eyes on!"

Raj came to life in the science lab; he pushed the bullies to the back of his mind and escaped into Doctor Dino's magnificent world of the dinosaurs and other oddities.

"I saw a Diplodocus, an Iguanodon, a Tyrannosaurus, an Allosaurus and a Triceratops." Raj answered smiling.

Professor Inchenstein danced around striking an odd pose with every dinosaur name mentioned, making his pupils laugh with joy.

"And where might I ask did you see these huge and wonderful bones?"

"In the Natural History Museum of course!" Raj replied with amusement.

"Yes yes, you are quite right Raj, there are not many places you can go nowadays to see the dinosaurs!" The lesson carried on like an academic roller coaster, and to all intents and purposes it seemed like a typical first day back at school. But the children had no idea that Professor Inchenstein would pick today to show a new student the black box, and their teacher had no idea that in doing so, he would change their lives forever. Year six would use any reason they could think of to get their teacher to open the black box, and an unbelieving Texan was as good an excuse as any.

"Show her! Show her! Show her!" chanted the class in a deafening din that became more and more wild. "Show her the black box! Show her the black box!" The chanting was now so frantic that Amber had to put her hands over her ears. She had never seen children behave like this! Her palms were sweating as the turmoil around her rose into an unbearable uproar and then Amber glanced at Serendipity for support, "Don't worry Amber, just wait and see!"

There was a rustling in the science cupboard, then slowly the door opened and one by one, three old fingers belonging to the Professor appeared on the cupboard door. As they all waited for the fourth finger, Alison screamed with anticipation, then, suddenly a horrific black claw came around the door. It was 7cm long, dark and shiny, like polished ebony. Professor Inchenstein then flung himself from the cupboard and ran around the classroom scaring all of the children, pretending to be a dinosaur. The children squealed and screamed, and Amber looked absolutely horrified.

"Yikes! What on earth is that?" she asked Serendipity with anxiety.

"That, my dear little red headed friend is a claw, from none other than one of the biggest beasts that ever existed on this planet!" The Professor was out of breath; all the galloping had taken its toll, (he was 65 after all).

"Who is the owner of this wondrous claw?" he bellowed, raising the claw above him in triumph.

The class screamed back; "Tyrannosaurus Rex!"

Amber looked at her teacher, totally shocked and flummoxed; she had never seen a teacher, dance or run around pretending to be a dinosaur and she had never seen a claw so big it was the size of her hand. She was absolutely flabbergasted.

"Where did you get it from Professor?" Arthur asked.

Arthur's question caused Professor Inchenstein to have a sudden flashback and the heavy weight that he carried around in his chest seemed to groan inside him. He managed to take a deep breath and force a wonky grin before any of his pupils noticed. Professor Inchenstein was just about to find a plausible story to explain the whereabouts of his claw when the bell rang informing them all that the fun was over, and it was time to go home. Everyone sighed with disappointment.

"Don't worry ladies and gentlemen, the wonderful world of the dinosaurs will be back next Monday at 3pm, until then my friends, get on with all those other inspiring subjects like "Math" he pulled a face "and French" he pulled another face and the class giggled once more. The Professor then rushed back into his cupboard, took the heavy wooden black box from the shelf and plonked it on the bench in front of Amber. The lid fell open with an almighty thud and the Professor placed his black claw inside on the soft velvet lining. Using both hands, he heaved the lid shut causing its metal hinges to creak with displeasure. The box securely closed he gazed sternly through his eyebrows at the girls and said, "Now remember children, no one, under any circumstance is to open this box."

Year six nodded obediently at their teacher and then hurried out of the science lab scraping the wooden stools in a clamour as they left. Raj went into the back room to tidy the test tubes as he always did after science lessons, while the rest of the pupils went home to their families. The only children that remained in the deserted science lab were Serendipity, Amber and Arthur. Arthur walked towards the two girls, leaned on the bench where Amber was sitting, propped his head on his hand and asked her, "Do you believe in the dinosaurs now?"

"Oh, gee I don't know. I am so confused." She looked across at Arthur, "Was that really a claw from Tyrannoporpis Rexer?"

"Tyrannosaurus Rex, you dummy! I don't know. I think if it was real it would be in a museum." Arthur pondered for a moment and then continued, "Even if it is fake, I definitely believe in the dinosaurs, there is so much proof!" Arthur stood up straight and looked in the direction of the cupboard door then back at Amber, his hazelnut eyes sparking mischievously, "I dare you to go and get the claw and have a look, close up, that way we can see if it is real or not!"

Amber looked very nervous, "Oh I don't think that is the right thing to do! The Professor said we are not allowed to touch it!"

22

"Oh, go on, I dare you, double dare!" Arthur cried.

Serendipity, who had never even had a conversation with Arthur before decided she was going to try and impress him, to show him that she was not scared. "I'll do it!" She said and rushed over to the cupboard where Professor Inchenstein kept all his fossils and specimens as he liked to call them. She slowly opened the door.

"Serendipity don't!" whispered Amber, her heart slamming against her chest as she watched Serendipity disappear into the black cupboard.

Serendipity was already in the cupboard and climbing on the bottom shelf pulling herself up to reach the top ledge and grab the black box. Amber and Arthur followed Serendipity into the cupboard and closed the door.

Serendipity cautiously opened the box, her fingers aching under the strain as she lifted the heavy lid. With the forbidden box finally open she said to Arthur, "Open the door it is too dark to see!"

"I am scared." said Amber.

"Stop being such a baby. Hold on I can't find the door knob." Arthur said as he fumbled in the dark trying to open the cupboard door.

Suddenly the door swung open and there was Raj, hands on his hips, imaginary fumes exploding from his ears.

"What on earth are you doing in the Professor's cupboard?" he cried angrily.

They all jumped, and Serendipity was so surprised that she dropped the claw which fell to the floor with a clunk.

"That fossil is over 65 million years old! What are you doing with it?" Raj continued crossly, pushing his glasses further up his nose in annoyance.

Serendipity, hands shaking bent down to pick up the claw.

"Who are you the teacher?" cried Arthur. "We were only looking to see if it is real!"

Raj glanced at Arthur and hesitated, he had never even spoken to him before let alone shouted at the bully that constantly tormented him, but Raj knew that the Professor would be livid if he found out, so he held strong and continued to scold the naughty children.

"Of course, it is real, now put it back before I tell Professor Inchenstein!" Raj retorted.

"Go on tell him see if I care." Arthur huffed back.

Serendipity was not listening to the others arguing because she was completely mesmerized by how big and heavy the claw was. It felt bizarrely warm in her hand and she started to rub it gently, brushing off any dirt, from when it fell to the floor. The warmth from the claw travelled from her hand up her arm making her body feel tingly and yet strangely calm at the same time. Then suddenly her vision became blurred and a bright white light, darted across her eyes like a nuclear explosion. She screamed out in fright, but her cries were silence by a whirlwind of dust that encircled the cupboard. In a flash, the four children disappeared, engulfed by a sea of blackness.

ΔΔΔ

The girls screeched uncontrollably as they fell and tried to grab hold of each other in the darkness. Serendipity kept on screaming louder and louder, afraid of the dark, she closed her eyes, but that was even more terrifying as she could see flashes of beastly looking monsters, jagged, pointing shapes, and then something spinning in the air. Just when they thought their brains would explode in their heads from the pressure they finally fell to the ground with an almighty thud.

Arthur was the first to stand up, coughing and shaking, all he could muster was a moan asking, "Where are we?"

He brushed the dust off his grey school trousers and looked up at the staggering fern trees towering above him. "Gosh it is so hot! Where on earth are we?" he repeated to himself as sweat poured down his brow.

As the dust around him settled he saw two bodies intertwined in a heap in front of him. Arthur helped the girls to their feet and they all gazed around in amazement.

"It looks like we are in some kind of rainforest. Do you think we are dreaming?" asked Amber in disbelief as she tried to push the exotic plants and wildlife around her away to no avail as they persisted on caressing her legs.

"It is possible we are having a group dream; I have heard about dreams like this from my parents. My mum told me that when they were on tour they would often close their eyes and go to a far-off place together full of wonderful and unusual sensations. Apparently, it is quite common in the music industry."

"Well wherever we are, there is no phone signal!" Arthur said as he spun around trying to catch a signal on his iPhone."

"Oh, why won't they leave me alone?" Amber cried as she frantically tried to escape the rough leaves of a strange plant that felt like they were clawing their way up her legs.

Raj frantically groped around on the floor looking for his glasses that he lost during the fall; almost blind without them, he felt his way forward crawling like a baby until his hand came upon what felt like a big, white, elongated melon.

"Come and look at this, quick look!" Raj shouted.

The others ran over to where Raj was, carefully avoiding moving tendrils of a very dangerous looking carnivorous plant on the way.

"They're huge snake eggs!" Serendipity exclaimed, "Like my dad's python only 100 times bigger, this is a land of giant snakes, we're DEFINITELY dreaming!"

"Your dad has a python?" Arthur asked impressed.

"Oh my, it looks like some kind of nest! I knew you shouldn't have opened that stupid black box and touched that stupid claw!" Amber said starting to cry as she peered into the nest below them. "What if the mummy snake comes!"

Raj eventually found his glasses amongst the huge snake eggs and placed them quickly over his eyes.

They were all so mesmerized by the shiny white eggs in front of them, that none of them realized that they were not the only ones admiring the nest's contents. A soft, rustling noise in the trees next to them started to get louder and then they heard a huge belch.

"Arthur, really, control yourself!" Serendipity said.

"It wasn't me!" An indignant Arthur huffed, scowling at Serendipity.

"Shhh be quiet" Raj whispered, watching the trees where the sound was coming from, "There is definitely something behind the trees."

They looked at each other in sheer panic and then Raj cried "Quick follow me." he grabbed Serendipity's hand and they all ran like greased lightning, vaulted over a dead log and threw themselves face down into the undergrowth under some low-lying ferns on the other side of the nest.

"Please please let's go back. I am scared" wailed Amber.

"Shhhhh, whatever it is, it is coming closer now be quiet and get down." Raj said assertively.

The rustling finally stopped, and the only sound to be heard were the children's thumping hearts and Amber's frightened, muffled sobs. Just as they were wondering if they had imagined the mysterious noises, the oddest-looking creature, with a curved parrot like beak, and miniature turreted horns all over its orange head, stepped out from the trees and gazed down curiously at the nest, admiring the unprotected eggs. The creature awkwardly crouched forward, bent its bumpy head down and snatched one of the eggs before running off back into the trees.

"What the hell was that?" Arthur screamed.

"It is a dinosaur!" Raj said in total disbelief, "a Pachycephalosaur to be precise."

"A what?" Arthur asked in utter amazement "A pachyo what?"

But Raj wasn't listening, he stood up slowly and watched the heavy headed dinosaur crunching and slurping the contents of the egg with fascination. "This is just incredible, look at its thick skull. It is about 25cm thick and it uses it to fight with other males or to defend itself! Isn't it incredible?"

The contents of the egg now gobbled up, the dome headed lizard came clambering back towards the nest and the children. Twice the size of a grown man, it wasn't the funny head, but the small, mean flickering green eyes set within it that made the children tremble with fear.

"Don't make a sound" hissed Raj, "It'll eat us next".

"How did this happen?" Amber said sobbing, "It must be that wicked claw. My father was right – it is the devil's work!"

Serendipity squeezed the claw tightly in her sweaty hand.

"It's not wicked, it's incredible" Raj said again. "We must be somewhere in the Late Cretaceous period." The other three looked at him as if he had just spoken double-Dutch. "Think of Jurassic Park, we are basically slap bang in the middle of Jurassic park, only a little later on, give or take 100 million years or so."

"What is Jurassic Park?" Amber asked innocently.

"Are you joking?" Arthur said, his mouth wide open with surprise.

Amber looked down at the muddy floor and shook her heard.

"But, but you are from America? Jurassic Park is one of Spielberg's most famous films!"

"Arthur, she has never seen it now let it drop." Serendipity said defensively knowing how embarrassed Amber could get.

Arthur was just about to retaliate when Raj said, "Guys, look, one of the eggs is moving!"

As they watched with eyes like saucers, a crack appeared in one of the egg cases and a little claw poked through, within 20 seconds a tiny dinosaur no bigger than a pigeon and covered in brown fluff, stumbled out.

"Look! Look, one of the eggs has hatched! What type of dinosaur is it Raj?" asked Serendipity.

"I am not sure, it has two hind legs and feathers – maybe it is some type of bird?"

"Is it a carnivore? Because I remember Doctor Dino said carnivores eat meat, i.e. us!" Arthur asked nervously.

What with all the excitement the children had forgotten to be quiet, and the Pachycephalosaur was slowly creeping towards them.

"Freeze!" commanded Raj, but the others were already deadly still. "Get ready to run when I shout run."

The girls held hands and took a deep breath. The Pachycephalosaur was less than ten meters away and its green eyes were staring transfixed at the four odd looking creatures in front of him. He lowered his knobbly head getting ready to charge when the little baby dinosaur wobbled out from the nest and walked towards the dinosaur. The Pachycephalosaur cocked its horny head and locked on to its new little prey with one of its hungry eyes. The dinosaur, looking forward to such an easy meal opened his mouth ready to eat the baby when an almighty roar erupted, so loud it felt as if it was coming down from the heavens!

Amber promptly fainted to the ground while the others looked up in the direction of the roar and to their horror saw a gigantic Tyrannosaurus Rex bearing down on the Pachycephalosaur. The egg stealer, caught off guard knew the game was up, it tried to turn around in time to defend itself, but the T-Rex was too quick. Blood squirted in every direction as 7cm long teeth pierced into the side of the Pachycephalosaur who squealed out loud in pain. The injured dinosaur had fallen to its knees in defeat and it waited for the inevitable moment when life would be extinguished. It did not have to wait long as the killer jaws opened wide and came crashing down on the back of the dinosaur, ripping the flesh and swallowing it whole. The mother T-Rex was not distracted by her victim's screeches and relished in eating the egg hunter alive. As this living nightmare played out in front of the sickened children, the baby T-Rex hobbled over to Serendipity and jumped up on her lap. Serendipity fell on her back in shock and dropped the claw that was in her hand. "Serendipity do something! Whatever you did that got us here do it again!" Arthur screamed at her. Serendipity grabbed the claw and started to rub it and blow on it hysterically. Within seconds, the blood, jaws and flesh were no longer visible as the earth below them disappeared and they drifted down in the same heavy blackness as before. The darkness that seemed so scary before was a thankful relief to the children and they let gravity pull them away to what was hopefully a safer place. The whirling and spinning finally stopped and they landed with another thump only this time the pitch blackness around them did not subside. "Where are we now?" Amber moaned, after regaining consciousness. Arthur fumbled around until he finally clutched something that felt like a handle and he turned the knob cautiously. Light shone through the open door, highlighting the stale dust in the air and they realized with great relief that they were back in the safety of Professor Inchenstein's science cupboard.

"Thank goodness!" sighed Arthur, "Did that really happen, did we really just see a Tyrannosaurus Rex?" he said, more to himself than anyone else, his heart still pounding in his chest.

"I am afraid it definitely happened!" Serendipity said.

They all turned around to look at Serendipity who was sitting down on the floor of the science cupboard and on her lap, was the baby T-Rex from the nest.

"Oh, dear Lord!" Amber cried, swooning once again to the floor.

2

The importance of a good rump

The children looked down at the peculiar, scaly creature on Serendipity's lap and thought it must be some terrible dream.

"Are you seriously saying that this is a baby Tyrannosaurus Rex?" Arthur said in total shock, his brown eyes growing wider with curiosity.

He picked up the baby dinosaur and held it up to his face so he could get a better look. "He does not look very scary; resembles more a scaly chicken with bits of green fluff than a dinosaur."

"You wait until he grows up and is 12 meters long and 7 tonnes! I would like to see if you would be scared then!" Raj retorted growing more and more confident.

The baby started wriggling in Arthur's arms and making noises, its amber eyes blinking in Serendipity's direction.

"Oh my, he thinks you are his mother!" cried Amber in despair.

Arthur handed the dinosaur back to Serendipity who took it in her arms and as soon as she held him he relaxed immediately.

"What are we going to do?" Arthur asked.

"Tell the teacher of course!" Amber suggested, "This monster belongs in a zoo!"

"Tell the teacher!" Arthur mimicked unkindly in his best girl voice. "You are such a baby!"

"Leave her alone Arthur!" Serendipity said defensively.

"Well do you want to tell the teacher?" he asked Serendipity.

Serendipity looked down at the cute little dinosaur in her lap and shook her head. "Maybe we can keep it?" she asked timidly.

"Now you're talking!" Arthur said grinning like a Cheshire cat, "I can't wait to show Rocky!"

Raj's tummy flipped at the mention of Rocky's name. There was no way he was going to let that bully see this precious dinosaur and torment it.

"We can't possibly keep it." Raj said seriously.

The other three turned to towards him. "Think about it for a minute, this is a dinosaur, a baby T-Rex that is going to grow to be taller than a house. How do you think you are going to be able to keep him?"

Arthur shrugged his shoulders in response and Serendipity continued to rock the dinosaur in her arms. Raj continued softly, "Look believe me, no one is more excited than me to be next to an actual dinosaur, but he belongs with his mother."

"I suppose you are right" Serendipity said sadly. "It's just he is so cute and sweet!"

Raj snorted with laughter, "You won't say that when he is 20 meters tall and has teeth the size of football!"

"So, what do you suggest, Brain?" Arthur asked Raj.

Raj coloured red and tried to ignore Arthur staring at him. "I suggest we take it back to its mother."

"Whoa, hang on a second!" Amber said suddenly. "Please don't tell me you are suggesting we go back to that place full of monsters?"

"They are dinosaurs not monsters dummy!"

"I really don't care what you call them! There is no way I am going back there!" Amber began to walk towards the science lab door; she could not handle any more drama on the first day of school, all she wanted to do was to go home and forget this ever happened.

"Amber wait!" Serendipity cried nervously.

Amber turned to look at her new friend.

"I, I, please don't leave me alone with it?" Serendipity looked panicked for the first time.

"OK but I am not going back there!" And Amber pointed towards the ominous cupboard.

"OK fine, we won't go back." Serendipity said reassuringly.

Raj was about to speak when Serendipity interrupted him, "Let's go back tomorrow. It's getting late and they will be locking up the school."

Raj looked sceptically at Serendipity and the dinosaur. Serendipity stared back beseechingly, "I promise we will go back tomorrow morning and leave him with his mother."

Raj sighed and agreed even though he felt it was the wrong decision. He felt happy that he was talking to other children in his class for the first time; he did not want it to end...

"Well Brain, what is the plan? How do we look after a baby T-

Rex?" Arthur asked Raj with his arms folded.

Raj thought for a second and then said, "Well his instinct is to hunt, so I suggest we feed him something before he decides to eat one of us!"

Amber crossed herself.

"What should we get him?" asked Serendipity.

"How about a good rump steak?" said Arthur.

"I know, let's go to Sainsbury's buy some steaks, feed him, he can spend the night with you and we bring him back to his mother first thing in the morning before school." Raj said decisively.

No one had a better plan so off they went to Sainsbury's.

"Remember we can't tell anyone about the dinosaur or we will never be able to take it home to its mother."

The others nodded in agreement and Serendipity placed the dinosaur in her school rucksack and gently put it on her back. She carefully kept the zip open so that air could circulate and off they all went to find a good rump steak. A blanket of nervous excitement surrounded the children as they walked down Chepstow Villas. Raj was feeling particularly warm inside; not only had he seen real live dinosaurs, but he was spending time with fellow pupils outside of school, something that he had never done before. He led the way and as they came towards Westbourne Grove he asked, "By the way does anyone have any money on them to buy the steaks?"

Arthur put his hands in his pockets and pulled out a miniature action man, a dice and eventually £3.

"I am not allowed to hold money" Amber said.

"Surprise surprise!" Arthur huffed.

"Oh, don't worry I can use my credit card." Serendipity said casually.

"You have a credit card?" asked Raj unable to hide his surprise.

Serendipity shrugged her shoulders and her cheeks flushed a slight hue of crimson. "I am only supposed to use it in case of emergencies, but if I buy food I have to buy organic." she added hastily.

"What's organic?" Amber asked innocently.

"Gosh you really are from Mars!" Arthur said teasing.

"It just means that the food is not grown with chemicals and fertilizers or fed antibiotics. My mum is really strict ever since she stopped acting she has started this health craze where we can only eat organic food. I have been a vegetarian all my life and since the summer we are all on this crazy raw diet!"

"Does that mean you have never had lamp chops?" said Arthur incredulously.

"Never!!"

"What about sausages?" Arthur was still in denial that someone had never savoured the succulent taste of home cooked meat.

"I know it's weird, but what can I do?"

Serendipity always struggled when she tried to explain how her family lived. The Magnum's were different, and she had to accept it, no matter how hard it was. She spent most of her childhood jet-setting between major cities all around the world from Hong Kong to Beirut within a week. Of course, in her eyes it was not jet-setting as so many people described her family's lifestyle; it was awfully boring. She would never see her parents, only nannies, babysitters and hotel staff. It was hard to make friends because they were always on the move; sometimes they would move into the Ritz in Paris for 2 months and then they would be in the Burj al

Arab in Dubai for six months, while her father and his band toured the Middle East. Serendipity and her brother Flo would hang around in hotel foyers and the only chance they would see their parents would be on the television. When The Smoking Nettles (her father's band) finally split up two years ago the Magnum family settled in Notting Hill. Serendipity was the happiest she had ever been because she was finally experiencing some sort of normality and routine. Serendipity loved coming home to find her father lying on the lime green lilo, floating in their indoor pool and writing music while her mother wore an apron and blended raw vegetables in the kitchen. This was as normal as it got for Serendipity and she was delighted to say the least!

"Actually, I think it is best we go to Planet Organic because if my mum does ever see the bill at least I won't get into trouble for buying cheap meat."

The boys looked at her strangely and Amber was still not clear on the meaning of organic but was too embarrassed to ask again. They all followed Serendipity further along Westbourne Grove until they arrived outside Planet Organic. "I can't believe steaks are so expensive! We just spent £105 on meat! This little dinosaur better appreciate it!" Raj said shaking his head in astonishment. Raj had never spent so much money before in his entire life, let alone just on meat!

"It is jolly expensive, but I suppose it is better quality." concluded Arthur.

Eventually they arrived outside Serendipity's home on the quiet street of Pencombe Mews. It was a typical London street, filled with white wedding cake Victorian houses, walls as bright as snow and huge pillars at either side of the dazzling coloured front doors.

"Wow you live here!" exclaimed Amber, "The whole house?"

"Yes! Now hopefully my mum will be downstairs in her studio doing yoga but if she sees the shopping bags, then they are for you. Whatever you do, don't let her see that we have brought meat into the house or she will have one of her animal rights fits." Serendipity stared hard at here new friends to make sure they understood how serious this was. "As soon as we get in we have to bolt up the stairs. OK?"

Raj and Arthur nodded in agreement and would have said yes to anything if it meant they could put the heavy shopping bags down. Serendipity turned her key in the sparkling gold lock and opened the large red door; she raced in and straight up the stairs. The door slammed shut behind the children and they made it safely onto the first-floor landing. Before they could catch their breath, they heard a voice calling from downstairs, "Serendipity, is that you darling?"

"Oh bother!" whispered Serendipity. She flung her head over the wooden banister and cried, "Hi mum, I am with some friends and we are going to do homework together in my room. We have a lot to do and we can't be disturbed." They all held their breath waiting for Serendipity's mum to respond.

"Are you sure you don't want me to bring you guys up some fresh cabbage juice?"

Arthur pulled a face that made Amber giggle.

"No! Thanks mum, we will come down soon. We just need to do our homework."

"Well if you are doing homework you should feed your brains first... come down here and have a fresh juice please."

"Mum!" Serendipity groaned embarrassed.

"Now dear, or shall I bring them up to you?"

"No!" Serendipity said loudly, "We are coming down."

She looked at her friends apologetically, "Give me the steaks. I will hide them in my room with the dinosaur."

Flustered, Serendipity raced up two more flights of stairs and hid the steaks in her wardrobe and then gently placed her rucksack on the bed, leaving the zip open so the baby dinosaur could breathe.

The children then hurried down to the kitchen to face Mrs. Magnum and her freshly squeezed cabbage. They walked into the kitchen and there was Serendipity's mum blending some gruesome green looking mixture in the blender; she had long blond hair the colour of custard and she was as skinny as a flag pole.

"Mum, meet my friends Raj, Amber and Arthur." Serendipity shouted.

Mrs. Magnum turned around and gasped, "Oh you made me jump. I did not hear you come in what with all the cabbage whizzing around!" she came over to Serendipity and gave her a hug. She then turned to the others and smiled. "Well you are the first friends Serendipity has ever bought home!"

"Mum!" Serendipity moaned again, cringing with embarrassment while her new friends looked at the marble floor uncomfortably.

"Well, sit down, sit down." Mrs. Magnum led the children towards the glass kitchen table and handed each one a large glass full of a pale green, lumpy liquid.

"So how was school? What is this homework you are going to work on?"

"Err, it is a project on em recycling." Serendipity said as she tried to gulp down the liquidized cabbage.

"Yes" added Raj, "we have to make a doll's house out of cardboard."

Mrs. Magnum raised her left eyebrow, "Well that is unusual but worthwhile I suppose. I think there are some old boxes in the den you could use."

"Great" Serendipity replied, finally seeing the bottom of her glass.

Amber was doing her best to hold her breath and swallow at the same time while Arthur just stared at his drink in disbelief.

"Come on drink up." Raj whispered to Arthur, "We need to build the doll's house."

"I know, but, it, it is green!" Arthur mumbled back.

Serendipity rolled her eyes and grabbed Arthur's glass forcing the mushy green vegetable down her throat, (she had drunk enough vegetables in the last ten years to not worry about the colour or taste anymore).

Cabbage drunk and tummies full, the four children raced down another flight of stairs to the so-called den to search for cardboard boxes.

Mrs. Magnum looked after at the children fondly as they raced out of the kitchen and down the stairs. She was happy that Serendipity was bringing friends home. She knew that her daughter found all the travelling that they did difficult and that she always complained how hard it was to make friends. The Magnum family had lived in Pencomb Mews for nearly two years now and Serendipity had blossomed ever since. Even though family life was turning out to be surprisingly harmonious, Mrs. Magnum did sometimes miss the exoticness of her previous life; the red carpets, the parties, the paparazzi, but the time had come to put her family first. Admittedly, she was secretly relieved when The Smoking Nettles announced to the world its imminent separation; they had after all been together for 16 years and generated over £7 billion for each of their band members. It seemed like the right time to lay their guitar strings to rest and start to enjoy family life and abundant supplies of homemade blended juices. Yes, Mrs. Magnum was extremely satisfied with the way life had turned out, calm as it may be for now. "Wow you have a set of drums!"

exclaimed Raj as he looked around inside the den in awe.

"Oh yeah, that is my dad's drum set."

"Wicked!" Arthur shouted grinning at the shiny drum kit that belonged to one of the biggest rock legends of all time.

Raj spun around in total bewilderment. Everywhere his eyes fell, he saw excess; a pool table, a table tennis table, a swimming pool, a 200cm flat screen, a running machine, there was even a disco ball hanging above the drum set. Raj had never been surrounded by so many exciting things. He was one of the rare pupils attending Pembridge Hall who was actually clever. Raj was so intelligent that he won the only scholarship the school offered that covered 100% of the fees when he was just six years old.

"How rich are you?" Raj said quietly, more to himself than to Serendipity.

"Here we are." Serendipity came from behind the pool table carrying a cardboard box and pretending not to hear Raj's question.

"Great that should do it."

The group of friends clambered up four flights of stairs, struggling not to fall over as they carried the large cardboard box to Serendipity's bedroom.

Raj gently took the rucksack off Serendipity's bed and opened the zip. The dinosaur jumped out and started to walk on the pale pink fluffy carpet making little noises and looking around curiously as he tried to make sense of his new surroundings.

"Open the steaks." Raj ordered and his new friends obediently started ripping open the packages. Raj then took a piece of Planet Organic's finest rump and threw it towards the dinosaur. The dinosaur hesitantly walked closer to the steak on the cardboard. The children were motionless as they watched the dinosaur devour the raw meat before them.

"Quick get another one!" Amber cried, "We don't want him to start on us!"

Arthur threw another steak on the floor and the dinosaur gobbled it up and then came over to Serendipity.

"Should I pick him up? Does he want more?"

"I think he has had enough. Go on pick him up." Raj reassured her.

Serendipity bent down and picked up the little dinosaur and held him in her arms.

"Just make sure he is never hungry." Raj advised.

"He is quite cute really." said Serendipity as she stroked his belly.

"You know I really should be getting home. I don't want to get into trouble." Amber said peering nervously out of the window.

"Do you live far?" asked Arthur.

"No, we are staying at my grandmother's place on Princes Square. She is sick, that is why we came over here." Amber replied.

"I thought you were American?"

"I am but my mum is English, she met my father on an Evangelical tour in Texas when she was 18 and lived there ever since. We moved to London in the summer because my Grandma Rose is sick, and my mum wanted to be near her."

"Well I will walk you back if you like, I am not far from Princes Square?"

"Sure."

Everyone agreed to meet at school the following morning at 8am in order to take the dinosaur back to its mother. Amber and Arthur said goodbye and as soon as they left Serendipity suddenly felt panicky again.

"Don't worry I will stay as long as you like." Raj smiled at her kindly and she saw the warmth in his pale blue eyes behind thick square spectacles.

Serendipity nodded in gratitude and then asked shyly, "Do many Indians have blue eyes like you? I just never noticed how pale they are."

Raj's neck became suddenly warm and without looking at Serendipity he replied awkwardly, "Em not sure really, I think most Indians have brown eyes, but my mother has blue eyes, so I suppose I got them from her."

The two children worked together to assemble the box in order to make a new home for their new dinosaur. The dinosaur was clearly excited by all the activity going on around it and was scurrying around amongst all the cardboard. It started to run around so fast that at one stage it slipped on a pencil and landed in a patch of discarded scotch tape!

"What a muddle you have got yourself in!" Raj said as he tried to cut the sticky tape off the baby dinosaur. "It's behaving like a puppy!"

"Shhh, don't worry little one, it will all be over soon." Serendipity cooed, trying to keep him calm as he wriggled in Raj's hands. "He should really have a name" she said as she stroked his scaly belly. "I know let's call him Tony."

"Really? Tony?"

"Why not? Tony the T-Rex!" Serendipity smiled mischievously.

"Well Tony it is." Raj said and placed little Tony (slightly bald now

in places) in his new homemade cardboard box. To make Tony's home more cosy Serendipity added a tissue box full of tissues as a bed and the odd cuddly toy as well as a rump steak just in case he got hungry and a bowl of water. They both sat on the floor and peered down at Tony who was exploring his new home.
Serendipity started to feel tired after all the excitement of the day. She looked across at Raj and asked, "How do you know so much about dinosaurs?"

Raj pushed his glasses up his nose and replied, "Oh I don't know. I suppose I find them fascinating really." Raj sighed before saying quietly, "I have this memory of playing with a toy dinosaur back in India when I was five with my dad and I remember being, well happy."

"Where is your dad now?" Serendipity asked gently.

"My parents live in India."

"Then who do you live with?" Serendipity asked finding it hard to hide her surprise.

Raj tried to hide his awkwardness by playing with a piece of string that was dangling over one of the walls in Tony 's new home. "I live with my Uncle Sohan. I won this scholarship when I was six to come to London to get an education, so here I am. "

"But what about your parents?"

"What about them?"

"Don't you see them, like on holidays or something?"

Raj did not want to tell Serendipity that his parents were so poor they could not afford the money to pay for a phone call, let alone plane tickets to see him. How would a girl like Serendipity ever understand that? He thought.

"They are pretty busy in India." Raj answered.

"You must miss them a lot."

"Suppose." By this time, the string that was firmly wound around Raj's finger was now so tight that his finger tip was glowing a vivid white.

Serendipity felt sad for Raj; she thought about all the time he spent alone in the science lab or teased by Rocky and his gang. She realised that they had been in the same class for two years and she knew nothing about him. She couldn't remember ever seeing him talk to anyone at school let alone hang out with someone.

She wanted to make him smile so she grabbed Tony and swung him around in the air causing Tony to squawk and wiggled his legs with excitement and surprise making Raj snort with laughter. He wished he could tell his parents what they had discovered…

ΔΔΔ

While Serendipity and Raj were busy preparing Tony's new home, Amber arrived at Princes Square and went straight to her room. She knelt down beside her bed and prayed:

"Dear Lord, please, help me to understand what happened today. I feel so confused. Please help me to find the answers to my questions. How did we travel back in time and why did we see so many monsters? What are the dinosaurs and why am I the only one who has no idea what they are? I want to fit into my new school and make friends, but I feel so different I just want to be normal.

Please look after my Grandma Rose, my parents and my new friends, Serendipity, Arthur and Raj.

Amen." Amber always felt better after she had said a prayer and spoken to the Lord, but that evening, she still felt very troubled and confused. She went down the stairs to see her parents and tell them about her first day at school. In the living room she found her mother calmly polishing her collection of brass buttons while her father read the Bible.

"Hello mother, father."

"Hello Amber, how was the first day of school?" Mrs. Bradshaw asked, not looking up from her buttons.

"It was really interesting. Everybody is very nice." Amber said.

Mr. Bradshaw looked up from the Bible and asked, "What prayers did you say at school?"

"In assembly it was the Lord's pray and before lunch we said Grace."

"Is that all, only two prayers all day?" Mr. Bradshaw closed the Bible and stared at his daughter.

"As soon as I came home I said a prayer." Amber tried to avoid her father's bullet shaped eyes.

"Do you hear that Dorothy? Only two prayers all day! The sooner we get back to Waco the better!" Mr. Bradshaw found the sudden illness of his wife's mother extremely inconvenient; but he had to do his duty, or he would not be seen as a good leader amongst his flock back home. He was sure that Grandma Rose would be safely with the Lord before Jesus' next birthday and everything would get back to normal.

"Father?"

"Yes Amber."

"Do you remember how you said that the dinosaurs were invented by the Devil?"

"Yes, I do indeed. Ridiculous! Dinosaurs! The Devil's imagination that is what the dinosaurs are."

"So, they never existed?" Amber asked quietly.

"Are you questioning me child?" Mr. Bradshaw said, standing up. "No, not at all, it's just one of the boys in my year mentioned..."

"Mentioned what exactly?" Mr. Bradshaw interrupted Amber before she could say anymore.

"Nothing." Amber said sheepishly.

Even though Mr. Bradshaw was only 140cm tall, he still managed to tower over his ten-year-old daughter, "Don't let me hear the D word mentioned again in this home."

"Devil or dinosaur?" Amber asked innocently.

"DINOSAUR!" Mr. Bradshaw shouted showing his daughter his tonsils.

"Yes father." Amber said cowering.

"Go and pray. Two prayers all day! Tut." Mr. Bradshaw said to himself, shaking his head with disappointment

"Yes father." Amber said quietly, happy to have an excuse to leave the living room. Amber slowly walked back up the stairs, making a special effort to stop the wood beneath her from creaking and finally arrived outside her Grandma Rose's door. The usual stuffy smell of lavender and stale air greeted Amber as she cautiously opened the door and walked into the room.

"Grandma, are you awake? Can I come in?"

Grandma Rose opened a crusty eye and saw her grandchild standing shyly in the doorway, she cleared her throat and tried to lift her head.

"Of course, my dear, come in and close the door." she croaked.

Grandma Rose knew she was dying; she was 85 and had lived a long, full life with few regrets; the only one being that she hardly knew her only grandchild. Now that she was dying, and her daughter decided to come over from the US to look after her, she was determined to stay alive as long as possible, so she could enjoy the company of Amber.

"Come over here my child and sit on the bed." Grandma Rose patted the pink pansy sheets softly with her feeble wrinkly hand.

"How are you feeling today?"

"So so, but enough about me, tell me all about the first day of school" Grandma Rose replied smiling, showing Amber her red gums.

Amber told her Grandma all about her day, the whispers behind her back when she told the class her father was a preacher, her new friend Serendipity and the lesson with Professor Inchenstein. She left out the part about her new name.

"Well it sounds like you have had a rather busy day." Grandma Rose said as she stroked one of Amber's red curls. "But why the long face? Why do you look so sad my child?"

Amber tried to smile at her granny, she did not want to show how upset she felt, "Do you know about the dinosaurs Grandma?"

"Well, I am not an expert, but I know a thing or two. Now let me think, there was Triceratops with the three horns and ah yes of course Tyrannosaurus Rex!"

As soon as the words Tyrannosaurus Rex were mentioned, Amber felt a shiver run down her spine.

"Why am I the only one in the world who knows nothing about them?" A tear fell down Amber's freckly cheek.

"There there, do not cry." Grandma Rose handed a hankie to Amber to dry her tears, "Life is all about learning, if we knew everything then life would be a dull old place."

"But father said they were invented by the Devil and never existed!

I looked like a fool in front of the whole class and now I know for a fact that they do exist! But father insists they were the devil's imagination and he just shouted at me when I asked him about it. Why did he react like that?"

All the excitement and the anxiety of the day finally found an outlet and the tears tumbled uncontrollably down her innocent face.

Grandma Rose thought long and hard before she responded; she let Amber cry and patted her head calmly, waiting for the tears to stop. Grandma Rose was not a fan of Amber's father, Mr. Bradshaw. She tried very hard to conceal her true feelings because she was afraid that they would go back to Texas and leave her alone if anyone knew how she really felt. There was something sinister in his demeanour, something that she could not quite explain because he was always so cordial. But Grandma Rose knew that his kindness was fake, she could just feel it. Mr. Bradshaw gave her the creeps, especially when he stared straight through her, wearing his fake smile, pretending to ask after her health! He always needed to control everything around him, especially his wife, which frustrated Grandma Rose immensely. Grandma Rose remembered her daughter before she met Mr. Bradshaw; she was outspoken and independent, bubbly and full of life, now she was a quiet, submissive housewife who would not say boo to a goose!

"My child, listen to me." she turned Amber's wet face towards hers, "Your father is a very religious man and his beliefs are very important to him. Evangelists are sometimes a little, em stiff, and they are certain that what they think is the truth, no matter what others say or what proof there is on the contrary."

"So, what should I believe?" Amber asked, blowing her nose loudly.

"Ah that is up to you to decide my dear."

Grandma Rose began to feel extremely tired and closed her eyes, "You must be strong Amber, seek out the truth yourself, you can't always believe everything you are told."

Amber quietly got off the bed so as not to wake her Grandma. She kissed her forehead and left the room, her head bursting with new questions.

3

Dealing with Fog and Log Head

The next morning the children gathered in the science lab as agreed at 8am. Everyone was there on time apart from Serendipity and Tony. Amber was pacing around nervously biting her nails while Arthur was sitting on the bench swinging his legs freely. "It is absolutely incredible what happened to us yesterday! Think about it, we saw two dinosaurs, one of them a gigantic killer T-Rex, I was dying to tell my dad, but he wouldn't believe me even if I did!"

"You must not say anything!" Raj said, closing his dinosaur book and looking at Arthur crossly, "We have to protect Tony."

"Don't get your knickers in a twist I did not say anything. I just meant that he would not believe me if I did!"

"My knickers are not twisted," Raj said annoyed, "But we should try not to talk about it, even here. Anyone could hear us, and they might take Tony away from us."

"Please don't argue, I am nervous enough as it is!" Amber stared at the big round clock on the wall anxiously. "Where is she?"

The door to the science lab swung open and in walked Serendipity. "I am sorry we are late!"

"How is he?" Raj asked concerned.

"Can we see him?" asked Arthur.

Serendipity took Tony gently out of her bag and placed him on the science lab bench. "I am sooo tired. It took Tony ages to fall asleep! In the end I had to let him sleep in my bed with me to stop him making noises!"

Tony was busy discovering his new surroundings not at all discouraged as he slipped and skidded along the wooden bench.

"Guys we are running out of time, let's take him back to his monster mother and then we can forget all about it." Amber said.

Raj was trying to stop Tony from sliding off the side of the bench, so Arthur agreed to go with Serendipity and get the claw from the cupboard. Amber peeped around the door keeping watch down the corridor. Five minutes passed, and no-one called Amber to come back in; to Amber five minutes seemed like a lifetime and as she waited and waited her gut told her that something was terribly wrong. She took a final look down the corridor to make sure the coast was clear and then she hesitantly opened the science cupboard door. Half of her was hoping they had gone to take Tony back without her, Amber had never expected such adventure when she moved to London and her nerves were at the end of their tether! She felt terribly guilty not being able to tell her parents and Grandma Rose what had happened to her, but she knew they would not understand and her father would be especially cross that she was talking about the dinosaurs. Pulling the door knob towards her, with her heart pounding in her chest, she looked inside the cupboard and saw her three classmates standing there in total silence their faces as pale as ashes.

"What is wrong? What is going on?" Amber asked softly. Amber glanced down at the empty black box and then back at her friends' puzzled faces.

"I am sure there is a perfectly normal explanation as to why the claw has gone walkabout, we just have to ask Professor Inchenstein where he put it." Raj said trying to keep the others calm.

"We don't have time! It is a quarter to nine, everyone is starting to arrive." Amber responded panicking.

"What are we going to do with Tony?" Arthur said alarmed. The children were becoming more and more overwhelmed with their situation; it felt absolutely hopeless. They had in their possession a baby Tyrannosaurus Rex that was growing faster by the minute and eating steak after steak and they had no idea what to do. Yesterday's plan to take Tony back seemed pretty logical; how could they have ever predicted that the claw would not be there when they returned the next day? Raj decided the best thing to do was to wait until they could find Professor Inchenstein. In the meantime, they would put Tony in Serendipity's locker, with the remaining steaks and go to class as usual. No one else had a better idea so they followed Raj's lead once again.

During the morning's lessons none of them could concentrate; out of habit Arthur sat next to Rocky at the back of the classroom and when Rocky started cracking a joke at Raj's expense, Arthur felt embarrassed for the first time. Raj kept his head down and thought about Tony. Nothing mattered anymore, only getting Tony back to his mother, he turned to look at Serendipity who smiled back at him and for the first time he felt less intimidated by the bullies at the back of the room. History seemed to drag on for a lifetime and finally when the bell rang for morning break the two boys ran to find Professor Inchenstein and the girls went to see how Tony was doing.

"I am terrible at keeping secrets. Maybe we should just tell Miss Bristlepott, she seems kind of nice, maybe she will understand." Amber said to Serendipity.

"Amber you must be strong, we must take Tony back to his mother, otherwise they will lock him up and he will spend his life scared and in a cage like the lions in a circus! The boys will find the claw, I am sure it will all be fine." She said, trying to convince Amber as well as herself not to panic.

As the girls checked that their new dinosaur had ample steaks left and was not too scared in the dark, the boys arrived outside the staffroom. Arthur hesitated before he knocked on the dark green door.

"Just do it." Raj encouraged him.

Arthur was usually a very confident boy but even he had his limits and knocking on the staff room door during break was one of them. There was a certain etiquette that had to be followed when disturbing a teacher during the morning break; firstly, it had to be some sort of emergency and secondly if no one came to the door after the first knock, then it was forbidden to knock again.

Arthur took a deep breath and knocked twice.

To the boys' delight the door swung open but delight quickly turned to dismay when Doctor Fog's rancid face peered around the green wooden door. Dr Fog, the Deputy Head, was officially voted scary teacher number 2 (no one could trump Log Head) at Pembridge Hall and a horror to behold in person. Her back hunched at the top of her spine, causing her head to jut forward which in turn made her bulbous nose look larger than it actually was. Thick black hairs poked out of her nostrils resembling the legs of dead flies as if tangled together in a great defeated heap. The same flies' legs also appeared on top of her head, but they gathered in unruly swarms and left smooth bald patches here and there which the children found fascinating yet terrifying to stare at. Another feature that the children always noticed but daren't focus on for too long were her three wobbling warts that appeared in an unusually precise Isosceles triangle on the right side of her jaw. Each wart had an angry looking hair thrusting out and on occasion all three hairs would meet in the middle making it very hard to look away! Dr Fog had a formidable reputation and was known for pressing down hard on her walking stick when it was purposefully positioned on a naughty pupil's toe. The walking stick was merely a prop to support the terror she emanated as she strolled effortlessly around the school; it was an instrument of intimidation and worked perfectly. The swollen blood vessels on her forehead were protruding more than usual as she scowled down at the two faces below her.

"Well?" she said, impatiently tapping her stick against the door as she glared at the two little boys who had the audacity to disturb her precious morning break.

"Sorry, err excuse me, sorry, err Doctor Fog, please can we speak with Professor Inchenstein?" Arthur said in almost a whisper as he tried with all his might not to focus on the terrorizing wart hairs that appeared to be growing right in front of him.

"Is it an emergency?" Dr Fog replied narrowing her eyes and tapping her stick more aggressively against the door frame.

"Yes." Raj replied looking down at his feet, fearful the bottom of Doctor Fog's stick would come crashing down.

"Boys?" Professor Inchenstein's kind, fluffy white head appeared around the door.

"Oh, thank goodness!" Arthur said relieved.

"What is the matter on such a glorious Tuesday morning? I was told it was an emergency?"

"Professor, what has happened to the claw?" Raj asked directly.

Professor Inchenstein could see the anxiety in their faces and wondered what on earth was going on. It was very unusual for Raj to be with another boy, especially Arthur who was considered one of the cooler ones.

"Come with me, come with me." He said reassuringly, putting his arms around the boys and guiding them in the direction of his science lab. He looked at their worried faces and said, "Well whatever is bothering you both it cannot surely be only about the whereabouts of my claw? Can it?" And he frowned causing his bushy eyebrows to obscure his view slightly. "I could ask you the question, how do you know my claw is not in the cupboard? But I won't ask that question as you both look like the location of my claw is going to save the world from some type of a cataclysmic event and it would be cruel not to relieve you of such an obvious anxiety."

He straightened his white coat and explained, "I took it to the Natural History Museum as they would like to use it in their special exhibition about the life of the tyrant lizard. It is a fairly significant exhibition and I do always enjoy being part of the National Centre for Science Education, I especially enjoy their breakfast club held once a month at the Park Lane Hotel!"

He walked towards the window and looked out onto the school lawn, "You see if I refused to donate the claw then it would have been frowned upon by my peers and I would not have been invited to the conference in April which I am very keen to attend..."

Professor Inchenstein continued to waffle on about the exclusive Palaeontology Club that he was a member of as he paced around the science lab. All the boys heard was that the claw was no longer within their reach. They darted out of the science lab in a state of sheer panic; what would they tell the girls? What was going to happen to Tony? Professor Inchenstein turned around and was just about to reassure them that the exhibition was only going on for three months and after that, the claw would be safely back in his science cupboard, but when he turned around the two boys had vanished. The Professor was baffled by the odd behaviour of the boys, but he was pleased that Raj had come out of his shell and made a friend at last. He was always a little worried about dear Raj, who reminded him of himself when he was a young boy; only interested in science and dinosaurs, no good at sport, being picked on by the other boys and always hanging around the science lab. He remembered how lonely he felt at school and he imagined that Raj must feel just as isolated as he did. Yes, it was good that he found a friend in Arthur even though they were very concerned about his fossilized specimen.... Professor Inchenstein had been teaching science at Pembridge Hall for 25 years and he was still surprised with how passionate young children could feel about what seemed to him the silliest of things. Moments later the boys arrived outside the girls' locker room and entered quickly before anyone saw them. They explained the shocking news to Serendipity and Amber.

"This is a disaster" said Amber, "Let's tell Professor Inchenstein the truth, he might be able to help us."

"Do you think we can trust him Raj?" asked Arthur.

"I think we could trust him, but look, I go to the Natural History Museum all the time, we can go there, find the claw and take Tony back to his mother like we planned."

Before the children had time to consider Raj's proposed plan the locker room door flew open and Bunny Bristlepott took over the doorway. The children gasped in fright and Amber felt close to fainting because Bunny's appearance up close was nearly as terrifying as the monsters she had seen the day before! Bunny stood glaring at the four naughty children, delighted with her find (she relished chastising the students, and boys in the girls' locker room was an unforgivable sin worthy of her uttermost rage).

"What on earth is going on in here?" She hollered at the naughty children.

Amber automatically shielded her face for protection and Serendipity instinctively stood in front of her locker, terrified that Log Head would discover their secret.

"If someone doesn't answer me they will be sorry, now speak wretched children. ANSWER ME!" she commanded.

Arthur, who was often caught doing something he shouldn't thought he would be brave and confront Log Head, head on.

"We are so terribly sorry Miss Bristlepott, but Raj and I were lost, and we came in here by accident." Arthur smiled as charmingly as he could under the circumstances.

Bunny was no fool, she knew something fishy was going on and she was determined to find out what.

She leant closer to Arthur and hissed "Do I look like I came in on the last Banana boat?"

Raj, imagining Log Head on a boat shaped like a banana, let out an uncontrollable snort much to the dismay of his friends and Bunny.

"Oh, you think this is funny, do you boy?" Bunny turned her bulging eyes to Raj who gulped down any remaining laughter and wished he had had more self-control.

Serendipity tried to help the boys out, "It's true they were lost, boys are so dumb sometimes!"

Bunny stared down at the terrified faces and considered carefully what punishment was worthy of such a crime, "You are all in detention tonight! I want you cleaning the toilets until they smell as sweet as forget-me-knots."

The children winced at the punishment but would do anything to escape Bunny's unforgiving glare.

"NOW GET OUT OF MY SIGHT!" Bunny screamed, and the kids scarped to safety. The children ran back to class, sweating and frantic as a result of their petrifying encounter with the school's Religious teacher.

"What bad luck being caught by Log Head!" Arthur complained.

"I was so scared I nearly peed myself!" Amber confessed.

"Well at least she did not find Tony!" Serendipity said.

"My plan is the only way out and now with Log Head on our backs we need to act quickly!" Raj said.

"How are we going to go to the museum and get the claw when we are supposed to be cleaning toilets after school?" Serendipity asked.

"Simple." Arthur replied. "We skive!"

Amber felt a nervous rumbling inside her; she had never been told off, never been put on detention and would never consider skiving a given punishment. She considered cleaning all the toilets herself and letting her friends go the museum without her, but she wanted to be liked and she wanted to be accepted. After much consideration, the children eventually concluded that Tony was more important than clean toilets and decided Log Head and her Forget-me-knots could wait! Amber swallowed her panic and nodded in agreement. While the children finished their morning lessons, Tony sat quietly in the pitch-black locker, squashed among Serendipity's smelly trainers; he was not happy at all and he was beginning to get hungry…

4

A Cultural day out

Finally, 3.20pm arrived and the school bell rang announcing the end of the school day. The four friends dashed out of German and sped to the girls' locker room, ducking and diving in case Log Head was prowling the corridors. Slowly, Serendipity opened her locker and Tony jumped out and into her arms making small whimpering noises. She did her best to calm him down, rocking him like a baby, until she was forgiven for locking him up in her stinky locker all day! Much to Tony 's annoyance, he was quickly bundled into Serendipity's rucksack and they ran out of the school in search of a black cab.

"Log Head is going to kill us!" Raj commented as they jumped into the first taxi they saw.

"We will just tell her we got the days wrong?" Arthur said, trying to act as if he was not scared of Log Head.

"Look, let's just focus on getting the claw, there is no point worrying about Log Head now!" Serendipity added wisely.

While they were in the taxi the children called their parents on

Serendipity's iPhone explaining they were going to each other's houses to work on a school project and that they would be home in an hour. They knew that lying to their parents was wrong but what choice did they have? The taxi whizzed through the streets of London as if it knew what an important mission it was on. They crossed over the Serpentine in Hyde Park and Tony enjoyed watching the swans and ducks waddling around the lake out of the window. Raj was the only one who had been to the Natural History Museum before, he practically lived there during the summer holidays and he knew it so well he could happily give a guided tour blindfolded. It was the only place in the world where he felt truly happy and safe, being surrounded by such almighty fossilized dinosaurs towering above him and all the stuffed exotic birds. His favourite was of course the Diplodocus that stood triumphant in the main foyer, his mouth slightly apart as if he was about to say, "Welcome to my humble abode," to the millions of tourists that came to visit him every year.

Raj turned to the others as they stood on the steps outside the entrance of the museum, "Now the only problem I foresee is that they like to search you when you enter."

"Well that could be a big problem mate, considering we have a dinosaur in one of our bags!" Arthur said sarcastically.

Raj saw Serendipity's rucksack moving in every direction on her back as Tony's legs pushed in rebellion at being held captive in another small, dark space.

"He is not happy!" said Serendipity, "He is wriggling too much!"

"I have an idea, give him to me." said Raj suddenly.

Serendipity took the rucksack off her back, opened the zip and pulled out an agitated Tony. Raj took him in his arms and said, "Let's go!" and he strode up the stairs two at a time.

"Are you mad?" cried Arthur.

"Trust me, no one will believe he is real, so he is not!"

Amber looked at Serendipity with concern and then quickly followed the others up the stairs.

"Well hello there young Raj, how are we today?" said the friendly security guard while stroking his overwhelmingly large belly. He then peered down over his protruding stomach and gasped, "What is this you have here?" the security guard stared in disbelief at Tony who was casually lying in Raj's arms.

"Oh, this is Tony, he is my new toy dinosaur, my parents got it from India!"

"Golly that is one hell of a toy! Looks real to me! It is amazing what the Indians can do!" He continued to caress his belly while staring transfixed at Tony who was behaving rather well. Gareth, the security guard checked the children's school bags and let them go through into the museum. "My my, you did not get toys like that in my day!" he murmured to himself with a mixture of disbelief and envy.

"Really Brain, you impressed me there." Arthur said slapping Raj on the back.

Raj grinned from ear to ear in triumphant that his plan worked and that they were closer to finding the claw. He held onto Tony and wrapped his blazer around him, so Tony was hidden but still had enough air to breath and not feel claustrophobic. The children gazed around at the splendid hall, admiring the coloured glass that filled the many arch shaped windows around the room. Amber's jaw dropped wide open as she stared unbelievingly at Raj's favourite dinosaur's skeleton.

"Please tell me that, is not real? I can't believe it!" Amber said crossing herself.

"Pretty cool don't you think? This is my good old pal Derek the Diplodocus." Raj smiled proudly.

"Derek?" Arthur said ironically as he looked up at the docile sauropod towering above them.

"Come on guys, don't get distracted, we are on a mission remember!" Serendipity said trying to catch her friends' attention.

"Follow me." Raj commanded and led the crew to the left of Derek and towards the entrance of the dinosaur exhibition. "Oh, my dear Lord there is another one?" Amber said stopping in her tracks as she saw a ginormous skeleton towering above her.

"Amber, you need to get with the programme." Raj said impatiently. "There are hundreds of diverse types of dinosaurs and believe it or not they lived on this planet, millions of years before you did."

Amber was finding it extremely difficult to digest what she had seen and understand what Raj just said. She had never been allowed to visit a museum before and she just could not understand why her parents had not told her about this other world, a world that was full of such extraordinary giants!

"Come on, it will be fun!" Serendipity said, grabbing Amber's sweaty hand and pulling her closer towards the Camarasaurus that was waiting to greet them at the entrance of the exhibition.

Arthur and Raj had already raced inside and were glued to the glass that was surrounding a Triceratops. "This is my favourite by far," said Arthur, pushing his nose on the glass and breathing mist patches, "Wouldn't it be great if we saw one of these next time we went back?"

"Shh! You must not talk about it, remember!" Raj whispered back.

"Alright, alright, I am just saying, this one is sick!" Arthur cleaned away the mist on the glass and looked at the massive horns sticking out of its head, "You would not want one of those prodding at your bottom, would you?" Arthur grinned cheekily at Raj.

"Come on, remember we are supposed to be looking for the claw." Serendipity nagged the boys as she and a bewildered Amber walked up the metal stairs. Walking slowly along the metal bridge, with life-size model dinosaurs and fossils on either side, the children were completely mesmerized.

"Look up there, there are some claws!" Serendipity said hopefully.

To the left of the children were two creepy arms hanging from the metal bars above, with claws the size of teapots leaning menacingly towards them.

"That is not the claw we want. They are from Deinocheirus, look here it is written, his name means Terrible Hand." Raj explained pointing to the description on the side of the bridge.

"That is more than terrible, that is petrifying!" Amber said as she gazed at the monstrous claws dangling in the air above her.

"Come on, let's keep going." Serendipity said trying to move the group forward.

"Brain, over hear, this one looks like a T-Rex." Arthur exclaimed pointing to the left at another life-size model.

"Yes, it does but it is not a T-Rex, it is similar but this one was way before T-Rex was alive, look it says here it is 147 million years old."

"A-ll-o-saurus." Arthur said out loud slowly, he then read underneath the name's meaning: "Other Reptile! Well that is unimaginative! Whoever found him must have been pretty boring."

Raj smiled back at Arthur; he was surprised with how much he was starting to like Arthur, he used to think Arthur was a mean idiot that just followed Rocky around like a dog, but the more time they spent together the more he found him really good fun to be around. Serendipity took Tony from Raj and again tried to hurry the group along the bridge to look for the magic claw.

"There it is!" screamed Arthur sprinting forward and leaning over the bridge.

"The claw? Where?" Serendipity asked excitedly

"Not the claw, but the head!" Arthur pointed at the enormous T-Rex skull that was suspended in the air and staring at the children.

"Do you seriously mean that Tony is going to grow to have a head that big?" Amber asked finding it difficult to believe that their little dinosaur could grow into such a monster.

Raj nodded, confirming Amber's fears and then flew down the stairs, "Come on, we have got to keep looking, it must be here somewhere!"

The children hurried down the metal stairs and arrived at a long black wall that had posters with information about Tyrannosaurus on it. They stopped in front of a jaw, one meter long with jagged teeth the size of carrots.

"Look here, where this tooth is missing," Raj said pointing to a gap in the mouth. His friends peeped over his shoulder to stare at the 7cm long daggers." Look closely and you can see a new tooth starting to grow in its place, isn't it fascinating? If they lost a tooth another one would grow back!"

Raj rushed further along the black wall, "You are going to love this bit! Come on, follow me!"

Arthur ran after Raj and the girls slowly walked alongside the black wall, more hesitantly than the boys. Eventually, Amber, Serendipity and Tony turned the corner and then Amber let out a piercing cry of fear, stumbled backwards and ran away as fast as she could.

The boys were in stitches laughing, "Go and get her will you, tell her it is not real!" Arthur said to Serendipity, clutching his belly.

"That is really not funny!" Serendipity said pretending to be cross but finding it hard to prevent a big grin from forming on her face. "You could have warned her!" Serendipity shook her head at the boys' bad behaviour and handed Tony to Raj so she could go and find poor scared Amber.

The children had arrived at the part of the exhibition that had heard more screams of fear than any other exhibition, (admittedly the screams usually came from children below the age of 5). At the other side of the ominous black wall was none other than a life-size, replica model of a T-Rex, moving and roaring as if he was about to pounce on the general public admiring him.

"Tony stop wriggling will you!" Raj said trying to keep Tony still.

"What is wrong with him?" Arthur said as he watched Raj struggle to keep hold of the baby dinosaur. "Keep him still will you, people are watching!"

"I am trying. Ouch! He bit me!" Raj let go of Tony who managed to climb through a gap in the metal fence and jump into the enclosure that surrounded the T-Rex.

"Oh wow, look Sally, look at the baby T-Rex moving around, gosh he looks so real!" a mother exclaimed to her daughter as they stared with fascination at the T-Rex and baby dinosaur.

By this time, Serendipity had finally convinced Amber that the T-Rex was not real and they appeared around the corner to see all the visitors pointing in amazement at Tony who was running around the pretend forest, jumping up at the model T-Rex "Oh my God!" Serendipity said out loud.

"Oh dear dear Lord!" Amber muttered under her breath.

Serendipity was livid, "What happened?" she shouted.

"Shh keep your voice down, he bit Raj! Tony went mental and bit Raj and ran in the enclosure!" Arthur said defensively.

Raj blushed not because he had dropped Tony but because it was the first time that Arthur had called him by his real name. Raj showed his hand to the girls trying to convince them it wasn't his fault.

"What are we going to do?" Amber said crossly.

"I am going in!" Arthur climbed up the metal rail and swung his leg over.

"Oh, Arthur be careful, watch out for the monster!" Amber cried.

"It is not real, dummy!" Arthur said rolling his eyes at Amber.

As soon as Arthur's feet had landed on the other side of the fence Gareth the security guard, puffing and sweating, appeared.

"Arthur, hurry, quick, grab him!" Raj whispered.

"Get out of there you toe-rag!" Gareth shouted.

Arthur continued to run around, ducking under the giant T-Rex trying to catch Tony who was acting as if he had just eaten a bag of candy and was suffering from a sugar rush.

"He is too fast, I can't catch him!" Arthur cried.

All the visitors had stopped in amazement to watch what was going on. Raj could see Arthur was not going to catch Tony on his own, so he flung himself over the metal bar and tried to help.

Gareth, recognizing Raj was flabbergasted.

"Never in all my time! Raj, get out of there, I am warning you two, get out or I am coming in!" Gareth was furious, perspiration was pouring down his brow and sweat patches were forming all over his white shirt. He was scowling at the naughty boys and shouting so loudly that all the other children were more afraid of Gareth than the roaring T-Rex. "Right," Gareth huffed, "I am coming in! Woe betide, which one of you I catch first!"

As mentioned before, Gareth was considerably over-weight; his quivering tummy had never moved so fast in the last twenty years and now it was being heaved over a one metre metal barrier. Gareth, one leg successfully over the bar was just about to bring the other one over to join it, when Serendipity instinctively grabbed it, causing Gareth to wobbly precariously and howl out in pain, his sensitive parts being squashed on the metal bar beneath them. While Serendipity was gripping hold of Gareth's leg, Raj managed to grab Tony and climb over the barrier at the other end of the enclosure.

"We have got him! Everyone run!" Raj screamed at his friends.

Serendipity happily let go of Gareth's leg, but she did this so suddenly that Gareth fell with an almighty crash over the bar and landed at the feet of the T-Rex, clutching his privates and groaning in agony.

"I am so sorry!" Serendipity cried as she saw Gareth rolling on the floor moaning. She quickly grabbed Amber's hand, who was standing as still as a statue and dragged her through the rest of the exhibition to find the exit. The children ran out of the museum, their adrenaline pumping through their veins and their hearts pounding in their chests. They stormed down the stairs and did not stop until they reached Exhibition Road; panting and gasping they finally leant on the bike racks to catch their breath.

"Well that was a disaster!" huffed Serendipity

"We were unlucky that was all!" Arthur said.

"That poor man!" Amber said, still in shock with what she had seen.

"I know, I wonder if Gareth will ever forgive me!" Raj said concerned, he had never meant for Gareth to get hurt.

The children flagged down a black taxi and stepped inside in silence, demoralized and de-motivated they headed back to Notting Hill.

5

Searching for Spinosaurus

A sense of hopelessness was starting to loom over the four children. The initial excitement of discovering Tony had soon subsided and they were overcome by stress and anxiety. Raj had no more bright ideas left so they all decided the best thing to do was to tell Professor Inchenstein. They headed back to Pembridge Hall, hoping to catch the Professor before he went home. Moments later the science door creaked open warning the Professor that some intruders were entering his lab.

"Goodness gracious, what are you still doing here?" The Professor asked smiling as he saw the four pupils enter his science lab rather dubiously. He could tell that something was clearly on their minds but what it was, he could never have predicted.

"Well come in, don't be shy, how can I help?" The Professor continued to smile at them but none of them could find the right words to describe why they were there.

The Professor glanced at the old clock above the door, he was planning to play bridge tonight with his friend Sebastian and the last thing he wanted to do was to hang around.

"You all look dreadfully pale, now one of you speak up. I can assure you that whatever it is, you will feel better for telling me." He hoped this was enough to get the dialogue going, he had never seen the children look so concerned. The Professor imagined that one of them had broken a test tube or the like and their silence was starting to infuriate him.

"Oh, come on folks, I have not got all day! I am 65 with high cholesterol, I could pop my clogs at any moment!" He dramatically clutched his heart for effect. "Now out with it!"

"Oh, just show him!" cried Amber, happy to shift the responsibility of their discovery onto a fully-grown adult.

"Show me what?" the Professor enquired starting to feel slightly curious.

Serendipity bent down, undid her rucksack and picked up Tony.

"By Jove! Einstein's nether parts!" Professor Inchenstein rushed forward and then fumbling, found his glasses hanging around his neck and aggressively tried to put them in front of his unbelieving eyes. He gasped for air, "Is this" he paused and gasped again, "But how?"

Before the children could find the words to explain, the Professor started to stumble around the science lab and eventually crashed down on the floor slumping in front of his desk, staring blankly at the wooden floor. Raj looked at Serendipity who looked at Amber who looked at Arthur. Arthur thought he should do something, so he decided to fill up a beaker with cold water and throw it on the Professor.

"Good God I am not dead Arthur!" Professor Inchenstein cried as he tried to dry his face with his lab coat.

"Sorry sir." Arthur said sheepishly hiding the beaker behind his back.

"Is this really what I think it is?"

Raj went over and helped the Professor to his feet, "Yes sir it is a baby Tyrannosaurus." Professor Inchenstein let his jaw drop wide open until saliva started to drip out of it and onto the floor.

"May I?" The Professor asked humbly as he reached his hands out towards the phenomenal dinosaur.

"Of course. Serendipity gently passed Tony over to the Professor. "We have named him Tony, he is very well behaved, but he does not like dark places." Serendipity fidgeted from one foot to the other.

"This is a miracle!" the Professor said quietly, tears of joy streaming down his wrinkled face. "For the love of fossils will one of you explain to me why I am holding a baby dinosaur?"

The pupils finally found their tongues and they talked and talked with such animation, finishing each other's sentences as they tried to explain what had happened to them over the last three days.

"Mary Anning eat your heart out! What an adventure! I am completely in awe with what you have shared with me and I thank you tremendously for picking me to share your secret." He gave them all a knowing wink. The Professor was overcome with so much excitement that he was dying to release it and thrust himself around the science lab doing the rumba. He nearly leapt into an advanced hip twist but managed to control his itching feet, he did not want to alarm the children. What excited him the most was if they were telling the truth, it meant he could see the dinosaurs too. He would go back to the prehistoric era and see the dinosaurs, in the flesh! It was every palaeontologists dream come true. "What should we do Professor?" Amber said in a very serious voice. At last she thought, someone sensible could take charge.

"Well is it not obvious?" He peered over his spectacles at Amber's relived face, "Every baby needs his mother and we need to find Tony 's!"

Serendipity's heart leapt with joy, she just knew the Professor would do right by Tony. Amber's heart on the other hand sunk like lead to the bottom of her stomach and sat their pessimistically. "But I suppose we need the claw and that is at the Natural History Museum, blast!"

The Professor was cross and started to pace around the science lab searching in his brain for a solution. After five minutes of pacing he leapt into his science cupboard bringing out a battered khaki rucksack.

"In here is everything an explorer could possibly need." he said more to himself than the children and he opened the bag on one of the wooden benches emptying its contents, "A compass, my digging tool kit, a torch, rope, morphine oh well that is just for adults."

Professor Inchenstein continued to mumble to himself excitedly as he looked at the contents of his bag; some of the items he had not seen for ten years or more, but he always knew he should keep them, they were bound to come in handy one of these days.

"Raj get me my encyclopaedia on dinosaurs from the book shelf – we should take this in case we meet some unusual ones along the way."

Doctor Dino straightened his bow tie and began to explain his plan, "OK listen up folks, I will go to the museum and get the claw and you dear children, you must get us provisions! Go into the school kitchen and ask Mrs. Melrose for food for ten men! Tell her Professor Inchenstein sent you and he is doing a very important experiment." The Professor turned to make sure the children had understood, "Don't hesitate she will help you, she has a soft spot for me you see!" and he winked at the boys.

Arthur and Amber dashed off to find Mrs Melrose to get the provisions.

"Oh, and don't forget plenty of bottled water!" Professor Inchenstein shouted after them.

The old man then star jumped in the air forgetting that the two other children were watching him. "When you get to my age it is important to keep the muscles active and sporadic jumping is the best way!" He gave Raj another knowing wink and skipped back into his science cupboard checking to see if he had forgotten some crucial lifesaving instrument. One minute later he came out of the cupboard holding some binoculars and a penknife that looked like it could open Fort Knox. Now you two wait here for me, I will jump in a taxi to get the claw and will be back in a jiffy. If anyone asks just say you are on detention!" He grinned at the two children who had never seen their teacher so animated before. Raj and Serendipity waited for the others to return in silence. They were watching Tony explore the science bench and laughed raucously when Tony fell into one of the sinks that was in the middle of the bench. Tony started to bleat like a little lamb looking at Serendipity unable to get out of the sink. Serendipity swooped down to pick him up, "Who is a silly little dinosaur!" she said in a funny voice like the way old people talk to babies.

Serendipity turned to Raj and asked, "Have you noticed how Tony has a pink blotch on the end of his tail?"

"Yes I did, it is like his pigments there are not fully developed, the rest of him is brown and green!" Raj was stroking Tony proudly when the science lab door swung open and Log Head's terrifying silhouette filled the doorway. Luckily Serendipity was standing in front of Raj, so Tony was hidden from Bunny's goggle-like eyes.

Bunny was furious! "You two are in the biggest trouble of your LIVES!" Bunny screamed causing saliva to foam at the sides of her mouth.

The children were speechless; how on earth were they going to get out of this one? Raj continued to stroke Tony trying to make him stay still.

"Please Miss Bristlepott, we tried to do your detention but, err, Professor Inchenstein put us on a week's detention and said that we should do yours afterwards." Serendipity hated lying but she had to try and appease Bunny before she exploded in front of them!

Bunny was outraged, she could not stand the nutty Professor and how dare he put his detention in front of hers! "Did he indeed!" Bunny whispered in a deathly quiet tone. "We will see about that! Now where is the old fool?" Bunny bent down so that her face was uncomfortably close to Serendipity's.

Petrified that Log Head would discover Tony behind her, Serendipity lied again and said that the Professor was in the staff room.

"Don't move you despicable beings, I will be back in an instant!"

In a flash, the doorway was once again a safe place to look at and Raj finally started to breath regularly again.

"Holy crap!" Serendipity sighed.

"This is bad, really bad!" Raj said putting Tony back in Serendipity's rucksack for safety.

"I know, Log Head will be back and then what will we do?" Moments later, Amber and Arthur arrived with all of the provisions.

"What is wrong?" Arthur asked, "You look like you have seen a ghost!"

"Worse. Log Head!"

"Crikey why can't she leave us alone?" Arthur huffed.

"She is coming back, any minute, we need to hide or do something!"

They all huddled inside the Professor's cupboard in case Log Head returned before the Professor.

Amber decided it was best to request protection from a superior force and clasped her hands together to pray.

Light suddenly infiltrated the cupboard and the children sighed with relief when they saw the grey fuzzy hair belonging to Doctor Dino.

"Why are you hiding in my cupboard folks?" The Professor enquired.

"Bunny found us and she is livid!"

The Professor gasped in fear, he was no match for Bunny and would do anything to avoid her looming bosoms!

"She is coming back we must hurry!" Serendipity whispered frantically.

As if summoned by an unknown force Log Head reappeared in the lab.

"Yikes she is here!" Amber screeched as she saw Bunny's brown dress move cautiously amongst the benches trying to find her victims.

The Professor closed the cupboard door as softly as possible and handed Serendipity the black shiny claw.

"Do your stuff my dear!" He whispered in Serendipity's ear. Bunny wrenched the science cupboard door open, prepared to pounce on the delinquents that she predicted to be inside but to her disappointment the cupboard was abandoned. She glared down at the dark space and spotted a tin of tuna on the floor. She picked it up and examined it intensely. Bunny could not stand being taken for a fool and that is exactly what had happened! She was determined to get revenge and she swore to herself that she would not leave the building until she had located the suspects in question. She threw the tin with rage smashing the test tubes at the back of the room in defiance. No one took Bunny for a fool and got away with it! While Bunny huffed and puffed as she searched the school for her culprits, the four children and Professor fell down to the safety of the pre-historic era. Serendipity braced herself this time and managed not to scream when the bright white light shot through her pupils and into her brain. She closed her eyes and let the ominous images flash under her eyelids, sharp shapes that looked like giant teeth and the same spinning rectangles as before.

Professor Inchenstein felt his insides shoot up his throat and escape out of his mouth in the form of a scream expressing both fear and joy. All five of them were expecting to land in the same location as before but to their alarm they never seemed to land at all. Suddenly the blackness transformed into a dazzling blue sky and the children and their teacher felt a warm breeze caress their faces as they continued to fall.

"Is this normal?" cried Professor Inchenstein totally unaware that this was anything but normal.

To Amber's complete surprise, she started to feel her body lifting strangely upwards and her cheek was touching a warm, soft worn leather. She finally regained her senses and realized she was soaring over the sea on the back of a gigantic bird like creature. Amber looked around in a panic to see where her friends were and just like her, they had all landed on these enormous birds, everyone that is apart from Arthur.

"Where is Arthur? Can anyone see Arthur?" she asked fretfully.

"Ahhhhh, I am down here! Help!" a faint cry was heard from below. Amber mustered all of her courage and looked down towards Arthur's cries. Amber gasped with fear as she saw Arthur dangling in the air with the handle of his rucksack hanging precariously on the tail of the bird.

"It is OK just stay still, you are safe!" Amber screamed back.

Professor Inchenstein was sitting upright on the back of his creature with his legs crossed like a Buddha, confidently gliding in the air above the others, "Higgs Bosom be found! This is a delicious atmosphere indeed!" He bent down to talk to the others, "Children we are riding on the backs of the biggest Pterodactyl that ever existed! We are the pilots of a 10-meter wing spanned Quetzalcoatlus! Woo Hoo!"

Amber could not bear to take her head away from the body of her Pterodactyl, her hands were clinging to the smooth body underneath her, her knuckles white with fear.

"Are we all OK down there?" Professor Inchenstein called down, suddenly aware that a ten-year-old could feel quite scared flying through the air 3000 meters high with only the great ocean below.

"Yes we are fine!" Serendipity shouted back.

Tony was deadly still in the rucksack.

"Are they really Quetzalcoatlus Professor?" Raj shouted across the wind, "I can't believe how big they are!"

"Yes Raj look at the crest on their heads, that's how you can tell!"

"I am not alright!" screamed Arthur, his words being swept away by the wind.

"What did you say Arthur dear," Professor Inchenstein asked looking perplexed; "You want a gang fight?"

Arthur repeated even louder "No, I am not alright!" He was feeling desperate, his tummy churning as he watched the sea beneath him whizz below.

"Well I think it rather inappropriate to start a gang fight hanging off the back of a Pterodactyl!" Professor Inchenstein shouted back, quite bemused with Arthur's request. "I suggest you stay still and enjoy the ride, you are quite safe. The handle of your rucksack is far up the tail, just think how jolly wonderful it all is!"

They flew and flew for what seemed like hours, the warm breeze caressing their cheeks and occasionally the odd cloud would engulf them feeling like soft satin sheets.

"Ahoy there! Look, look over there, I see land! Ha, I see land."

"Thank Goodness." Amber sighed under her breath, thankful her prayers had been answered.

"About time!" a fed-up Arthur replied.

"Yes, quite right Arthur lad, it is indeed sublime." The Professor agreed. The land ahead slowly came into focus and the children saw jagged rocks along the coastline that seemed to be bobbing up and down. Professor Inchenstein squinted through his spectacles trying to decipher why the coastline was bouncing so vigorously. "Hold on children," he cried, "it looks like we are about to land."

The ginormous Pterodactyls did indeed appear to slow down and start to glide, nose down towards the moving rocks. Amber closed her eyes and thought of her Grandma Rose while Arthur felt himself slide further along the tail as his Pterodactyl dived down to land. As the rocks became larger and in focus Professor Inchenstein realized what was making them move so unusually.

"How splendid! Children," he called, "we are about to land in the middle of a Pterodactyl mating ritual!"

The children looked towards the grey rocks and saw the mammoth Pterodactyls, flapping their wings up and down, screeching loudly trying to attract a mate. "I hope we don't take part in it!" the Professor chuckled to himself as they started to circle above, trying to find a spot to land amongst the crowded rocks.

"Why are they taking so long to land Professor?" Serendipity asked, starting to feel dizzy as she and Tony flew round and round.

"Location, location, location! It is all about location! You see the Pterodactyl with the best location is more likely to attract a mate. Female Pterodactyls like all females are extremely fussy and hard to please. They tend to choose a mate with the strongest genes and the one in the best location! Just think of a man with a house in Notting Hill versus a man with a house in Croydon, who gets the lady, eh?" The Professor winked at Serendipity and continued to shout, "This is a perfect example of the survival of the fittest theory."

But before the Professor had time to explain Darwin's theory his Pterodactyl swooped down and landed on a large rock. The Professor quickly tumbled down and waited for the children to land. Everyone else soon landed apart from Arthur's Pterodactyl who seemed to be struggling to find space.

"Come on Arthur!" cried Raj.

"Ha!" retorted Arthur, who did not appreciate Raj's humour, "Do you really think I have control over this overgrown bat?" he shouted back as he whizzed through the air hanging helplessly. Eventually, Arthur's overgrown bat, as he called it seemed to give up and he fell despondently into the sea.

"Hang all the elements!" The Professor cried out in fright as he watched Arthur sink below the crystal water.

"Do something Professor!" Amber pleaded.

"You see, perfect example of the theory I was about to explain!" Professor Inchenstein said running over to where Arthur's unfit Pterodactyl had fallen. "ARTHUR?" he hollered loudly.

"There he is!" screamed Amber, "Help him please!"

Doctor Dino opened his ten-year-old rucksack and pulled out a fraying coil of rope and threw it down on Arthur's wet blond hair. Arthur grabbed hold of the crusty rope and felt himself being pulled towards the rocks. The children helped him to dry land and they watched as Arthur's poor overgrown bat floated on the surface of the sea waiting for its inevitable death.

"What will happen to it sir?" Arthur asked shivering and gazing sadly into the ocean.

"Well Arthur, it is unlikely that he will make it I am afraid. You see he was not as fit as the others, he could not find a space to land and he ran out of energy and just seemed to give up. Creatures only survive if they are the fittest, the world is designed to get rid of the weak ones and keep the stronger ones."

The children could barely hear the Professor's explanation of Natural Selection as they were surrounded by squawking Pterodactyls. "I suggest we find somewhere safer to dwell, we do not want to be caught in the middle of fighting male Quetzalcoatlus! Follow me children."

The Professor commanded and they wound their way between the giant, screeching creatures in search for a safer spot. Finally, they escaped the temperamental mating ground and sat down on a rock, sheltered by trees and out of the broody beasts' way.

"Oh, children just look around you, look at this amazing Sequoia towering above our insignificant heads." Professor Inchenstein rushed up to the tree and pushed his left cheek against it and wrapped his arms around the trunk. "Come on kids, come and hug this wonderful living life-form."

The children got up and walked slowly towards their tree hugging teacher, "Yes that's it, gather round, give it a big cuddle. Join hands and smell that brilliant bark."

The Professor inhaled deeply while Serendipity let the rough bark caress her rosy cheek. Even with each of their arms stretched wide around the Sequoia tree, they were only half way around it. After three long minutes of tree hugging the Professor relaxed his arms and sat down at the base of the impressive tree. The children, a little relived that the hug had finally ended sat around Doctor Dino.

"Well I don't know about you, but I am rather poached." The Professor said leaning against the tree.

"I am starving too! We were flying for hours." Raj said his tummy rumbling.

"Well let us eat Mrs Melrose's feast!"

The children eagerly opened their rucksacks and devoured a mixture of tuna sandwiches and scotch eggs. Tony gobbled up three steaks and then sat calmly on Serendipity's lap digesting.

"He is really quite remarkable and tame!" Professor Inchenstein said admiring the quiet disposition of their baby Tyrannosaurus. "Tell me Serendipity how much does he eat a day?"

"Now he eats around twelve rump steaks a day."

"Yes I am not surprised, they are said to grow extremely fast as size is their biggest source of protection. And how marvellous that he is covered in brown fluff just like a baby chicken! You see Raj, dinosaurs are connected to birds and this only confirms it! Oh, how I wish I could show the world!" He glanced down at the children who looked back at him alarmed, "Oh don't be silly of course I never would, I am just saying that this little creature would answer so many questions."

The Professor became quiet and thoughtful as he stared down at little Tony. He then rummaged in his rucksack and brought out a pair of scissors and a sealed tub. Rolling up his sleeves he gently cut a bit of Tony 's fluff off and placed it in the tub. "Don't look so worried it is merely to do some tests afterwards, we can learn a lot from DNA as Raj here will tell you!" He said smiling at Serendipity who was looking down at Tony's new bald spot on the back of his neck.

"Where are we Professor?" asked Raj.

"Very good question," replied the Professor with a mouth full of sausage roll. "We are in the Late Cretaceous period, around 70-65 million years ago."

"Wow! That is awesome!"

"Yes Arthur I tend to agree that it is rather awesome." the Professor replied grinning.

"But are we in America, or Europe, or could we be in Africa?" Raj asked excitedly.

"Well dear boy it is hard to tell, you see those magnificent Pterodactyls that we flew on for so long have only be found in the US, but scientists recently discovered that Pterodactyls would migrate all the way across the Atlantic Ocean and reach modern day Spain in order to mate."

"What, so we could be in Magaluf?"

"It is possible Arthur." The Professor said his eyebrows furrowed.

"That is no good!" huffed Serendipity. "Tony is a T-Rex and they only lived in the US, if we are to find his mother there is no good being in Magaluf!"

Tony feeling the tension in Serendipity stood up and started to growl. "Shhh my little Tony, mummy is not cross with you." Serendipity gave him a kiss on the nose and rubbed his belly until he stopped growling.

"You are quite right my dear, quite right." Professor Inchenstein said wearing one of his rare, serious expressions and pondered what the best thing to do was.

Before he had found a solution, Amber disturbed his thoughts by asking, "Professor, is Tony really going to grow into the biggest killer that ever lived? He just looks so harmless; it is hard to imagine that he could eat us all."

Everyone stared in Tony's direction with a sense of uneasiness.

"I cannot deny that the Tyrant Lizard was named appropriately! They were feared by every creature on the planet – no one could challenge a T-Rex, only another one. But Tyrannosaurus Rex was not the biggest killer that ever lived."

The children were captivated, what could possibly be more ferocious than a T-Rex?

The Professor, enjoying the attention from his audience continued his tale with vivaciousness, "Oh yes, there was a dinosaur that would have made a T-Rex think twice before he approached!" He paused for effect, "A dinosaur that had a head 2m long and in that ginormous head were 7cm long teeth!"

The children were hanging onto their teacher's every word.

"And those mighty teeth belonged to a dinosaur that was 20m long and 6m tall. He would tower above the other creatures watching them quiver in fear."

At this moment Professor Inchenstein stood up and prowled around imitating the almighty beast that he was describing, "He would walk on his hind legs but his most remarkable feature was his two-meter sail that soared across his sturdy back." The Professor then humped his back demonstrating where the sail would be.

"This magnificent beast would spend his days sailing around swamps and rivers, hunting the unassuming fish in the chilly water! In fact, he is the only known dinosaur that was able to conquer both land and water!" Doctor Dino paused and thought about how wondrous these dinosaurs really were.

"Has anyone guessed what I am describing?" He asked, straightening his back and peering down at the terrified children.

"Are you talking about Spinosaurus sir?"

"Excellent! Yes, Raj the magnificent Spinosaurus was the ultimate hunter and killer."

The Professor sat down and had another swig of water before he continued his tale. "You see my wife and I decided it was going to be our mission in life to find one of these rare and unusual creatures." He wiped the sweat from his brow, cleared his throat and said, "The Germans were the first to come across a fossil belonging to Spinosaurus back in 1911, but then the Second War broke out and the English bombed Munich's state palaeontology museum by mistake and the fossils were blasted to smithereens, lost forever!"

The Professor threw his hanky in the air demonstrating the impact of a bomb exploding in Munich. "It was not until fifty years had gone by before another fossil was discovered and that my dear friends, was discovered by my wonderful wife!" Professor Inchenstein was beaming down at the children who could not take their eyes off their teacher.

Arthur broke the silence by asking, "You have a wife?" finding it hard to hide the surprise in his voice.

"Yes, my dear boy, I have a wife and surprisingly enough I have a life outside of Pembridge Hall as well!" Professor Inchenstein smiled kindly at Arthur.

"Tell us how she found it Professor." Raj asked keenly.

"Well it was back in the mid-80s, you know the time of mass consumption and hedonism. Yes, it was in 1982 when I met Mavis for the first time on a dig in Montana. We were searching for anything really, no particular species in mind, we just longed to find old bones. Mavis and I instantly connected; she was a beautiful geek, curly blond hair, mysterious brown eyes and I was, well just a geek. She had many admirers amongst the palaeontologists on the dig but for some reason that I could never explain she chose Boris Inchenstein."

The Professor's eyes shone brightly as he remembered the first time he had met Mavis and how she had changed his life forever.

"One of striking things about Mavis was her determination. When the woman got something in her head that was it, she would not stop until she got what she wanted! Stubborn as an ox she is! She intimidated some of the other men but I was completely mesmerized by her. After we became close she told me her secret ambition to find a Spinosaurus."

The teacher paused for effect and then continued in a low gentle voice, "I felt instantly concerned, you see children, the fossils found by the Germans were out in the Sahara Desert in Morocco, the deadliest desert there is."

He then took another gulp of water and carried on his story, "Excavating in the desert is the hardest environment for a palaeontologist to endure; the dryness, the scorching heat and the sandstorms, oh the dreadful unforgiving haboobs. Imagine every hole in your body filled with hot jagged sand!"

The children's minds were working overtime as they tried to picture the scene that Professor Inchenstein had described.

"That sounds awfully uncomfortable!"

"Yes, Arthur it was jolly uncomfortable! And don't get me started on the sand bogies! Yes, it is rather tricky to be gentlemanly when in the desert."

The Professor gave a knowing wink at the boys before adding, "But Mavis could I? Indeed, I could not! So, we joined a team of excavators from across the world and organized a trip to Morocco. We had only been together for five years before we set off on our trip but those five years were the happiest of my life."

A tear crept down a wrinkle on the Professor's face but he managed to brush it away before the children had noticed. "Seven months we were out there, searching and searching, digging and digging and nothing was found, it was hazardous, absolutely hazardous! The days were like Dante's inferno and the nights were so cold it was like we were sleeping on sheets of ice. The sun blinded our eyes even though we wore the blackest sunglasses we could find and the flies, oh those frightful flies, sucking our sweat like ravished vampires. It was really hell on earth, but Mavis kept going and her determination motivated everyone else and we kept at it, week after week.

One morning I arose a little later than usual and Mavis had already left the tent. It always made me worry when she went off on her own, so I scurried out into the sand dunes like a nervous dung beetle in search of my mate. I asked all the other excavators who were finishing their breakfasts if they had seen her, but nobody had. Just as I was beginning to panic I heard a cry from above the cliffs, "I have found it! I have found it!" I looked up and there was my beautiful Mavis waving at her beloved husband. I was overcome with joy for her. But how on earth did she get up there I said to myself. I shouted back, I am coming, I am coming my love, stay still. I am not sure if she heard me because she kept on waving and jumping which terrified me, her red shirt billowing in the breeze; she was so very high up on the rock face."

The Professor took a deep breath and looked above the heads of the children out to the horizon as he continued his story, "And then out of nowhere there was a wretched haboob; the winds swept in all directions, lifting thousands of those jagged molecules into the air. I tried to keep looking at Mavis, but the sand was scratching my eyes, I kept them open with all my might, braving the incisions until I nearly went blind, so regrettably I shut them".

The Professor closed his eyes for a moment, in a soft and calm voice he said, "Eventually the winds died down, I looked up to where Mavis had been standing and I could not see her anywhere." The Professor opened his eyes, "My heart raced in my chest, I screamed her name as I ran towards the bottom of the cliff."

Silence fell amongst the children as they sat deadly still listening to their teacher's tragic tale. "Eventually I arrived scrambling on the rocks like a mad man or, so I was told after. I looked down and to my horror my fears were confirmed. My poor Mavis was lying motionless at the bottom of the rocks in a heap. I cried out, but no sound was heard, it was as if my lungs were drowned with sand and I could not speak. Every quark in my body was engulfed by the dreadful fear of loneliness."

He looked down at the children and realized they were all crying. "Oh, my dears I did not mean to upset you! Please do not cry." He said blowing his nose on his spotty hanky and swallowing his grief.

"What happened to Mavis, Professor?" sobbed Amber

did not care about jagged sandstorms or sand bogies; she was determined to find the elusive fossil and I could not let her go there alone, lowing in the breeze; she was so very high up on the rock face."

The Professor took a deep breath and looked above the heads of the children out to the horizon as he continued his story, "And then out of nowhere there was a wretched haboob; the winds swept in all directions, lifting thousands of those jagged molecules into the air. I tried to keep looking at Mavis, but the sand was scratching my eyes, I kept them open with all my might, braving the incisions until I nearly went blind, so regrettably I shut them".

The Professor closed his eyes for a moment, in a soft and calm voice he said, "Eventually the winds died down, I looked up to where Mavis had been standing and I could not see her anywhere." The Professor opened his eyes, "My heart raced in my chest, I screamed her name as I ran towards the bottom of the cliff."

Silence fell amongst the children as they sat deadly still listening to their teacher's tragic tale. "Eventually I arrived scrambling on the rocks like a mad man or, so I was told after. I looked down and to my horror my fears were confirmed. My poor Mavis was lying motionless at the bottom of the rocks in a heap. I cried out, but no sound was heard, it was as if my lungs were drowned with sand and I could not speak. Every quark in my body was engulfed by the dreadful fear of loneliness."

He looked down at the children and realized they were all crying. "Oh, my dears I did not mean to upset you! Please do not cry." He said blowing his nose on his spotty hanky and swallowing his grief.

"What happened to Mavis, Professor?" sobbed Amber quietly.

"She was still alive." the Professor replied.

"Oh, thank goodness!" sighed Serendipity.

"But she was not well, not well at all. We flew straight to Rabat on a helicopter and they tried to save her. After six months she stabilized but she has been in a coma ever since."

Professor Inchenstein blew his nose again trying to pull himself together; he rarely spoke about his personal life, especially the horrific moment when his wife fell to her doom.

"So, she has been in a coma, for what 25years?" Raj asked astonished.

"Yes, yes it has been a long time." Professor Inchenstein

confirmed, "However, I see her every day, I tell her all about you lot!" he smiled fondly at his pupils through his sad eyes.

"That is the saddest story I have ever heard." Amber said quietly looking at the Professor with a mixture of pity and admiration. "I will pray for you, I will pray for Mavis every night."

"We all will." Serendipity confirmed squeezing Amber's hand.

"Thank you dears." Professor Inchenstein cleared his throat and tried to lift the spirits of his friends, "But the good news is, is that Mavis did what Mavis does best and she uncovered the largest Spinosaurus fossil every to be discovered!" He beamed proudly thinking how lucky he was to have a wife like Mavis. The sun was slowly descending on the horizon, filling the sky with the richest hues of reds, oranges and gold that the children had ever seen.

"I think my dears, we should be getting back. If we are in Magaluf there is no point whatsoever in staying here. As Serendipity correctly pointed out we need to be in the US to find Tony 's mother and unless we want to fly on the back of a Quetzalcoatlus I suggest we go back to Pembridge Hall and try again tomorrow."

The children's eyelids were weighing heavily over their eyes and they agreed it was best to go back to London. The adventurers huddled together, and Serendipity rubbed the claw. The ground quickly disappeared below them and gravity pushed them along their way in the same mysterious dark space as before, until they arrived in the science cupboard at Pembridge Hall.

"Good gosh children look at the time!" Doctor Dino cried as he closed the cupboard door.

Amber's stomached flipped violently, she had no idea how she was going to explain to her father why she was so late. Raj turned to look at the large wooden clock in the lab and to his surprise the time was 4.45pm: according to the clock they had been gone for no more than 3minutes.

"But Professor, according to my watch we have been gone for three hours!"

"I know Raj this is rather strange, fabulous but still rather strange." The Professor's eyebrows moved up and down excitedly. "It means that one-hour prehistoric time equals one minute in real time!"

Professor Inchenstein put on his tweed jacket and said enthusiastically, "Well, I can still meet Sebastian for bridge after all! I don't know how I will concentrate!"

They all agreed to meet in the science lab at 8am the next morning so that they would have plenty of time to take Tony back to his mother once and for all.

7

Escaping Troodons

"SERENDIPITTTTTTYYYYY!"

Serendipity bolted upright in her bed with her heart slamming against her chest. She heard a thump and a stomp and before she had time to react her bedroom door swung open and there was Mrs Magnum, scowling at her daughter. Serendipity just had time to throw her duvet over Tony and hold him down before her mother had the chance to spot him.

"Can you please explain to me what Ming Wong has found in the recycling bin?" Mrs Magnum was red in the face and she was carrying a plastic bag at arm's-length, pointing it accusingly at her Serendipity.

Serendipity knew exactly what was in the bag and her brain was racing to try and find a plausible excuse.

"Mum, I can explain, please don't be cross." She said while desperately trying to keep Tony from leaping out from beneath the covers

Mrs Magnum emptied the contents of the bag on the floor and as

Serendipity had predicted, out fell all the steak packets that she had been feeding Tony.

"I am looking forward to an explanation that can justify the killing of other INNOCENT ANIMALS!" Mrs Magnum screamed.

Serendipity had never seen her mother so cross.

Sweat was bubbling on top of Serendipity's nose as she searched rapidly for a viable excuse, "I wanted to try meat. There, I just wanted to try it." Serendipity said quietly.

Mrs Magnum took a deep, deep breath and considered that maybe the strict vegan diet that she had forced on her family was the cause of her daughter's extreme carnivorous behaviour.

"But how on earth did you cook it? Ming Wong said she never cooked meat in this house, she swore to me she had stayed true to the Magnum family values and I believe it. So young lady, please educate me how you ate them."

Serendipity was now drenched in sweat as she struggled to hold Tony down, "Raw, I ate them raw, like the French!" she added hastily.

This was enough to throw Mrs. Magnum over the edge, "R-A-W?" she choked back at her daughter in disbelief. "But there are more than ten wrappers here?!"

"Mum I am so sorry, I hated it, I just had to try it. All the kids were picking on me, so I said I ate it, it was only to try it. I hated it and I will never, I promise never eat it again."

Mrs Magnum's felt a sudden pang at the thought of her daughter being bullied at school and her initial shock started to subside, "Well at least it was organic."

"I am so sorry mum, please forgive me."

"You know I can never stay cross with you for long!" Mrs Magnum stepped over the steak wrappers as if they were nuclear waste and suggested they have a forgiveness hug. Serendipity was so relieved that she was no longer in trouble that she hugged her mum back, smelling the familiar scent of Chanel No. 5. However, this harmonious moment did not last for long, Tony was finally free and jumped out from under the duvet cover roaring with all his strength at Mrs Magnum who he was sure was attacking his Serendipity. Mrs Magnum reacted as most mothers would when a baby T-Rex jumps out from under their daughter's duvet; she screamed so loud her tonsils burned and then she collapsed on the floor in a heap on top of all the deadly steak wrappers. Serendipity grabbed hold of Tony before he had a chance to jump on her mother and she threw him in her wardrobe and shut the door.

"What on earth is going on in here?" Mr Magnum asked rushing over to his wife who was lying on the floor. "Serendipity tell me what happened. NOW!"

Her father was so distressed his hands were shaking as he stroked Mrs Magnum's silky yellow hair, but Serendipity could not find any words to describe why her mother was lying motionless on the floor. Mr Magnum raced out of the room and came back with a cup of water from the bathroom and hurled it on his wife. To everyone's relief Mrs Magnum sat up, her hair sticking up on her head as if she had just experienced an electric shock. "Maggie, baby, tell me what happened." Mikey said softly holding his wife in his arms.

"I, I saw, it was I am sure, I saw it, there in the bed." She stood up and nervously looked under the duvet.

"Saw what sweetie, what did you see?"

"A baby dinosaur!"

Mr Magnum was not expecting to hear this; he raised his left eyebrow and looked at Serendipity hoping to find some clarity. Serendipity in return shook her head and shrugged her shoulders.

"Baby have you taken all your homeopathic pills this morning?"

"What? Mikey, I am not crazy I saw it!" she turned frantically and looked at her daughter, "Tell your father what happened!"

"I am sorry mum, I did not see anything." Serendipity said staring down at her bare feet unable to look her mother in the eye, sweat now dripping from her every pore.

"You must be in shock Maggie, you are upsetting Serendipity, look come with me lets lie down and I will get Ming Wong to make you some fresh mint tea with a shot of Remy Martin in it." Mr Magnum managed to pull his wife from Serendipity's bedroom and down the stairs.

ΔΔΔ

"You are kidding!" Raj said in total disbelief.

"I wish I was. Oh, Raj it was a nightmare.! Serendipity said starting to cry.

Raj had no idea how to react to a girl that was crying so he awkwardly put his hand on her shoulder and patted it gently. Tony also started to bleat nervously sensing that Serendipity was unhappy.

"How are we my dears on this splendid Thursday morning, are we ready for another adventure of indescribable scale?" Professor Inchenstein waltzed into the science lab at exactly 8am with an even bigger rucksack on his back than before. "Oh, what is wrong? Why do I see little droplets of H_2O on your cheeks?"

Serendipity told the Professor what had happened to her that morning. "I see, that must have been quite a shock! Listen, do not worry, your mother will recover and forget all about it. She will put it down to a late trip from the rock n' roll days and it will all be forgotten. We will find Tony 's mother today, I promise, and everything will go back to normal. I assure you." He smiled through his bushy white eyebrows and Serendipity felt calmer even though she did not know what a late trip was, she trusted the Professor and hoped he was right.

"He is just growing so big, I can't hide him anymore and what with all the disruption this morning I did not have time to feed him."

"Don't panic, I am well prepared!" The Professor pulled out a whole cow's thigh from his rucksack as if he were pulling a rabbit out of a magician's hat and they all watched as Tony gobbled it down greedily. Amber and Arthur arrived shortly after and they all prepared for their next adventure back to the Late Cretaceous period. "Now I suggest you rub exactly where you rubbed the very first time so that we try and land back in the nest." the Professor advised Serendipity.

Serendipity closed her eyes and slowly rubbed the bottom of the claw; falling like abandoned feathers, they rocketed through the black air. This time the blinding white light did not surprise Serendipity and she tried to concentrate, to focus on the shapes that popped up behind her eye lids; the same sharp objects, they reminded her of the teeth that she saw at the Natural History Museum, thick and spiky with serrated edges. Just as the form was becoming more in focus Serendipity landed with a hefty thud.

"It worked! We are back in the nest."

"How do you know it is the same one Raj, how can you be so sure?"

Raj was rummaging on the floor between all the broken egg shells.

"Ah ha! Because here is the tea-towel I was holding when we fell last time!"

"Why, may I ask did you have a tea-towel with you at the time?" The Professor asked confused.

"Because I had just finished cleaning all the test tubes and was putting them back in the cupboard when I found these three messing around with the claw!"

"Alright dear, no need to be agitated." Doctor Dino said quickly to calm Raj.

"Well done Serendipity you rubbed the right spot." Arthur beamed.

The Professor crouched down and examined the nest, counting all the broken eggs, "Look children, it seems that Tony has four brothers and sisters. Now nobody knows if dinosaurs cared for their young, but my prediction is that they stuck together until the young were able to look after themselves. We need to find the mother T-Rex's tracks and follow them until we find Tony 's family."

"Here is a foot print sir, look it is massive. Gosh it is, twice my height!" Arthur was pointing down in shock.

"Well done Arthur dear you have indeed found the mother's footsteps and what a big mama she is!" The Professor took out his compass and hurried forward, "Come on chaps we have a lot of ground to cover!"

The four children and little Tony rushed after their teacher trudging through mud and leaves in the sweltering heat. They walked for fifteen minutes in silence. Every now and again the Professor would raise his hand in the air to stop his troops so that he could observe some unusual plant and take a sample for his research. Tony stayed close to Serendipity and his little legs went twice as fast as the rest in order to keep up. After another 15mins the Professor stopped and leant against a tree, wiping his brow with his red and white spotty hanky.

"We have been walking for more than half an hour and we have not come across any dinosaurs. What bad luck!"

Amber on the other hand was thinking what good luck it was and could not believe how irresponsible the Professor was being.

"Maybe it is because we are in the forest and the trees are too close together for big dinosaurs to walk in." Raj suggested.

"That is not a bad point Raj but you would think we would see some small Bambiraptors or an Ornithomimus. And Tony 's family did manage to navigate their way through here because we are following their tracks."

"I am sure you will see one soon Professor." Serendipity said realizing the Professor's disappointment.

"Yes, I am sure you are right, I must be patient, a watched pot never boils, eh? Let's keep going folks."

The explorers continued their trek through the forest following Tony's mother's footprints intensely. The footprints eventually led the party of six to a vast opening and to the Professor's joy they could see a watering hole in the distant. The water was being drunk by practically every type of dinosaur that Professor Inchenstein could remember from the Late Cretaceous period. "Oh, my my my my my! My pot has boiled indeed!" Professor Inchenstein yelped with joy! "Scorching hot it is too!"

The Professor took out his binoculars and zoomed in at the spectacle a hundred meters from them. "This is the most fascinating view ever to befall the human eye!"

It was becoming hard for him to see anything as his eyes filled with happy, amazed tears. The four children were mesmerized by the creatures they saw; a herd of Triceratops with horns the length of broom sticks, groups of smaller dinosaurs running around in between the gigantic tree size legs of a herd of Alamosaurus, their long necks reaching the middle of the watering hole.

"Wow!" Arthur whispered to himself pushing his hair out his face so he could take a better look.

They were soon jolted out of this tranquil moment by Serendipity who suddenly cried, "Oh no, Tony has gone! He has run off towards the waterhole!"

Indeed, their little friend had scarpered off to join his fellow dinosaurs. Serendipity decided to run after him but the Professor had just enough time to grab her hand and stop her.

"My dear, you cannot go running out there, it is too dangerous, there is no protection for a start."

"We can't just leave him there; he does not know anything about this world." Serendipity sobbed.

Raj was looking through the binoculars at Tony, "Don't be so sad Serendipity, look here, Tony is drinking at the water hole like the others, maybe he wants to make friends."

Serendipity calmed down as she watched her little baby Tony drinking the water and walking happily around with the other dinosaurs. She sighed deeply. The inevitable moment had come around too soon, she would have to part from her beloved pet dinosaur, forever. Despondently she handed the binoculars to Arthur and sat down thinking back to the first day when she had met Tony.

"Oh, don't look so forlorn my dear, it is for the best that he is with his own kind!" The Professor gently patted Serendipity on her head.

"I know but I wish I had time to say good bye. And we did not find his mother like we promised!" A big soft tear fell down Serendipity's cheek.

While the Professor tried to comfort his student, Arthur felt the binoculars start to slip in his sweaty hands until they fell to the floor with a clunk and made the group jump.

"Be careful you young whippersnapper! This old thing is a

collector's piece and not to be thrown about like a rugby ball!" The Professor said annoyed as he brushed the dirt off his binoculars.

Arthur paid no attention to his teacher's scolds, he just pointed towards the watering hole in a stunned silence. Doctor Dino positioned his binoculars where Arthur was pointing and let out a sudden cry.

"What is it? What is going on?" Serendipity asked clambering to her feet.

Serendipity grabbed the binoculars off her teacher and with her hands shaking she looked towards the waterhole, searching frantically for her baby. "Oh my God, he is being chased by two dinosaurs!" she cried with alarm.

Serendipity knew what she had to do, no matter what the danger was, she had to save Tony from his inevitable death. Just as she was about to leap out on the plain, Doctor Dino dived after her and, once again, grabbed her arm just in time.

"No! No!" she wailed, "Please let me go!"

The Professor wrapped his arms around her waist so that there was no chance of her escaping. "Professor do something!" screamed Amber. "The monsters are going to eat him!"

Professor Inchenstein snatched the binoculars back with his free hand and saw two dinosaurs, no bigger than an ostrich, running on either side of their fluffy Tony.

"What are they Professor?" Raj asked.

"Oh, do something, please, they are gaining on him, they are going to kill him, please!" Serendipity screamed again, stamping her feet on the ground to no avail. Professor Inchenstein's arms were as sturdy as steel.

The three racing dinosaurs were heading closer and closer to the children and their teacher. Tony was doing everything he could, darting from left to right avoiding the gnashing jaws of his chasers. Arthur sized up the two dinosaurs and thought that they did not look too scary. As they came closer he sprung out from the bushes and ran in the other direction screaming, "Pick on someone your own size you over-grown turkeys!"

"Christ! Arthur come back here!" Professor Inchenstein shouted with despair. He released Serendipity at last and watched Arthur's blond bob disappear at top speed. Sweat poured down the Professor's brow as he imagined the scene when they returned to Pembridge Hall and he would have to explain to Arthur's father that his son was eaten alive by a pair of Troodons!

The Troodons stopped for a split second distracted by the odd human creature that had jumped out of the bushes. They looked him up and down and decided he would be a more satisfying meal than the little runt of a dinosaur that they had been chasing, their direction changed and they hurled towards Arthur at top speed.

"Arthur, head for the trees, climb a tree!" Professor Inchenstein cried towards poor brave Arthur. Tony finally reached them and jumped up into Serendipity's arms.

"Poor thing he is shaking." Amber said.

"Shhh, calm down little one, you are safe now."

"Well not exactly." Raj said trying not to scare the girls.

The Professor saw what Raj was worried about and shouted, "Now I do not want to panic you but RUUUUUUUNNNNNNNNNNNN!"

The Professor vanished into the forest like an angry rhino, "Head for the trees" he hollered over his shoulder.

The children ran as fast as they could trying to keep up with their teacher, Serendipity lagging behind, struggling to run and hold a wiggling Tony at the same time. Not far behind them was Arthur's red sweaty face, followed by two greedy Troodons, heading right for them. Professor Inchenstein stood at the bottom of a ginormous tree with low hanging branches. "Come on kids I will help you up." he said.

Amber was the first to arrive at the tree and the Professor lifted her up to the first branch and told her to climb as high as she could go. Raj was next to reach the safety of the tree and he jumped onto the first branch with ease. The Professor grabbed Tony and gave him to Raj and then lifted Serendipity up the tree.

Amber was screaming for Arthur to run faster, her view from the tree's branches enabled her to see one of the monsters so close to her friend that she was sure in a few seconds Arthur would be eaten. The Professor climbed up the tree and he leant down ready to grab Arthur. "Come on son, not far to go." He cried.

"He is not going to make it!" sobbed Amber hiding her face behind her freshly scratched hands.

"Come on Arthur you can run faster than that!" Raj cried trying to force Arthur to run even faster.

Arthur, his heart thrashing in his body and his lungs gasping for breath made one last effort to sprint towards his teacher's outstretched arms. He leapt up towards the tree and gripped hold of Professor Inchenstein's arm but his hands were so sweaty he slipped and fell down. Doctor Dino swung down and grabbed Arthur, hurling him up the tree safely onto the branch. Just as the Professor was reaching up to clutch the branch for his own safety, he felt a sharp pang in his side and he fell to the ground. The Troodon's claw had scraped the teacher's side and now the dinosaur was about to pounce on the injured Professor. The Troodon's saliva dripping mouth, opened wide ready to consume the beloved Professor. Doctor Dino quickly clutched his binoculars that were dangling around his neck and thrust them into the open jaws of the beast above him. The Troodon, who was expecting a tasty meal, was taken by surprise at having such a hard, clunky object between his teeth. Not sure whether to chew it or swallow it the Troodon shook his head in confusion. Unfortunately for the Professor, the strap of the binoculars was still around his neck, and he was flung from left to right like a rag doll.

Raj snapped off a small branch and started whacking it on the head of the Troodon with all his strength to try and save his teacher. The Troodon, not used to this type of defence from his prey was most perturbed. The Professor was tossed to the other side of the tree and finally set free from his binoculars.

"Get up Professor, quick get up now and climb the tree." Arthur yelled.

"Get up, get up!" The children shrieked with anxiety.

The Professor, who was slightly stunned from his fall, woke from his daze by the children's cries. He jumped up and climbed the other side of the tree in a frenzy.

"Up, up we have to keep climbing" the Professor shouted across the tree. He could see that the other Troodon had joined his mate and they were trying to grip the trunk with their curved claws.

"I thought you said they can't climb trees?" Raj shouted down to the Professor.

"Well I bloody well hope they can't!" Doctor Dino peered down at the Troodon and watched it try to pull its scaly body up the tree. "Up, up come on kids, we need to go as high as we can!" The Professor shouted while wincing with pain as he heaved his old bones up the tree.

They climbed and climbed until they were about 30 meters high. Amber finally stopped and sat on a thick branch trying to catch her breath. Her friends soon joined her and last but not least the Professor came panting up the tree. He looked down and to his relief he could not see the boggling yellow eyes of the hunters who came so close to devouring himself and Arthur. Sweat dripping off his chin, the Professor checked that his team of adventures were OK, "Well Arthur might I say you have impressed me with your braveness and stupidity! Really Arthur I entreat you to refrain from confronting a pair of hungry Troodons or any dinosaur for that matter!"

Serendipity moved across the branch to Arthur and gave him a big hug, "Thank you for saving Tony."

Arthur's face flushed an even deeper shade of crimson, "Well we could not let them eat the little mutt now could we!" And he stroked Tony's soft belly.

"Are you hurt Professor?" asked Raj concerned.

"Oh, it is just a graze, nothing to worry about." The Professor replied, smiling at the children as he felt the blood trickling out of his side and sticking to his shirt.

"What are we going to do Professor?" Amber asked panicking.

"I am afraid Amber that we are in a bit of a pickle. Do you know what distinguishes a Troodon from other dinosaurs?"

"I read somewhere they can see in the dark." Raj answered.

"Yes, that is true, well done boy. They can see in the dark which gives them a competitive advantage over their prey as they tend to hunt during the night. But not only is their vision incredibly advanced but they are the most intelligent of all dinosaurs. Compared to other dinosaurs, their brains are the biggest in relation to their body size."

"How does this affect us?" Amber asked, not really wanting to know the answer.

"Well my dear it means that these cunning Troodons know we are up here, they know the only way to escape is down and they know that we can't stay up here forever!"

"Oh gee, what are we going to do?" Amber said feeling queasy with panic.

"I suggest we all have a sausage roll and enjoy the view." The Professor replied.

"Good idea, I am famished!" said Arthur.

"How can you talk of sausage rolls when we are stranded up a tree with two Trodons below?"

"Troodons." Raj corrected her.

"Whatever! There is no way down and I don't want to live in this tree!" Amber huffed.

"Keep calm Amber dear, I will think of a solution but in order to do so I need to feed my brain and some processed pork will do the job nicely." the Professor said stuffing a roll in his mouth.

7

Professor Inchenstein's Secret

Amber was frustrated with Professor Inchenstein; he was a teacher, an actual adult after all and yet he behaved as childishly as Arthur did sometimes. She did not want to be seen as the uptight boring girl from America, but she was finding the lack of responsibility shown in the others especially their teacher, incredibly inappropriate. Amber was just about to suggest that the most sensible thing to do would be to go back to the safety of Pembridge Hall when Arthur got their first and asked the Professor a question, "Professor where did you get the claw from? Did Mavis find it too?"

Professor Inchenstein hesitated, he was secretly hoping that Arthur would forget the question he had asked him on the first day of school, but seeing the determined expression in his pupil's face, and considering that they had just fought a pair of Troodons, he felt that he owed the children the truth.

"Well I suppose being 30 meters high and stuck up a huge prehistoric tree is a good a time as any for a story." Professor Inchenstein straightened his purple velvet bow tie and said in a rare serious tone, "Children, I ask you this only once. Can you keep a secret?"

The Professor's eyebrows frowned down at the children.

They all nodded simultaneously desperate to hear another one of their teacher's amazing stories and find out the secret behind such an unusual, magical claw.

"To answer your second question Arthur, no, Mavis did not find it. My dear Mavis had already started her long sleep and she had been dreaming for fifteen long years."

The Professor looked around at his audience and began to tell the tale of the claw, the truth had never been told before this moment.

"I had been an incredibly dutiful husband," he begun "I stopped all excavating and started teaching at Pembridge Hall so that I could visit my love every day and bring her fresh flowers every week." The Professor then glanced at his students to make sure they all understood what a good husband he had been.

"But after a while I started to get itchy feet. I longed to dig and search and find million-year-old bones. I could not crush the longing I felt inside my loins, so I asked Mrs Bromelow for a sabbatical and bought a ticket to Montana.

I explained to Mavis that I would be gone for no more than three months and I wrote my new phone number on her arm in case she woke up.

I cannot tell you children how excited I felt to be back on the field! You see the tail bone of a T-Rex had just been unearthed and I was on my way to find the spine and whatever else might be there!" The Professor's eyebrows moved enthusiastically up and down revealing his sparkling blue eyes. The children were absolutely captivated; they were so engrossed that they had all forgotten where they were and that two hungry Troodons were waiting to eat them below.

"So off I went with this very same rucksack" he said, patting the familiar rucksack before him. "To my delight the dig was well underway and more of this beautiful creature had been discovered, a thigh bone five meters tall and part of the spine too. Of course, it was not the same without Mavis! I would call her every night; the nurses would put the phone to her ear and I would tell her all about my day and how I wished she was digging by my side like the good old days." The Professor quickly blew his nose into his spotty hankie to distract the children from noticing the tears that were swelling in his eyes.

"A month into the dig and nearly the whole skeleton had been discovered which was unheard of! The only missing bits were part of the skull, teeth and right arm." The Professor tapped his head with his hand, bared his teeth and wiggled his right arm demonstrating theatrically all the missing bones from the T-Rex skeleton.

"As one of the most experienced excavators on the field, I was asked to guard the sacred bones during the night. I stayed in a little tin caravan on site with a sleeping bag and a copy of Anna Karenina to keep me company during the long lonely nights. Then one night, I was reading the part when a heart-broken Anna was about to jump in front of a train when the most incredible noise shook the tin walls around me. I thought it was an earth quake the vibrations were so severe! I was not concerned for my own well-being only the splendid bones that lay, vulnerable out on the rough terrain.

"I leapt out of my tin like a frog on acid and to my horror I saw a ruddy helicopter about to land right on top of our newly found T-Rex!"

The children around him gasped in shock, "But why would a

helicopter do that?"

"I asked myself that very same question Raj, and still to this day I have no blooming idea!

My tin caravan was a mile away, so I ran and screamed and yelled for them to turn off the propellers that were whirling and spinning causing all the bones to scatter uncontrollably. But they could not hear me because the revolving din was so deafening. By the time I arrived at the precious fossils the helicopter was already beginning to take off, so I never managed to find out what it was doing! A prank of some sorts I suspect!

Oh, but what a terrible prank, a prank of unimaginable consequences! You see children so many bits of bone were lost, and I was to blame! I was supposed to be keeping watch!"

"But it was not your fault Professor!" Serendipity said sympathetically.

"Oh, I wish that the rest of the team and the sponsor were as understanding as you my child. I explained what happened, but they were not interested in my excuses, all they were concerned about was the fact that half of the skeleton had suddenly disappeared. I was asked to leave the site, I was officially dismissed! Oh, the shame the shame! I locked myself in the tin caravan for two hours refusing to budge but, in the end, they forced the door open and two local ruffians escorted me off the premises."

Professor Inchenstein lowered his voice before saying, "I was man-handled!"

He took a swig of water and continued, "Shaking the rough locals off me I went to have a tinkle before I got on the bus. As I was relieving myself, my urine splashed on the sand and it revealed something black and shiny."

"The claw!" Arthur shouted.

"Yes, the claw! I was so upset by the way I had been treated that I grabbed it and shoved it into my boot!"

"You stole it Professor?" Amber's innocent eyes fixated on her teacher in disbelief, causing the Professor to shift uncontrollably on his branch.

"Well Amber, technically speaking when you find a fossil you can keep it, finders keepers and all that." The Professor replied trying to avoid Amber's eyes.

"That is not technically true Professor." Raj said. Everyone turned to look at him, wondering what he was going to say next, "If the site is a registered fossil site then every fossil found belongs to the state."

"Oh Raj, you are too clever for me!" A defeated Professor said, sighing deeply.

"Did none of you hear what happened? He was sacked, and it was not his fault! I don't blame you Professor." Professor Inchenstein tapped Serendipity appreciatively on the head.

"Then what happened?" Arthur asked

"Well, I travelled back to London to see Mavis, my tail sheepishly between my legs. When I arrived at the hospital all the nurses behaved in a rather uneasy manner. My instincts told me something bad had happened to Mavis! My whole body trembled with guilt; if anything had happened to her while I was away, I could never have forgiven myself."

"What happened to Mavis?" A worried Amber asked.

"Mavis had woken-up! She had gained consciousness for ten minutes and I had missed it!" Professor Inchenstein shook his fluffy head from left to right remembering how devastated he had felt when he found out. "I immediately demanded the nurses why they had not called me. They claimed they tried and it went to voicemail, apparently, she had woken up while I was on the plane! What rotten luck. If I had arrived a day earlier I would have been there, or if I had not been dismissed then at least we might have spoken for a few minutes before she fell back into her persisting slumber. I blew it!"

Professor Inchenstein blew his nose again, trying to control his emotions; he had kept this secret locked inside his chest for ten long years, and by telling the children, the heavy weight that swung persistently around his neck, felt suddenly lighter.

"Don't cry Professor." Serendipity said.

"Oh, don't pay any attention to me, I am a silly waffling old fool! I did not know whether to love the claw or hate. I kept it hidden in my home, not daring to tell anyone in case someone worked out what I had done. But ten years later I had a brainwave."

The grey spiders' legs that perched so messily above the Professor's eyes moved excitedly up and down revealing the familiar sparkle in the blue eyes beneath.

"I announced to the world that I had found the claw in one of Mavis' old wash bags and that she must have found it on one of her previous digs and never told me. The Daily Mail even wrote an article about me, they took my photo and everything! The headline read something like, Nutty Professor found T-Rex claw in wife's wash bag!"

Doctor Dino stretched his arms above his head and concluded, "Yes children, I had my five minutes of fame."

Serendipity put her hand in her pockets and squeezed the claw tightly and said, "What an amazing story."

A blushing Professor gracefully took a bow making the children giggle as he nearly lost his balance and fell off the branch he was sitting on.

"Did Mavis ever wake up again?" Amber asked.

"No, she has not. She is being very stubborn indeed!" The four children felt extremely privileged that their teacher had confided in them; they promised to keep his secret and not tell a living soul. Amber chose this moment of silence to bring everyone's attention back to the problem at hand.

"So, what are we going to do?"

The Professor was so absorbed by his reminiscing that he was thrown by Amber's direct question, "Do about what dear?"

"About being stuck up a tree with two monsters waiting to eat us at the bottom!" Amber's frustration grew even more; she could not believe her teacher was being so slow!

"Ah yes that problem!" Professor Inchenstein frowned conveying that he was thinking of a solution.

"I think it is obvious what we need to do." Amber continued, her fellow pupils and teacher waited expectantly, "There is no way down, we cannot live in this tree so we should go back to Pembridge Hall."

"I must admit that does seem like the sensible thing to do." the Professor said. He glanced at Serendipity's worried face and continued, "However, we are in a rather awkward situation, the life of dear Tony is our responsibility and I do not want to let you all down."

"We are so close to finding his mother, if we leave now, we will never find her."

"Quite right Serendipity." the Professor agreed.

"And he is too big to keep at home, my mum almost died of a heart attack when she saw him. I will never be able to take him back home!" Serendipity felt the warm tears as they slowly fell from each eye.

"Don't cry, we can take him to a zoo and he will be safe." Amber said softly.

Raj who had been unusually quiet stepped in, "Amber, we are not taking Tony to a zoo for people to poke and prod, he needs to live a normal life in the wild and I will stay up this tree until those wretched Troodons leave and we find Tony 's mother like we said we would." His cheeks glowed red with a mixture of fear and pride. Serendipity smiled warmly at him through her tears and wondered why she had never noticed Raj at school before. The awkward silence was broken by Tony who started to growl softly.

"You see now you are all upsetting Tony," Serendipity said, stroking his belly trying to calm him down.

"Much as I do think Tony is a sensitive fellow, I doubt he actually knows what we are talking about. I think the growling is more to do with the 25m long Alamosaurus that is munching away at the leaves on our tree behind you."

The Professor was right; a head the size of an elephant was ripping off leaves and swallowing them briskly.

"Blimey, he is humungous!"

"Yes, Arthur he is a fine, fine specimen."

The Professor and the children forgot the moral dilemma they had been debating because their eyes were transfixed on the jaws of this new giant that moved methodically from side to side, only three feet away!

"Ha! I knew that sausage roll would produce a brain wave!" The Professor said grinning, "I know how we will get down this tree and the Troodons, clever as they are will have no idea!"

His eyes sparkled with mischief staring at the giant in their tree.

"Please tell me it has nothing to do with this saliva munching monster." Amber asked in disgust.

"Saliva munching monster! Goodness gracious what a thing to say! Amber my dear, that is no way to describe our saviour."

The Professor walked slowly towards the Alamosaurus, so close if he reached forward he would touch the dinosaur's face.

"Look Professor, there are more over here!" screamed Raj in delight.

"One, two, three, perfect." Professor Inchenstein counted the sauropods and then explained, "For those of you that are not following my genius sausage roll inspired idea, let me enlighten you. We are going to escape the Troodons by riding on the heads of these marvellously large herbivores."

"Excellent!" Arthur was grinning from ear to ear and he stood up and stroked the cheek of the Alamosaurus that was closest to him.

Amber's mouth was wide open in utter disbelief. "Oh, Professor you must be kidding me?"

"Have faith in me Amber, we can hold onto the large spike jutting out of his head and we will be away from the flesh eating Troodons in no time. Think of it as riding an elongated elephant!"

Amber gulped hard in horror as she watched the others slide across the branches, closer to the elephant size heads. The Alamosaurus did not seem to feel a thing as Raj slowly climbed up the face of the dinosaur and pulled his body onto its head. He sat down on the right side of the spike that was standing on top of the head, "Come on it is easy." he shouted back.

"Serendipity there is room for you on the other side of the spike, up you get, go on." The Professor helped Serendipity put Tony in the rucksack and then lifted her onto the nose of the Alamosaurus. Professor Inchenstein waited until Arthur and a very reluctant Amber had climbed onto the other Alamosaurus and then he clambered up his own giant head. For another ten minutes the herd of Alamosauruses continued to munch on the trees, chomping and swallowing tones of vegetation. The pupils and their teacher clung onto the spike next to them and waited patiently.

"Why are they so big Professor?"

"Very good question Arthur, it is still a mystery but there are many theories. Some scientists believe the sauropods grew so big because of the levels of oxygen in the atmosphere, the availability of nutritious food and the lightweight construction of their bones. Other views are that their long necks enabled them to reach more nutritious foods causing them to grow bigger. You see they swallowed large amount of leaves without much chewing, which would make them grow in size at a rather fast pace." Professor Inchenstein wiped his glasses with his spotty hanky and continued to explain the debated theories about the giants beneath them. "Look at the way they are scoffing down these leaves, have you ever seen anything like it children! Absolutely marvellous. But do you know what all scientists agree on? It is that the enormous size of the sauropods gave them protection." Professor Inchenstein cleared his throat and said conclusively as if he was addressing an auditorium of palaeontology students, "In my opinion, there was no single cause for the observed trend in body size, but rather an intertwined mass of pressures and constraints which shaped the evolution of these dinosaurs—a constant interplay between what was evolutionarily possible and what was advantageous to local conditions at a given time."

The children tried to digest what their teacher just said.

Fascinated, Arthur quickly asked another question, "How can a massive sauropod be the same as a red robin?"

"There are more similarities between red robins and dinosaurs than you could imagine."

The Professor always enjoyed explaining the facts about these wondrous creatures especially the connection between the terrible lizards and the gentle loving birds flying around in today's world.

"You see birds use gizzards, little stones, to digest the food that they eat. Birds have no teeth remember so they can't chew. And what is fascinating and answers your point Arthur is that these huge sauropods swallowed pebbles, just like birds did to help them digest all the rough leaves that they gulped down their long necks."

"I thought that dinosaurs used chemicals to break down their food in their stomachs?" Raj asked.

"Very good point Raj, many scientists would agree, but it has never been proven and the gizzards have!"

"This is no time to debate the digestive system of these Alamama." Amber said crossly.

"Alamosaurus." Raj said.

"Not the time!" Amber snapped as she sat uncomfortably on the scaly hard head, squeezing Arthur's hand in fear.

"Can you hear that?" Raj asked.

"What?"

"That, there, listen!" A low humming sound was indeed heard hovering amongst the tree tops and then suddenly the herd swung their heads slowly from the trees and started to move.

"Hold on kids, looks like we are off!" the Professor cried with glee as the giants came together.

Twenty or so giant heads, popped up above the tree tops in response to the low humming that vibrated amongst the forest. The heard of Alamosauruses stomped towards the plain.

"Oh, dear lord they are starting to move!" said Amber clutching onto the horn beside her for dear life. Tony popped his head out of the rucksack to see what was going and fidgeted uneasily as he saw the tree tops bob along under his nose.

"Don't worry Amber this is probably the safest place we can be." Professor Inchenstein said reassuringly. "Nothing can harm us here. We are kings of the world!"

8

Battle of the Mothers

The children felt like they were riding the most exciting and dangerous ride in the fairground; their stomachs lurched every time their "saviours" stepped forward on their earth trembling legs. As scary as the ride seemed at first, the children soon agreed with their teacher; it was indeed the ride of a lifetime. The soft breeze caressed the Professor's white tufty hair and he gulped down the clean air and muttered repeatedly, "marvellous, absolutely, blinkingly, marvellous!"

Amber had placed her hand tightly on top of Arthur's when their dinosaur started to move without realizing it and after twenty minutes she shyly took her hand away.

"Feeling less scared now?" Arthur said grinning at Amber over the spike that was sitting between them.

"Yes, sorry about that." Amber replied as she watched Arthur shake his hand trying to get the blood circulating again now that it had finally been set free.

"No worries!" Arthur smiled at Amber. "You know you should try and relax a bit more, we are very safe here."

All Amber could think about was what would happen if she slipped or the inevitable moment when they would have to try and get down. But she did not want to come across as a complete wimp, so she smiled back and decided to distract her worrying thoughts. "So, your dad plays cricket for England?"

"Yes, that's right, he is captain too this year."

"You must be proud. Do you and your mum go and watch him play a lot?"

Arthur shifted uncomfortably on his side of the spike, he forgot that Amber was new to Pembridge Hall and did not know his family history, he always hated explaining it. "I go a lot," he looked across the tree tops in the distance and sighed, "my mum left us last year."

"Oh boy, I am so sorry." Amber felt terrible. "Do you mind if I ask why?"

Arthur swallowed hard, fixating his vision on the top of their dinosaur's head; he did not usually explain to his friends what happened between his parents, mainly because he was embarrassed and ashamed: embarrassed by his father's infidelity and ashamed by his mother's abandonment. But strangely he felt he could trust Amber and he told her what happened, how his mother said she could not stand the lies and the cheating anymore, "She said my dad was an addict and a womanizer."

Amber was not sure what a womanizer meant but she understood that it must have been pretty bad for Arthur's mother to leave her father over it.

"But why didn't she take you with her?" Amber asked softly.

"Beats me." Arthur replied quickly, "She says she needs time. Whatever the hell that means!"

Amber put her hand back on top of Arthur's, this time not in fear but in support. Arthur turned his head to the right and looked at his new friend through his blond floppy hair and smiled. "I don't usually like girls, all they care about are hairstyles, make-up and Hollyoaks, but you are different from the others."

Now it was Amber's turn to gaze far in the distance pretending to focus on the horizon her cheeks flushing a light red. She knew she was different from the other girls in her class; she had no idea what they were going on about half the time and she hated feeling so left out, but now she was pleased that she did not know the difference between lip gloss or lipstick or who was cheating on who in Hollyoaks, because Arthur liked her, he liked her exactly how she was. "Ahoy their children, it looks like we are slowing down." Professor Inchenstein shouted.

Raj stared out into the distance and saw the sun reflecting calmly in the ground. A hundred meters or so ahead of them lay another watering hole. The water was surrounded by various different types of dinosaurs, all drinking contently around the edge of the water just like modern day animals would do in the Kenyan plains. As the herd plodded closer towards the water Raj noticed something that made his stomach summersault uncontrollably, "There, there she is." he whispered.

"There who is?" Serendipity asked curiously.

Raj pointed to the far side of the water towards some rocks "The mother, we have found Tony 's mother!"

Serendipity squinted hard at the rocks, shielding her eyes from the blazing sun and then she suddenly jumped in her skin at the sight of Tony 's mother, "Gosh she is massive!" Serendipity said to herself, as she watched the outline of a T-Rex, the size of two double decker buses form.

"Professor, Professor, look over there!" Raj cried.

Professor Inchenstein could hardly sit still at the prospect of seeing other dinosaurs up close.

"I can't hear you Raj dear!" The Professor shouted back as he looked at a herd of Triceratops and Edmontosaurus drinking the fresh water. He slowly looked around the water, absorbing every fascinating detail with delight and then he gasped and nearly slipped backwards off the head of his Alamosaurus. "We have found them! Look children, I can see a family of T-Rexes by the rocks, basking leisurely in the sun." Professor Inchenstein started to wave and point frantically in the air in the direction of the rocks. "Good grief, what a fine beast, a fine, fine beast indeed!" he muttered under his breath.

Not only was there a T-Rex the size of two London buses but four other smaller T-Rexes lying down sleeping next to their mother. Tony yelped with excitement inside the rucksack. As the Alamosauruses came closer and closer to the water the other dinosaurs moved out of their way so as to avoid being crushed. "Hold on fellows!" Professor Inchenstein shouted as the lengthy necks swooped down to reach the fresh water. They all screamed with a mixture of fear and excitement; it felt like the finale of the roller coaster and the children's tummies were filled by uncontrollable butterflies. "OK chaps now is the time to jump off, it is not deep look." and Professor Inchenstein hurled himself down into the shallow water with ease.

They all followed suit apart from Amber, "I can't I am too scared! I can't swim!"

"Nonsense!" Professor Inchenstein cried back, "It is no more than a meter deep. It is remarkably refreshing now jump down while you have the chance or you will spend the rest of your days on that scaly head!"

"Come on Amber I will catch you." said Arthur smiling.

The Alamosaurus shook his head from side to side trying to shake, what felt to him like an irritating beetle off his head. Amber caught off balance went flying through the air over Arthur and splashed down in the muddy part of the watering hole. She stood

119

up gasping for breath wiping the mud from her eyes. Serendipity, Raj and Arthur were in stitches, even the Professor stifled a chuckle when Arthur compared Amber to a "turd monster!"

"It is not funny!" Amber said spitting mud from her mouth and trying to clean her face. Professor Inchenstein suddenly realized that the next part of their adventure was going to be incredibly dangerous; deep down he never thought that they would find Tony's mother but as if by fate behind the rocks she lay. He puffed out his chest and commanded, "Everyone hold hands and follow me. Serendipity zip up your rucksack, we can't have a repeat of what happened at the last watering hole!"

The children were surprised by how stern their teacher had become. They stopped laughing at Amber and quickly held hands and followed the Professor towards the rocks where Tony's family lay sleeping. On reaching the rocks they crouched down and the Professor slowly peered over the top to get a better look at the terrifying 12m tyrant lizard snoozing no less than 10m from them.

He sat back down next to the others and said softly, "Now this could turn ugly children." He looked at them all making sure that he had their full attention before he continued, "We do not know what is going to happen, the mother might reject him or even worse might kill him."

Serendipity gasped in shock.

"Yes, it could turn ugly indeed." The Professor paused for effect before continuing. "Serendipity please tell me that you have in your hand the claw that brought us here?"

"Yes Professor, I have it here." She replied clenching the claw tightly.

"Now I know how fond you are of dear Tony, we all are. But this is going to be the moment of truth." He frowned down at the children through his fluffy eyebrows. "We did what we had to do, we found Tony's mother and we must let nature take her course." He paused and puffed out his chest even further, "So if anything, bad happens you must rub that claw!" He pointed assertively at Serendipity. "We must leave Tony here and go back. No matter what!"

The children had never seen Professor Inchenstein so serious. "Promise me Serendipity that when I say rub the claw you will do it?"

Serendipity obediently nodded in agreement, "I promise Professor."

Serendipity took her little dinosaur that she had mothered for four days out of her bag and squeezed him tightly; she stroked his belly and cooed in his ear that she will always think about him and will miss him very much. Professor Inchenstein placed his hand gently on her shoulder and said softly, "It is time."

Serendipity sighed deeply and wiped the snot and tears from her face. With Tony in her arms, she slowly crouched down and edged her way to the end of the rocks. She gave Tony one last kiss on his scaly head and then pushed him gently out into the open towards the snoozing double decker bus. Tony strolled forward a few meters and approached the sleeping pack of dinosaurs in front of him.

The children and Professor froze like icicles behind the sun-drenched rock, watching Tony 's every step. Tony continued to walk forward more confidently, unaware of the danger he was about to awake.

One small yellow eye opened and focused on Tony; the head containing the eye titled upwards and then the T-Rex slowly stood up. This dinosaur was only another meter taller than Tony and must be one of his brothers or sisters. Tony plodded forward, curious to see another creature so similar to himself. Tony and his brother stood still facing each other silently. The children and the Professor were so preoccupied watching the two young dinosaurs interact, that none of them noticed that an even bigger amber eye had opened and was watching the scene in front of her. The mother T-Rex snorted loudly causing Amber to cry out in fear, Tony to jump backwards and his new-found brother to scurry away behind his mother. Her two-ton head lifted slowly off the ground and then the rest of her body followed suit. Tony arched his head up as high as he could, watching the ginormous dinosaur towering above him. Tony stumbled backwards as the mother T-Rex lowered her head and sniffed hard, inhaling the intruder's scent.

"I can't watch!" squeaked Amber, her muddy stained hands covering her eyes. "What is happening, why is it so quiet?" she whispered to Arthur.

The deathly silence was broken by an almighty ROOOOOAAAAAARRRRRRR from the mother T-Rex. Tony squealed with fright and ran back towards Serendipity and Amber dropped to the ground unconscious.

"Rub the claw, rub the claw!" cried the Professor.

Serendipity froze.

The twenty-ton mother lumbered forward following Tony, causing the floor below them to tremble and all the other dinosaurs around the watering hole to scatter.

"Rub the claw, for the love of fossils rub the ruddy claw!" Professor Inchenstein screamed even louder.

Serendipity suddenly woke up from her trance and ran out from behind the rock towards Tony. "Heavens be damned get back here!" choked Professor Inchenstein. Never in his life had he felt such panic and fear. He knew he should go after her, but he could not make his legs move, they were too scared.

"What is she doing?" whispered Raj in total shock as he watched his class mate stand directly in front of a Tyrannosaurus Rex as if it was a mundane lamppost. Tony on the other hand was relieved to have Serendipity's legs to protect him and he cowered between them in gratitude. Serendipity held the claw bravely up to the T-Rex shutting her eyes and praying that she would not be crushed between the dagger-like teeth gleaming above her. Tony's mother slowly put her head down close to Serendipity and sniffed the claw in her hand. Serendipity could feel the dinosaur's hot breath steaming down through its colossal nostrils. The mother then bent down further and sniffed Tony again, who slowly came around from behind Serendipity's quivering legs.

"Look Professor, she is missing a claw! Your claw must have come from her!" Raj exclaimed.

"You are right Raj, this is extraordinary. It is even more extraordinary that Serendipity has not been gobbled up!" the Professor answered wiping his sweaty brow with his drenched spotty handkerchief pointlessly.

Amber regained consciousness peeped over the rocks to see what was going on, saw Serendipity standing face to face with the biggest monster she had ever seen in her life and soon swooned again to the floor in complete disbelief!

The mother T-Rex then stood up to her full height, turned around and slowly walked away. The group of baby dinosaurs who were wide awake at this stage, dutifully followed their mother leaving Serendipity and Tony alone. Tony instinctively went to follow the pack of T-Rexes and then he stopped in his tracks and turned to look back at Serendipity. Her heart was swelling in her chest and tears building in her eyes as she ran towards him and swopped him up in the air squeezing him tightly. Tony licked her face and squealed in delight. The mother T-Rex who was waiting a few meters in the distance turned around and snorted loudly. Serendipity put Tony down and pushed him towards his real mother then she walked away, back towards the rocks, her tears flowing uncontrollably. Serendipity flopped down against the hot rocks exhausted; her friends stared at her in complete awe.

"That was awesome!" Arthur said.

"I don't know what came over me." Serendipity replied, truly confused as to what made her confront a terrifying Tyrannosaurus.

"You gave us all quite a fright." The Professor said sternly frowning at Serendipity but finding it hard to remain cross. "Amber here fainted with fear!" The Professor pointed down at Amber's slumped body.

"Twice!" Arthur confirmed grinning, "She fainted twice!"

"Sorry, I, I did not mean to scare you. I just had to do it." Serendipity felt the warm claw slipping in her sweaty palm. "The claw, it was the claw, it made me do it."

Professor Inchenstein raised his over grown eyebrows unbelievingly, "Well it was very brave that is for sure. Brave and daft!" he said smiling again.

Amber regained consciousness and asked, "What did I miss?"

Her friends and teacher laughed out loud, "Amber you missed a sensational moment. Somehow, Serendipity communicated to the full-grown T-Rex that Tony was her son and that she should take him with her. It was really exceptional viewing!"

Amber looked at Serendipity in amazement, "It was wicked, absolutely wicked!" Raj confirmed.

"Wicked as it was, fellow friends, I believe the time has come to go back to the safety of Pembridge Hall. I don't know about you, but I have had enough drama for one Thursday!" Professor Inchenstein put his arms around the children and said, "Serendipity, please rub that magnificent claw!"

9

Back to reality

Compared to their first week of school, the rest of the autumn term passed unexceptionally for the four adventurers and their teacher. Professor Inchenstein bought a safe for his home and locked the claw securely inside, along with the other specimens he had brought back from their pre-historic visit. He told his comatosed Mavis everything that had happened to him, acting out so many of the scenes, causing the nurses to wonder whether he had gone mad. The children had no need to tell anyone of their tales as they had each other to confide in. They would race out of school and go to Serendipity's house where they would talk none stop about everything that had happened, going over the stories again and again. Having escaped Troodons, ridden on the heads of Alamosauruses and confronted a Tyrannosaurus Rex, suddenly everything their peers gossiped about seemed incredibly dull. Arthur still hung out with Rocky and the cool gang in school, he tried to talk with Raj a few times when no-one was looking but one-time Rocky saw and pushed Raj so hard that he fell on the floor and his turban fell off.

Arthur wanted to help him up but everyone in the class was watching, especially Rocky. From that moment the boys kept their distance in school and waited until they were at Serendipity's house to hang out. Despite Rocky and the gang, a bond formed between the four children so incredibly strong that even on Christmas Day the friends insisted on meeting up much to the dismay of their respective families, apart from Raj's Uncle. Uncle Sohan did not believe in celebrating anything; birthdays, Easter, even Christmas! As a result, Raj and his Uncle spent the day eating a Sainsbury ready meal and watching EastEnders repeats until the pub opened. As soon as The Cock and Bottle's doors swung open, Uncle Sohan scuttled off to enjoy a pint of cider and a packet of his favourite pork scratchings. With his Uncle finally gone, Raj hurried to meet his friends at Serendipity's house, just in time for mince pies and charades.

ΔΔΔ

The weary winter months slowly drifted into spring, and eventually the once frozen cricket pitch was overcome by soft, billowing, green grass. It was on a mild spring morning when the boys of year six were led out onto the cricket pitch for the first time that year with their P.E. teacher, Mr Wainsworth. Mr Wainsworth was a very uninspiring teacher; all he talked about was fishing and cricket and was constantly campaigning to make fishing a sport that should be taught at Pembridge Hall. Dr Fog referred to Mr Wainsworth's fishing passion as nothing more than an idle hobby, and would tell him to teach real sports, sports that will win their school more silver trophies for their victory cabinet. As so many other teachers, Mr. Wainsworth did not view Dr Fog in a favourable manner, but she was the deputy-head after all, so he consoled himself with his infatuation with cricket, and trained his team of ten-year olds as if they were taking part in the Gillette cup. Raj dreaded sport's lessons, mainly because his hand eye co-ordination was practically non-existent and all of year six knew it. As a result, he was always the last to be picked for any team. Always. Raj skulked to the back of the crowd waiting for the humiliating moment that was sure to come. Everyone soon joined either Arthur's team or Richard's as their names were called out by the captains. Raj was the last boy standing as usual and joined Arthur's team by default.

"What bad luck!" Rocky shouted loudly which made Raj wish he could just disappear. But there was nowhere for him to hide, so he slowly walked to the far end of the cricket pitch and intended to stay well clear of the ball. The game commenced, and Arthur started bowling so fast that Raj could barely keep track of the ball; it seemed to whizz in the air like a tornado, splitting wood as it reached the opposition's quivering bat. Fifty boring minutes passed and from what Raj could gather, their team was doing pretty well, although Raj did not feel like he was contributing much to it. All he seemed to be doing was standing around; the ball never came his way so he let his mind wander from the whizzing tornado, and onto Tony and their adventure. He thought back to when he was sitting 30m high in the sky, riding the head of one of the largest creatures that ever walked on the planet. Suddenly, he heard his name being shouted from all directions.

"RAJ catch it!!"

Raj's stomach shot up into his throat as he realized the whizzing tornado was zooming towards him high. He could see out of the corner of his glasses Arthur's blond bob, rushing towards him, but he knew he would never make it in time, so Raj thrust his arms in the air and prayed for a catch. The sun's rays conspired against him and blared down on Raj's light blue eyes and try as he might to keep them open, for fear of going blind he had to shut them. He felt a heavy thud strike him on the chest, which he was sure must have been a meteorite because it left a burning sensation in his torso. He fell backwards trying to bare the throbbing pain he was feeling in his upper body when he heard cheering all around him. He looked around to see Arthur lying at his side with his hand in the air clutching a red ball.

"What happened?" Raj asked bewildered, trying to get up but wincing with pain.

"We caught it! The ball hit your chest and flew towards me and I managed to grab it before falling to the floor! I have never seen anything like it!" Arthur exclaimed panting. "Mate, we won!"

The rest of the team rushed towards them and lifted them in the air cheering. Raj had never experienced anything like this in his life; he did not know what it was like to be popular and he had certainly never been the reason why any team had won any match. He looked over at Arthur who was very relaxed being hurled in the air. Arthur grabbed Raj's hand and cheered, "Hip hip hurray, hip hip hurray! Let's hear it for Raj for the best deflect I have ever seen!"

Raj blushed the same deep crimson as the whizzing tornado and ceased to feel the burning in his chest; all he felt was pride and joy. The only boy that was not overjoyed by the team's victory was Rocky. Arthur saw him standing on the side-lines, scowling at Raj being thrown in the air. For the first time, Arthur looked at Rocky and wondered why they were friends? The euphoria from the cricket pitch was carried through to the changing rooms and into lunch break. By the time the boys had told the girls what happened during cricket practice the story had elaborated so much that it did not even make sense. But it did not matter if events were slightly exaggerated Raj told himself, as fourth years were slapping him on the back in the corridor and calling him a cricket legend! No one used to talk to him and now suddenly everyone noticed that he was there, he was no longer invisible and felt over the moon with his new popularity. Serendipity and Amber became incredibly close, an intimacy formed between the two girls that neither of them had ever experienced before. Serendipity was introduced to Amber's parents and her Grandma Rose who lay weak and feeble in her bed. Serendipity never felt quite at ease when she visited Amber's house; she found Grandma Rose charming and sweet, but Amber's parents gave her the creeps. Amber's mother, Mrs Bradshaw would never look Serendipity directly in the eyes and she would shy away from all questions, replying, "Ask Mr Bradshaw, he knows best." Mr Bradshaw was a very small, ugly man at 143cm tall; he had strands of mousy brown hair that were swept to one side of his shiny pale head. As if to compensate by the lack of hair on top of his head he grew a thick, even, rectangle shaped moustache that would have been exactly like Hitler's had it been a little shorter and darker. Unlike Mrs Bradshaw, Mr Bradshaw would stare, unblinkingly at Serendipity as if he was accessing her innermost thoughts with his beady eyes. When the Bradshaw's arrived from Texas to look after Grandma Rose, they redecorated immediately, covering the blue and pink flowered wallpaper with a thick coat of grey paint. The interior of the Bradshaw household was now extremely austere and was just as intimidating to Serendipity as Amber's parents. The only decorations to interrupt the monotonous grey walls were a simple wooden clock and a crucifix. Everything was extraordinarily neat and tidy, not a cushion un-puffed, not a speck of dust to be seen. The organization of the home and its constant state of perfection is what made Mrs Bradshaw feel relaxed and calm inside. As long as everything sat comfortably on a doily Mrs Bradshaw was happy. Serendipity had never even seen a doily until she stepped into Amber's home and watched with amusement as Mrs Bradshaw served everything on a white piece of paper with patterned holes in it; whether it was a biscuit, a cup of tea or a teaspoon, it had to be on a doily. One Sunday evening the Bradshaw family and Serendipity were sitting around the dining room table surrounded by dreary walls about to have their roast dinner.

"Amber dear, recite the Lord's prayer" Mr Bradshaw said closing his eyes and joining his hands together.

Amber obediently recited the Lord's pray. Serendipity closed her eyes and fidgeted in her chair in a nervous manner. She was thinking about how she had tried to explain to Mrs Bradshaw that she was a vegetarian, and how Mrs Bradshaw had refused to understand. Amber's mother did not say that the word vegetarian was invented by the devil, but it was certainly considered sacrilegious in the Bradshaw household. Serendipity realized that tonight was the first night she would taste what her mother had spent her whole life preventing.

Serendipity opened her eyes to see roasted vegetables and potatoes; glistening peas with butter melted on top and watched in horror as Mr Bradshaw was proudly carving a mound of meat at the head of the table. An extra-large portion of beef was served onto Serendipity's plate and she watched the red juices drowning her cooked vegetables. Mrs Bradshaw splashed gravy over the serving and waited impatiently to see Serendipity try her home cooked roast.

"Come on dear, eat up before it gets cold." She said watching intently.

Serendipity was never concerned that her food would get cold as for the last nine months the Magnum family had been eating nothing but raw food. Serendipity forgot what cooked food tasted like and her senses were aroused by the smells seeping up her nostrils. Serendipity slowly sliced a portion of beef and placed it in her mouth. She let it sit on her tongue unable to make her teeth move. Feeling all the Bradshaw's eyes watching her, waiting for her to eat it she took a deep breath and swallowed, trying to smile at the same time. As soon as the meat fell down Serendipity's throat the rest of the Bradshaw's began to eat their dinner too.

"So Amber tells me that your father is a successful musician." Mr Bradshaw said in his long American droll, scrutinizing his guest with his unwavering, grey eyes.

"Yes, he is." Serendipity replied politely while trying to eat an overcooked carrot.

"Classical music I assume?" Mr Bradshaw said, slapping his lips loudly as he chewed his food.

"Kind of, it is more classic rock." Serendipity mumbled.

"How absurd! Classic rock! Dorothy did you ever hear anything like it, a rock musician?"

Mrs Bradshaw raised her eyebrows in response but managed to keep her eyes focused on her plate at the same time.

"You are pulling my leg, come on what does he really do?" persisted Mr Bradshaw.

Serendipity was becoming more and more uncomfortable; Mr Bradshaw's questioning was clearly unkind, and the hot food and dead cow were sitting obstinately in her stomach, which was rumbling loudly.

"Well he is retired now, he mainly writes for other people."

"Retired! He can't be older than me? What about your mother, I assume she stays at home to look after the family?"

Forcing a brussel-sprout between her teeth Serendipity replied, "She is an actress." Serendipity had an uncanny feeling that Mr Bradshaw would not approve of her mother's profession.

"An actress! How adventurous? Dorothy did you hear that? An actress and a rock musician for parents!"

Again, Mrs Bradshaw tried not to take her eyes off her plate and shrugged noncommittedly in response to her husband. Mr Bradshaw shook his head in a condescending manner, looked towards the ceiling and crossed himself.

Amber cleared her throat to try and break the tension, "Serendipity has lived all around the world, Hong Kong, Dubai, and Kuala-Lumpur." She smiled encouragingly at her friend.

"And where may I ask did you worship in these non-Christian countries?" The beady eyes had left the ceiling and were piercing down on their pray, like a hungry snake waiting to catch a mouse about to leave its hole.

Sweat was gathering on poor Serendipity's nose and she felt an unusual, grumbling coming from inside her. Serendipity could not even remember the last time she went to church in London, let alone when they were touring in the Middle East. She opened her mouth not sure what reply would come out but instead of words a mixture of undigested carrots, brussel-spouts and lumps of red meat spilled onto the dining room table. Mrs Bradshaw let out a quiet cry and frantically tidied the table trying to rescue her beloved doilies from Serendipity's spew!

Shortly after this incident Serendipity left the Bradshaw home and headed to the safety of Pencombe Mews. As she walked along Pembridge Villas she was surprised by how much she was actually looking forward to one of her mother's raw vegetable shakes.

ΔΔΔ

On the other side of the pavement Professor Inchenstein was making his way to the hospital to visit his wife. He walked along Prince's Square and passed by the Bradshaw home, unaware of the tension that was bubbling from within the grey walls since their guest had left! Professor Inchenstein was not looking forward to seeing Mavis and his heart skipped a beat as he came closer to St Mary's Hospital. He had some exciting yet guilty news to share with his wife and he was not sure how she would respond; well, he knew that her physical being would not respond as it had not moved in 25years, but he was sure that her mind was still active, and even though in a coma he was terrified of what she may think of his news. He opened the hospital doors and the familiar smell of sterilized bleach, which he used to find comforting, made him want to wretch.

"You are looking a bit peaky Professor." commented Mandy the receptionist.

"Peaky, oh no, all is well. How is my sweetheart?"

"Still snoozing." Mandy replied, kindly looking the Professor up and down. "You going on some kind of safari?"

Professor Inchenstein suddenly remembered that he must look awfully strange; he wore beige shorts with large pockets that were bulging with pen knives and other useful pieces of equipment, a bum-bag, sleeveless green jacket, red socks pulled up to his knobbly knees, and a red straw hat with flying corks, dangling over his eyes.

"Well yes, I am off on a trip, kind of like safari, only a little more adventurous."

"Will you send us a postcard?" Mandy said as she tidied the papers on her desk.

"Certainly." Professor Inchenstein replied and tipped his straw hat in the direction of Mandy, before hurrying up the stairs to see Mavis. He greeted the nurses on the third floor with the same familiarity as Mandy, trying not to notice the unusual glances his attire was attracting. He sat down next to Mavis and clasped her clammy hand in his and pressed his lips down hard. The Professor looked up from the lifeless hand and turned towards his wife and began to cry. The tears trickled down his wrinkled face gathering at his chin.

Oh, for God's sake Boris pull yourself together he murmured, and he blew his nose on his spotty hanky trying to control his emotions. The last few months had been extremely taxing for the Professor; the mundane routine that his life encompassed was slowly eating away at his insides, like a termite devouring a sturdy oak. His life consisted of teaching at Pembridge Hall, playing bridge with Sebastian and visiting Mavis at the hospital. Until he visited the Cretaceous period he was quite content with his little life, and he hoped every day that his dear wife would wake from her coma and enjoy the last years of her life in her husband's devoted arms. But since Tony, everything had changed. Professor Inchenstein could not find his inner peace; he felt anxious and nervous as if he suddenly became aware of his life trickling slowly away, and he felt a kind of desperation that he did not understand. He had spoken to Mavis about his depressive feelings, but nothing was helping him, that is, until he made a decision. Now, he had to tell Mavis what his decision was, and it was this decision that terrified him and excited him at the same time. He sighed deeply and began to explain to Mavis why he had come to such a decision, and how it was impossible to change his mind.

"I hope and pray that you will understand Mavis my love, but I have to do it." He bent down and kissed her damp forehead. He took one long look at her peaceful face, which had hardly aged in the last 25 years and said "Farewell."

10

The Wall of Hullabaloo

It was a fresh Monday morning, the larks were singing in the trees and undisturbed droplets of dew were calmly hanging on the soft grass, enjoying the moments of peace before the residents of Notting Hill would awake and trample them on their way to work. Raj's little feet skipped to school and he felt the dew drops splash against his bare legs as he crossed Pembridge Hall Square. It was 7.45am when Raj arrived at Pembridge Hall and he loved the way the school was so quiet at this time; no scraping of chairs, no banging of doors and no bullies to be seen, just quiet. Raj was always the first to arrive at school and the last to leave; he would do anything to spend as little time as possible at Uncle Sohan's gloomy flat, for Raj, school was a sanctuary. He whistled to himself as he walked down the long corridor until he arrived at Professor Inchenstein's science lab. The old door creaked on its hinges in a familiar way and Raj replied, "Good morning to you too!"

Raj went to the back of the room and turned on the stiff copper taps, added a glug of Fairy liquid and watched the sink fill up with soapy water. Raj continued to whistle as he cleaned the test tubes that Professor Inchenstein had left out for him and he thought to himself that this was the happiest he had felt in a very long time. For the first time he had friends, real friends and he felt an unusual warm feeling inside, a feeling that told him that he was no longer alone in the world. Half an hour later he had cleaned all the tubes and they looked sparkling new as they dried on the bench next to the sink. All Raj had to do now was put them in the science cupboard and then he would go to the library to read the next chapter of Oliver Twist (Oliver had just been shot by Mr Giles and Raj was terribly impatient to find out what happened next). Raj opened the science cupboard door and let out a little cry when he saw what was inside. Raj's eyes slowly adjusted to the darkness of the cupboard and two skinny legs wearing red socks lying. His eyes travelled up the red socks to the knobbly knees, to the yellow bum-belt and eventually reached the straw hat that was sitting on a cloud of familiar white hair. Raj gasped as he looked down at his teacher slumped on the floor of the cupboard and panic rushed through his veins as he thought the Professor must be dead. Raj's fear soon dissolved as the Professor let out a loud snore indicating that he was just asleep and not a cold corpse. Raj put down the test-tubes and started to shake one of the Professor's skinny legs.

"Professor, wake up!" he whispered.

The Professor continued to sleep letting out a muffled snore every other breath. "Professor, wake-up now!" Raj said louder this time shaking both of his teacher's legs.

The Professor started, suddenly aroused from his intoxicating slumber and said, "What! Woof! Brrrrrh!" His old eyes focused on Raj's worried face and he exclaimed, "Oh Raj, did we make it? Are we there? Oh, pray are we there?"

The relief Raj felt on seeing his teacher wake-up soon dissolved back into anxiety, "Are we where? You are not making any sense! What are you doing in here?"

The confused Professor looked around himself, slowly recognizing the familiar objects in his cupboard and let out a loud groan. He then shook his fluffy head, placed his wrinkled hands over his face and said in a pitiful tone, "Oh I am such a fool, I am an old, old silly fool" and he started to sob loudly.

Raj crouched down and patted his teacher on his shoulder, "Professor, what is wrong, you are not making any sense. You are frightening me."

"I am such an old fool." was all Raj could make out between the Professor's heaving sobs. The Professor then bent his knees towards his chest and gave himself a cuddle, rocking back and forth. As he did this Raj noticed something black and shiny lying on the floor; he picked it up and looked in disbelief at his teacher.

"Where you trying to go back Professor?" Raj asked incredulously.

The Professor stopped rocking and looked up at his pupil sporting the same expression that a naughty child would wear if he were caught with his hand in the forbidden cookie jar. After 30seconds of silence the Professor swung around onto his knobbly knees and clasped Raj's shoulders, he then peered into the worried pale blue eyes and he started to explain himself.

"Raj, I don't expect you to understand but I will try all the same to make you."

Raj froze in his teacher's frantic grasp, he had never seen the Professor acting so odd and the wild look in his eyes made Raj feel frightened.

"I have found the last few months incredibly hard. I don't sleep, I don't eat. Ever since Tony, I just can't deal with normal life. All I can think about is that unknown world and I dream about it from day to night, I dream about the dinosaurs and I long to see them again. I crave it."

The Professor's grasp tightened on Raj's shoulders. "Raj, there is so much we don't know and I could find out all the answers, if only

I could go back, just one more time."

The Professor then let go of Raj and slumped back down on the floor in a defeated stupor.

Raj realized what was going on and the happy butterflies that had been fluttering around so leisurely inside him all morning closed their wings one by one. Professor Inchenstein was the closest person that he had to a father figure and he did not want the Professor to go back to the Cretaceous period, it was far too dangerous. Raj could hear his fellow pupils starting to arrive and he did not want anyone to see the Professor in such a vulnerable state.

Raj placed his hands on his hips and shouted, "Get up Professor! Pull your socks up and get up. Pull yourself together." Raj's face flushed red as he shouted at his teacher.

Professor Inchenstein, looked up startled at his pupil, who he had never heard raise his voice in the last four years. It was so out of character that the Professor jumped up at once, pulled his socks up to his knees, rushed to the sink and dunked his head in the soapy water. Patting his face dry with a tatty brown towel, Professor Inchenstein, placed his hands-on Raj's shoulders once again, this time in a gentle and fatherly manner.

"Raj, I am a silly old fool. Please Raj dear, don't tell the others, I don't want everyone else to know what a fool I am."

"I promise Professor." Raj handed the claw back to his teacher and was thankful that their roles had reversed back to normal again.

The Professor looked at the clock and said, "Oh blast it is 8.45am, I won't have time to get changed! Oh well everyone thinks I am barking mad, so they should not be too surprised by my attire!" He winked fondly at Raj who felt relieved to see his teacher cracking a joke and acting normal. "Now hurry along Raj or you will be late for the register. You don't want to keep Log" he cleared his throat,

"Miss Bristlepott waiting!"

Raj grinned and quickly scurried out of the science lab, turned one last time to check on the Professor who was busy putting the test tubes back in the cupboard and ran to his classroom. Raj was feeling uneasy all morning, his friends kept on asking him if he was "OK?" and he would reply that he did not sleep well, but he was fine. He could not concentrate on any of the morning lessons because he could not get his favourite teacher rocking on the floor of the science cupboard with the claw at his feet, out of his mind. Of course, Raj had dreamed of going back to visit the Cretaceous period; he would imagine all the new adventures that they would have and all the dinosaurs that they could meet, but it was just a fantasy for Raj. It was so dangerous the first time, they were lucky to get back alive; it would be madness to go back. He was also wondering why the claw did not work when the Professor rubbed it. Raj glanced across at his friend Serendipity and wondered why when she rubbed the claw, it took them to the pre-historic period but not when anyone else did. Before this adventure with Tony, Raj himself would often go to the Professor's cupboard before school and touch all his specimens, especially the claw, and nothing unusual had ever happened to him. He also thought how odd it was that Serendipity did not get eaten by Tony 's mother; he remembered that Serendipity said that it was the claw that made her confront the mother, but none of it made any sense.

"Raj Grewal, would you mind sharing with the rest of the class your thoughts which are obviously so much more interesting than the theories of Pythagoras!" Dr Fog bellowed at Raj.

The class sniggered apart from Arthur, Amber and Serendipity who looked at their friend in a concerned manner.

"Nothing Dr Fog."

"Sheer emptiness, is that what you mean to say? That your mind was full of emptiness?" Dr Fog had come so close to Raj's desk that he could smell her morning breath.

Raj stared down at his desk afraid to catch a glimpse of the dreaded wart hairs that were lingering ominously above his head. Raj thought that silence was his best defence and hoped that his submissiveness was enough to appease Dr Fog's wrath. Dr Fog banged her walking stick on Raj's desk making his insides shoot out across the classroom with fright. Dr Fog, satisfied that she had made her point walked to the front of the classroom as if nothing had disturbed her lesson at all and continued talking about Euclidean geometry. Raj could hardly eat his lunch because he was too preoccupied, wondering how the Professor was doing. He moved his spaghetti around his plate and hoped that the Professor's state would improve in time for their science lesson. After lunch Year six entered the science lab with the usual commotion.

"Come on kids, settle down. Settle down my fine specimens!" the Professor said as he sat on his desk at the front of the classroom swinging his legs in the air.

Raj immediately felt relieved when he saw the good humour that the Professor was in. When every bottom was firmly seated on a wooden stool, the Professor began the class. "Now, today my lovelies, I am going to introduce to you the Wall of Hullabaloo!" The Professor beamed down at his pupils' excited faces. He suddenly swung his red socks across to the other side of the desk and jumped down, he grabbed a piece of chalk and scribbled on the blackboard:

"THE WALL OF HULLABALOO!"

An excited whisper spread like wildfire across the science lab. The Professor leapt back on his desk and faced his class, "Ladies and gentlemen, the Wall of Hullabaloo is one of my many genius creations." He then swooped down making an exaggerated bow as if expecting to be applauded. The Professor quickly stood up straight and began to explain to the children the meaning of his very special wall. "The point of the wall is so that we all understand that everybody makes mistakes. Even the geniuses amongst us make the most incredible mistakes."

The Professor's eyebrows moved up and down in an excited fashion, causing his class to giggle with delight. "This is no laughing matter!" the eyebrows quickly frowned emphasising the seriousness of what the mouth was saying, "Indeed, the Wall of Hullabaloo is a very severe wall indeed."

Professor Inchenstein sat down on his desk and swung his legs aggressively, "Let me explain the rules and then we will begin."

The teacher took his red and white spotty hanky from his pocket and wiped the sweat from his forehead. "The rules are simple, all we need to do is think of mistakes that great scientists have made throughout time and we write those mistakes on the Wall of Hullabaloo, it is as simple as that. Now who would like to go first? Who can think of a scientific error that a scientist made?"

Raj's arm shot up in the air like a bolt of lightning.

Rocky hurled a rubber at Raj and it hit him bang onto the back of his turban. The class sniggered. The Professor did not see what had happened but guessed it was something against Raj. He thought it best not to bring any attention to it as that would probably make it worse for his pupil, so he carried on as if nothing had happened. "Go on Raj, tell me."

"We used to think that the world was flat?" Raj said.

"Fantastic! You are quite right Raj; the ancient cosmologies did believe that the world was flat. Excellent!" The Professor swung around, bounced down off his desk, and wrote on the blackboard, THE WORLD IS FLAT.

"It was not until the fourth century BC, when the ancient Greek philosophers, Aristotle in particular, proposed the idea that the Earth was, in fact, a sphere!"

The Professor rubbed his hands together in glee, he then picked up an orange pencil in each hand, swung his hands from left to right as if he was leading an orchestra and said out loud, "THE WORLD IS FLAT - a load of hullabalooooo."

The class looked back in silence at their teacher not sure what to do, Serendipity leant over towards Raj and whispered, "Is it me or does Doctor Dino seem to be extra nutty today?"

"Come on class follow my lead, THE WORLD IS FLAT - a load of" he paused and grinned at the children encouragingly. They all cried out harmoniously together "HULLABALOO!"

"Now that's what I'm talking about kids. Excellent. Now give me another one?"

The children were enjoying the game but none of them could think of another mistake a scientist had made. "Alright I'll help you out, Ptolemy, a second century astronomer, believed that the Earth was the centre of the universe! He believed that the Sun orbited the Earth! This is definitely one for the wall!"

The Professor jumped down and wrote underneath the world is flat, that the Earth is the centre of the universe. Armed again with a pencil in each hand, the Professor shouted, "THE EARTH IS THE CENTRE OF THE UNIVERSE - a load of .... "

"HULLABALOO" Year six screamed out with delight.

At this very moment, Dr Fog was walking past the science lab door and overheard the screams of hullabaloo. She rolled her eyes, shook her head in dismay and thought that it was about time Professor Inchenstein retired!

"Any more for any more? Ah I have one, Creationism! People believed that mankind was created by God along with everything else in 6 days! This indicates that-mankind is only 6000 years old and I can tell you all now that modern humans have been walking around this round Earth for over 200,000 years!"

The Professor jumped down and wrote on the board MANKIND – 6000 YEARS OLD, he swung around to face the class and cried, "a load of?"

"HULLABALOOOOOOO!"

The class was having the time of their life during this science lesson; they always had more fun with Dr Dino than any other teacher. Everybody was smiling and laughing except for Amber who felt confused with what the Professor had told the class. She shyly raised her hand in the air to ask a question, "Oooh another one yes please Amber tell us a mistake!"

"Oh, I don't have another one for the wall Professor."

The Professor's bushy eyebrows frowned down on Amber and waited, "Well go on dear what is your question?"

"It's just, I have been taught that humans were created by the Lord above, and that we are 6000 years old! How can there be two theories, which one should I believe?"

"My dear little buttercup, let me explain; there are often conflicting views between religion and science; the biggest conflict being evolution and the birth of mankind".

Professor Inchenstein sat back on his desk, pulled his red socks up and crossed his legs like a Buddha, "You see Charles Darwin published his famous book called The Origins of Species in 1859, which is the foundation of evolutionary biology. What does that mean you might ask? It means that we evolve, all creatures evolve from other creatures, and us humans shared the same ancestor as another animal! Anyone know what that animal is?"

"Apes!" Raj shouted.

"Exactly. Humans and apes evolved from the same ancestor!"

Amber was even more confused than before which obviously showed in her eyes because the Professor said kindly, "Don't look so alarmed Amber dear, it doesn't mean that we are a bunch of chimps, it just means that we share the same DNA and ancestors." The Professor continued his explanation, "You see before Darwin, nobody knew where we came from and man turned to the Bible for explanations."

"So, does that mean that the Bible is incorrect?" Amber could barely believe the words that were coming out of her mouth. All her life, she was told to believe every word in the Bible; whenever she needed advice, her parents told her to read the Bible, whenever she was sad she found solace in the Bible and whenever she was bored she would become engrossed in the fables and Biblical stories. If what Professor Inchenstein said was true, then Amber's world was going to be turned upside down.

At this moment the bell rang, and the class sighed with disappointment. "We will carry on this exciting discussion tomorrow; in the meantime, I would appreciate it if you could find the time to read the first two pages of Chapter 6! Oh yes, tomorrow we are going to take a trip." His eyebrows started to flash excitedly again, "A trip around the marvellous universe!"

11

The helicopter ride

"You must agree that the Professor was acting rather strange today?" Serendipity asked Raj as they walked home to Serendipity's house for dinner.

"I guess so." Raj remembered his promise to his teacher and avoided catching Serendipity's eye.

"I wonder what is wrong with him." Serendipity said concerned.

"Oh, I am sure it is nothing and he will be better tomorrow." Raj replied trying to reassure himself as well as Serendipity that their favourite teacher would be alright. Partly to change the subject, Raj asked his friend a question that had been troubling him ever since he found Professor Inchenstein on cupboard floor. "Don't you think it is odd that the claw only works when you rub it?"

Serendipity, taken a bit by surprise by Raj's question, which seemed completely random and nothing to do with what they were talking about, stopped in her tracks and said defensively, "What do you mean?"

"Well it is just a bit odd that you are the only one who is able to take us to the Late Cretaceous period. Just think of how many other people who have rubbed the claw and touched it and nothing strange happened to them." Raj pushed his glasses up his nose, an action he often did when he was uncomfortable, "It is just a bit odd. That's all."

"Do you mean I am odd?" Serendipity asked, starting to feel upset.

"Of course not, I am not saying you are odd. I just meant that it is odd."

They both continued to walk slowly towards Pencomb Mews. "I mean I have touched that claw so many times and nothing ever happened, and I bet the Professor has touched it and rubbed it, and well it did not work with him either."

"What are you suggesting?" Serendipity asked quietly.

"Look don't get all upset, I think it is fantastic, I wish I was the one who was special!"

"I am not special!" Serendipity retorted feeling more emotional at being called special than odd. Raj stopped walking, took hold of Serendipity's hand and stared at her, "Well I think you are special. Claw or no claw, you are special to me." Raj smiled kindly at her. The two friends continued to hold hands and walked towards Pencomb Mews in silence, each engrossed with their own thoughts and the meaning of their conversation. After dinner, Raj reluctantly went home to Uncle Sohan's while Serendipity rushed straight up to the top floor attic, which belonged to her brother and knocked firmly on the door. Serendipity's brother, Flo, was four years older than Serendipity and had arrived at the awkward adolescent phase that all parents dread. Heavy metal music was being blasted from the speakers within the attic, so Serendipity opened the door and stuck her head inside. The curtains inside the attic were drawn, even though it was only 7pm, and the only light was a warm, rustic red glow that was coming from a 2-meter-high laver lamp in the corner of the bedroom. Flo was flopped on the bed, reading The Catcher in the Rye. Flo was an incredibly

146

confident and stylish teenager; his black hair was always coiffed in an arrogant quiff, held steady with a tonne of gel. His skinny jeans were held up precariously with a leather belt, allowing the top of his pink branded designer boxer shorts to peep out and admire the view. A silver skull with diamond encrusted eye sockets swung on a thick heavy silver chain, draped around his skinny neck

"What are you doing in the dark?"

"What are you doing in my room?" Flo responded, not even looking up from his novel.

"Can I come in?"

"Of course, you can little sis."

Serendipity entered the dark attic and sat on the end of the bed silently.

Flo turned down the music and asked, "Did you come up here just to admire me?"

"Do you ever feel different?" Serendipity asked in earnest, trying to hold the tears back in her eyes.

Flo looked up from his book at his sister, observed her worried expression and placed his book down and lit a cigarette. After a long drag, Flo smiled and said, "Of course we are different. You are called Serendipity and I am called Flo – it takes a strong character to carry off names like ours!" He blew out the smoke causing Serendipity to cough.

"Look, when our parents throw a dinner party they invite the Jagger's and McCartney's. Your God-parents are the Osbourne's for Christ's sake! Of course, we are different!" He could see that his little sister was still concerned so he prodded her in the ribs with his foot trying to tickle her and make her laugh.

"I know we are different like that." Serendipity said quietly.

"Then what is the problem?" Flo said, taking another long drag on his cigarette.

"You know you are not supposed to smoke!"

"Don't be such a snitch." At this point Flo was beginning to feel bored with the conversation and picked up his book ready to continue with Salinger's ramblings. Serendipity stood up and walked towards the door. "We should be grateful that we are not named after our place of birth like the Beckham's, I would be Kuala Lumpur and you would be named after some desert!" Flo grinned mischievously at his sister.

"I was born in a desert?" Serendipity asked bewildered.

"Yup." her brother answered, not raising his eyes from his book.

Serendipity opened the door, wondering why no one had ever told her before that she was born in a desert. "Could be worse," her brother shouted after her, "We could be named after fruit like the Martins! Bye banana!" and he snorted to himself between the pages. As Serendipity walked down the narrow stairs, her thoughts were completely preoccupied with what her brother had told her. How could she be born in a desert and nobody had ever told her before? And what desert? At least she forgot about her original concern of why she was different, but her tummy started to churn uncomfortably. She raced down the stairs, determined to find out where she was born and the story behind it. Serendipity flung the living room door open to find her parents relaxing by the open fire; her father lying on a sheepskin rug, with his head leaning against the sofa while he read the paper, and her mother was resting on the cream leather sofa watching the television.

"How is my Princess of Darkness?" Mickey Magnum asked smiling at his daughter.

"Why was I born in a desert?" Serendipity asked, her arms folded and looking as serious as she could at her parents. "You told me I was born in America!"

"Honey, relax, come here." Maggie Magnum said softly, pulling her daughter onto her lap.

Her father put down his paper and leant towards his two favourite girls. "You were born in America. It is true."

"But in a desert?" Serendipity asked, raising her left eyebrow.

Serendipity's sudden severe disposition made the Magnums laugh, "Don't look so cross at us, when your mother gave birth to you it was the most exciting night of my life!" Mickey then sat on the sofa and touched Serendipity fondly on the nose. Serendipity looked back at her father expectantly waiting for an explanation.

Mickey Magnum cleared his throat and began, "The band had been going strong for a few years but we were just picking up momemntum, our US tour was totally sold out! Your mother was eight and half months pregnant, but she insisted on coming on tour with us."

"I would not leave my baby." Maggie said, stroking affectionately her husband's ponytail.

"It was a warm summer's night and we had just done a concert in the Sonoran Desert! The fans were screaming at us, the adrenalin was pumping so fast I was sure I could fly!" Mickey gazed into the fire, thinking back to the time when adrenalin pumped so naturally around his body. "But after the concert, your mother was getting tired, so we cut the party short, jumped in the helicopter and made our way back to the Four Seasons hotel in Scottsdale.

The sky was dark and clear with bright jewels of light blinking through the darkness. Do you remember that sky Maggie, baby?"

"Oh, how could I forget!" Maggie exclaimed, enjoying the trip down memory lane.

"Just thinking of it makes me want to write a song!"

"Ahem!" Serendipity said impatiently.

"Right, the helicopter! We were all calming down after the buzz from the concert, gazing at the stars and then your mother screamed like a bayoneted whale!"

"Oh Mickey!" Maggie threw a cushion at her husband pretending to be offended.

"Go on what happened next?" Serendipity asked.

"What happened is that you decided you wanted to come out and look at the stars!" Mickey winked at his daughter, "Your mother continued to howl making everyone feel very nervous."

"I did not howl!" Maggie said trying not to smile.

"Honey, it was a distinctive howling!"

"Well I would like to see what you would say 21000m in the air and having contractions!" Maggie threw another cushion at her husband.

"Ok so you were howling, then what happened?" Their eager daughter asked.

"Well your mother was so stressed and in so much pain she asked the pilot to land. The pilot was in such a panic, he had never had a woman giving birth in his helicopter before and he was freaking out!" Mickey took a swig of Guinness and continued, "The pilot was trying to persuade your mother to wait until we reach the hotel, but then her waters broke, and you were determined to see the stars as soon as you could!"

Mickey smiled fondly at his daughter, "Your mother refused to stop howling unless the pilot landed so he eventually obeyed. We were flying over the middle of the desert, there was no landing pad, but the pilot managed to find a safe spot to land.

It was getting cold, so we wrapped your mother in my cashmere poncho and waited. Instead of ceasing to howl as she had promised, your mother screamed so loud it sounded like someone was being murdered!" Mickey threw a grin at his wife who smiled softly back at her husband.

"And then what?"

"Well the pilot and I delivered you into this wonderful world" Mickey lifted Serendipity up over his head and then cuddled her.

"So, I was born in a desert?"

"You weren't just born in any old desert; the helicopter had landed on some fossil site full of old bones! Do you remember that baby, all those old bones?"

Maggie nodded and put her hand to her chest, caressing the end of her necklace fondly. As soon as the words had come out of her father's mouth, Serendipity felt a dryness in her throat and her palms started to sweat.

"What sort of bones daddy?"

"Oh, I don't know, at the time we had no idea what they all were, we thought they were rocks but then some nutty man started screaming at us and shouting something about fossils and bones, some dinosaur I think."

"As soon as you were born we jumped back in the helicopter and flew to the nearest hospital. The man who shouted at us went quite ballistic when the propellers started moving again! Ha ha ha." Mickey started to laugh out loud as he remembered the funny sight of the man in his pyjamas running around frantically and screaming at the new parents to turn the helicopter off.

"Did I ever show you this?" Maggie said taking her necklace off and handing it to Serendipity.

"This is what you always wear." Serendipity said, finding it hard to understand the significance of what her parents had told her.

"I know, look at it closely." Maggie and Mickey exchanged a

knowing look as Serendipity studied her mother's gold necklace. "You would never know but it is actually a bit of old bone that your father gave me!"

"I just thought it was a rock that I took as a souvenir but turns out to be part of a dinosaur bone! I covered it in gold and gave it to my beautiful wife." Mickey bent over and gave his wife a kiss.

Serendipity was hardly listening anymore; her mind was racing. She had just found out that she was born in a desert, on top of a dinosaur and left in a helicopter. Her mind instantly darted back to the moment when she was on the top of the tree and Professor Inchenstein had told them how he had found the claw. Could it be true? Could it have been her birth that had caused the Professor to be fired and steal the claw?

ΔΔΔ

That very same evening a worried Amber walked with Arthur to Princes Square.

"You are very quiet tonight." Arthur said to Amber, kicking a pebble as he walked.

"Every time I have a science lesson, I just feel upset."

"What do you mean, you don't like Doctor Dino?"

"Of course, I like him, that is why I want to believe him and that is why I feel upset."

"I still don't get it. Why are you upset?"

"Didn't you hear what he said, that the Bible is not completely true? That modern humans have been on the planet for two hundred thousand years?"

"So?"

"I knew you would not understand!" Amber said crossly and

walked off in a huff, leaving a bewildered Arthur standing on the street wondering what he had done wrong.

When Amber arrived home, she ran upstairs to pray, hoping that the comforting safe feeling would return once she had finished. Unfortunately for Amber, the heavy feeling in the pit of her stomach remained. She stood up from her bed and walked down the corridor to see if her Grandma Rose was awake.

The grey door creaked open, "Grandma?"

"Well hello my dear, come in, come in, close the door."

As soon as Amber heard her Grandma's voice she felt reassured.

"Why the sad face, not another science lesson?" Grandma Rose smiled at her grandchild.

"I just wish someone would tell me the truth!" Amber said starting to feel cross for the first time.

"That is more like it! That's the same spark your mother had before she met..." The dying old granny managed to stop herself in time and quickly asked, "What happened today dear?"

"The word evolution happened!" Amber said, her arms crossed.

"That is one big word!"

"Well according to Professor Inchenstein, we, you, me, mum, dad, we all came from apes!" Amber was sure that this could not possibly be true – it was absurd. She knew her father disagreed with her teacher, but she needed to see what her grandmother would say, and she was praying that her grandma would agree that the word evolution was a big fat joke.

Grandma Rose could see what was happening to her grandchild and she was secretly ecstatic. At last someone else was having an influence on Amber apart from her father. This Professor Inchenstein was waking up her granddaughter and the frail old lady could not be happier.

"Oh yes, evolution is a common theory believed by most people." Grandma Rose said, her eyes sparkling.

This was the confirmation that Amber was dreading.

"So, Professor Inchenstein must be right!" Amber said out loud, more to herself than to her granny. This time, Amber did not cry, she just felt cross; cross that her father had been hiding all these theories, cross that she was not allowed to study science in Texas and cross at herself for feeling so confused about everything. Grandma Rose watched Amber's reaction intensely and looked forward to Professor Inchenstein's next science lesson.

12

Bunny Bristlepott

The next morning, Professor Inchenstein was feeling more composed, he not only felt composed but looked composed too. The red socks and bum-belt were left at home, neatly in his adventure drawer and he wore his best green tweed jacket and bright purple bow tie. The Professor sat at the front of the classroom waiting for Year six to arrive and as he waited he spun a green Cantaloupe melon that was sitting on his desk.

"Come in, come in, sit yourselves down!" Professor Inchenstein said beaming down at the children arriving for their science lesson. The Professor continued to spin the melon in silence, even after the class had settled.

"Why are you spinning a melon Professor?" Arthur shouted from the back of the class.

The Professor grinned at Arthur, still managing to spin the melon at the same time, "Very good question Arthur! Can any of you fine young whippersnappers guess what this melon represents?"

"The earth?" Raj said hesitantly.

"Ooooooohhhh close Raj dear, but it is not the correct answer!"

The Professor energetically leapt on top of his desk and held the melon high above his head with both hands, almost touching the ceiling.

"This tasty fruit represents the beginning of the universe!"

The melon was then hurled from the front of the classroom towards Arthur who managed to catch it, however, he did slip off his stool in the process. Professor Inchenstein jumped off his desk with a clamour and raced down between the wooden benches until he landed behind Arthur. He stuck his feathery head over Arthur's shoulder and glared at the melon.

"It is true indeed! The ever-expanding universe was once so dense and compressed that it was no bigger than this Cantaloupe! In fact, it was smaller than this melon, imagine the size of a melon seed and even then, we don't come close to how small the universe once was!" The teacher paused for a second and then continued, "The Universe was so flaming hot that it would roast you to ashes in a millionth of a millisecond!" Professor Inchenstein quickly spun around then said, "Share the scorching melon Arthur, don't let it burn you, go on share the universe!" Arthur passed the melon to a confused Rocky who rolled it along the wooden bench to Alison.

"How big is a melon seed?" James asked the teacher.

"Do you not know my boy?" The Professor asked in wonder. "Have you never tasted the succulent sweet juices of a Cantaloupe?"

James shook his head.

"Well that won't do!" The Professor cried.

He grabbed the melon off one of his pupils and ran into his mysterious cupboard. Moments later he flung the door open waving an ancient Japanese machete.

The class gasped. Dr Dino threw his paper work and stationary off his desk dramatically and placed the melon in the centre. The children winced as they watched their teacher raise the sword above his head with both hands. Amber hid her eyes behind her hands. The Professor swung down the sword with exceptional dexterity and slit the melon in half down the middle.

Wiping his brow, he turned to the class, "Don't look so alarmed! Have you never seen an old man slice a melon before?" He grinned mischievously at his students and beckoned them to come and observe the size of the melon seeds.

The Professor distributed slices of the melon amongst his pupils and gave them time to settle back into their seats and eat the delicious fruit. Once consumed Doctor Dino ran up to the front of the room, threw himself over his desk and landed on a heap the other size, out of sight from his pupils.

The children waited impatiently to see what their teacher would do next. A low bellowing sound was heard from beneath the desk as Professor Inchenstein put his hands over his mouth in order to amplify his voice and yelled. "Who knows what made the melon (aka universe) explode?"

Raj's hand shot up in the air. The Professor did not need to peep over his desk to know whose hand was in the air. "Tell us Raj!"

"The BIG BANG!" Raj shouted.

The moment the words left Raj's mouth, Professor Inchenstein exploded from behind his desk causing year six to scream and laugh out loud. "Excellent lad! The melon quite literarily exploded spreading matter and non-matter out into the vast space which then became our universe!" Wiping the sweat from his forehead with his spotty hankie, the Professor then asked, "What is your favourite sandwich Alison?"

"Cheese and pickle." Alison shouted back laughing.

"Excellent taste Alison dear, one of my favourites too!" The Professor winked at Alison and then turned to the rest of the class, "Well imagine the time it takes to make a cheese and pickle sandwich and that will tell you the time it took for the Universe to be born."

The Professor took a swig of water from an old beaker and then continued his lesson with extra enthusiasm.

"Now, does anyone know how long ago the melon exploded? Take a guess kids, don't be shy."

Alison answered, "10 million years ago?"

Professor Inchenstein shook his fuzzy head and waited for more guesses.

"A billion years ago?" another pupil shouted out, but still the friendly cloud at the front of the classroom shook from side to side.

"Ten billion?"

Another shake.

"Ladies and gentlemen, you have exceeded your number of guesses!" The Professor raised his right hand in the air to silence the class. "It was 13.7 billion years ago when the big bang exploded, and our glorious universe began."

Professor Inchenstein rushed to the blackboard and scribbled with pink chalk UNIVERSE = 13.7 billion years old.

"So, if the universe began 13.7 billion years ago, how old is our planet Earth?"

The class like before continued to guess random numbers until their teacher put his finger to his lips and then swung around facing the blackboard and wrote. EARTH = 4.5 billion years old.

"Now kids, the next question. When did life begin on our lucky planet and what was the first species?"

This time Amber knew the answer and her hand shot up in the air enthusiastically. "Yes Amber, take a guess."

"Oh, I don't need to guess! Adam was the first species on the planet, 6000 years ago!"

The Professor's chalk snapped in half as he begun to write the letter A on the blackboard.

The Professor hesitated, "Now, Amber, dear we have talked about this before, remember?"

"Not really sir, before you said we evolved from Apes or some Ape ancestor, well Adam was the first human to evolve."

Amber had never looked so determined before; she had been waiting for this moment all morning. Everything the Professor had said in their last lesson had been spinning in Amber's confused head. She had done her utmost to find a logical explanation that combined evolution and the Bible, and she believed she had cracked it once and for all!

The Professor smiled kindly at Amber; he had never had a pupil challenge him before and usually he would relish the challenge and debate aggressively until science triumphed, but he could see that Amber was suffering and he wanted to be gentle. "Well, we do not know who the first human was; we have found many skeletons of the first human species that was called, Australopithecines."

Professor Inchenstein picked up his broken chalk and started to write Australopithecines on the blackboard. "Anyone know when these unusual looking ancestors roamed the planet?"

This time nobody guessed so the Professor wrote on the board Australopithecines = 4 million years old.

"But before our hairy ancestors went from this," Doctor Dino jumped onto his desk and crouched down, swinging his arms doing his best to imitate an ape, "Into this."

The Professor then slowly lifted his body up, straightening his spine, vertebrae by vertebrae, trying to show the process of evolution from ape to modern human.

"What was the first sign of life on our planet? It certainly was not humans!" He concluded, his pale blue eyes smiling softly at Amber.

"Fish?" Raj guessed.

"Not a bad guess Raj old boy, but not right!"

The children's necks arched back to see their teacher who was still standing on his desk, towering above the class. "The first life form did begin in the mysterious depths of the ocean, but it was not a common salmon or tasty cod, no! It was…." The eyebrows moved excitedly on their teacher's animated face, "CELLS! Simple cells kids that was all there was, simple boring cells, blobbing about the oceans."

Professor Inchenstein then wrote above Australopithecines, SIMPLE CELLS = 3.8 billion years ago. The Professor stepped back from the blackboard admiring the pink chalk and said, "What a timeline eh?"

"But what about us sir, when did we evolve?" Arthur asked.

"Well my child, we, you, I, your parents, my wife, even Dr Fog," the class sniggered, "are all called Modern Humans!" The Professor straightened his bow tie, "Homo Sapiens to be precise!"

Doctor Dino took off his spectacles and tried to clean the lens with his silky hanky. Once clear he asked the class "But what I want to know is WHEN modern humans started traipsing along the earth? Any ideas chaps?" And he struck a warrior two yoga pose to face the class.

The class stared back mesmerized.

"All blank in the head, are we?" their science teacher asked in reaction to his pupils' silence.

"Well goes to show how much you lot listen to me eh? I only told you last Thursday!" Professor Inchenstein put his best cross-face on as he pretended to glare at his class. "Come on, Raj can you take an informed guess? Come on I can't hold this pose forever!"

"200,000 years ago?" Raj shouted out.

"At least one of you were listening!" Dr Dino mumbled as he rolled his eyes at the class. Pink chalk in hand he scribbled on the board under Australopithecines,

MODERN HUMAN = 200,000 years ago.

The children's eyes were transfixed on the blackboard, "Well don't just stare at it admiringly, write it down in your books, write it down. A fine, fine, timeline indeed!"

UNIVERSE = 13.7 billion years old

EARTH = 4.5 billion years old

SIMPLE CELLS = 3.8 billion years ago

AUSTRALOPITHECINES = 4 million years old

MODERN HUMAN = 200,000 years ago

"Any more questions wonderful people? I guarantee there is an answer up here!" The Professor arrogantly tapped his head with the pink chalk.

"Why did the melon explode?"

In response to this question the Professor fell dramatically to the floor as if he had just experienced a violent seizure. Year six was in a complete state of panic; Doctor Dino was ancient in their eyes and the fact that he had collapsed on the floor could only mean one thing. Raj rushed to the side of his favourite teacher and shook him violently. "Professor, Professor are you dead Professor?""

"What a silly question Raj! If I was dead, then I would hardly be able to articulate an answer!" Their teacher replied, his eyes still firmly shut. The class sighed with relief but were still not sure what was wrong with their teacher.

"I have chosen to lie on the floor in shame."

"But why?" Amber asked.

"Because I don't have the blasted answer to Arthur's question! It is the one thing I don't know. The one thing no scientist knows!" The Professor opened his eyes to see twenty concerned faces gazing down at him. "The fact is Arthur we just don't know!"

Amber broke the silence, "Maybe…"

"Yes Amber, go on what do you think?"

"Well, if humans don't know what made the universe begin then maybe we should ask someone else."

"Interesting. Who should we ask?" The Professor pushed himself up leaning on his elbows.

"Well God of course!"

The Professor finally rose fully and patted Amber on the head, "That is not such a bad idea, not such a bad idea!"

The bell rang forcing the dramatic lesson to come to an end, "No one can leave unless the fabulous timeline is inscribed into your science books! I will be inspecting your books at the door and only ones with the fabulous timeline written will be able to escape!"

Professor Inchenstein quickly skidded to the door and star-jumped in front of the doorway, preventing his pupils to leave unless he moved out the way. ** An over excited year six ran out of the science lab and hurried down the corridor towards Bunny Bristlepott's classroom. "I have something to tell you." Serendipity whispered to Raj as they walked down the long chilly corridor.

"What is it?" Raj said.

"I can't tell you here." Serendipity replied feeling uneasy.

"What is the matter?" Raj stopped to face his friend.

Serendipity knew she could trust Raj, but she wasn't sure if she was ready to tell anyone her secret yet. "It doesn't matter. I will tell you later." She carried on walking behind the rest of her class leaving a baffled Raj behind.

"Why are you all so late?" Bunny Bristlepott howled at the children who rushed into the classroom. The difference in welcome between Professor Inchenstein and Bunny Bristlepott was highly visible; there were no spinning fruits, no grins and no flashing, bushy eyebrows. Bunny Bristlepott did, however, have extremely thick dark eyebrows that were angrily set above her acorn coloured eyes. "I am sorry, did you not hear my question? Why so late? Where have you come from?"

"Professor Inchenstein would not let us out the door until we showed him our…"

"Enough Alison, do not say another word!" Bunny Bristlepott glared at Alison, her big round eyes twitching irately. "Don't say anymore!"

It was clear to year six that their Religious Education teacher did not like Professor Inchenstein. None of them understood how anyone could not like the Professor, but Log Head clearly had a reason.

"Now that you have decided to finally honour me with your

presence I suggest you open the Bible and hope the Lord forgives your tardiness!"

Amber eagerly opened her Bible and started to flick through the pages inhaling their familiar scent. Even though Amber found Bunny Bristlepott somewhat terrifying, she loved spending time reading the Bible, she always felt a sense of peace that nothing or no-one else could compete with.

Bunny Bristlepott placed her large, brown rimmed glasses in front of her eyes and said, "I suggest we start with Genesis."

A rustling of pages was heard as the children flipped through the Bible's pages.

"Do any of you have any idea what the word Genesis means?" The teacher's owl-like eyes were enlarged behind her spectacles and they gazed down doubtfully at her pupils.

Amber put her hand in the air and said, "The beginning."

Bunny Bristlepott's board like figure turned slowly to face Amber and a sly smirk formed on her thin lips.

"That is correct. Amber perhaps you would like to start."

Amber felt a flicker of pride, she could recite Genesis in her sleep, but she did not want to make a mistake and started to read out loud, "In the beginning God created the heaven and earth. And the earth was without form, and void; and darkness was upon the face of the deep. And the Spirit of God moved upon the face of the waters. And God said let there be light and there was light."

"Thank you Amber, Alison, please continue." Bunny Bristlepott demanded.

The lesson continued in this fashion with the pupils taking it in turns to read Genesis. It happened to be Raj's turn to read day five, "Let us make mankind in our image, in our likeness, so that they may rule over the fish in the sea and the birds in the sky, over the livestock and all the wild animals and over all the creatures that move along the ground."

"James, continue please."

"Excuse me Miss Bristlepott." Raj said, raising his arm in the air.

"Wait until day six Raj before you interrupt the class!" An intimidated James continued, finally reaching day six, "God saw all that he had made, and it was very good. And there was evening, and there was morning—the sixth day."

"Now you may speak Raj."

The inexpressive form of Miss Bristlepott had edged her way closer to Raj, so uncomfortably close that he could smell her stale musk scent seeping from her body.

"I just wanted to err ask you when it all happened?"

"When it all happened? What kind of an outrageous question is this?"

"I mean how long-ago Man was created?"

"Might I say that I find this question highly inappropriate, but I will oblige you and answer this time only." Bunny Bristlepott did not like questions. Any questions.

"Adam was created by God along with all other living creatures 6000 years ago."

Miss Bristlepott ignored Raj's arm that shot up into the air and continued reading herself. Raj who was usually very silent like the rest of the class in Miss Bristlepott's lesson, surprised himself by obstinately keeping his arm in the air.

"Raj I do not know what has come over you today. Honestly another question already?" Log Head asked bemusedly.

"Yes, another question. If Adam was the first human, then how come there have been human skeletons found that are 200,000 years old?"

Bunny Bristlepott was beside herself; never in all her teaching days had anyone questioned her or the Bible. She was speechless. Before she could find the appropriate words to scold Raj another question was thrown at her from the ring of children.

"And what about evolution? Professor Inchenstein said that it took millions of years for species to evolve. Did it really happen in just six days?" Amber asked innocently.

The rest of the class held their breath in fear, they all knew the rules; no one was allowed to mention Professor Inchenstein's name during Log Head's lessons.

"I beg, I beg, your pardon young lady!" Bunny Bristlepott was gasping for breath and red flames were forming on her pale face. Amber realized she had made a terrible mistake!

"Did you question ME? Did you question the BIBLE?" Year six had never seen their teacher so cross and scary.

"No, gee, I am sorry I am just confused. The Bible says one thing, science says another I am just so"

"HUSH!" Bunny Bristlepott scowled so intensely that Amber could not bear to look her in the eye.

"It just does not make sense." Raj continued much to the disbelief of his teacher and peers, "Simple cells were living on this earth 3.8 billion years ago and the modern human evolved 200,000 years ago so if the Bible says that man was created 6000 years ago, well I am sorry it does not add up." Raj pushed his glasses up his nose before concluding, "Someone has got their facts wrong!"

"Goodness gracious, never in all my time." Bunny Bristlepott's hands were shaking and sweat was dripping from her bushy head, trying to put out the fire that was raging on her face.

"It is a load of," Raj paused and then cried indignantly, "It's a load of hullabaloo!"

"Hullaba!" Bunny Bristlepott staggered backwards, choking as she tried to pronounce the word Raj had used.

Their teacher could not believe what she had just heard.

She had no words left to scold; there was only one option left.

"You two follow me!" Bunny hissed menacingly.

The classroom door was flung open with such vehemence that the hinges shook with terror.

Raj jumped down, but a scared and anxious Amber was not able to move from her wooden chair. Bunny Bristlepott's flaming head reappeared in the doorway and whispered, "You do not want to keep Doctor Fog waiting!"

An even bigger gasp than before was heard; year six knew what would happen if someone was reported to Doctor Fog and they would not wish it on their worst enemy. Rocky gave a thumbs-up to Arthur showing he was pleased that Raj was in trouble, but Arthur looked away and pretended he did not see him. Arthur was impressed that Raj had stood up to Log Head, but he was worried what would happen to him now. Amber, her legs wobbling like jelly managed to move between the desks and follow Raj out the door.

13

The Preacher's Wrath

The naughty pupils were waiting nervously outside Dr Fog's black door while Bunny Bristlepott was inside the chamber, explaining what had happened. Amber had to lean against the wall for support, she was so scared she thought she might faint; she had never been in trouble before. Raj was doing his best to be brave even though his toes wriggled nervously in his shoes. The black door suddenly creaked open, and a low mellow voice was heard from within, "Enter."

Raj walked past the black door with Amber shaking in his shadow. They shuddered like ghosts as the door slammed shut behind them. Their noses were greeted with the mixed stench of stale potpourri and burning wax. The office was very dark inside, and this darkness existed simply because Dr Fog did not like light. The only light that Dr Fog could tolerate was from an inoffensive candle flame. The flickering flames caused unusual black shapes to move around the room, darting from the walls to the ceiling in a horrifying manner. The children's eyes slowly adjusted, and Dr Fog's face appeared amongst the shadows, the flames illuminating her features from below; a terrifying sight to behold.

Bunny Bristlepott was nowhere to be seen.

"I am outraged. Absolutely outraged by such disrespectful, inconsiderate, impertinent behaviour!"

"I am sorry Dr Fog, but if I could just explain." Raj said.

Dr Fog's stick thumped down on her desk making the candle wicks quiver with fear. "There is no explanation for such behaviour. Miss Bristlepott tells me you bombarded her with questions, inconceivable questions!"

"Professor Inchenstein says learning is all about questions." Raj mumbled under his breath.

If there had been more light available, the children would have seen their teachers' cringe uncontrollably as soon as Professor Inchenstein's name was mentioned.

"Education is about listening! Obedient listening!" Dr Fog stood up slowly causing more ominous shadows to fly around the walls and she walked towards the children, her ferocious stick hovering threateningly in the air.

"And don't think just because you are not saying anything that I do not know you are there!" Dr Fog, swept across the room and stood in front of Amber. Amber tried to find her voice to say something, but her throat was blocked with fear and no words would come out. "I have no idea, and nor do I wish to know, what they teach in the New World, but I can tell you now that in English schools, schools with history and heritage we do not disrespect our teachers."

"I am so sorry, I do respect teachers! I did not mean to cause a problem, I only wondered…"

A familiar voice from the back of the room said, "Well your wondering has caused fellow students to doubt the Bible, which is imposturous!"

The children jumped nervously around but it was so dark that all they could see were Bunny Bristlepott's spectacles gleaming between the shadows.

"But I believe in the Bible – I do very much, I believe in God, I just wondered why the dates and times were so confusing."

"That's because the Bible has got its facts wrong. The world was not built in 6 days, and it took 4.498 billion years before humans were on the planet and ahhhhhhhh!"

Dr Fog could not take anymore, she was feeling so vicious and angry thinking how these two rotters had upset her friend Bunny that she let her stick crash down on Raj's foot and leant her weight down on it until he begged her to stop.

"That is quite enough out of you! Honestly, I do not know what has got into you these last months, but I don't like what I see!" She reduced the weight on Raj's foot but kept the stick still touching his shoe in case he retaliated. "What happened to the quiet, studious Raj that was honoured with a scholarship to Pembridge Hall? He seems to have turned into a questioning rebel! A rebel that this school could do without!"

This last comment frightened Raj more than anything else Dr Fog had said.

"Sorry Doctor Fog." Raj mumbled inaudible.

Dr Fog sat back down at her desk, leaned forward so that the candle flame was almost singeing her extra-long wart hair and stared at Raj. "If I see you in my office one more time you will be on a plane to New Delhi quicker than you can say Bollywood!"

He ceased to feel the throbbing in his toes and his mind raced thinking how awful it would be if he was expelled from school and sent back to India. What would his parents say? Sweat started to bubble uncontrollably on Raj's neck.

"Letters will be sent home to your parents." Doctor Fog concluded.

The children were transfixed on the Deputy Head's hideous face and were thinking hard about the consequences of what she had just said. They were so mesmerized that they jumped in their skin when they felt a soft tickling against their cheeks. Bunny Bristlepott's beaver like head had reappeared between the two children's, her soft curls caressing the frightened children like hairy spider's legs. "Now get out!" Bunny hissed.

The punished children bolted out of the dark chamber as quickly as they could, their hearts thrashing in their chests and sprinted down the corridor to safety, Raj struggling to keep up as he hobbled behind Amber.

ΔΔΔ

"I am sure she is not allowed to do that." Arthur said.

Raj winced as he pulled his sock off and showed his friends the purple bruises that were forming on his toes. "I have no one to tell anyhow." Raj said sadly.

Serendipity came into the den with a pack of frozen peas, here try this. She placed the peas gently on Raj's swollen foot.

"Ahhhhhhh! It is freezing!" Raj screamed.

"Of course it is freezing, they are frozen peas, now keep still!" Serendipity forced the peas down on Raj's foot and eventually the wriggling stopped, and the peas began to sooth the wound.

"What is going to happen now?" Arthur asked.

"Well nothing much to me, Uncle Sohan doesn't care about school. He doesn't care about anything to do with me really." Raj said matter-of-factly pushing his glasses up his nose.

"Count yourself lucky! My father is going to kill me! I am so scared I daren't go home!" Amber said sobbing into her hands.

Serendipity put her free hand round Amber's shoulder whilst keeping the peas in place.

"I am sure it is not as bad as you think. Once you explain."

"But I am not allowed to explain. I am not allowed to even answer him back." Amber's face was now bright red and covered in blotches, "I will never get the chance to tell him my side of the story." Amber continued to cry out loud and her friends felt extremely worried too, they had never seen Amber so upset before.

"I think that you should try and talk to him, maybe he will listen." Serendipity said hopefully.

ΔΔΔ

Amber was not the only one that did not sleep well that night; Professor Inchenstein tossed and turned in his bed as if he were sleeping on red hot coals. His mind was exploding with different ways to take him back to the Late Cretaceous period, but each idea would not work without Serendipity. How could he go back without endangering her life? Professor Inchenstein could not find the answer and as the clock struck 3am he surrendered; he had lost the fight with sleep and resolutely put on Mavis' red silk kimono and went to the kitchen to make a cup of hot milk. He did not wear Mavis' red silk kimono because he liked the soft satin against his skin, (that was just a bonus) he wore it because it was the only clothing belonging to Mavis that he could fit into, and by wearing it, it reminded him of his dear wife. He gave it to his wife on their wedding day and it reminded him of that very special day. Sitting in the drafty kitchen at his rickety wooden table, the Professor grabbed a piece of paper and started writing feverishly. He was going to build a case, just as if he was going up in front of a tribunal. A case that would convince himself, as well as his friends why it was imperative to go back to the Late Cretaceous period once more.

ΔΔΔ

The next morning Amber's anxious eyes watched the mail box keenly. "Drink your juice dear and eat your porridge. You will be late for school if you don't hurry up." Mrs Bradshaw said as she peacefully did the washing-up.

The flap in the door jutted open and a pile of envelopes fell to the floor like hand-grenades. Amber knocked her chair to the floor as she leapt to the door and scanned the post for Dr Fog's letter. She found the grenade and clasped it to her chest, relieved. Smiling, she swung around to find her nose facing her father's stomach.

"Expecting something were we?" And he snatched the letter from his daughter's hands. "Interesting, it is addressed to me and from Pembridge Hall." He walked into the kitchen and said to his wife, "Dorothy we have a letter from the school, perhaps it is an invitation to speak during one of their religious ceremonies."

Amber was dying inside; her legs were shaking so badly that she forced herself to pick up her chair and sit down, never taking her eyes away from her father's face. Mr Bradshaw took his favourite ivory handle knife and let the serrated edges cut across the freshly sealed envelope. Mr Bradshaw tossed the envelope dismissively, causing the safety pin to drop carelessly to the floor.

The smug expression that was often found on Mr. Bradshaw's face slowly faded as he began to read Dr Fog's letter. Time was up; the grenade had officially detonated. He glared at his daughter and then frantically reached across the table trying to grab hold of her arm. Amber saw the fury raging in her father's eyes and anticipated his move, she jumped back just in time and ran out of the kitchen and up the stairs. Mr Bradshaw missing Amber's arm gripped hold of the table cloth and hurled it to the floor screaming, "Don't you run away from me child!"

Mrs Bradshaw, who had calmly been tidying the cutlery drawer screamed out in fright as she saw the breakfast table contents flung to the floor; crockery crumbling and glasses smashing under the soles of her husband's shoes as he raced out the room after his daughter. Mrs Bradshaw immediately dealt with the problem at hand and tried to salvage her doilies and tea-set amongst the debris. Amber flew up the stairs two at a time and exploded into her Grandma's room, jumped over the bed where her startled granny lay and hid between the bed and wall for protection.

"Well good morning dear, what is going on?" Grandma Rose asked sitting up slowly and watching the fearful expression on her granddaughter's face.

"It's not as bad as it sounds, if I could only explain." Amber said, her hands trembling.

Before Grandma Rose had the chance to enquire further, her door was flung open again and an infuriated Mr Bradshaw landed in the room, clutching the letter in his fist.

"How DARE you?" he strode towards the bed, shaking his fist in the air. "How dare you, my only child question the Almighty?" Mr Bradshaw spat the words at his daughter over the bed.

"Father, please, I did not, it was a misunderstanding. Please father let me explain." Amber pleaded.

"The humiliation. The shame. Oh, wretched child, I will make you sorry." He stared with so much hatred that Amber immediately looked at the bed sheets afraid to see the anger burning in her father's gaze. He lowered his voice to a sinister whisper and repeated, "I promise, you will be sorry." He started to undo his belt.

"No father please, not that, I am sorry. I did not question the Bible, I promise, I questioned science not the Lord. I believe and love the Lord, no daddy please!" Tears were streaming down Amber's cheeks, but they had no effect on Mr Bradshaw; his heart was as cold as Saturn and he smacked his leather belt on the wall with relish.

"Clive, please, do not hurt this child." Grandma Rose sat up fully in her bed and put her frail arm in front of Amber for protection.

"Stay out of this Maureen! I will discipline my child how I see fit!"

"Clive I am begging you, calm down. Let's talk about this, let's hear what Amber has to say."

"She has said enough already. Embarrassing the Bradshaw name in front of her entire year. A letter home from the Deputy Head! Let's read the letter shall we, let's see if I am over-reacting."

"I regret to inform you that your daughter, Miss Amber Bradshaw has behaved inappropriately during her Religious Education lesson and that this type of behaviour will not be tolerated in the prestigious institute, Pembridge Hall."

Another thrash of his belt was whipped against the door frame causing Grandma Rose and Amber to quiver in fear.

"Wait for it, it is going to get real good now!"

"Amber was found questioning her teacher, Miss Bristlepott in an unruly and disrespectful manner. She not only questioned her teacher but questioned"

Mr. Bradshaw stopped and crossed himself before continuing:

"the Bible, instigating doubt amongst her peers!"

"Father I promise, it was not like that, please let me explain."

"Enough out of you! Enough out of you! I will beat you silent! I will beat you silent!" Mr Bradshaw screamed so loudly that the veins on his temples looked like they were going to blow-up. Mr Bradshaw leaned over the bed, attempting once again to grasp his disobedient daughter.

"I promise you Clive, if you lay one finger on Amber then I promise you I will live longer! I swear it, I will stay alive and keep you away from Texas for longer than you could imagine."

Grandma Rose was now facing Mr Bradshaw, posing as a barrier between father and daughter. Mr Bradshaw took a deep breath, he was not willing to tackle an eighty-five-year-old granny to reach his daughter.

"You are right Maureen, I have over-reacted." Mr Bradshaw, sweat slithering down his face, slowly put his belt back through the trouser loops.

"Come with me child. Let me hear your side of the story." And like a skilled hunter, luring its prey from the safety of its burrow, Mr Bradshaw convinced his daughter to leave Grandma Rose's bedside and accompany him down the stairs.

Even though Mr Bradshaw made sure Grandma Rose's door was firmly shut, the wood was not thick enough to drown out the screams and cries from Amber as her father's belt lashed down on her bare back.

ΔΔΔ

Amber still went to school that morning, every time she put one of her feet in front of the other a burning pain would shoot up her back where the fresh scars from her father's belt blazed. She could not bring herself to tell her friends what had happened, more than anything she felt like they would not understand, and she felt an embarrassment that she could not explain. Serendipity could see that her friend was unhappy and she imagined that her father had told Amber off and upset her, but she had no idea the pain that Amber was quietly bearing. As the three friends sat on the school lawn during the afternoon break Serendipity said, "Why don't you all come back to mine after school and we can go swimming if you like?"

"What about Arthur?" Raj said quietly as he stared at Arthur and Rocky across the playground.

"I'll send him a text." said Serendipity. "Amber, are you in?"

They both turned to look at Amber who had not yet responded.

Amber blushed red in the face, "I would like to, it is just," she stared down at a daisy that she was pulling the petals off, "I can't swim."

Tears started to pour down Amber's cheeks; she was not crying because she could not swim as her friends thought, she was crying because she could not block out the pain that was dancing around her back like the tip of a knife doing the mamba.

"Oh, don't cry! Amber I will teach you!" Serendipity said and went to hug Amber, but Amber pulled away to prevent Serendipity from touching her back. Serendipity grabbed Amber's hand and said again. "Don't cry Amber, you have friends and if you don't want to swim you don't have to! Please don't be so upset."

Amber blew her nose and felt better after a good sob, "Oh don't pay any attention to me! I would love to learn how to swim" she said, smiling through her tears at her friends.

"Why do girls always cry?" Raj asked Arthur as they walked towards Arthur's house.

"Beats me! I don't know much about girls."

"Yeah me neither." Raj said, pushing his glasses up his nose.

"When my mum was here she used to cry a lot and now my dad's new girlfriend cries sometimes." Arthur sighed before concluding, "They just make it look so easy! Honestly I find it quite hard to cry."

"Yeah me too, I never cry." Raj agreed even though he often cried himself to sleep because he missed his parents so much.

A short while later they arrived at Arthur's house. Raj waited on the pavement while Arthur rushed inside to find two pairs of swimming trunks. Moments later Arthur appeared in front of his house, ran down the front steps swinging two pairs of swimming trunks in each hand. He threw one pair at Raj who was not expecting it and it slapped him in the face making both the boys' chuckle and they soon forgot about crying girls, mothers and girlfriends as they headed towards Serendipity's home. By the time Arthur and Raj arrived at number 16 Pencombe Mews, the girls were already changed, and Serendipity was showing Amber how to do front call. Amber was sitting on the edge of the pool wearing two sets of orange armbands and a neon rubber-ring as she watched Serendipity carefully.

Mrs Magnum let the boys in and took them down to the indoor swimming pool, "So boys, what can I get you? You must be thirsty after a long day at school?"

"Oh no not thirsty or hungry at all." Arthur replied hoping he did not sound too rude.

"And what about you Raj dear, do you like beetroot?"

"Err, I am not sure." Raj replied sheepishly

"Well there is only one way to find out!" Mrs Magnum opened the door to the den and showed the boys where to get changed, "I will be down in a mo with some excellent beetroot juice that will definitely get your bowels going!"

"Mate, you should have told her you are allergic to beetroot!" Arthur said crossly, because he knew that his bowels would be moving just as efficiently as Raj's if Mrs Magnum had her way.

"Sorry, it is just she is so nice, I don't want to offend her." Raj said.

"Well you have offended my stomach! It is already cramping up at the thought of beetroot juice! Yuk!" Arthur said making a face that made Raj laugh.

Once changed the boys ran as fast as they could and dive-bombed into the pool causing floating Amber to be flung to the other side of the pool and Serendipity to scream out in excitement.

The cool water gently caressed the red-hot strips of pain on Amber's back and for the first time all day she forgot what her father did and had some fun with her friends.

"Your mum is threatening us with beetroot this time!" Arthur said as he threw the ball to Raj. Raj unable to swim with his glasses on, jumped in fright when the ball splashed down in front of him.

"What can I do?" Serendipity said shrugging her shoulders, "You should try it, it is good for you!"

As if by premonition, Mrs Magnum waltzed into the den with a tray containing four glasses filled with a luminous pink liquid, "Come on kids, you will be able to swim much faster with six beetroots inside you!" Serendipity's mum said smiling down at the children.

"Thanks mum we will have them later."

"I don't think so dear, best to drink up when they are fresh!"

Arthur sunk under the water trying to hide from Mrs Magnum's fluorescent juices causing the other three to giggle uncontrollably. Mrs Magnum had many qualities, and persistence was definitely one of them; she held out a towel dressing gown for each of the children so they would not get cold while they drunk their high fibre juices. She waited patiently for Amber to take off all the rubber rings and arm bands that she was wearing and gasped out loud when she saw the state of Amber's back making the children jump.

"What is wrong mummy?" Serendipity asked as she swallowed a mouthful of beetroot. Maggie saw in Amber's forlorn face that she did not want the others to notice so Mrs Magnum quickly wrapped her in the dressing gown and said, "I have left the oven on! I must turn it off right away!" And the juice bearer disappeared much quicker than any of the juices would.

"But you don't even cook!" Serendipity cried out confused after her mother.

"So, did you get Dr Fog's letter yet?" Arthur asked sipping his drink reluctantly.

"Yes, I gave it to Uncle Sohan and he used it for roll ups." Raj said between gulps.

"What does that mean?" Serendipity asked.

"He basically smoked it" Raj explained.

"How cool!" Arthur exclaimed.

"I wish my father smoked my letter." Amber said sorrowfully, the throbbing in her back suddenly feeling more painful.

"Well I have something to tell you all." Serendipity said having finished her drink.

Amber was relieved to have the attention directed away from her and Dr Fog's letter.

"What is it?" Raj asked.

"Well, I asked my parents to tell me where I was born, and it turns out there are a lot of strange coincidences..."

"What do you mean?" Arthur asked still struggling with his six beetroots.

"Basically, I was born in the Sonoran Desert in America."

"That is pretty cool." Arthur said nodding.

"But it was no normal desert; I was born on a fossil site. A dinosaur fossil site!"

The three listeners put their glasses down and stared at their friend completely engrossed with what she was saying.

"Are you serious?" Raj asked putting his glasses on, so he could pay more attention.

"Yes I am. But wait, it's going to get even more weird."

"How can it be weirder than being born on top of a dinosaur?" Arthur asked pushing his wet hair out of his face.

"My parents were in a helicopter and it landed onto a dinosaur fossil and that is where my mother gave birth to me."

"Professor Inchenstein!" Raj exclaimed.

Serendipity nodded, "I think it could be, do you remember which fossil site it was?"

"I don't think he mentioned the name, but it was definitely in Montana."

"Guys I am not following this at all. What are you going on about? What does Professor Inchenstein have to do with you being born on a fossil site in a helicopter..." Arthur's face turned from confusion to comprehension mid-sentence, "Oh my God! You are the reason the Professor got fired and stole the claw!"

"Shhh keep your voice down." Serendipity looked towards the door to make sure her mother would not come back in, "I think it is probably true. I feel bad for him, it is my fault." Serendipity looked down at her hands and both of the boys were worried that she was going to cry, Raj could not handle two girls crying in one day!

"Don't be upset, it is not your fault, if anything it is your parents' fault and I am sure Professor Inchenstein will understand." Amber said comforting her friend.

"Yes, I suppose you are right, it just feels strange." Serendipity said looking up at her friends.

Before the children could continue their conversation further, Mrs Magnum arrived in the den and insisted that Amber get her clothes because she had something to show her upstairs. The four friends knew better than to resist the will of Mrs Magnum so Amber grabbed her clothes and followed Mrs Magnum up the stairs.

While Serendipity and the boys continued their discussion passionately, Mrs Magnum led Amber up to her bedroom, told her to lie on the bed and soaked the raw red scars on her back with Neosporin lotion. Amber winced with pain, but she trusted Mrs Magnum and she prayed the pain would go away soon, "You must keep dry until they heal, no more swimming OK?"

"Yes, I will."

"Do you have someone who can rub this on your back?" Mrs Magnum asked kindly.

Amber thought about her Grandma Rose but then thought it best not to worry her; she could try asking her mother to do it as long as her father did not notice. Amber shook her head and the tears rolled steadily down her cheeks.

Mrs Magnum did her best to comfort Amber without touching her back and then said, "Come here straight after school, every day and I will put the cream on your back until it feels better, OK?" Maggie wiped the tears away from Amber's face and smiled reassuringly. Amber nodded, blew her nose and wiped away the tears and remaining snot. She had never been as grateful to anyone before as Mrs Magnum and her kindness.

ΔΔΔ

While the four friends were enjoying swimming and discussing the unusual circumstances of Serendipity's birth, Professor Inchenstein continued to write a list of questions; questions that no scientists could answer. He was determined that the scientific world needed answers, in fact the world needed answers, and the only way anyone would find the answers was if he went back one last time. Just one last time. Yes, he convinced himself that it was a matter of scientific discovery and the world would thank him and his name would be in the text books along with Einstein's and Lyell's. Professor Inchenstein became so excited that he even acted out the ceremony where he would receive a Noble Prize, bowing down gracefully in Mavis's silk kimono with an onion in his hand representing the prize.

14

Dwarf Planet

After lunch year six eagerly left the playground to be early for their next lesson; no-one wanted to be late for Professor Inchenstein's class. James still regretted being five minutes late one time and he missed the moment when Doctor Dino created his own volcano by decomposing ammonium dichromate. The Professor refused point blank to repeat the experiment for James claiming that "If one wants to see a volcano erupt in life then one must be early. Simple."

Amber had no idea what to expect from the Professor's lesson, but she intended to go in with an open mind and not be nervous. Her back felt slightly better today and her father even said hello to her at the breakfast table. Amber had the feeling that today was bound to be better than yesterday. It had to be. "I like to see a keen class! You are early! Come in, come in! Welcome oh hopeful youths!" Professor Inchenstein said to his pupils. "In fact, don't sit down, I am bored with this room, and for this lesson we need space! Ha! Pun intended!" Professor Inchenstein straightened his pink and blue spotty bow tie and cried, "Follow me troops!" as he ran out of the classroom towards the school lawn with an excited year six on his tail.

Pembridge Hall's pristine lawn was soon trampled on by the students as they tried to keep up with their teacher. Eventually the Professor came to sudden halt and bent over, clasping his knees for support. The children gathered around their teacher waiting for him to recover.

"Who wants to be the sun?" a gasp was heard coming from under the fluffy head.

No one understood what he meant.

Professor Inchenstein raised his head and stood tall, towering above his students. "I said who wants to be the SUN?"

Amber, who was determined to be less shy today, raised her hand.

"An excellent choice for a sun, indeed! Come here my child stand in the middle." Professor Inchenstein crouched down in front of Amber and said, "We could not live without Amber, our Sun is what gives us life and without it, we would all be decaying skeletons feeding the worms, and then of course the worms would die, and life would be no more."

He jumped up to face the rest of the class, "Now for those of you that are a little slow, let me explain."

The Professor's eyebrows lifted-up high above his shining eyes and he exclaimed, "We are going to create... drum roll anyone?" No one obliged the teacher. "The Universe, planet by planet!"

He spun theatrically and then instructed everyone apart from Amber to stand out the way so that they had enough free space to create the Universe. "Now, who knows what planet is closest to the sun? It begins with M, m, m, m, m. Yes, Alison go on."

"Mercury!"

"Well done! Alison, get over here, you are going to be our first planet, Mercury! What an honour!"

Alison came rushing over to the Professor, "No don't touch me!" screamed the Professor, "You are far too hot, you would burn my body to ashes quicker than I could say 'Get thee to a nunnery!'"

A baffled Alison took her place next to Amber and waited for instructions.

"Now ladies and gentlemen, who wants to be the planet of Loooovvveeee?" The Professor said winking at the boys causing them all to snigger awkwardly. "Arthur, you will do, come over here and stand further down from Alison, be Venus, there is a good lad." Arthur reluctantly accepted and skulked forward aware of the muffled giggles behind his back. "It is true, the planet is named after the Goddess of Love, but I can assure you now there is not much love-making happening on this sizzling planet as it is 400° Celsius hot!"

The lesson continued in this fashion until eight children were in line representing the planets. When each child became a planet, the Professor would inform them of some scientific fact relating to the planet that they became.

"Right well I think we are in order, excellent! Now it is time to orbit!" The Professors eyebrows moved up and down so intensely they looked like they would fly off his wrinkly face at any moment and into the universe.

"What about Pluto sir?" Raj asked.

The Professor spun around to face Raj, "Good question, good question!" Professor Inchenstein bounded towards Raj like an over excited rabbit, "Let me speak in laymen's terms. The scientific community have been in constant debate as to whether Pluto should be considered a planet or not, at one point in its history it was accepted and benefited from all the perks a planet gets."

"What perks do planets get sir?" Asked Alison.

"Well being a planet is an honourable thing indeed! All schools are taught about the planets, planets are featured in most text books and scientific journals, you get much more exposure being a planet then a comet or moon for example!"

Professor Inchenstein straightened his bow tie before concluding, "Anyhow, the pundits that are part of the International Astronomical Union decided that Pluto does not qualify to be part of the planet family due to the fact it is too small and cannot clear its obit. As a result, Pluto is known as a Dwarf Planet!" The Professor mopped his brow, "Brutal I know!"

"Now come on kids the fun is about to begin, let's get orbiting!" Doctor Dino skidded as fast as he could to Mercury. "Just to explain the planets that are closest to the sun orbit the sun much faster than the ones furthest away. Anyone know why?"

The Professor saw the familiar hand in the air and said, "Yes Raj tell us."

Raj answered, shouting across the lawn, "The gravity from the sun makes the planets nearest to the sun move faster."

"Exactly, well done boy! So, the planet furthest from the sun like Neptune all the way back there, will move slower than Mercury here! In fact, it will take Neptune 164.79 years to do one orbit around the sun and during the same time Mercury would have already been around the sun 683 times!"

"Now just before we start the orbit all the planets must be aware of one more very important fact." The Professor paused for effect to make sure the class was listening and then continued, "Planets do not orbit in a circle, they orbit in an oval shape, because when they get closer to the sun, the sun's gravity is so powerful that it pulls the planets closer to its heart. So Amber remember when the planets do their orbit you need to pull them closer to you."

Amber was wondering if she had to actually physically do anything but was too shy to ask and then suddenly the planets started to circulate.

"That's it around you go you beautiful celestial bodies!" the Professor shouted admiringly.

"Slow down Venus you are over taking Mercury! Arthur this is not a race, you can't speed up just because you want to! Now slow down!"

The children/planets continued to orbit the sun until Neptune had done one orbit which took about five minutes.

"Professor I am feeling dizzy." said Alison who had the unfortunate role of being Mercury and having to run the quickest.

"What can I say Alison, you are Mercury and you must behave like Mercury. Being a planet is no easy task! Now don't worry Neptune has nearly done a full orbit."

Eventually Neptune (James) completed his orbit and the children and teacher cheered while Alison fell flat on the floor to try and stop her head from spinning.

"OK kids, now the field work is done we have to write it up."

A groan was heard in response to this which made the Professor start abruptly, expressing complete an utter shock on his face, making the children giggle. "No more groans please, I promise it will not be too painful, the fun is not over until you leave the science lab remember!"

And then the Professor sprinted off the lawn in the direction of the classroom.

Year six ran after their nutty Professor; Raj was running as fast as he could to keep up with everyone but suddenly he felt something hit his foot and he tripped forward landing flat on his face. Holding back the lump that rose in his throat, Raj refused to cry as he gazed up and saw Rocky turn around and wink at him. No one else had seen what had happened so Raj picked himself up, brushed away the blood from his freshly grazed knees walked to the science lab. By the time the hot and sweaty planets and their spectators arrived in the science lab their teacher was already scribbling away on the blackboard. "Ladies and gentlemen, I am about to introduce you to another one of my amazing creations." Professor Inchenstein stood to the left of the blackboard and pointed proudly at what was written. "If you can remember this, you will never forget the order of the planets. Now repeat after me:

"Marvellous volcanoes erupt mysteriously, jerking sea-beds, upsetting nature."

"And again:" The Professor bellowed.

"Marvellous volcanoes erupt mysteriously, jerking sea-beds, upsetting nature." The children chanted reciting from the blackboard.

"I can barely hear you! AGAIN!" The teacher cried with his hands behind both his ears.

"Marvellous volcanoes erupt mysteriously, jerking sea-beds, upsetting nature." The children screamed as loud as they could.

"Now that's more like it!" Professor Inchenstein said beaming down at his class.

"OK now write it down like this in your note books:

Marvellous = Mercury

Volcanoes = Venus

Erupt = Earth

Mysteriously = Mars

Jerking = Jupiter

Sea-beds = Saturn

Upsetting = Uranus (The Professor stifled a giggle at this point then quickly composed himself before continuing)

Nature = Neptune."

Professor Inchenstein looked fondly at the blackboard and then turned to his students, "Come on hurry up write it down, write it down."

Year six obediently wrote everything down in their books before being dismissed for their next lesson. As they left the classroom they were all harmoniously reciting the new phrase down the corridor.

"Now that is what I call education!" Professor Inchenstein said over their heads as they hurried to their next class, proud that his phrase had worked so well.

As soon as year six were out of sight he hurried back to his desk at the head of the classroom and continued to write down a list of questions, questions he hoped would be the reason why his life would change forever.

ΔΔΔ

At 3.20pm sharp Raj arrived in the science lab to clean the test tubes. He liked the silence in the lab, he liked to be away from the other kids and out of Rocky's way. He was safe in the science lab. Just as Raj was about to turn on the familiar copper taps he started.

"Raj my friend!"

Raj turned around in a fluster to find Professor Inchenstein behind him. "Professor, you made me jump!"

"Oh, I am sorry, did not mean to, did not mean to."

The Professor had a look in his eye that Raj had never seen before, and it worried him, "What is wrong Professor?"

"Wrong? Nothing, nothing. Absolutely nothing wrong." The Professor mumbled nervously.

"Come on Professor you can tell me?" Raj said encouragingly.

The Professor smiled at Raj and gestured that they should both sit down. Raj perched himself on a stool and so did Professor Inchenstein. The Professor clasped his hands together and stared down at the wooden bench in front of them. The science teacher had been thinking long and hard how to say what he wanted to say, but now the moment came, he faltered, unsure how to start what he had practiced so many times in his mind. He cleared his throat for the third time before saying, "Raj, I would like your advice." He then paused and looked at Raj directly, their pale blue eyes fixing on each other; one pair surrounded by old wrinkles the other by smooth dark skin. Raj waited patiently wondering what on earth his teacher would say next.

"Now I know you know my little secret and I appreciate you keeping it." The Professor tapped his nose in appreciation.

"I haven't told anyone that you tried to go back sir." Raj said in earnest.

Professor Inchenstein held his hand up to silence Raj. "I know." He paused again as old people often do when they are thinking and then said, "Raj since our little adventure, I have been wondering about all that is unknown in this prehistoric world." The teacher stood up suddenly and began to pace around the room. "Raj there is only so much a scientist can discover from fossils, if I could get real live specimens and do proper research I would be able to transform the scientific world for the better, for the better."

"What do you mean?" Raj asked pushing his glasses further up his nose.

"Raj listen to these questions and tell me if you know the answers, if anyone does:

Q: Were dinosaurs cold or warm blooded?

Q: Was T-Rex a hunter or scavenger?

Q: Was T-Rex a cannibal?

Q: What killed the dinosaurs and made them extinct? Was it really the meteorite or was there something else?"

As Professor Inchenstein recited his list of questions he thought would interest his pupil, he leaned on the bench, towering over Raj for emphasis. Raj looked up at his teacher, his eyes wide open not sure if it was his turn to speak.

"Raj," Professor Inchenstein whispered leaning forward, "Don't you want to know the answers?"

ΔΔΔ

Raj never finished cleaning the test tubes. The Professor's questions whizzed around his head and he could think of nothing else. He decided to go home and think about everything Doctor Dino had told him. If he had to make a decision, then it needed a long debate in his mind and he needed to concentrate so he took the long way home and headed to Umbridge House. Raj looked up at the depressing council estate where he and his Uncle lived; he observed the decaying brown bricks, broken up with dirty white window frames and thought about Pencombe Mews. He smelt the familiar smell of cannabis seeping from the Watler's flat on the ground floor as he made his way up the urine stained stairwell. Finally arriving at flat six, he turned his key in the yellow door and heard Tom and Jerry playing loudly in the lounge.

"Hi Uncle Sohan"

Silence as usual.

"How was your day?" Raj asked as he put his school bag down on the thick orange carpet. Raj could see his uncle's bald head sitting above the sofa, glued to the telly.

Silence as usual.

As Raj had taken the long way home it was almost 5pm and he was hungry. He walked into the kitchen and opened the freezer door.

"Do you want me to heat you up some food Uncle?"

Silence as usual.

Raj was used to this behaviour from his Uncle and it did not bother him anymore, in fact he quite enjoyed the quiet. He placed a bubbling hot vindaloo next to his Uncle on the sofa and took his meal to his room. Raj needed to be alone and he needed to decide what to do about the Professor's questions.

Could they really go back just one last time to do research? Would it be safe? What would Serendipity and the others say? What should he do? Raj thought.

Raj knew the Professor confided in him because he wanted him to talk to the others, but what was the right thing to do he wondered. He trusted his teacher and he felt excited at the thought of seeing more dinosaurs, but they only just managed to escape alive the first time. Was it worth risking their lives to go back again? Young Raj closed his eyes and wished he had someone he could talk to; he longed for the first Sunday in May when we would be able to speak with his parents on the phone, even if it was for only ten minutes, it was the best ten minutes he had each month. A tear escaped from his rare blue eye and lay quietly on his pillow.

ANNIE WHITE

15

The Plan

Raj felt nervous all morning. He waited until lunchtime before he confided in Amber and Serendipity telling them exactly what the Professor had talked about and he emphasized that he did not know what to do.

"Arthur should be hearing this." Amber said.

Raj looked towards Arthur sitting on the round table in the middle of the hall with all his mates and felt a pang of disappointment. Serendipity followed Raj's gaze and decided to go up to Arthur in front of everyone.

"Wait Serendipity!" Raj hissed, "Don't bother we can catch him after school."

But Serendipity was already walking over to Arthur, her friends watched on with trepidation.

Just as she reached the table she hesitated, maybe this was not a clever idea she thought to herself but before she had time to turn and go back it was too late.

"Oi Arthur, looks like you have an admirer!" Rocky shouted.

Arthur turned behind him grinning and then noticed Serendipity and swallowed hard. The entire dining hall had become silent and was watching.

"Well what does Metal Mouth have to say?" Rocky shouted.

"I, I wanted to tell Arthur something." Serendipity whispered.

Arthur was completely torn; on the one hand he wanted to talk to Serendipity and Amber and Raj, but there was no way his friends would let him, and then they would pick on him too.

"Go on then!" Rocky demanded enjoying watching Serendipity squirm.

Arthur looked at Serendipity and tried to smile.

"Forget about it." She said and walked away.

"METAL MOUTHS IN LUUUUUVE!" Rocky shouted for the whole hall to hear and made loud kissing noises.

Serendipity blushed crimson and Arthur let his head drop. His hands were wet with sweat and he wished he could just go over there, to his friends and say, What's up? Why was it so hard? Why did he care what Rocky and the gang would do? But he did. And he hated the fact that he did.

Serendipity plonked herself back down on her chair and played with the food left on her plate.

"He doesn't mean to." Amber said quietly.

"Mean to what?" Serendipity said crossly and threw down her fork.

"You know, be unkind."

"Just send him a text and we can meet him after school." Raj suggested.

"No. I am fed up sneaking around. If he is that embarrassed by us, then maybe we should not tell him what is going on. Maybe we are better off without him!" Serendipity huffed. After school the girls went to Serendipity's and Raj said he would meet them there later, he did not tell them, but he wanted to wait for Arthur. Raj had no phone, so no way of getting Arthur's attention. He thought about writing him a note but that would be silly right? He decided to bravely wait by the school gates and hoped Arthur would notice him. Raj waited patiently, every now and again looking over his shoulder hoping he would catch Arthur's attention. After a few minutes, Raj recognised Arthur's blond hair coming around the corner. Raj held his breath and prayed that Rocky would not appear. Arthur finally looked up and saw Raj and nodded. Raj smiled and felt relived, Arthur knew he wanted to talk. Raj turned around for a split second but when he turned back to look at Arthur, his legs turned to led; his eyes locked with Rocky's and he knew he was in for it.

"Quick! He is outside the school we can get him real good this time!" and Rocky bolted towards Raj followed by his troops.

Raj knew he needed to run but his legs would not move. He saw them coming, he knew it was too late, there was too many of them, it all became a blur and then something woke up inside him and he ran.

He knocked past a man and his dog, he swung around the corner and crashed into a bin but got up quickly and tried his best to sprint down the path but he was no match for Rocky and he began to pant trying to catch his breath. He daren't turn around, he did not have to, he could hear them. And then he felt it; a heavy push on the back.

"Why are you running Brain?" Rocky said as he pressed his foot into Raj's back. Rocky waited for the others to arrive; he liked an audience.

"I asked you a question." Rocky repeated when his mates had joined them.

"What's the point in running when you know you are going to get caught?" Rocky grabbed Raj by the collar and dragged him to his feet then threw him against the brick wall.

Raj, defeated, fell against the wall and cried out as the concrete smacked against his bare arm. Rocky moved closer to his victim so there was no way he could escape and then grabbed hold of Raj's turban and ripped it off his head and threw it over the wall into someone's back garden.

The gang roared with laughter, everyone, that is apart from Arthur.

"Oi what's your problem?" Rocky suddenly said turning towards Arthur.

The gang turned their attention now to Arthur who stood on the outskirts of the ring of bullies.

"Are you going soft or something?" Richard asked.

Arthur felt his face flush crimson. "SHUT-UP!" he shouted at them.

"Oooooooooooh" Rocky whistled mockingly.

Rocky pushed through the crowd until he reached Arthur, "What's your problem?" he said menacingly.

"I don't have a problem, mate, I am just bored." Arthur replied. "I mean look at him." he said pointing towards Raj, "What's the point? He's pathetic and not worth my time."

Raj quickly looked down at the floor not wanting the bullies to see the tears swelling in his eyes.

"He's right," one of the bullies said, "Let's go to Nando's I am starving."

"Yeah come on let's get out of here." Richard agreed.

The group began to disperse apart from Rocky, who walked up to Raj and spat in his face before following his friends to the restaurant. Arthur lingered.

"Oi you coming or what?" Rocky hollered.

Arthur stared at Raj who was trying to tuck his shirt in his trousers and then followed Rocky down the path.

ΔΔΔ

"What happened?" Serendipity asked as soon as she opened the door and saw Raj standing on the steps.

Raj, head down walked into the house and muttered that he did not want to talk about it.

"Where's your turban?" Amber said shocked, she had never seen Raj without it, nobody had.

"It was that idiot Rocky wasn't it?" Serendipity said crossly. "I have had enough of them!" and she thumped her fist on the glass table causing the half-drunk celery juices to wobble. "Are you hurt?" Amber said softly, "Oh gee you are bleeding!" she exclaimed as she noticed the blood on Raj's elbow.

"Leave it I am fine." Raj snapped.

The girls looked at each other surprised, they had never heard Raj snap at them before.

"Was Arthur involved in this?" Serendipity asked crossly.

"Leave it alone." Raj said.

"Come on guys drink your celery up!" Mrs Magnum glided into the kitchen, "Oh Raj, hello."

Maggie Magnum glanced at her daughter enquiringly. Serendipity shook her head. She knew Raj would not want her mum asking questions about his missing turban.

Maggie realised something had happened to Raj; she noticed the blood on his arm, the tear in his shirt and above all she could see how hard he was trying to keep it together.

"Raj my dear, do you enjoy a squashed celery?"

This sounded so silly that both the girls laughed out loud and Raj let a small smile form on his face. "I honestly don't know!"

"Well there is only one way to find out!" Maggie beamed kindly at Raj and handed him a glass of watery liquid with wiry green strings poking out the top.

The doorbell rang.

Maggie left the children to answer the door and swooped back into the kitchen with Arthur behind her. Mrs Magnum poured Arthur a juice and subtly left the children alone.

Arthur placed Raj's turban on the table. The girls were silent, everyone was watching Raj.

Arthur shifted uncomfortably from one foot to the other, "Look, man, Rocky is an idiot."

"Der!" Serendipity interjected.

Raj continued to stare at his turban and refused to look up at Arthur.

"Hey, listen, I" Arthur flicked his hair nervously, "I am sorry about what happened."

Raj suddenly stood up to face Arthur. He felt the anger erupting inside of him and said, "You just stood there and watched them!"

Arthur saw the girls look at him horrified and he hung his head in shame.

Raj grabbed his turban and went to the bathroom under the stairs. Amber could see how upset Arthur was feeling and she wanted to hug him, to make everything better, but she knew it would probably make things worse.

A few minutes later Raj walked back into the kitchen with his turban fixed firmly on his head, he looked calmer, more composed.

"We have something to tell you." Raj began.

Arthur, understanding that they could move on from what happened sat down and was surprised with how grateful he felt drinking a juiced celery. Things were normal again.

Raj explained to Arthur what the Professor wanted to do.

"Wicked! I am definitely up for it! Count me in!" Arthur said loudly.

"Shh keep your voice down, we don't want mum to hear." Serendipity said looking around anxiously. "Does the Professor really want to go back? Was he serious Raj?" Serendipity asked glancing at her friend unsure of how she felt about the prospect.

Raj pushed his square spectacles up his nose before replying, "I think he really thinks it would be worthwhile to go back. Not go back for long," he added, "Just long enough for him to do his research."

Serendipity raised her left eyebrow and Raj knew her well enough to know that she was not convinced.

"Think about it, there are so many questions that no one can answer about the dinosaurs, for example, was T-Rex a cannibal? What killed all the dinosaurs? Don't you see we could find out what happened and tell the world!" Raj now realised what his answer would be, forgetting about Rocky and his bleeding arm. All that mattered now was the dinosaurs, he could see that now. After listening to what everyone else was saying, Amber now spoke, "Won't it be awfully dangerous? Arthur nearly got eaten last time by the monsters or have you forgotten already?" Her cheeks flushed red as she spoke. She was sure that no good would come to them if they returned to such a hideous land.

"Yes but I did not get eaten! I am fine and just think what an amazing experience it would be. I think we would be mad not to go back one last time." Arthur said smiling at Amber reassuringly.

"Oh I am not sure; my tummy is churning just at the thought of it." Amber said worriedly.

"Serendipity? You are not saying much." Raj said watching his friend intently.

"Well I still feel guilty about what happened to Professor Inchenstein when I was born, maybe this could be my way of making up for it." Serendipity looked round at her friends hopefully.

"Does that mean you are IN?" Arthur said, ready to dance around the table.

"Only if Amber feels sure." Serendipity replied.

All three turned and looked at Amber expectantly.

"Oh gee, I don't know. Do you all really want to go back and see all those scaly monsters?" She asked timidly.

"Dinosaurs." Arthur corrected.

"I think we owe it to the Professor, let him do his research. We will be back by tea, no one will notice anything." Raj said gently.

Amber stared back at her three new friends and it felt good that they were all together again and the boys had made up. Maybe this experience would bring them closer and make Arthur realise that he did not need Rocky and the gang anymore, that the four of them were enough,

"OK I am in!" Amber said her tummy fluttering uncontrollably.

Arthur jumped up, grabbed hold of Amber and swung her around the kitchen. Amber screamed with excitement and Raj grinned at his friends. He could not wait to tell the Professor!

ΔΔΔ

The children had to wait for an entire day of lessons to pass before they could speak with the Professor. Finally, the last bell rang and they rushed to the science lab in order to tell their teacher the good news. They opened the science lab door and hurried inside but to their disappointment Professor Inchenstein was nowhere to be seen.

"Where could he be?" Asked Arthur deflated.

"Maybe the staffroom?" Serendipity suggested.

"Shhh, I can hear something." Raj said as he walked towards the science cupboard door. The others listened keenly and heard the following tune coming from that direction:

"I have got a lovely bunch of coconuts didilideedee.
There they are all standing in a row.
Bum, bum, bum.
Pink ones, green ones, some as big as your head!"

"Professor?" Raj said loudly as he opened the cupboard door.

"Oh goodness gracious, don't scare an old man while he sings in his cupboard. Dear, dear!" The flustered Professor said clasping his chest dramatically. He peered over Raj to see the other three pupils standing behind him and he suddenly realised that this could be a very important moment.

"Sorry sir, we did not mean to." Raj said.

"What? Oh, not at all. Not at all! I am a silly jumpy old fool. Now, how are we?" he said beaming at the four children flashing them his yellow stained teeth as he came out of the cupboard.

"We are good sir." Serendipity said.

The Professor held his breath, afraid he would burst with anticipation.

"We wanted to talk to you about something private." Serendipity said in a very serious voice as she closed the door.

The Professor continued to hold his breath and nodded encouragingly.

"Well Raj told us what you wanted to do, you know, to go back to do research and we have talked about it." Serendipity continued in her overly serious tone.

The Professor felt like he was about to pass out from the lack of oxygen reaching his lungs yet he daren't breath out until he had heard what the children's decision was. He promised himself that if they said no then he would not try and persuade them.

"Just tell him he looks like he is about to burst." whispered Arthur in Serendipity's ear.

"Well we are pleased to say yes, we will go back with you one last time!" Serendipity smiled at her teacher, her braces reflecting the sun that shone through the science lab windows.

The children stood still, frozen, waiting for the Professor to react. The Professor was now turning the same colour as the liquid beetroot that Mrs Magnum so often forced down the friends' throats.

"Professor say something." Raj said concerned.

Finally the Professor managed to alleviate his lungs and gasped out so loudly that Amber jumped in surprise. Doctor Dino was so astounded by the children's decision and what that would mean for him that he could not find any words at all to express how he felt. The children continued to stare at him, their faces becoming more and more anxious as the silence continued. Eventually Professor Inchenstein managed to pull himself together and spat out at the top of his lungs, "FLABBERASTIC!"

"Flabber what?" Arthur asked surprised.

"Celestial bodies eat me for breakfast!" The Professor dabbed his eyes and exclaimed, "You do not know how happy you have made an old man." Tears of delight danced in the Professor's eyes and soon sprinkled down his wrinkly cheeks. The children smiled back feeling just as elated as their teacher. "Well, sit yourselves down, we need to plan, yes we need to plan, plan the adventure of a lifetime!"

ΔΔΔ

Once the five adventurers had agreed on a plan of action, Professor Inchenstein ran to St Mary's Hospital to speak to Mavis and tell her the dramatic news. For seven long months he had been trying to devise a way to travel back to that unusual world where so many magnificent dinosaurs lived. This would be his chance to make history, this would be his chance to educate the world, but most of all this would be his chance to be remembered, forever; Professor Boris Inchenstein. Twenty minutes later, with sweat dripping down from every pore making his usual frizzy locks somewhat limp and frazzled, Professor Inchenstein arrived at the hospital.

"What on earth is the matter Professor?" Mandy the receptionist asked as the Professor staggered into the foyer.

"Only good news Mandy my dear, only really splendid news!" Professor Inchenstein responded as he leapt up the stairs two at a time.

At Mavis's bedside the Professor sat down and seized her hand in his kissing it uncontrollably. "Oh, Mavis my love, if only you could come with me, if only you could." Professor Inchenstein quietly sobbed into his wife's hand. After five minutes he took a deep breath, wiped the tears from his face and blew his nose on his favourite purple and green spotty hankie.

"Well where do I begin?" He asked his wife and then rampantly talked about the plan to go back to the Late Cretaceous period. He spoke to her about the research he was aiming to accomplish and all the wonderful facts he would tell the world. "The plan is to go back on Saturday morning at 9am and return by 5pm at the latest, it will give us 20 days which will be ample time. If everything goes to plan we should be back by lunch. Now I know what you are going to ask, what will the children tell their parents? But good old Boris has thought of everything!" He smiled at his wife's unresponsive face and was not at all deterred by her lack of enthusiasm. "I am going to pretend to organize a school trip to Stonehenge so that the parents give permission for their children to be out all day! Genius!" He said out loud. "Now I know what you are going to say, one should not tell porky pies, but surely this is worth a white lie? I promise to be responsible and look after the children. Nothing bad will happen."

The Professor continued to waffle on excitedly until darkness enveloped the hospital windows and his belly started to rumble. He stared down at Mavis and promised himself that he would never forget a cell on her face. As the Professor left the hospital he saw the familiar silhouette that belonged to Bunny Bristlepott appear from the shadows and head into the hospital. Boris tipped his head politely in her direction but alas received no response, she would not even look him in the eye.

Professor Inchenstein left St Mary's and walked back slowly towards his flat. His mind was racing with things that he needed to do for their trip; he would have to be able to make fires, (but that was easy, he used to be a boy scout) and they would need food for at least five days which he would have to carry and then he would need to take samples and bring his equipment. Yes, there was a lot to do, a lot to do indeed he thought as he skipped in the air with exhilaration. The four children were just as excited as their teacher, even Amber felt less nervous and was looking forward to their trip. They all managed to get the permission letters signed by their parents and Uncle Sohan for the trip to visit Stonehenge. Amber found it incredibly difficult lying to her father, she was sure he could tell that something was wrong, but he still signed the form and quickly got back to reading the Bible without asking any questions. Amber sighed with relief when Mr Bradshaw handed back the signed letter and then ran upstairs to see her Grandma Rose.

"Grandma?" Amber asked quietly to see if she was awake.

"Amber dear, I have been waiting for you. Come in and have some fruitcake." Grandma Rose put on her spectacles and looked hard at her daughter, "You look excited! Tell me what is going on?" Grandma Rose grinned widely exposing her red gums at her grandchild.

Amber sat carefully on the bed next her dying Grandma, took a piece of cake and explained all about the trip to Stonehenge.

"Oh that is exciting! Stonehenge! Yes, full of history and still nobody knows how they did it!" Grandma Rose smiled broadly then said, "When you are older, promise me you will read Tess of the D'Urbervilles by Thomas Hardy; a beautiful but tragic story. You will be thankful you have been to Stonehenge once you have read it, makes the ending all the more real!" She gave a wink to her granddaughter and thought about the tragic life of Tess.

Amber hesitated, she was not sure what her Grandma was talking about but she felt so ashamed lying to her Grandma Rose that she wondered if she could trust her and tell her the truth.

"Grandma, can I trust you to keep a secret?"

"Well of course." Grandma Rose replied as she stuffed a portion of fruitcake in her mouth. "I only ever see old Stella next door and she can barely hear!

"It is just we are not really going to Stonehenge." Amber said shyly.

"Oh, well where are you going then?" Her grandma asked intrigued whilst munching her cake.

"We are going somewhere magical, somewhere no one else has

ever been!" Grandma Rose was not sure what her grandchild meant but she waited patiently to find out.

"We are going to see the dinosaurs." Amber said seriously.

Grandma Rose was so taken aback that she began choking on the fruit cake.

"Are you OK Grandma?" Amber said worriedly, softly patting her Grandma's frail back.

Grandma Rose gulped down some water and eventually managed to dislodge the cake from her throat. She turned to look at her granddaughter and asked, "Whatever do you mean?"

Amber realised that it was too late to back-track now and she could not lie either so she told her Grandma everything; she told her what happened on the first day of school with the claw and all of the adventures that they had experienced.

When Amber had finished telling her story she looked at her Grandma waiting for a response, she was expecting questions or to be told it was too dangerous to go back, at the very least she was hoping for some kind of advice. But her Grandma's only response was silence.

Surely, she is making this story up. Grandma Rose thought. She could not have possibly done all that! It must be her imagination and what an imagination, yes, she will do well in this world. Even though Grandma Rose was sure that her daughter could not be telling the truth she was extremely impressed with the level of detail within the story. She knew she had to say something but what can one say to such a fanciful tale?

"Well what an adventure you have had." The old Grandma said at last.

"Grandma I am telling the truth, I swear" Amber said.

"Darling you have worn me out with your tales, but I cannot wait to hear about your next trip, when are you going again?"

"This Saturday." Amber replied confused, "Does that mean that you think I should go back, you do not think it will be too dangerous?"

Grandma Rose was happy to play along with her Grandchild's imagination, "If you are with the Professor I am sure you will be OK." She replied patting Amber on the head.

16

Stonehenge

Suzy knew nothing about children; she did not know how to talk to them, she did not know what to do with them and if she was honest with herself, she did not really like them. At the age of twenty-four, she was now faced with her new boyfriend's ten-year-old son and she had no idea how to handle him.

"So today is the day you are going on a school trip?" Suzy said to Arthur rubbing his hair awkwardly.

"Yep, off to Stonehenge with the Professor." Arthur replied as he pulled away from Suzy's hand.

"You are taking an awful amount of stuff for one day!" Suzy commented as she lugged the heavy rucksack onto Arthur's back.

Arthur shrugged in response. He was never very responsive towards Suzy. Suzy had been living with Arthur and his father for two months now and even though she tried to be nice, Arthur knew she did not like him. He missed his mum and since Suzy had moved in and started picking up the phone when it rang, Arthur's mum called less and less. Suzy used to work at a Costa Coffee stand at Lord's cricket ground when she met Arthur's father, Christian, and now she did not work at all; she spent her time between the massage pallor and shopping trips to Harrods.

"Where's dad?" Arthur asked sulkily.

"Cricket practice." Suzy said, tapping her acrylic nails impatiently on the side table as she waited for Arthur to leave the house so she could start her day in peace (child free).

"Oh well say goodbye from me then." Arthur said as he looked around the kitchen.

"Bye, bye." Suzy said opening the door for Arthur to leave while she applied another layer of lip gloss distractedly.

Arthur stepped out through the front door and observed the familiar houses on his street questioning if he would ever see them again. Before Arthur had a chance to move forward Suzy had shut the door, which pushed on Arthur's heavy rucksack causing Arthur to lose his balance and stumble quickly down the front steps.

He walked towards Pembridge Hall through Princess Square and wondered if Amber had already left. He daren't knock on the door knowing how her father would react to a boy calling on his daughter, so he sat on a small wall and waited for five minutes to see if she came out. "You better get shifting or you will be late for your trip." Grandma Rose said while wiping some saliva that was dripping down her chin.

"Do you think it is a good idea?" Amber said hoping her Grandma would tell her to stay at home. "Of course! If it is anything like the last adventure you are in for quite a ride my dear." Her Grandma replied smiling, wondering what all the fuss was about.

Grandma Rose seemed so relaxed about the trip that Amber felt calmer inside, "OK Grandma, I better go, don't want to keep the others waiting." Amber hugged her Grandma so tightly that Grandma Rose felt like she was being squeezed like a lemon and had to ask her granddaughter to loosen her grip.

"Now you have a fantastic time! I can't wait to hear all about it!"

As Amber closed the bedroom door all she could remember was

her Grandma's red smiling gums. What could possibly go wrong? she asked herself as she walked down the stairs and out the front door.

ΔΔΔ

Professor Inchenstein arrived very early at St Mary's and begged Mandy to let him into see Mavis. Even though it was three hours before visiting time, Mandy could see how distressed the Professor was, so she indly gave her permission. Professor Inchenstein muttered many "thank yous" as he galloped up the stairs. He cautiously approached the ward where his comatosed wife was laying fast asleep. Seeing his wife lie motionless on her bed, the Professor knew he was making the right decision. He sat in silence for a considerable time before sobbing into his hankie, his words barely audible, "If I could see another way I would take it! But I can't carry on any longer, I can't. I must take this opportunity and I know we will meet again soon. We will meet again soon."

ΔΔΔ

"Why are you being so soppy?" Mrs. Magnum said as she tried to make an avocado smoothie while listening to her daughter go on about how much she loved her.

"I don't know, just like that." Serendipity said quietly as she played with her hair.

"How is my little Princess of Darkness?" Mikey Magnum said as he strolled into the kitchen to refill his coffee cup.

A tear crept down Serendipity's face and she sniffed too loudly for it to go unnoticed by her father.

"Pumpkin, what's the matter?" Her father put down his cup and crouched down in front of his daughter. Mrs. Magnum stopped whizzing the blender and turned towards Serendipity concerned.

"It's nothing, I am fine, I am just feeling homesick."

Mickey and Maggie Magnum looked at each other then Maggie said, "Sweetie, if you don't want to go on this trip today then you don't have to, you know that right?"

Serendipity took a deep breath and thought of her friends and the Professor; they needed her, she had to go.

"I am just being silly." Serendipity said, "I can't wait to see Stonehenge!" She grabbed her rucksack, kissed and hugged her parents, rushed to the front door and shouted over her shoulder, "I will be back by five!"

The red door slammed shut and Mr and Mrs Magnum carried on with their day as normal, completely unaware of the journey their daughter was about to embark. With their hearts quickly beating in their chests Serendipity, Amber and Arthur arrived outside Pembridge Hall at 9am as planned. Raj was already their waiting for them waving excitedly.

"How long have you been here?" Serendipity asked.

"Not long." Raj lied. He did not want the others to know that he had been there since 8am just waiting and reading his dinosaur magazine.

The children did not have to linger for long before they saw the familiar cloud of hair appear from around the corner. The Professor was skipping with so much momentum that his boisterous locks resembled bird's wings that were just about to take off towards the sun. The four friends found it hard not to laugh as they watched the colourful spectacle that they knew to be their teacher (as it could be no other) bounce towards them.

The Professor was kitted out in his best safari outfit; new bright purple socks replaced the previous red ones and covered his skinny legs, arriving just below his knobbly knees; light green shorts adorned the rest of his legs, bulging with the usual equipment and the familiar yellow bum-belt was tightly fastened below his belly. Newly painted multi-coloured corks dangled down from his red straw hat that was perched on his feathery head, and to finish the ensemble he had bought himself a brand-new silk bow tie, fuchsia pink with yellow spots. The Professor looked such an oddity that the locals would stop and stare, unable to ignore what had just passed them. Just before he arrived at the gates, a tourist actually asked Doctor Dino for a selfie which of course the Professor posed for with his best pout.

"Apologies for my tardiness, apologies, apologies." Professor Inchenstein said as he arrived panting outside the school gates.

He slowly unzipped his yellow bum-belt and pulled out a long brass key which shimmered in the morning sunlight. Inserting it into the iron-gate, the children and their teacher heard a loud click as the key unlocked the old gates and they creaked open. He turned to look at his pupils raising his eyebrows with eagerness "Follow me chaps." An excited energy took over the four children as they followed their teacher to the science lab and closed the door. Even though the school was deserted, the Professor waited for the door to be firmly closed before he beamed down at the four eager faces below him. "OK folks let's get this show on the road. But," he paused for effect, "before we take this unpredictable road, let us first check we have all the necessary equipment!"

The science teacher then inspected all of the children's rucksacks to make sure that they were well equipped for at least 2 days' worth of adventure. After a thorough assessment he finally zipped up Arthur's rucksack and concluded, "Friends, it is time."

His blue eyes sparkling mischievously in their sockets and he leapt like a fire bellied toad into the science cupboard and waited for the others to follow. The door closed tightly shut and the only noise to be heard was the heavy breathing from the five nervous friends. Serendipity felt something cold and heavy slide into her sweaty palm and she knew what she had to do. Feeling the familiar claw slowly heat up in her hand and the soft tingling creep along her limbs, she knew there was an extraordinary connection that only she had, Raj was right, she was special.

"No time like the present! No time like the present!" Professor Inchenstein whispered in Serendipity's ear.

Serendipity nodded in response and rubbed the magical claw.

ΔΔΔ

The science cupboard floor disintegrated into a mysterious abyss and the children and their teacher fell helplessly to the unknown world that only they knew.

"Porridge oats and pumpkin pie!" The Professor yelled out as loud as he could while he flapped his arms in mid-air.

"What did he say?" Arthur cried as the wind blew his blond hair in every direction.

"I think he is hungry!" Raj replied baffled, trying to keep his own breakfast in his stomach.

Amber found it hard to cross herself in mid-air so resorted to clasping her palms together and saying the Lord's prayer over and over.

While her friends were busy praying and screaming Serendipity closed her eyes and let her mind focus on the vivid shapes that flashed before her eyelids; she was determined to work out what they were once and for all. As she concentrated harder she could clearly see the same spinning rectangles, they were going so fast, rotating in a circle they were almost a blur, and then a colossal amber eye like a snake but the size of a bowling ball appeared, blinking confidently in the darkness. Serendipity kept staring at the eye waiting to see what would happen next but the vision shattered as her bottom fell to the ground; earth had found them once again. "Brrrrh! By Jove what a ride!" Professor Inchenstein said loudly as he gazed up in awe at the towering ferns spinning above him.

The four children followed their teacher's gaze and observed the ginormous trees sway gently over their bodies. The leaves formed an opaque canopy of green, which protected the life below it from the sun's scorching rays.

"Hypnotic as this feels, I think it is time, my fellow Marco Polo's to start our travels!" Professor Inchenstein grasped the hands of his pupils and pulled them to their feet. "All in one piece I assume?" He asked glancing at everyone to check that all their limbs were correctly attached. "Good good." He mumbled as he retrieved his compass from his rucksack. "Now follow me! North we shall go!" he exclaimed and strode off into the depths of the forest.

Before the children had time catch their breath and ask who Marco Polo was, the conspicuous red straw hat was almost out of sight!

ΔΔΔ

For an hour the children followed their teacher through the forest in a curious silence. They observed everything around them; the unusual plants that covered the ground and caressed their legs as they passed by, the tropical sounds that bounced off the many tree trunks but seemed to have no source and the thousands of insects that scurried below the undergrowth.

"What are we looking for exactly?" Arthur said as he leant on his knees trying to catch his breath.

Professor Inchenstein halted in his tracks and turned to his fellow explorers. He held out a transparent plastic bag full of foliage, soil, bark and leaves. "Arthur dear, everything around us is a scientific discovery of some sort". He wiped his sweaty brow and said, "In fact all of you should be collecting specimens, as you have sharper eyes than mine!" he then wrestled with his giant rucksack and threw more plastic bags at the children so they could begin their own collections. "And of course, need I say it but we are hunting! Hunting the most exotic, wondrous creatures that ever stepped on this planet!" His eyebrows moved so fast that sweat sprayed onto Amber's face who was unfortunately standing the closest to the teacher.

"But we are not hunting to kill dinosaurs, are we?" Raj asked his mouth dropping open in horror.

Professor Inchenstein spun round to face Raj and crouched down so their blue eyes were level. The teacher replied softly, "Raj my friend, I would never harm a dinosaur! It was only an expression of speech, a more appropriate word would be find we need to find the most beautiful creatures in the world and learn from these magnificent living organisms!"

Raj sighed with relief and the old man of 65 and his crew of ten-year-olds continued on their exploration in a forest that was over 65milllion years old. The four friends felt more relaxed now they had something to do and were enjoying breaking off bits of bark, picking up odd looking stones and collecting anything that took their fancy. They were all so distracted that none of them noticed that in such a brief time five Marco Polos had become four.

"Guys, guys, where is the Professor?" Amber said concerned as she scanned the forest looking for her colourful teacher.

Her friends stopped what they were doing and looked around too for the red straw hat that had been guiding them north for the last two hours.

"He can't just disappear!" Arthur said scrutinizing the forest.

The children's hearts descended further and further towards their stomachs as they waited and waited for the friendly cloud of grey hair to appear between the ferns.

All the exotic sounds of the forest seemed to diminuendo until the only noise to be heard was the drumming of their four sunken hearts.

"PROFESSOR!" Raj called out as loud as he could. "PROFESSOR!" he screamed again with wretched panic.

"Over there!" Serendipity whispered, pointing towards the distant, "I am sure I saw something red move."

"Follow me!" Arthur said bravely. He grabbed a long stick from the undergrowth and stepped forward to lead his friends in the direction of the red something.

They all held hands with Arthur at the lead and Raj keeping the rear. They tried to be as silent as they could but the more they tried, the more they sounded like a herd of elephants traipsing on top of exploding fire crackers!

In no time they reached a clearing and Serendipity pointed again, "Look behind that tree, there is definitely something red behind that tree." she whispered. Her friends crouched to the ground and watched the tree in question attentively, all of them praying that the red something was indeed their teacher's hat and nothing else. Even Amber was concentrating so much on the tree that she forgot to pray. What seemed like a lifetime but in reality, was only five minutes the ominous red something appeared slowly from behind the tree.

"Oh, thank goodness!" Amber said out loud as she saw the familiar red hat appear. She closed her eyes to thank the Lord but could not finish her prayer because Serendipity started screaming from the top of her lungs.

Raj flung his hand around Serendipity's mouth to silence her cries and held her close to his chest. Amber, shaking all over, could only find the courage to open one eye. She stared in the direction of the tree and to her horror saw what could only be one of those monsters the others referred to as dinosaurs. The monster staggered forward with Professor Inchenstein's straw hat in his mouth. The Professor was nowhere to be seen.

Arthur clenched his stick the best he could with his sweaty hand, ready to defend his friends.

"Everyone keep calm." Raj whispered.

"Keep calm!" Amber exclaimed. "How can we keep calm when that monster has eaten Professor Inchenstein?"

"Listen to me." Raj commanded. "I don't think the Professor has been eaten. If I am right and I hope I am, that dinosaur is an herbivore."

"What has that got to do with anything?" Amber asked shaking.

"It means that this dinosaur does not eat meat, only leaves." Raj explained.

"Then where the hell is Professor Inchenstein?" Arthur asked thrashing his stick on the earth with frustration.

"Has anyone seen my hat? Lost it back there somewhere! What are you all doing on the floor?" Professor Inchenstein looked down at his pupils with interest; he observed Amber's nervous state, the fact that Raj's hand was gripped tightly over Serendipity's mouth and that Arthur was clenching a rather threatening looking stick. He raised his right eyebrow waiting for an explanation and Arthur pointed his stick towards the tree. "There is your hat Professor!"

"Hail to the comets!" The Professor yelped with surprise as he crouched to the ground to join the others. "Oh, what glorious luck! My hat is being consumed by a Parasaurolophus! Oh, what a privilege!"

Serendipity pushed Raj's hand away from her mouth and said with a rather cross tone, "Luck? We thought you had been eaten! Where did you go?"

"Yes! We thought that monster had eaten you up!" Amber said her voice still shaky.

The Professor momentarily glanced at his angry pupils and then back at the incredible Parasaurolophus, its crest shimmering under the sunlight. "Don't be cross with me, I thought you were all behind me, I turned around to check on you and could not find anyone! I have been searching for your ever since. I lost my hat and my friends all at once!"

Serendipity's frown subsided, "Well stay closer from now on."

"Oh, don't look so forlorn! How could this marvellous beast eat me when he is an herbivore? Raj should have told you that."

"I did try." Raj mumbled.

"Just don't get lost again!" Serendipity concluded.

"Very sensible. We must all stay closer from now on." The scolded teacher agreed. Now that the children's initial panic had abated, they stared with amazement at the 1.5m Parasaurolophus eating the red straw hat. Professor Inchenstein took out his camera and started to snap the beast in front of them as softly as he could and made a quiet commentary at the same time.

"Observe that this Parasaurolophus must not be fully grown as he is only 1.5m tall and adults can grow to up to 3m. And what an outstanding crest! You know his name means crested lizard and rightly too! That crest is something to shout about!"

The children listened to the Professor's fact file and watched transfixed as the crested lizard soon swallowed the last few pieces of red straw, the hat was gone.

The dinosaur, completely unaware that he now had a fan club watching him, decided to walk further into the thick of the forest in the search of more exotic red hats. The Professor placed the camera around his neck and held one end of Arthur's stick and tugged it gently.

"Come on chaps, this is why we are here to observe the exoticness of this world! Everyone hold hands and keep as quiet as a gorilla's constipated backside!"

The children giggled quietly as they held hands and followed their teacher through the condensed forest after the hat eater. Finally, Arthur's stick prodded him in the chest; the Professor had stopped and held up his hand to halt his team. Professor Inchenstein fell dramatically on all fours and started to crawl forward. The children released each other's hands and crept slowly forward, smelling the rich scent of soil underneath them.

"At last my dreams have been answered!" The teacher said as a smile as large as a rainbow appeared on his face.

Undeniably it was a sight that was worth tears; the Parasaurolophus had led the explorers to a herd of Triceratops, quietly grazing on the surrounding greenery.

"Wow! My favourite!" Arthur exclaimed as he watched the dinosaurs chomp and munch, chomp and munch, while their great big horns gleamed in the sunshine.

"I understand Arthur boy, why this dinosaur would be your favourite, I really do!" The Professor said as he continued to click with his camera. "They do look impressive with their three horns jutting out from their fabulous headdresses, ready to ward off any intruder, but in today's world they are the equivalent of a mundane cow!"

"No way!" Arthur said in disbelief. "They are so big and fierce, how on earth can they be like a cow!"

"Oh don't look so upset, they are still a good favourite but as I said, they don't do much apart from graze like a cow. There were thousands of them and they were the staple diet for most carnivorous dinosaurs."

"I don't know what the cows look like in England but that looks nothing like the cows we had back home in Texas!" Amber said confused.

"He did not mean that they look like cows, just that they take on the same role as cows do in our animal kingdom today!" Raj said with assertiveness.

"Well there is only one way to find out if they really are like cows and that is to hop on their backs and see what they do!"

"How do you suppose we hop three meters high?" Serendipity asked with her right eyebrow raised critically.

"He does not really mean that we are going to get on those beasts' back." Amber said looking at her Professor for assurance.

Her glance was met by a flash of mischief in her teacher's eyes and Amber knew that they were indeed going to hop and hop high!

17

Don't follow the herd

As Amber had correctly feared, the Professor, followed eagerly by the boys, was doing his best to climb a nearby tree in order to land on the back of one of the Triceratops.

"You are crazy!" Amber shouted. "Serendipity please tell them they are out of their minds if they think that I am getting on the back of one of those monsters when I have a choice!!" Amber continued loudly with her arms folded in protest.

Before Serendipity could decide who to side with she was lifted in the air by Doctor Dino then pulled up by Raj who was already sitting comfortably on the back of one of the Triceratops.

"There is no way I am getting up there, no way!" Amber said with complete horror as she watched Arthur tapping the space behind him.

Professor Inchenstein's fluffy head descended rapidly towards Amber's and halted as soon as their eyes were level. "Amber do you trust me?" he said solemnly holding out his hand.

Amber stared at her teacher's outstretched hand and then up towards her friend's encouraging faces. She knew it was an unnecessary risk to ride on the backs of these huge and wondrous creatures when they could easily follow them on foot, but at the same time she did not want to stop the other's adventure. To tell the truth, Amber was feeling fed up with being the serious one, the cautious one, the only sensible one. She placed her hand in the wrinkly palm of her teacher's and decided it was time to have some fun! "Oh gee! Oh my!" Amber cried out as she felt the hard scales of the dinosaur beneath her.

"Wicked isn't it?" Arthur said happily as he fondly stroked the frill of his Triceratops. "Just grab around my waist and hold tight."

Amber timidly put her arms around Arthur and once her hands joined, she sealed them tightly shut with all of her might.

"How are you going to get up Professor?" Raj asked.

"Oh don't worry your little cotton head about me. I intend to climb this tree like an agitated monkey and then hurl myself off and onto the back of that lonely looking one over there!" He pointed at a Triceratops who was minding his own business eating some roughage. Two minutes later, the Professor did his best agitated monkey impression and clambered up the tree in question at top speed. When he was above the dinosaur he leapt forward shutting his eyes while he was in the air. Doctor Dino opened his eyes just in time to catch his balance as he landed on the almighty back of the unsuspecting dinosaur. The dinosaur did not even flinch.

The morning sun became stronger and the forest leaves sparkled like scattered diamonds around the adventurers as they sat patiently waiting on the scaly backs.

"What now sir?" Arthur asked wiping the sweat off his forehead.

"Well first things first, we must name our new and honourable friends."

The boys and Professor took this task very seriously and thought hard for an appropriate name.

"OK everyone, please say hello to Rambo!" Arthur said grinning proudly.

His friends obediently said hello to Rambo the Triceratops.

"Raj any ideas?" The Professor asked.

"Meet Boudicca!" Raj replied, stroking her frill fondly.

"Oh yes a fantastic historical women warrior! Boudicca the queen of the British Iceni tribe, led an uprising against the occupying forces of the Roman Empire! She did not have a happy ending though, flogged by the Romans when her husband died!"

"What about yours Professor?" Serendipity asked.

Professor Inchenstein straightened his bow tie before proclaiming, "My Triceratops will also be named after another hero brave enough to stand up against their oppressive Roman rulers! Children," the Professor did a gracious bow, "Let me introduce you to the one and only Thracian Gladiator, Spartacus!"

Once the children introduced themselves to Spartacus, the Professor instructed everyone to observe the herd and marvel at their exoticness.

"Yes lovelies, we must observe and there is no better way to observe than to record it, now say CHEESE."

After the photo-shoot, Professor Boris Inchenstein sat upon his Spartacus with a proud straight back and looked around at the rest of the herd; there must have been about twenty or more he guessed, all grazing calmly in the soft breeze. Life does not get any better than this he thought to himself as he stroked the small horns that bordered the frill of his dinosaur's headdress. "If only my Mavis could be behind me with her arms around my waist, then life would really be most perfect." he muttered under his breath.

"It's skin feels like sand paper." Serendipity observed as her soft hand felt the hard-knobbly skin below.

"It is not very comfortable!" Amber complained as she cautiously shifted around trying to get comfortable.

"Their thick rough skin is to defend the soft tasty flesh below!" Their teacher commented.

"Isn't that what the horns are for?" Arthur asked.

"Well of course, the horns will protect him to some extent, but what if he is attacked from behind?" the Professor said.

"I read that some scientists believe the horns were not for defence at all but used to find a mate and fight off other males" Raj noted.

"Quite right Raj chap, quite right!" The Professor confirmed, "However, nobody really knows, it is all speculation. But what excites me the most, what really gets my blood surging is the fact that we are about to discover the truth ourselves!" He held onto his Spartacus's frill as if it were about to gallop off into the wilderness and find a mate, however, his dinosaur did not look remotely interested in copulation and continued to devour the shrubbery around him.

While the Professor sat ready and waiting to find Spartacus's soul mate the children dutifully observed the dinosaurs around them from their elevated positions. While they waited and observed, the sun's rays blasted down on the children's backs in a merciless manner causing them most discomfort.

"I feel like I am being boiled alive!" Serendipity moaned as she felt her t-shirt stick to her back as if it were soaked in melted butter.

"Yes, the sun is rather unforgiving this morning!" The Professor agreed shaking his limp locks from side to side to remove some of the residue.

"They don't seem to be doing much." Arthur complained, "I thought there would be more action!" He said disappointingly, looking at the docile herd of herbivores around him.

"Be patient, you young whippersnapper!" His teacher replied, "It is a privilege of the highest order to be seated on the back of a living creature that is 65million years old, even though it does feel like we are being barbequed!" He grumbled.

Calm and lethargy fell over the five hot adventurers and they each drifted off into their own quite world. Doctor Dino continued to document everything he saw, scribbling away whenever he had a spare minute. His sweat kept on sliding down his nose and then splashing onto his notes causing him to mumble gentle obscenities under his breath. Raj never bored of peeping over Boudicca's headdress to stare at her eyes; they were like bottomless black marbles the size of golf balls surrounded by a bogey green iris. Arthur imagined charging at a T-Rex at top speed and stabbing the carnivore in the belly with Rambo's pointy horns. Serendipity decided to pass the time by counting how many Triceratopses she could see, she counted number 22 when Amber broke the silence and asked the Professor a question that had been bothering her for weeks.

"Why was Bunny Bristlepott so mean to me and Raj when we asked her questions?"

Professor Inchenstein looked up from his watery notes and noticed the earnestness in his pupil's face. He had heard through the grapevine in the staff room that two students from year six had upset Bunny, but he did not realise who it was and what it was about. He wiped the sweat from his tangled eyebrows and proceeded with caution, "What did you ask her?"

"I only asked her about the beginning of life. Why the Bible's timeline is so different from what you taught us." Amber said quietly with a hurt look in her eye.

Professor Inchenstein winced quietly to himself; he now

understood what had happened and he felt extremely sorry for Amber who was so innocent and so troubled.

"I am sure Bunny Bristlepott did not mean to be so cross." He replied clearing his throat as he spoke.

"Yes she did, she went mental!" Arthur added.

"Now Arthur, don't exaggerate! I do not believe that Bunny went mental." Their teacher said frowning.

"She was pretty cross Professor." Serendipity confirmed.

"Well she definitely lost her marbles when I said the Bible was a load of Hullabaloo!" Raj said. Professor Inchenstein nearly fell off his Spartacus he was so shocked by what Raj had said. "You said WHAT to Bunny Bristlepott?" he choked.

"He said that the Bible was a load of Hullabaloo!" Arthur said grinning, "That was when she went mental!"

Once the Professor caught his breath he asked, "But why would you say such a thing?" and for the first time he looked disappointed in Raj.

They all noticed the sudden change in their teacher's humour.

"That is what you taught us, remember? That Creationism is a load of Hullabaloo!" Raj retorted aware he had done something wrong but not entirely sure what it was.

The Professor winced out loud this time as he realised now exactly what had happened and he felt completely responsible. "But I never said that the Bible was a load of Hullabaloo!" He said with his face falling south in despair. "Did you tell Bunny that is what I taught you, that the Bible is a load of Hullabaloo?"

Raj could not bear to look his teacher in the eyes; he had never seen the Professor look so troubled.

Everything suddenly made sense to the Professor, for weeks he had been trying to work out why Bunny was more hostile towards him than usual; the snide comments behind his back in the staff room, the disapproving looks from Doctor Fog and her outright refusal to share her Belgium chocolates with him when she let all the other teachers try one – now he knew why.

"But you misunderstand me boy." The Professor said softly to Raj.

The Professor thought long and hard before he attempted to explain and correct the wrong that had been done. He was indeed an Atheist, he believed in facts; he was a scientist after all. He thought back to the lesson when he introduced his magnificent Wall of Hullabaloo and considered that he might have gone a step too far. He had never meant for Bunny to get hurt.

"Right all of you listen to me." He said with such authority that the children stopped noticing the dinosaurs around them and stared transfixed at their teacher. "You cannot take everything that I say completely literally."

"But you are always right sir" Raj said quietly.

"Nobody is always right! Not even me!" He smiled softly at his pupils.

"What makes our world such a wonderful place is the fact we have our own freedom to think, speak and most importantly believe! It is up to us to find our own truth! There are thousands of different types of religions and belief systems in the world. Some people choose to believe the Bible word for word, others choose to believe in its messages and values. But what is the most important of all is that we must, absolutely must, respect other people's beliefs. Even, if we do not believe them ourselves." He concluded, looking sternly at Raj who was about to say something but then thought twice about it.

"Yes, but I was very respectful to Bunny Bristlepott, all I did was question her." Amber said, thinking back to the injustice that befell her and her father's terrifying reaction.

"I am sure you were my buttercup, but you must understand that we adults do not always get it right, and we do not always behave correctly either!" The Professor replied, smiling fondly at Amber.

"Err Professor?"

"Yes Arthur what is it?"

"I think we are on the move!" Arthur said enthusiastically.

"Oh dear Lord!" Amber sighed as she felt the tree trunk legs begin to move slowly under her. She squeezed Arthur so tightly that he thought his lungs might explode.

"About time!" The Professor shouted with relish. "Now hold on tight to your reins and stay together!"

"How are we supposed to stay together?" Serendipity asked but the question was lost in the excitement as Spartacus, Rambo and Boudicca started to lurch forward, leg by leg, thud by thud into the wilderness. With every shudder, with every tremble, with every vibration the explorers and their exotic rides advanced further towards the gleaming sun. The dust that was once so quiet and undisturbed exploded in the air and gushed around them; it was so thick, it loomed over them like a swarm of bees, stinging their eyes as the wind blew. The boys gripped the headdresses that framed the 2.5meter long skulls in front of them with all their strength and the girls clung onto the boys with a mixture of fear and excitement. Doctor Dino causally had one hand on his steering wheel while the other was recording the scene on camera.

"This will make Jurassic Park look like amateurs' work! Ha! Imagine Spielberg's envy when I show him my footage!" The Professor said as he enjoyed recording the magical moment. Professor Inchenstein knew that the film he was making was going to be a best seller, it would go on that tube TV thing he had heard so much about and be seen by the world's population; it might even win an Oscar he thought! He decided to do some commentary (David Attenborough style) to add value to the filming so he began to describe what he could see in a low gentle voice:

"It may be hard for you to imagine while you sit at home on your sofas, but I am in fact filming from the back of a Triceratops! Oh yes and a real one at that! Don't believe me, do you?" He asked as he peered deep into the camera lens. "Well take a look around and let's see if I can persuade you otherwise!"

The Professor continued to describe the scene to his future audience and luckily for his film, the dust started to settle and he could show the world that he was actually telling the truth. Raj's glasses were slowly slipping down his face but he was too frightened to take one of his hands off the frill in order to push them back up.

"Where do you think we are going?" Serendipity whispered in Raj's ear.

"No idea! Maybe to find more food or water." Raj replied.

Amber had her face buried into Arthur's back and did not dare look up she was so afraid.

"Have you opened your eyes yet?" Arthur asked cheekily, guessing that his friend behind him had them tightly shut.

"Certainly not!" Amber muffled.

"Come on, you are safe up here, Rambo and I will protect you. Open your eyes Amber, you will never forget what you see." Arthur said reassuringly.

Amber knew he was right. Amber agreed that there was not much point choosing to ride on the back of a gigantic dinosaur if she was not going to take a peek and look around at the view she had. Very slowly, she opened one anxious eye and peered over

Arthur's shoulder.

"Gee whizz!" She sighed out load.

"Aren't you glad you looked?" Arthur asked.

Amber could not believe her eyes; everywhere she turned she saw intimidating horns; behind her, to the right, to the left and in front, all raging forward with purpose.

"They look so angry." she observed.

"I don't think they mean to, but I am not sure how a dinosaur with 50cm long horns jutting out of its head is going to look friendly." Arthur replied.

"I guess." Amber said quietly as she fixated on the three daunting horns that were bobbing up and down behind her.

While the children observed in awe the spectacle around them, their teacher continued to capture it and was commenting on the Triceratops's behaviour.

"If you look closely ladies and gentlemen you will see that these splendid Triceratopses have organized themselves in some sort of orderly fashion. Minutes before they were grazing in a large group and now they have formed a line that is four thick. If I just stand up, we will be able to see what is going on ahead." The Professor put the camera around his neck, keeping the film rolling at all times and carefully crouched down bending his old knees; he then edged slowly forward so that when he stood up his knees leant against the headdress and would hopefully hold him steady.

"Ah, observe, that we are quite near the back indicating that the Triceratops that we chose to ride are not very old and not very important! Oh well never-mind." Doctor Dino continued.

"I don't believe it." Serendipity shouted out loud.

Raj looked round in excitement but unfortunately could not focus on anything because his glasses had practically slipped off his nose.

"What, what is?" he said frantically worried some danger was approaching.

"Look at the Professor!" Serendipity cried.

Raj took a deep breath and quickly took his right hand off the frill and pushed his glasses back up his nose so he could see his teacher.

"You have got to be kidding me." Raj exclaimed when his blurred vision finally cleared.

"He is off his rocker!" Arthur yelled when he noticed the Professor nonchalantly standing in a surfing stance on the back of Spartacus.

Doctor Dino did not have a care in the world; all that mattered to him was that he could take the best film possible, and by standing up tall, he could see everything that was going on with their herd of Triceratopses.

"Oh, how fascinating!" His commentary continued. "The smaller Triceratopses are walking in the middle of the herd so they are protected just like elephants do to protect their young from ravenous lions. We don't have to worry about hungry lions snatching the young, oh no! Our dreaded enemy is the biggest, most ferocious T-Rex! Oh, I do hope one tries to attack us and that I catch it on camera!" He babbled irresponsibly.

Before long the herd with their new friends had been riding together for over an hour. They had left the luscious green forest behind them many miles away and were slowly walking through the open plains. Nothing new was happening so the Professor decided to take a seat and relax for a while. The boys also slackened their grip on the dinosaurs' headdresses allowing the blood to flow freely again on their white knuckles. Even Amber stopped squeezing Arthur so tightly enabling him to breathe more regularly. Doctor Dino was wondering what else he could say about Triceratopses for his film when they heard an unusual moaning sound that seemed to be coming from up ahead. The Professor cautiously stood up in order to get a better view of what was going on, keeping his camera recording in case something interesting was about to happen. He zoomed in to achieve a closer look in front and to his horror of horrors he witnessed a massive panic amongst the herd.

"Blast the Cotswolds!" the Professor uttered under his breath.

The dinosaurs seemed to be disappearing one by one as soon as they reached a certain point. Alarm vibrated through the teacher's veins as he realised what was happening; the herd had fallen into a mud pit and were trampling on top of one another and then sinking into the thick brown depths below. He knew he had to act fast if he was going to be able to save himself and the lives of his pupils.

"What is going on Professor?" Raj asked nervously sensing something was seriously wrong because his teacher's legs were wobbling uncontrollably.

"Right it seems we are in a bit of a pickle," Doctor Dino explained. "I need you to do exactly, EXACTLY as I say do you hear me?" He shouted firmly at the children.

The blood quickly drained away from the children's faces leaving them an ashen hue as they realised that something must be terribly amiss. The Professor had a crazy idea that was full of risk but he had no time to think of another one. He frantically took his rope out of his rucksack and tied a hoop at one end; he then tied the other end around one of the horns belonging to Spartacus using a fisherman's knot.

"Now I am going to throw this at you Arthur my brave lad and you are going to put it around Amber's waist." The Professor carried on shouting, ignoring the abject fear that appeared on his pupils' faces. "DO AS I SAY!" The Professor screamed.

Amber was debating whether to faint or not as the thought of having a rope tied around her waist that was attached to a horn of a neighbouring monster. It was more than her nerves could handle, but her teacher shouted so loudly at her that she forgot to pass out and quickly put the lasso around her body.

"Now when I say jump you are going to leap into my arms." The Professor rolled up his sleeves ready to catch Amber. "Arthur if she doesn't jump you had better push her, understood?"

Arthur squeezed Amber's hand tightly trying to reassure her.

"NOW JUMP!" The Professor cried.

Amber's legs sunk deep into the back of Rambo like pillars of led into cement – she refused to budge. The Professor nodded towards Arthur and then Amber gulped with fear as she felt a strong push from behind and realised that she was floating through the air towards her teacher's outstretched arms. Spartacus was only two meters away from Rambo but because Amber was pushed instead of jumping herself, she quickly descended and was about to hit the hard side of the dinosaur. Luckily Doctor Dino clasped her arm just in time and swung her up so fast that she landed with a thud behind the Professor.

The Professor did not have time to check to see if Amber was alright; he grabbed the rope from around her waist and flung it back to Arthur. Arthur knew what he had to do and as soon as the rope touched his hand he tugged it hard, walked to the back of Rambo and then ran as fast as he could along its back and leapt into the air towards the safety of the Professor.

"How are you going to get the others Professor?" Arthur cried as he landed next to a quivering Amber.

A sadness overcame the Professor and he did not reply immediately because the truth was, he was not sure how to save

Raj and Serendipity. They were on the other side of Rambo and they could not possibly jump to reach the Professor. Doctor Dino could feel the adrenalin racing through his veins as the mud pit up ahead came into sight and he knew that the chances of them all surviving would be extremely low. He placed his hand on Arthur's shoulder and gently said, "Now Arthur, we do not have a lot of time so you need to listen to me." Arthur nodded trying to be brave while Amber sobbed quietly behind him.

"You and Amber need to jump off this wonderful beast and you need to run far away from the herd. They are all sinking into a mud pit up ahead and we are in imminent danger."

Amber now aware of the hazard could not control herself and started sobbing loudly.

"Be brave both of you. Run to trees and shelter. Take my rucksack too it has everything you need in it to survive." The Professor jammed his camera in the top of the bag and then threw his rucksack off the dinosaur and the two children watched it clunk to the floor. He kissed both the children on their heads and then pushed them gently off Spartacus. Doctor Dino swiftly turned to his other pupils and shouted, "Don't panic I am coming to save you!" Raj and Serendipity had been watching intensely how their teacher saved their friends. They were both relived that Amber and Arthur were now safe, but they were not sure at all that their own fate would be so fortunate. If they tried to jump down they would surely be trampled to death as there were dinosaurs on either side of Boudicca and many more behind her. Doctor Dino undid the rope from Spartacus's horn and wrapped the rope over his head so it rested on one of his shoulders, he then stood like a sprinter ready to take off and run the 100meters.

"Professor, don't, you won't make it!" Raj cried out as he saw what his beloved teacher was about to do.

Doctor Dino paid no attention to his pupils' objections and flung himself onto Rambo's back. His right foot, however did not manage to land properly and he twisted his ankle causing him to land flat on his face, but at least he did not fall to the floor. Serendipity cried with relief as she watched the grey fluffy head slowly rise and the Professor gave himself a shake and wiped the blood away from his face.

"Stand back folks I am COMING…" The Professor shouted as he leapt into the air towards Raj and Serendipity. Serendipity screamed out loud as she saw her teacher hurl towards her mid-air. This time the Professor had a firm landing and both his feet hit the back of Boudicca. Once steady, he then grasped the children in his arms with delight.

"Now we have no time for sentimentalism." He said as he brushed a tear away from Serendipity's cheek.

"Professor I think it is too late! Boudicca is almost in the mud!" Raj cried.

The Professor looked up and watched with dread as he saw the once proud herd drowning miserably in thick gooey mud. One by one the horns started to disappear.

"Why don't I rub the claw?" Serendipity asked timidly, knowing that if she did Amber and Arthur would be lost in this unknown world forever.

"Don't worry dears, I promise you our end will not be now!" The Professor said solemnly, "We will make it out of this little trifle and join our friends in no time, so let's not resort to the claw at this stage! The most important thing is not to land in the mud, do you understand?"

Raj and Serendipity nodded that they understood and slowly stood up with the help of their teacher. "Now you need to follow my lead. We are going to casually leap on the backs of the sinking Triceratopses until we reach the edge of the pit over there." The Professor pointed to where the ground was not sinking. "Just image these are giant rocks in a river and we are going to hop on them like stepping stones to the other side." He smiled at the children's pale faces, "Follow me!" he shouted and soared in the air until he landed on the back of another sinking dinosaur. By this time Boudicca's legs were completely out of sight. Raj stroked her head softly and said goodbye while Serendipity jumped as high as she could following her teacher.

"Come on Raj don't dilly dally!" The Professor shouted over his shoulder as he tried to guide the children to safety.

Raj quickly hurried after the others and soon caught up with Serendipity, he held her sweaty hand and they started to jump together. The Professor turned to watch his pupils making sure they were safe. "Come on kids, we are almost there. Just make it to me and then we can jump to dry land!" He cried feeling some hope at last. The Professor had already reached the last dinosaur that was on the edge of the pit and the next jump would lead him to safety. Serendipity and Raj were not far behind and they leapt as high as they could to reach the dinosaur next to their teacher's; Raj landed firmly on the sinking back, but Serendipity's foot slipped and she screamed with fright. Luckily Raj still had hold of her hand and he tried with all of his strength to pull her up but his feeble arms could not stand the strain. Raj could see the fear in his friend's eyes and even though his arm felt like it was being wrenched slowly away from his armpit, he was determined not to let her fall to her death. "Put your foot on the dinosaur's shoulder and try and push up on his face!" Raj screamed.

The Professor felt like he was about to have a heart attack when he saw Serendipity slip; his lungs were gasping for breath and his legs wobbled like jelly. It would be impossible for him to jump back and save Serendipity because his sinking dinosaur was much lower than the one the children were on; all he could do was watch in dismay as Raj struggled to pull Serendipity onto the face of the dinosaur. The Professor felt the dinosaur that he was kneeling on slowly sinking down and he knew that he did not have long before he would drown too.

Serendipity swung her left leg with all her strength onto the face of the Triceratops and with her left hand she managed to grab hold of one of its horns. Raj still held onto her other hand in desperation, pulling her up as much as he could. Serendipity did her best to haul herself up and towards the dinosaur's headdress. Finally, she placed her left hand onto its frill and let go of Raj in order to push herself over the headdress and onto the back of the dinosaur. Serendipity could feel her energy waning, but she knew if she could just push herself up and over then they would be safe. Raj was standing on the dinosaur's back with his arms open ready to catch his friend. Serendipity slowly edged her bottom onto the top of the frill and swung her legs over ready to jump down.

"Fantastic you are almost their now jump." Raj cried.

Serendipity smiled at Raj's kind face and jumped. The Professor croaked with dread as he saw Serendipity's rucksack get stuck on the dinosaur's headdress and his pupil's feet dangle 30cm above the dinosaur's back. Raj lunged forward and tried to pull Serendipity's arms out of her rucksack's straps, but the rucksack was fastened with a belt around her waist and the clasp was jammed.

"It's no good!" Serendipity sobbed wriggling her arms frantically "I am stuck!" She cried with tears streaming down her face.

Doctor Dino felt the mud gently caress his knees and he knew that the game was up; he let his head fall in shame at the thought of Serendipity sinking into the mud with the other dinosaurs.

Raj, however, was not going to let his first and best friend die like this; he rummaged in his own bag and was overcome by gratitude as he felt the cold edge of his blunt penknife against his hand. He wedged it open and frantically tried to cut the strap around Serendipity's waist.

"Raj it's OK just go!" Serendipity yelled at him in anguish.

Raj ignored his friend's screams and continued to gnaw the strap with his knife; he did not even feel the red blisters that were beginning to form on his hand. The mud had started to stroke Raj's ankles, but he did not care because the strap started to fray and he thought if he just continued for a bit longer he could set his friend free. Serendipity watched admirably the top of Raj's head and appreciated how determined he was to cut her lose. She placed her hand on his turban and stroked it fondly. Raj could barely see the blade because his eyes were filled with hopeless tears, "Just keep going." he said to himself, "Just keep going." Raj shouted out loud in surprise as he felt his friend fall on top of him, "It worked!" Serendipity shouted. She flung her arms around Raj and squeezed him tightly.

"Oh profound protons he saved her!" The Professor sobbed to himself as he watched the friends embrace on the sinking dinosaur.

"There is no time to loiter now grab this rope and tie it round the two of you and I will pull you out the mud."

The two friends looked at each other with complete relief and swiftly threw the rope over their heads and tied it tight and jumped. Doctor Dino pulled with what strength he had left and eventually they reached dry land. Raj tried to wipe the mud off his glasses but quickly gave up and he lay back on the cracked earth with the others, staring at the clear blue sky. They had made it.

Suddenly Serendipity sat up and gasped so loudly the Professor shielded his face expecting an imminent danger.

"What's wrong?" Raj asked concerned.

"It's the claw." She replied meekly, "It, it is in my rucksack!"

18

Carboniferous tales by the fireside

Amber and Arthur approached the drowning herd with trepidation. It was depressing to watch the slow death that was overcoming the herd; the silent panic that flashed across their green eyes, the mud being snorted out from their protesting nostrils and then the inevitable moment when the dinosaurs would admit defeat as the slushy mud conquered their persistent struggle. As Arthur and Amber drew closer to the newly buried herd all that could be seen were pairs of horns reflecting the sunlight.

"I feel sad." Amber said quietly.

Arthur squeezed Amber's hand as he led her around the mud trying to find their friends and teacher. They had no idea what had happened, the last thing they saw was the Professor leaping in the air like an over excited Lima. Amber was muttering the Lord's Prayer hoping that her friends had made it and not had the same terrible fate as the floating horns surrounding her.

"Look over there! I see them!" Arthur shouted with excitement.

Amber sprinted forward and was overwhelmed with happiness as she saw Serendipity, Raj and the Professor sitting in a small circle at the edge of the mud pit, head to toe in mud! Arthur tried his best to keep up with Amber, but the weight of the Professor's rucksack was proving more than he could bear so he threw it to the floor and raced at top speed to see his friends.

"Oh, thank goodness you are safe! We were so worried!" Amber shrieked as she hugged Serendipity with relief, knocking her to the floor. Serendipity was the first girlfriend Amber had ever really had and she was so frightened that she would lose her. Amber was so busy hugging everyone that she did not pick up on the tension felt by her rescued friends. Arthur on the other hand arrived seconds later and he saw the concern in Raj's eyes.

"What's wrong mate?" he asked slapping Raj on the back with affection.

Raj looked at Serendipity, who in turn looked at the Professor. Doctor Dino, being the eldest, thought it was only right that he should break the shocking news to Amber and Arthur.

"Sit down my fine young adventurers, sit down." The Professor pointed to the solid earth next to them.

Amber slowly let go of Serendipity and stared at her teacher.

"What's going on?" She asked worriedly.

"Well the rescue of your two friends was not without a huge amount of drama and action." He attempted to straighten his spotty bow tie, but it was caked in mud making his attempt completely futile.

"You see we have a slight problem, a problem with the most concerning consequences." His hands moved again towards his neck then quickly dropped down again. "However, I am sure that there will be a way out, there is always a way out!" The Professor continued to babble.

"What on earth are you talking about Professor?" Arthur asked impatiently.

"It's the claw" Raj whispered, "It fell in the mud."

Arthur's jaw dropped so low that none of his friends had ever realised what a large mouth he actually had until this moment.

"Is this some kind of sick joke?" Amber asked turning to Serendipity hoping to see a cheeky smile form on her friend's face.

Serendipity looked down at her fingers and watched her tears fall to the floor making dark patches in the dusty dry earth.

"Not to worry children, it is really nothing to worry about." The Professor said sheepishly knowing full well that worry was the most appropriate emotion to be feeling at this point in time.

The pupils and their teacher sat on the same spot for a considerable amount of time without talking. They watched the few remaining horns poking up from the depths of the mud and contemplated their situation gravely. Serendipity was feeling extremely culpable and so was the Professor, for it was his idea to ride on the backs of the Triceratopses and it was his idea that they should revisit the Late Cretaceous period. Yes, it was very clear to the Professor that he was responsible for this mortifying situation and he felt a growing dread within him as he searched for a solution that deep down he knew did not exist. Once all the horns were finally out of sight the Professor stood up and said, "Let's move away from this eerie graveyard and find a place to shelter." He then straightened his extremely creased tweed jacket and fastened the front buttons. "Where is my rucksack Arthur?"

Arthur pointed in the distant towards a black blob that stood out against its sandy surroundings. The Professor walked silently towards his rucksack and the children followed behind him despondently.

ΔΔΔ

The five adventures trudged forward with sunken hearts and followed Doctor Dino into the forest. The Professor was shattered and slumped down in front of an extremely large Sequoia tree. The tired crew dropped to the floor and leant back on the jagged bark of the tree. The Professor looked at the forlorn faces of his young friends and decided it was up to him to change the mood into a more positive one.

"Well chaps as my Great Aunt Meldrith always said, when one is feeling down, one should eat some Bakewell tart! And guess what I have squashed in the bottom of my rucksack?" He grinned mischievously at the children making them giggle despite their situation, "Only the finest Bakewell tart in the whole of London! Oh yes Gail's Bakery would make the French squirm with envy!" And he pulled out from the darkest depths of his rucksack a transparent plastic bag burst ing with icing and sponge, and not resembling a cake in the slightest.

The smell of a freshly baked cake soon reached the children's hungry nostrils and their bellies suddenly remembered that they had not eaten in hours. The Professor broke off a bit of bark from tree they were leaning on and scooped a piece of cake into his pupils' outstretched hands.

The five weary adventurers consumed the cake with greed and then sat back against the tree and enjoyed the sugar rush that is always so delightful after eating too much cake. The forest floor slowly became darker and the Professor realised that night was soon going to arrive. He instructed the children to stay near this tree and not to move under any circumstance. He handed Raj his whistle and told him that he is to blow it if anything bad happens and advised that they should climb a tree if any untoward dinosaurs were to approach.

"I thought you said we were not supposed to move!" Arthur questioned cheekily.

"Don't be facetious Arthur!" The Professor replied frowning.

"Where are you going Professor?" Amber asked nervously.

"I am going to search for wood to make us an atmospheric fire to keep your little toes toasting warm!" And with that he disappeared into the forest. The children waited in silence for the Professor to return. Raj wondered if they were really going to have to live in the Late Cretaceous period for the rest of their lives while Amber thought how sad it was that she would never see her Grandma Rose again. Arthur decided that the best way to pass the time would be a game of good old-fashioned eye spy and set off with the letter P. While the children looked for something beginning with P the Professor hurried as fast as he could to collect the wood needed to build his atmospheric fire. He wanted to be quick, as he was worried if he stayed away for too long another disaster could befall his pupils and he did not think that his ticky ticker could take any more drama. He hummed the first song that came into his head which happened to be Old Abram Brown is Dead and Gone whilst he gathered as many twigs and roughage that he believed would burn well.

Ten minutes later and holding as many bits of branches and bracken as his arms could carry the Professor scurried back to the large Sequoia tree. Darkness was slowly enveloping everything in her path making it near impossible for the children to see anything let alone something beginning with P.

"There is really no point in playing this game when we can hardly see our hands!" Serendipity huffed.

"Don't get stroppy!" Arthur replied. "It is very easy to guess, I don't know why you are all taking so long and you should use your other senses to guess it, if you know what I mean!" Arthur gave a wink to Raj.

Amber, Raj and Serendipity racked their brains and used their ears and noses to try and guess what Arthur could see that began with P.

"It is almost pitch black now." Amber said anxiously. Arthur slipped his hand into Amber's and she felt reassured.

"OK I will give you a clue." Arthur said starting to get frustrated with how slow his friends were being. "It is something that we all do and it happens to be on the bottom of Raj's shoe!" Arthur grinned like a Cheshire cat and his teeth glowed brightly under the moonlight.

"That is disgusting!" Serendipity cried. "Typical of you to think of that!"

Arthur thought the combination of the girls' disgust and Raj's embarrassment as he sniffed the bottom of his trainer incredibly funny and he started bawling with laughter. His laughter became contagious and all the nervous energy that had been circuiting around the children's veins suddenly released itself and the silent forest was permeated with uncontrollable laughter.

The Professor heard the loud noises coming from where the children were and his heart began to race in his tired chest. He decided the only way to scare off the deadly predator about to attack the children was to sing Old Abram at the top of his lungs and wave the largest branch that he was holding with as much aggressive gusto as he could fathom.

The children heard a crackle in the near distant and Raj quickly shushed his friends, "Did you hear that?" he whispered nervously.

Amber felt her throat dry up and she squeezed Arthur's hand extremely hard.

Raj placed the whistle to his parched lips ready to blow when they all screamed with fright as the Professor jumped towards them from the undergrowth brandishing a threatening branch and singing at the top of his lungs "HE USED TO WEAR AN OLD BROWN COAT THAT BUTTONED DOWN BEFORE!"

Serendipity ran off behind the tree in fear and Raj blew the whistle so loudly he nearly burst his ear drum. Doctor Dino, convinced they were under attack, increased the volume of his song putting his old lungs under immense strain and thrashed around in the dark with his stick hoping to swipe the intruding dinosaur across the face.

It was Arthur who finally got a grip of his senses and the situation and shouted at the Professor.

"Professor what is wrong, stop it Professor!" he shouted.

But the Professor was singing so loudly that he only thought Arthur's protests were that of fear and distress and consequently he swung his branch more vibrantly.

Arthur at this point thought the Professor had gone utterly mad and the only way to shut him up was to tackle him to the ground. He crept up behind his raving teacher and dived at him rugby style clasping the Professor's legs and knocking him over.

"I have been taken from behind." The Professor screamed, "RUN! Save yourselves!" and the Professor accepted the fact that he was soon to be gobbled alive.

"Professor for goodness sake it's me Arthur. Nothing is attacking us apart from you!"

The Professor finally stopped wriggling and groped in the air towards Arthur, "Why in Darwin's name have you tackled me boy?"

"You were behaving like a lunatic and scared the crap out of us!" Arthur panted.

"Now now, no need for obscenities. I thought you were under attack! You were all screaming!" The confused Professor replied.

"We were laughing sir." Amber explained.

They were all now surrounded by the blackest night they had ever known so the Professor turned towards Amber's voice and said, "Well I did not think of that, laughing eh? What was so funny?" Once the fire was lit and burning strong the children told the Professor their joke and the teacher chuckled kindly, even though he did not find it funny at all. He was more interested in the poo in question on the bottom of Raj's shoe and hastily scraped it off and put it in a sealed jar causing the children to squeal with disgust. The Professor looked up at them in surprise causing his friends to burst into laughter once again.

"There is nothing wrong with a bit of dinosaur poo! You should feel very proud Raj lad, not many boys your age can say they have trodden in Dinosaur dung!" Doctor Dino held the jar up to the fire so that he could get a better look at the sludgy brown substance inside. "I am longing to find out who it belongs to!" And he moved his eyebrows up and down so fast that the children's giggles floated high into the air and tickled the night sky. The burning branches warmed their toes and momentarily calmed their worried souls. The auburn flames flicked across the blackness illuminating the children's faces and casting dark shadows around them. The provisions that they packed for their trip would last no more than five days, so Amber and Serendipity prepared a meagre meal for the boys and Professor, consisting of ham sandwiches, raw unpeeled carrots (noone thought to pack a peeler) and two Smarties each. Minutes later, with the sandwiches and carrots gobbled up and their bellies still rumbling persistently, the Professor took it upon himself to tell them all a story in order to distract them from their hunger and unfortunate circumstance.

"Now I imagine that your four brains believe that dinosaurs are rather large and wondrous creatures, am I right?" The teacher asked his pupils peering between the darting flames to see their innocent faces. Their heads nodded in unison to this question.

Satisfied that the children were already engrossed with what he was saying and distracted from their perilous situation, the Professor continued in an overly zealous manner.

"Well let me open your worlds and imaginations to an even more peculiar time; filled with monstrous insects and millipedes the size of crocodiles!"

The four friends were absolutely captivated and hung on their teacher's every word.

"Boys and girls," he whispered, "Open your minds to the Carboniferous Era" and he threw a branch on the fire causing the flames to dance erratically and the children's hearts to pound harder in their chests.

"We must go even further back in time than we are now. You see as we sit here near the fire light we are in an age that is around 65million years old! But in order to be with the gigantic insects we need to rewind the clock to 358 to 299 million years ago!" Doctor Dino waved his hands dramatically in the air.

"Indeed this land was pretty exotic to say the least. The forest floors were covered in swamps and marshes, sodden to the ground with slushy mud and murky water. The air was filled with buzzing insects more than a million-different species, swarming between the trees like hungry locusts."

The Professor gulped down a precious glug of water and continued his story, "But no insect was safe in the air because out of nowhere the mother of all bugs would zoom in the air and dive and swirl and catch every living creature within her grasp. Anyone know what I am talking about?" the Professor did not give the children any time to respond but burst the answer into the air and accidently spat all over the fire! "Meganeura – she was a giant alright, like the modern-day dragon fly but the size of a wild boar; wings as long as hockey sticks and eyes the size of avocados! No one messed with Meganeura and lived to tell the tale that's for sure!"

The children stared at their teacher's face between the fire's flames and tried to imagine a dragon fly the size of a wild boar with wings as long as hockey sticks and eyes the size of avocados."

"You are pulling our legs sir!" Arthur said.

"I can assure you that I never joke about the Carboniferous period." And their teacher frowned so seriously that he seemed just as scary as the Meganeura he had been describing. Professor Inchenstein undid his weary, muddy, bow tie and laid his head down by the fireside. "Lie down children and count the stars that are glistening in the sky above us."

The children followed their teacher's advice and lay down on their backs and stared up at the magical black sky. The monotonous sheet of darkness was broken up by the biggest, brightest stars the children had ever seen; they twinkled and sparkled and seemed to return the children's gaze with a sympathizing wink.

"Oh overwhelmingly beautiful luminous spheres of plasma, we are not worthy to be under you." And with that the Professor fell into a heavy slumber and snored so loudly, the four friends were sure that if any dinosaur were to approach them they would be scared away directly.

19

Mother to the Rescue

Counting the twinkling stars soon made their eyelids feel extremely heavy and one by one they fell into a deep sleep. The night's hours passed by slowly drifting into morning. Raj was dreaming of being on holiday with his parents; he was playing cribbage with his father on the beach and his mother was walking towards them holding quench thirsting lemonade. Raj could feel the scorching heat on his face from the sun and drops of the wet lemonade falling temptingly on his dry lips. He slowly opened his eyes and to his confusion could not see anything because everything seemed misty and cloudy. He wiped his wet mouth with his sleeve and took off his glasses that had completely steamed up and cleaned them the best he could with his fingers. He put them back on, looked through them and then his heart stopped beating for 3 whole seconds before his glasses steamed up again. Raj froze deadly still and thought that he must still be dreaming. He wondered if he should wipe his glasses again or just close his eyes and think of lemonade and cribbage? Another blob of liquid fell on his mouth but this time he knew it was not lemonade and it only confirmed that what he saw for three seconds was in fact real. Raj thought back to all the adventure books he had read and movies he had watched to try and help him come up with an escape plan; but nothing he had ever read or watched told him what to do when a T-Rex's head was inches above your own and it was breathing hot air on your glasses preventing you from seeing and its saliva was dripping onto your mouth. Raj was indeed in a pickle and he had no idea what to do so he shut his eyes decided to think of cribbage and lemonade. The Professor stretched his old arms above his head and groaned slightly as he felt every muscle in his body ache due to the adventures of yesterday. He poked the fire with a long branch as the flames had nearly all turned to cinders, and then he saw it. His body tensed like dry cement and he looked imploringly towards Raj. He had no time to think, he only had time to act. He grabbed a branch from the fire that was still alight and jumped into the air. He wacked the T-Rex on the head and screamed from the top of his lungs YOU'LL NEVER SEE HIM MORE! HE USED TO WEAR A LONG BROWN COAT THAT BUTTONED DOWN BEFORE!" and he ran as fast as he could into the depths of the forest. His distraction worked and the 2tonne T-Rex's head swung from Raj's misty glasses and turned towards the Professor. The light from the branch could still be seen in the forest as it darted frantically from left to right. The T-Rex moved its hind legs forward nearly crushing Raj and the dinosaur lurched forward after the Professor, its tale caressing the fire and knocking Amber as it went. Serendipity jumped over the fire and grabbed Raj who lay limp on the floor.

"What's wrong with him?" Arthur asked as he also crouched beside Raj's motionless body.

"I think he is in shock!" Serendipity said.

"Oi Raj get up!" said Arthur shaking him violently.

But still Raj was as floppy as a rag doll.

"You don't think...?" Amber asked nervously.

"Of course he is not dead!" Arthur said and tugged at his friend's arm.

Serendipity asked Arthur to stopped shaking Raj and bent down to kiss him on the lips. The kiss only lasted a second, but it was long enough for Raj to sit bolt upright in a fright and take off his misty glasses. He looked up at his friends' blurry faces and said, "Guys, I was having the weirdest of dreams… I was on the beach with dad playing cribbage and then there was this massive T-Rex staring down at me and then I could hear a funny song and then I was drinking lemonade and then I felt Serendipity…" And with this last vivid part of the dream Raj blushed and fell silent.

"Dude you were not dreaming!!!" Arthur said with impatience.

With his glasses now clean and back in front of his eyes Raj gazed at Arthur and asked, "Which part was true?" And he then glanced nervously towards Serendipity who in turn began to study a leaf on the floor intensely. Amber wanted to box all of their ears together she was so frustrated with them! "What is wrong with you all! The Professor saved your life and is being chased by the biggest monster in the world and you are sitting here wondering if Serendipity kissed you!"

Raj quickly figured out that there had been a T-Rex lurking over him, he gulped hard and quickly stood up "We have to help the Professor! Which way did he go?"

The children ran as quietly as they could which was near impossible considering that every leaf they trod on seemed to crunch with a noise as loud as exploding fireworks. They sprinted towards the danger not thinking how they planned on saving the Professor; all they knew was that they had to try. After five minutes Raj stopped so abruptly that Arthur crashed into the back of him and Raj stumbled out onto an open space where they witnessed the most horrifying sight.

Towering high and almost reaching the height of the fern trees stood as Amber quite rightly described the biggest monster in the world.

"What's he doing?" Whispered Arthur.

"Where is the Professor?" Serendipity asked just as quietly. "Are we too late?"

The children watched the gigantic dinosaur shake his head and roar so loudly that Arthur automatically put his arm around Amber. The killer's feet were the size of a small car and at the end of its three scaly toes, black shiny claws curved sharply downwards and tapped the ground ominously. Its mouth drew back showing off its gnashing teeth that were dripping with saliva, the same saliva that Raj had mistaken for lemonade.

The children watched fascinated as the gigantic beast kept on smashing its head on a decaying log that was lying in the middle of the open space. Every time the colossal head crashed down, the dead tree would bounce high in the air and groan loudly as it descended with a crash.

"What is that noise coming from the log?" Amber asked nervously.

"Oh my God!" Raj exclaimed, "The Professor is in the log!"

"What are we going to do?" Amber asked terrified at the prospect of the enemy they were about to face.

Raj pushed his glasses up to the top of his nose and swung round to face his friends. "We need a plan, that log is not going to last much longer, it is already starting to crumble, we don't have a lot of time!" He huddled his friends close to him and told them his plan to try and save the Professor.

There was no time to say goodbye or share any other sentiments because the T-Rex banged his head with such violence onto the log that the log snapped in half and the Professor shot out onto the floor, shielding his eyes with his hands and humming loudly. The children took this opportunity to save their teacher and they all screamed with all their might and ran in four different directions, waving their arms in the air as they headed for the trees. The T-Rex who was about to gobble up the humming Professor turned his immense head towards the screaming children and snorted with vehemence in their direction. He left the Professor trembling on the floor and started to run in the direction of the children. His legs were so heavy that he barely slumped forward, and the children thought that they could easily outrun the beast behind them and reach the safety of the neighbouring trees. But within minutes the scaly legs gained momentum and began to chase one of its victims with such speed that there was no way the child he chose to chase would escape unharmed. The four friends had no idea which one of them was being chased as they daren't look behind them; each one of them gasped for breath as they headed for the safety of the trees up ahead and prayed that they were not the one that the T-Rex had decided to eat.

Serendipity could feel the lactic acid circulate around her body weighing her legs down and making her muscles sting and shake like jelly. She was staring at one tree about twenty meters away; if she could just reach that tree she would be safe but her hopes were shattered because she heard an almighty roar behind her and she tripped over her own feet in fear and fell flat on her face. The T-Rex was meters away and roared again as it flung its head towards Serendipity's limp body that lay in the mud; its mouth open wide with saliva frothing aggressively between its teeth. Just as its jaws swooped down ready to swallow its much-deserved breakfast another roar echoed from the forest and the killer T-Rex was hurled suddenly to the floor having been ambushed from the side by another T-Rex.

Serendipity had no idea why she had not been eaten and she did not intend to find out! Without looking behind, her she pulled herself out of the mud and raced towards the tree, climbing its branches with such speed that in no time she was twenty meters in the air. Only when she felt she was out of danger did she dare look down to see what had happened to the dinosaur that was so close to ending her life.

Raj, Arthur and Amber had already reached the safety of the forest and climbed so high that they had the perfect view to see the battle of the T-Rexes. The one that had leapt out of the forest was much smaller than the T-Rex that had tried to eat the Professor and Serendipity. Even though it was half the size of the T-Rex it fought, it did not seem intimidated at all and kept on attacking and attacking, thrashing its head and teeth on the side of the T-Rex.

Serendipity nearly fell out of the tree when she saw the battle that was happening below.

"Oh my God, it's Tony!" She screamed. "Look! Its tail is pink like Tony's!"

The other children heard Serendipity's cries but could not make sense of what she was saying apart from the word Tony. Tony was at a clear advantage because he caught the giant T-Rex by surprise and he was fighting with such aggression and determination that the other T-Rex could not believe that his morning breakfast was so hard to come by. The T-Rex was already bleeding from the side but they were only superficial wounds, Tony just scratched the surface, he was not strong enough to penetrate the dinosaur's hard, thick skin. Tony 's advantage did not last long, and the hungry T-Rex finally got his balance back and roared so loudly with annoyance that Amber nearly peed her pants. It was now Tony's turn to retreat but the T-Rex was so agitated that he had lost another chance at breakfast that he was not going to let his attacker get away scot free. He roared again and thrashed his head in the air so violently that snot the size of donuts flew through the air as fast as bullets. Serendipity watched her dear little Tony, (who was not so little anymore) walk backwards as he observed the T-Rex's every move. She knew Tony did not stand a chance against the T-Rex who was three times as big as he was, and she felt big blobby tears stream down her face. At this exact point in time the Professor sat up and thought to himself "How very curious life can be. One minute you are certain to be consumed and the next you are sitting twiddling your thumbs and wondering what is for breakfast!" He stood up and wiped the dust and mud from his khaki shorts when he heard a raging roar coming from inside the forest. His survival instinct told him to run as fast as the speed of light, but the adventurous child inside made the Professor sprint like a mad man towards the danger. When the Professor arrived, Tony had already been knocked to the floor and he had blood dripping from his gaping mouth.

Serendipity saw her multi-coloured teacher standing out amongst the greenery and shouted down to him explaining the situation and Tony's imminent danger. Doctor Dino knew he had to try and save Tony so he shouted and jumped to try and distract the killer T-Rex. Having been fooled twice already, and feeling immensely hungry and frustrated, the T-Rex ignored the bouncing bait and pressed down his foot on Tony's side holding him to the floor with his sharp claws. The children watched in horror as Tony wiggled and squirmed desperately trying to escape but to no avail. With a triumphant roar the T-Rex opened his mouth wide aiming for Tony's neck, but low and behold another T-Rex the same size this time as the one that was about to eat Tony lunged forward, (nearly squashing the Professor) and hurled herself at the T-Rex and knocked him to the floor. This was far too much drama for Amber who was trembling so violently that the branch she was standing on was in jeopardy of breaking and falling to the floor.

"Newton's Nether Regions!" The Professor exclaimed and instinctively turned on his camera that was dangling around his neck. He refused to move an inch, even though he was microscopically too close for comfort to the three-way T-Rex battle that was developing next to him.

"Suck on this Spielberg!" Doctor Dino whispered smugly to himself.

Raj and Arthur were transfixed with the battle unfolding below them. Raj thought there was something familiar about this new T-Rex that had just showed up, and then it hit him why he recognized her and screamed to his friends.

"It's Tony's mother! Look everyone, she is missing a claw!" he hollered from his tree top.

The Professor could not believe his luck! Not only was he watching a ferocious battle between T-Rexes, but a mother T-Rex came to the rescue of her son. This was a miracle! The Professor was so completely overwhelmed by how sophisticated these creatures were that his hands began to tremble with awe, but he soon controlled himself as he did not want his footage to be shaky and for the viewers to mistake his excitement for fear! Serendipity was nervously biting her nails as she saw Tony pull himself back on his hind legs and begin edging towards his attacker with a new-found confidence now that his mother was by his side. Tony's mother roared indignantly showing her superiority and then leapt forward and smashed her head against the neck of the T-Rex. Before the T-Rex could recover she opened her jaws wide and bit aggressively into the neck of her enemy and crunched down as ferociously as she could. Tony stood back and watched the battle from the side-line. It was clear who was winning as chunks of flesh and blood from the T-Rex now under attack were whirling through the air. With his neck split open and blood dripping onto the mud, the T-Rex knelt down and accepted defeat by bowing his head towards the ground. Tony roared with triumph and his mother turned towards him and snorted in acknowledgment. But just as she released her hold on the dinosaur to look at Tony he lashed up in one last attempt at survival and bit hard into the stomach of Tony 's mother. Serendipity screamed with horror and Amber covered her eyes, barely able to keep her balance on the branch. Tony leapt forward to help his mother and bit hard into the T-Rex's neck, ripping it apart in his strong jaws. The T-Rex, now drenched in his own blood, fell completely to the floor and groaned with agony as life drained slowly away from him. As soon as the T-Rex's eyes stared blankly at the treetops, Tony relaxed his jaw and turned to his mother who had knelt onto the ground. Raj pushed his glasses up his nose for the hundredth time and felt goose bumps all over his skin as he saw the dark red pool of blood pouring on the floor from Tony's mother's stomach. Tony touched his head gently on his mother's side with affection.

"Professor, Professor, can't you do something to save Tony's mother?" Serendipity asked imploringly, having climbed down the tree to be nearer to the dying dinosaur.

"I am afraid we must let nature take her course." The Professor said solemnly, tapping Serendipity on the head.

By the time Amber, Arthur and Raj joined the scene; Tony's mother collapsed onto the floor and was slowly waiting for the moment when life would be no more. Tony stood closely by, watching his mother sadly; he was deadly still which frightened the children. The girls and boys held hands and stared at the tragedy in front of them. The Professor's camera rolled on recording every moment and waited for the inevitable point in time when Tony's mother would lose too much blood and her heart would stop beating. Serendipity's wet tears left streaks like dirty canals down her dusty cheeks. And then the moment they had all been waiting for with such dread finally arrived. The giant stomach heaved for the last time and the enormous amber eyes filled with water and stopped shifting nervously as they finally found peace. Amber burst into tears and buried her head in Arthur's chest. Serendipity did not take her eyes off Tony.

"Do you think he knows who we are?" Arthur whispered.

"Of course, he does, he saved my life!" Serendipity sobbed.

"I know it's just he is the size of three elephants after all and pretty scary." Arthur added as he watched the huge Tony tap his black shiny claws on the ground with grief.

The four adventurers gazed at Tony waiting to see what he would do next.

"It is hard to imagine we used to keep him in your smelly locker during lessons!" Raj said thoughtfully.

The thought of this massive dinosaur in Serendipity's school locker made Arthur snort out loud and he was about to break out into a raucous laughter when Tony suddenly turned his head to the five friends and instead of laughing, Arthur held his breath in fear.

Amber quickly jumped behind Arthur and Raj stumbled backwards, the camera continued to roll capturing every extraordinary moment.

"Colliding Protons! Serendipity get back here." The Professor cried as he saw Serendipity walk boldly up to Tony.

Serendipity lifted her arms towards Tony and he responded by bending his gigantic head down to meet Serendipity's arms. Raj bravely followed Serendipity, ready to step forward and protect her if Tony turned nasty.

20

Professor Inchenstein's decision

Deep crimson blood covered the forest bed like a river. Chunks of flesh dangled precariously in the trees and torn organs lay abandoned amongst the ground. It was the most gruesome scene the children had ever seen and Amber was doing her best not to throw-up and contribute to the stench around them. The only person that was completely unaware of the blood bath was Serendipity, who stood close to Tony waiting for him to react. Tony pushed his head forward lifting Serendipity up into the air. Serendipity screamed with excitement and held on for dear life.

"Are you all completely crazy?" Amber hissed.

"Shhhh!" The Professor replied, "I am still recording!"

"Am I the only one that has a problem with Serendipity behaving with this monster as if it was a puppy dog?" Amber crossed her arms annoyed. "Look he might eat her by accident and then you will all be sorry!" she huffed.

"Amber chill out. It is Tony!" Raj said, "He won't hurt her, he saved her."

Amber relaxed a little when Tony lowered his head gently so that Serendipity could stand again on the floor. Serendipity rubbed his nose and Tony snorted.

"This is ridiculous! He could gobble her up in a second" Amber placed her hands over her eyes.

The Professor continued to record every magical moment.

"What's happening?" Amber demanded.

"Not sure really. He has his head down next to Serendipity and it looks like they are having a conversation." Arthur replied sceptically.

"This is not the time for jokes Arthur Clifton!" Amber huffed, "Just tell me what is happening and stop messing around! What are they talking about, the weather?"

"If you don't believe me you know what to do." Arthur replied.

Amber knew Arthur liked a good joke, but she had a horrible feeling that this time he might be telling the truth. As he so rightly pointed out the only way to know for sure was to take her sweaty hands away from her eyes and take a peek.

"Now do you believe me?" Arthur asked grinning as he watched Amber's reaction.

"What on earth is she saying?" Amber asked in disbelief.

"Beats me!" Arthur sighed under his breath. "Catching up on old times perhaps!"

Moments later Tony walked over to his dead mother, bent his head downward and opened his mouth wide.

"Hang all the elements!" The Professor said with astonishment, "He is going to eat his own mother!"

"Oh how dreadful." Amber cried and firmly placed her hands over her eyes again.

"Wicked!" Arthur said in response looking forward to some more blood and action.

"It looks like he is starting with his mother's arm." The Professor commentated with a grimace on his face.

Tony lifted his head and in lodged between his teeth was his mother's arm, hanging limply and drooling blood from the broken socket. Tony then walked back towards Serendipity and plonked the arm in front of her on the floor. Serendipity swung round to face her friends with tears of joy and relief in her eyes and sobbed, "We can go home!"

She expected her friends to jump with joy, but all that met her merriment were looks of confusion and disbelief.

"What do you mean?" Raj asked, his legs still trembling.

Serendipity ran back to the abandoned dinosaur arm and picked it up causing a deeper grimace to form on her teacher's face and for Arthur and Raj to shout "Yuk!" simultaneously.

"What? What is going on now?" Amber yelled.

"Don't look, whatever you do, don't look!" Arthur replied firmly.

"Guys, the claw! Der!" Serendipity shouted waving the arm in the air, completely oblivious to the blood that was splattering all around her.

"Bring back the ice age!" The Professor exploded as he worked out what Serendipity was going on about. "We are saved!"

They all gathered around Serendipity and the bleeding dinosaur arm, even Amber managed to pull herself together and join the group.

"So, let me get this straight." Raj said slowly, "You think." He paused as Tony snorted loudly overhead. Hesitating, Raj continued, "Sorry, you and Tony believe, that his mother's claw will take us back to the 21st Century."

Another snort from above was heard. "Exactly!" Serendipity said beaming at Tony.

"Well I suppose it makes sense." Professor Inchenstein said.

"Makes sense! Yes of course, this all makes sense!" An indignant Amber muttered to herself sarcastically.

"Well it is worth a shot." Arthur said hopefully.

Serendipity let her hand move down the scaly dead arm to the black shiny claw that was curved like a parrot's beak and she felt the cold bone touch her soft skin. Her heart flipped suddenly as she felt the same warm sensation run through her veins as it did the first time she stepped into the Professor's cupboard.

"It will work. I just know it will." Serendipity said excitedly. The Professor, for the first time since he arrived at the battle of the T-Rex's, let his hands fall down and turned off the camera. He looked down fondly at his four students and took a deep breath; he knew what he had to do, he just hoped he had enough courage to go through with it.

"Professor," Raj said concerned, "What's wrong? You should be happy! We are going home."

The four innocent faces looked up at the solemn Professor, even Amber momentarily forgot about the monster towering over her head as she looked worryingly at her teacher. Doctor Dino wondered how he was going to tell them his plan; he had become so fond of them all since their adventure began, especially Raj who was always close to his heart.

"Children, Tony," he began, glancing up at Tony to make sure he was paying attention, "I do not feel that I can come back to London with you." As he said this, he took his spotty hanky out from his pocket and mopped his brow and face trying to compose himself.

"What are you talking about?" Raj asked, suddenly feeling goose bumps all over his body.

"You are having us on!" Arthur said flipping his hair nervously away from his face.

"Tell us you are joking." Serendipity pleaded.

The Professor stood motionless and stared at the four young faces below his.

Amber slipped her hand into her teachers which made the Professor choke down a large sob.

"But why?" Raj asked, swallowing his emotions as best he could.

Professor Inchenstein heaved a heavy sigh and said, "I do not expect you to understand me. Not now. But maybe one day you will, and you will forgive me."

He looked round at his friends hopefully, but his eyes were met with so much emotion and disbelief that the Professor quickly stared at his shoes and continued his explanation.

"As you know my dear beloved wife has been in a coma for the last 25 years. I have waited. I have waited so very long." The Professor coughed loudly trying to concealhis need to cry.

"I have come to accept the inevitable." He paused. "She is not going to join me again in this world. We have to wait for the next and I have finally learned to accept that."

He now took the courage to look up at his students and he smiled at them through his glossy eyes. "You see dears, I will not be able to live a normal life after this adventure. You four have all your lives ahead of you but the best part of mine is behind me now. Since we arrived here in the Late Cretaceous period the weight that has been crushing my heart for the last 25 years disappeared. I feel happy for the first time since Mavis's fall and I just, I just want to be happy again."

"But how will you survive?" Arthur asked curiously.

"I intend to hand out with Tony here, if he will have me?" The Professor glanced up at the giant T-Rex.

Tony snorted in agreement.

The children knew there was nothing they could say to change the Professor's mind, so they stood in silence and tried to understand his motives, that is everyone accept Raj. "What about me?" He cried, unable to contain himself.

"My boy, do not look at me like that!" The Professor begged, "I do not mean to hurt you. I will miss you terribly. You have been the son I never had, and it breaks my heart to do this, but I must." Their teacher choked. He then sputtered between his tears, "I will go mad if I go back. Please, don't make me." And with this final plea, he knelt to the floor, took his hand from Amber's and covered his face as he cried.

Raj's heart throbbed in his chest as he thought about all the happy times they had spent together in the science lab. He was overcome with sadness at the thought of not seeing the friendly fluffy head every morning in the lab. Raj bottled up his emotions best he could, but he could not bear the thought of losing the Professor, he was like family. Raj hadn't seen his parents for the last four years after all and being with the Professor made him feel safe. Raj crouched down to his teacher and whispered in his ear. The Professor jumped up so suddenly that Amber shrieked spontaneously and made Tony snort so loudly that she shrieked again.

"You certainly will not!" The Professor shouted out loud, his tears miraculously stopping as he stared aghast at Raj.

"I am and that is that!" Raj shouted back defiantly.

Serendipity, Arthur and Amber were completely taken by surprise; they had never seen Raj raise his voice, in fact they had never heard him shout at anyone before let alone the Professor.

"What is going on?" Serendipity asked seriously.

"Well, will you tell your friends what you told me?" The Professor said crossly to Raj, raising his bushy eyebrows disapprovingly.

Raj kicked the floor and mumbled, "I am staying too."

"What!?" Arthur exclaimed with shock, "Don't be silly mate, this is a joke, right?"

"Of course he is joking!" Amber reassured everyone, "I mean, I don't get the joke, but then again I never really do." She concluded, smiling nervously towards Raj.

"Raj look at me." Serendipity said sternly.

"You are not going to change my mind so just don't bother! I am staying with the Professor." Raj replied, it was his turn to stare obsessively at his shoes.

"It is out of the question my boy. OUT of the question." Professor Inchenstein repeated firmly.

"Raj." Serendipity said softly, "Talk to me Raj, why don't you want to come home?"

Raj kicked the earth sulkily and muttered, "None of you would understand."

"Try me." Serendipity said calmly.

"What do I have to come home to?" Raj shouted, looking up at his friends and teacher with tears in his eyes. "It is alright for you, you have family/ I, who do I have?" He choked. "All I have is my lousy Uncle who never says a word to me and Rocky at school who beats me up once a week."

Arthur hung his head in shame.

"I speak to my parents once a month for 10 minutes. That's all they can afford; a ten-minute phone call. Have you any idea how" he paused and looked down at his shoes again before finishing, "how lonely I am all the time?" Amber, Arthur and Serendipity had no idea that Raj felt so miserable; he often had a smile on his face and he never complained about anything. But the more the three friends thought about it, the more they realized that his misery was just well concealed. Arthur thought about how Raj would never want him to come to his house, they always met at Arthur's; Serendipity recalled how often Raj would stay behind in the science lab, but she thought it was because he enjoyed being there, she never thought that it was because he did not want to go home, and Amber remembered the time when she arrived really early at school and found Raj in the library as it was the only room open, but she just assumed he liked reading, she never thought his passion for Dickens was in fact escapism. Serendipity approached, "I have never had real friends until now. I have spent my whole life trying to fit in and kids just want to know me because they want to meet my dad! As soon as they do, they lose interest in me and I am left back where I started. With you, well, you never cared about that." Serendipity gently put her arms around Raj; she squeezed him tightly and as she did Raj buried his head in her neck and sobbed quietly. This was the only hug he could ever remember having in his entire life. The others watched the hug in silence and Amber prayed that Raj would not stay in this terrorizing world surrounded by so many monsters.

ANNIE WHITE

21

Bunny's Lair

Bunny enjoyed a startling cold shower in the morning; she delighted in feeling the harshness of the freezing droplets pound against her head and shoulders.

Shivering but clearly revitalised from the night's slumber, Bunny stepped out of the shower and wrapped a dark brown towel around her body and then stared at her reflection in the mirror. Her owl-like eyes glared back and observed her dark, drenched hair. She sighed deeply, turned from her familiar forlorn face and walked to the bedroom to get dressed. For Bunny it seemed that joy was not a sentiment that she should be allowed to feel and as a result a constant state of sadness overcame her. All happiness and pleasure were sucked out of her on June 20th, 1976 and it never returned. The only remaining feeling that was left was that of wretched hopelessness. Placing a brown pinafore over her crisp white shirt, she looked in the mirror again, hoping to see a glimmer of the old Bunny, but sadly no. All she saw was brown; her dress, her hair, her eyes, her glasses, even her expression was a depressive, mushy brown.

"Brown is better than black!" She said comfortingly to herself and repeated it again and again as she creaked down the wooden stairs on her way to school.

ΔΔΔ

Every teacher plays a role amongst their pupils' lives; some are good, and some, are unfortunately not so good. Some teachers are remembered as the friendly one, the strict one, the funny one, the weird one, the boring one and some are the out-right terrifying one. It was easy to guess which description befell Bunny. She had not always been so severe but over the years Bunny found it harder and harder to smile, resulting in the tips of her lips to bend down slightly and over time, gravity pulled them down further, until they rested in a permanent position of disdain. Bunny would watch with a bizarre satisfaction as pupils would change their direction when they noticed her at the other end of the corridor. Bunny understood her role and she was happy to play it.

"Bunny!" hissed Dr Fog as soon as Bunny walked into the school reception. "Bunny! Have you heard the news?" Dr Fog motioned excitedly to her friend to come closer so she could share the latest gossip.

"What is going on?" Bunny asked intrigued, (she always did enjoy gossiping about the other teachers, especially the old cronies from the math department).

"He has vanished!" Dr Fog exclaimed raising her stick in the air enthusiastically (demonstrating that its use was purely recreational).

"Who?" Bunny asked impatiently.

"The old fool! The Professor has gone!" Dr Fog revealed smirking candidly.

"Gone? What on earth do you mean?"

"Sent me this letter!" the Deputy Head explained and waved the letter in front of her friend. "Listen!" Dr Fog read the letter for Bunny's benefit. "Dear Dr Fog, It is with regret that I hand in my resignation as the Professor of Science at the wondrous institute Pembridge Hall. Yours Professor Boris Inchenstein" Bunny snatched the letter and re-read the simple words not quite believing what they signified.

"At last he and his ridiculous chaotic lessons have departed! Well good riddance!" Dr Fog added vehemently.

"Is this all he said?" Bunny asked baffled.

"That's all he wrote and after everything you did for him! He would not even be here if it weren't for your recommendation!" Dr Fog added.

"That's it. Gone. Given up?"

Dr Fog, starting to feel annoyed with Bunny's lack of enthusiasm and boring questions. She straightened her collar and said, "You need to give up too Bunny, move on. If the Professor can then so can you!" and with that Dr Fog swiftly exited the hall. The Professor's letter fell gently to the floor.

Bunny picked it up and whispered "Never," so silently it was barely audible. For the rest of the day Bunny's head was fuzzy; she could not focus, she could not even find words to tell Jeremy Sheldon off when she caught him sticking gum to her desk (much to Jeremy's delight). The day was a total and utter blur. When the bell struck 4pm she just had to go and see the lab, just to see if it was true, if old Boris had in fact given up and left. The door creaked open and Bunny looked around at the orderly lab; everything tidy and in place. She walked to the front of the classroom and leaned on the large wooden desk. She felt the tears well up in her eyes as she saw the engraving MI on the old oak. Her rough finger caressed the two letters and she just wished for things to be as they once were. Bunny took a deep breath and was about to leave when she heard a rustling coming from the Professor's cupboard. She crept closer, relishing the thought of finding a naughty pupil (that was just what she needed, the chance to scold a mischievous child), she opened the door swiftly and saw to her surprise, Raj crouched on the floor, head buried in his hands and sobbing quietly.

Bunny's heavy chest heaved softly with sympathy as she watched the poor boy. Overcome with unusual emotion, Bunny managed to slide herself opposite to Raj without making any noise at all. Raj so preoccupied with his own sadness did not notice this new company in the cupboard and continued to release his disappointment over the Professor leaving. Raj played those last moments back over and over again in his mind. Why did I come back, I should be with him and Tony! I know I would be happy there. But then he remembered Serendipity's hug and Arthur and Amber and he felt so confused! He glanced up and then started so fiercely at seeing Bunny that he jolted backwards and banged his head.

"Come." Was all Bunny said and beckoned to Raj to approach.

Against all Raj's better instincts he crawled towards the most terrorising teacher in the school and let his head fall against her chest. Bunny patted his turban and tried to calm him best she could whilst he cried.

A considerable amount of time passed in this way and eventually the sobs died down and Raj lifted his head and looked Bunny in the eyes.

"Why did he leave me?" he questioned with such torment Bunny did everything she could to hold in her own erupting emotions.

Bunny clasped Raj's hand in hers and replied, "My boy, he did not leave you. He needed a break from life as life can ware even the spirited of spirits down. He will come back one day, when he is ready."

"You don't understand!" Raj cried, the sobs gaining momentum again, "He is NEVER coming back!"

Raj then rushed out of the cupboard knocking a stool over in the process as he left the lab.

Bunny looked around her, gazing up at the cupboard full of oddities and then at the fallen stool. "I am always cleaning up after him!" she said to herself as she picked up the stool and slammed the cupboard door in anguish!

∆∆∆

The four friends did their best to cope with the loss of the Professor; his absence made their friendship even stronger as they found solace in each other's company. It was hardest on Raj as he really did love the Professor, but he knew the Professor was happy and that gave him some peace. Amber on the other hand was not so sure that the Professor made the right decision; she could not comprehend why any sane person would choose to spend their life in the company of hideous, frightening monsters. Serendipity and Arthur were a great support for Raj; between them they invited Raj to their homes for dinner to ensure that he never had to have Vindaloo again with his Uncle Sohan. At school Arthur did his best to manoeuvre Rocky away from Raj and the bullying reduced slightly. Raj appreciated Arthur's efforts, but all he really wanted was for Arthur to want to hang out with him at school. And so, the days became weeks and weeks became months until the battle of the T-Rexes and the disappearance of the Professor became a distant but constant memory for the children. The sudden departure of the Professor effected more people than the old teacher could have ever imagined, the most surprising of all being Bunny Bristlepott.

"Any sign?" Bunny asked as usual as she walked pass Mandy.

"Nope not a peak." Mandy replied shrugging her shoulders.

"Any chance you might have missed him?"

Mandy raised her overly plucked eyebrows and said, "Lady, that old boy could not get past me! His appearance is not what you would describe as err subtle!"

Bunny nodded in agreement, thanked Mandy and walked slowly up the hospital stairs to Ward 4.

Nobody likes hospitals, but Bunny, hated them more than most people; she detested that sterile smell, a stench that would envelope her nostrils and linger for hours after she had left the ward. She hated the eerie silence in Ward 4 and she hated to watch the hopeful, helpless visitors that would sit for hours by the beds of their loved ones, waiting, waiting, waiting for a glimmer of life that never came. But despite all this hatred, she still came every day to see her beloved sister. Sometimes she would talk about her day, the school gossip, the dramas in the staff room etc. and sometimes she would just sit there. Silent. Loving. Waiting.

Today was one of her silent visits and it was during this quiet silence when she felt something touch her hand. She quickly dismissed it as an irritating insect of some sort but then she felt it again and her heart skipped a beat. She looked up at her sister's face, straining her eyes, desperate to see some change. The nurses had warned her about sudden twitches of the muscles and how this meant nothing, but she was sure what she felt was different. "Ah!" She cried and then held her breath dramatically as she felt another soft yet determined squeeze on her hand.

She looked again at her sister's motionless face and back at her soft limp hand. Again, a squeeze.

"Holy Mother of Mary!" Bunny whispered.

She turned to look at the nurses, busy chatting away and drinking coffee down the corridor. Should she say something? She daren't. What if she was dreaming? What if she was being a hallucinating old fool? She should give up, like the Professor did, like Dr Fog told her to. But low and behold another squeeze, this time harder than all the others. Bunny tried to speak but it was like her throat was full of dry coal. No words came. She refused to take her eyes off her sister's face. Come on Mavis, come back to me! she yearned.

Bunny prayed, Bunny loved, Bunny hoped like she had never done before. Her life had been so miserable, she refused to let herself be happy, not with her sister lying death-like for so many lonely years. But now she felt it, she felt a joy and a hope that had been crushed by years of defeat. "Come back to me!" she croaked, the words muffled by raw emotion Slowly, ever so slowly Mavis' eyelids flickered. They clenched, then flickered again, they opened slightly then closed shut.

"Come back to me!" Bunny cried this time, spitting the words out in earnest.

At last, as if there had been a whole debate going on behind her sister's eyelids, the lids finally opened revealing the winner; two magnificent, sparkling brown eyes. The same dreamy eyes that captured the heart of the old Professor so many years ago.

22

The Awakening

To say that Bunny was beside herself with overwhelming joy and happiness was an understatement. She was thrilled. Her younger sister Mavis, who had been in a paralyzing coma for the last twenty-five years had finally, against all the odds, despite all the doctors' opinions, awoken.

Mavis' first quiet words to her sister were, "Why are you so gloomy?"

Bunny frantically ruffled her hair and wiped her nose trying to look less gloomy for her sister. But she did not really care what she looked like, all she cared about was Mavis, her precious Mavis was back.

"No seriously, why are you dressed like a nun?" Mavis insisted.

"Mavis! My darling. I am overjoyed." Bunny sobbed.

"Oh Bunny you always were so emotional!" Mavis tried to heave herself up in her bed but struggled due to her weakened muscles. Bunny jumped up to help her sister by plumping a pillow behind her.

"Bunny, what's going on? Why am I in here? I can't feel my legs." Their brown eyes met, one pair full of questions the other full of sorrowful answers.

Bunny began the story and held her sister's hand tightly as she explained why twenty-five years had passed by in a blur.

ΔΔΔ

"We need to do tests Bunny, standard tests, nothing to worry about but you need to give us some space." The Doctor said calmly but firmly to Bunny.

"Don't go away!" Mavis said startled by the numerous white coats surrounding her.

"Mavis, I am right here, I will not move an inch!" Bunny reassured her sister as she was ushered to the side of the room.

Mavis closed her eyes. Was it all true or was she dreaming? She felt people lifting her arms, watched them tapping her knees with a metal instrument and forcing her eyes to open. Her body felt weary, tired, yet extremely light at the same time. She still could not move her legs. It seemed like yesterday when she was in Africa looking for the mysterious Spinosaurus. She remembered finding what she thought to be a bone from that mighty jaw and then, nothing. Just blank, darkness.

The bright white lights were too strong for her eyes and all the questions felt like a kind of torture; "Can you feel this, can you see this, does this hurt!"

It was all too much, Mavis had to show them that she was not to be messed with, "For God's sake stop poking and prodding me about! I am not a dissected frog!"

The white coats halted abruptly and stopped their curious investigating. The lead Doctor motioned for the others to step back a moment, "Mavis, we need to establish what your capabilities are?" She came closer and said, "Please be patient and let us do our work. We are so happy to see you awake that we need to make sure you," she paused, "that you will stay with us."

Mavis took a deep breath and allowed them to continue. She went over everything Bunny had just told her again and again and then the most obvious question came to mind. She called for the doctor to get her sister immediately.

Bunny appeared, chirpy and slightly flustered, her eyes damp from all the happy tears.

Mavis stared at her sister and asked firmly, "Where is Boris?"

Bunny gulped, she knew the question was coming and she knew her reply would not be good enough for Mavis.

"What do you mean gone?" Mavis asked. "Since when?"

"Oh Mavis I am so sorry. He has been here these last twenty-five years; waiting for you, visiting you, loving you. But a few months back he handed in his resignation at the school and just vanished. Not a word more."

"Don't you think that is a bit odd?" Mavis asked, scrutinising her sister.

"Well he always was a little odd dear." Bunny said facetiously.

Mavis paused and thought for a moment.

"Bunny something must have happened recently to make him leave. Can you think of anything?"

Bunny knew she had let her sister down; she had been watching over the crazy old Professor for the last twenty-five years, making sure he stayed out of mischief; she gave him a job at her school just to keep him close and at the last moment, when it really mattered she had lost him. "Mavis, you know we have never been very close, but I did my best to look after him."

Mavis squeezed her sister's hand, "I know you did Bunny."

Then some random thought came to Mavis and she asked Bunny

if the Professor had any children.

"No, oh no Mavis, he was incredibly faithful to you. He never found another Mavis and he never had any children. Why do you ask?"

"It is just I remember things. I used to think I was dreaming but it must have been Boris talking to me."

"What was he saying, do you remember?" Bunny asked intrigued.

"I don't remember anything in particular detail but he kept talking about these children."

"Well he is a teacher."

"Yes, but this was different, he was talking about the same child all the time and..." Mavis trailed off, she was worried Bunny would not understand.

"What is it Mavis?"

"He kept on talking about the dinosaurs!"

"Well there is no surprise there! He was always raging on about those giant reptiles!" Bunny replied disapprovingly, she could never understand her sister's and Boris' obsession with those wretched giants and ever since her sister's accident she blamed them wholeheartedly and would never forgive them!

"No but this was different, it was like he was telling me something, like he had actually met one!"

Bunny took off her spectacles and blinked at her younger sister, "Mavis, you have been in a coma for the last twenty-five years! You are clearly confusing reality and fantasy. Boris was probably inventing stories to entertain you and himself!" Bunny put her spectacles back on and hoped such nonsense would not be mentioned again.

Mavis knew Bunny would not indulge her anymore so she chose

to keep her thoughts to herself, but she knew that something strange was going on and she strained her brain, hoping to remember something that would help her understand what had happened to her husband. The doctors continued to examine the miracle that was Mavis Inchenstein; they called in specialists, they inspected, they discussed, all trying to work out what the best support going forward should be. Mavis was eventually prescribed an intense session of physiotherapy and given the good news that she had no permanent damage and was considered a medical marvel!

ΔΔΔ

Time slowly drifted by for Mavis and Bunny; each day Mavis became stronger; her mind was so determined that the speed in which her body healed astonished the medical world once again. Mavis worked hard during the day on her muscles, building their strength and at night she worked hard on her mind; trying to piece to gether the stories that her beloved Boris had told her.

It was not long before Mavis was discharged from hospital and moved in with her sister. Bunny was over the moon to say the least, but she was concerned about Mavis, who never seemed to be at ease. Mavis was up all night, every night scribbling notes, frantically trying to make sense of the dreams that she had during her coma. For Mavis it was as if remembering Boris' story would solve the mystery of his disappearance. Bunny of course thought that Mavis was barking mad and she would report back to the doctors who did not seem to take Bunny seriously at all.

One morning as Bunny was getting dressed for school, Mavis walked loftily into her sister's room and sat on the bed, she looked troubled and Bunny's concern for her sister's welfare grew and grew.

"Do you have keys?" Mavis asked, as she read her notes from the night before.

"Keys to what dear?

"Boris' place?"

Bunny hesitated, she began to resent Boris more and more. His absence was causing her sister's progress to regress; physically she was doing well, but her mental state was questionable. After some time, she walked over to her chest of drawers, opened the top drawer and handed Mavis a set of keys. "The address is on the key-ring." Bunny said, "But to be honest with you, I really don't see the point."

"Bunny, he is my husband, he might be in trouble. Maybe I will find a clue as to what happened?"

"I have already been to his flat and there is nothing of interest there!"

Bunny took a deep breath, she hated snapping at Mavis. "Look, he is probably playing Bingo in Bognor-Regis with not a care in the world."

"Really? You think he is playing bingo? You don't think that after seeing my picture on the front cover of every paper in England that he would not pop in to check to see how his wife was doing?"

"OK it is strange, but perhaps he is in the Arctic with no access to the news – that would explain everything." Bunny said reassuringly.

"So one minute he is in Bognor-Regis playing bingo, the next in the Arctic looking for polar bears? Come on Bunny, it is about time you start taking this seriously!"

Bunny did not reply, she did not like to see Mavis worked-up, so agreed to go with her after school to Boris' place to look for clues. She would do anything to keep her sister happy. After a busy day at school Bunny hurried to Boris' flat to meet Mavis. When she arrived, the door was already unlocked, so she pushed it open and walked up the staircase. She prayed that this visit would offer some kind of closure to the whole Boris episode. Bunny looked around at the sparse kitchen; a small wooden table and one lonesome chair in the corner of the room, one teapot and one chipped cup stood on a wonky shelf above the sink. She heard a creak and a sob coming from the other room and she rushed in to see what was going on.

"Mavis, what's the matter?" She asked panicking as she saw Mavis sitting on the bed, clutching a red silk something and crying into it.

Mavis threw her silk kimono at Bunny and explained that Boris had given it to her the night of their wedding.

"Oh, my dear sister", Bunny said emotionally as she knelt down beside Mavis. "He chose to leave, he chose to move on."

"But look at this place! Just look at it! There are cobwebs as thick as pillows!" Mavis said hopelessly as she stood up and threw her arms around the room in despair. Bunny followed Mavis' arms around the room and agreed that the Professor had led a very simple life.

"It is not simple! It is depressing! How could he have lived like this?" Mavis asked despairingly.

"It is all my fault! Boris lived like a hermit in this hell hole waiting for me to wake up and now after 25years I decide to join the living and he is nowhere near this pitiful place!"

"Now you listen to me," Bunny said firmly as she grasped her sister in her arms, "None of this is your fault!"

"You don't understand. It was my arrogance that led to my accident! I insisted we dig in the most dangerous terrain in the world; it was my choice to wake up early and go off on my own. I am to blame for everything!" And Mavis sobbed so vehemently that Bunny found herself crying too.

The two sisters cried together until night fell and the little apartment grew ghostly dark.

"Come on my love, let's go home." Bunny said softly and kissed the top of Mavis' head.

Mavis' legs did not want to move. Against their will they walked slowly towards the miserable looking wardrobe in the corner of the bedroom.

"What are you doing now?" Bunny asked impatiently. "There are clearly no clues here Mavis, he has gone!"

Mavis ignored her sister and reached inside the closet looking for a hanger to hang her silk kimono. Her eyes had already adjusted to the dark and she noticed a large gap in the floorboards under the wardrobe. She crouched down to get a better look and yanked up the wood which came lose surprisingly easily. Bunny took a deep breath. It was almost 8pm and she had not had any supper, her stomach began to rumble, and she could feel her patience being consumed by her ravished famine.

"Mavis! We need to go home. Enough of this clue searching! I am off!"

Bunny was just about to strop off out of the bedroom to make her point when Mavis asked, "What would he need a safe for?"

"A safe? What nonsense!"

"Bunny get over here. He has a big black safe under the floorboard of his wardrobe!"

"Well I never. What could the old fool have in there?" Bunny wondered. "Can you open it?"

"No." Mavis replied disappointingly "We need a key."

Mavis looked so determined that Bunny knew she would not listen to reason, so much to the dismay of her stomach, she searched high and low for the wretched key! After an hour of endless searching Bunny was at her wits' end; she threw herself down on the bed in Boris' bedroom and stared at the cracked ceiling above her.

Bunny heard her sister rummaging, still frantically throwing things out of drawers and looking under the thread beaten rug again and again trying to locate the elusive key.

"Mavis it is clearly not here. He must have it with him. Please, please can we go?"

Mavis let her head fall in defeat.

Bunny heaved herself off the uncomfortable bed, grabbed Mavis' hand and led her out of the Professor's flat.

∆∆∆

Bunny watched her sister deteriorate and it was destroying her; she felt like her insides were sewn up by rusty wire and she could not breathe anymore. Mavis refused to go to her physio lessons and there were even days when she refused to get out of bed. She would mope around the small flat in her silk kimono, staring out the window watching life pass by below. Mavis's behaviour terrified Bunny. What if she were to slip back into a coma? Bunny would ask herself, and she would have nightmares about losing her sister again to a deadly sleep where she never awoke. If only there was something that she could do to find that nutty Professor and bring him back to her sister! She would do anything to see that fluffy cloud of hair again! The next morning Mavis refused to get out of bed again and Bunny left for school with a heavy heart. At lunch time it was her turn to supervise the children in the playground so she sat morbidly on a wooden bench and watched the care-free children run around playing ball and chasing each other with glee. Suddenly her ears pricked up as she overheard some of the children talking about the Professor.

"Do you think about him much?" Amber asked her friends.

"Of course." Serendipity said. "I think about his crazy hair and his colourful bow ties all the time. It always makes me smile."

"Do you remember the sinking mud and how he saved us all?" Raj said fondly.

"He was our hero." Amber said smiling.

"I miss him." Raj added sadly.

"Do you think we could ever visit him?" Amber asked.

"Even if we did go back, we would never find him." Serendipity commented.

"He is with Tony. Tony will keep him safe." Raj said quietly. He knew he would never see Doctor Dino again, but the fact that Tony was looking out for him made Raj feel better.

Bunny felt like she had been buried in sheets of ice; goose bumps ran riot all over her body and her hands started to tremble. "What are they talking about? Is it just fantasy? And who in the Lord's name is Tony?" Bunny demanded. She stormed out of the playground to find Mavis and tell her what she had heard.

It did not take long for Mavis to sit bolt upright in her bed and demand Bunny to repeat again and again what she had heard. Bunny obeyed and repeated the children's conversation again and again until Mavis had written it down word for word. Mavis then leapt up and frantically looked through her notes.

"I am sure it is all idle chit chatter. Kids have very excitable imaginations you know, you should hear what some of them come out with!" Bunny said more to herself than to Mavis.

"Bunny look here, look, I wrote it down, the name Tony. We have to find out who Tony is and then we will find my Boris." Mavis sighed with relief; finally, the mystery surrounding her husband's disappearance was unravelling.

"Bunny, these kids are the same kids that Boris spoke to me about, they must be! What are their names?"

Much to Mavis' joy and Bunny's confusion the names Raj, Arthur, Serendipity and Amber were familiar to her. "Bunny you must believe this is strange?" Mavis asked imploringly.

"I agree it is slightly unnerving, but these kids might not have all the answers and you must be prepared for that." Bunny said with concern.

"I have to meet them." The next day after school Bunny led Mavis to the Professor's science lab. The old door creaked open and invited them inside. Bunny pointed towards the back of the classroom and said softly, "Hello Raj."

Raj jumped in his skin as he turned and saw Bunny Bristlepott standing in the doorway with a strange woman that looked a bit like Bunny only blond and smaller.

"I was just tidying the lab. I am sorry Miss Bristlepott for disturbing you."

Bunny smiled which unnerved Raj even more and she cautiously approached the worried pupil.

"You are not in trouble Raj, please, we just want to talk to you, that is all."

"OK." Raj replied but still carried on drying the test tubes.

"I would like to introduce you to my sister, Mavis."

Mavis stepped forward and stretched out her hand towards Raj. Awkwardly, Raj put the damp grey cloth on the bench and shook the outstretched hand.

"Hi Raj, I hear you know my husband well."

Raj stared at the blond lady and then at Bunny completely

confused.

"Sorry Madame, but I don't know any husband." Raj replied shyly.

"Raj, this is Mavis Inchenstein."

Raj felt his hand loosen, he could not stop it, he just let go, he did not even realise until the test tube smashed to the floor and the glass sprayed across the tiles like spilt sugar.

"But you were in a coma?" he said softly.

Mavis moved closer and bent down so that her eyes were level with Raj's. "I woke up."

Raj's nose was sweating so much that his glasses practically fell off.

"I need your help to find my husband."

"You will never believe me." Raj replied.

"Try me."

23

Yucatan Peninsula

While Raj was trying to convince an eager Mavis and a disbelieving Bunny what had happened to the Professor, Amber had just arrived home and was heading up the stairs to see her Grandma Rose. She glanced up at the top of the stairs and she saw her mother sitting there, her head leaning on the wall and tears falling quietly down her cheeks.

Amber raced to the top of the stairs and touched her mother's shoulder; she had never seen her mother cry before, "What happened mommy?"

Amber racked her brain trying to think what would have made her mother cry and then her eyes stared frantically at her Grandma Rose's door.

"No! No! Anything but grandma, not my grandma, not yet, we need more time!" She wailed as she burst open the door and stood motionless in the doorway.

Grandma Rose lay on the bed under the pink floral sheets and she looked like she was in a peaceful sleep. Amber walked closer to the bed; she was not afraid at seeing a dead body she was just so incredibly sad that she did not get the chance to say goodbye and tell her Grandma how much she loved her.

Carefully, Amber pulled herself up on the bed and lay down next to her Grandma, she clasped the cold lifeless hand in hers and she prayed. Amber finished her prayers and kissed her Grandma Rose softly on the forehead. Amber's wet cheek touched the wrinkly skin of her Grandma and a feeling of hopeless overcame her. She thought back to all the stories she told her; describing all the adventures she had with her friends and the monsters. No matter what was on Amber's mind, her Grandma always listened, albeit sometimes she fell asleep while Amber talked, but she knew this was because of old age and not boredom!

Who would she talk to now? She wondered sorrowfully.

Amber was jolted out of her thoughts when her father shouted up the stairs that supper was ready. A grieving Amber walked sullenly down the stairs and into the kitchen.

"Mommy, I am not hungry, do you mind if I skip dinner?" Amber said, her eyes now swollen and puffy from all the crying.

"Sit down." Was her father's response.

Reluctantly Amber sat at the table. She stared at her father who was reading the paper and she noticed a sparkle in his eyes; a sparkle that she had not seen since they left Texas. She stared more intensely at him, there was something odd about him, she could not work it out and then all of a sudden it hit her, hard in the face; he was happy.

Her Grandma Rose, her only Grandma had passed away not more than a couple of hours, lying dead upstairs above them all and she was supposed to sit down, eat her dinner and watch the smirk grow on her father's face. For the first time in her life Amber wanted to rebel.

Mrs Bradshaw put a plate of cod and mash in front of her daughter.

"I don't want it." Amber said fiercely and pushed the plate aside.

Mrs Bradshaw, so taken aback by her daughter's behaviour let out the word "Oh!" before her brain could stop her.

Mr Bradshaw wacked his paper on the table making the doilies tremble, "What did you say, you ungrateful child?"

"Grandma Rose is upstairs. Dead!" Amber cried between sobs.

"Your point being?" Mr Bradshaw answered with pursed lips.

"And you are happy!"

"You should be happy too! She is with the Lord Almighty. Now stop your nonsense and eat your dinner or I will give you something to cry about!" Her father held his daughter's gaze, making sure she understood the consequences of continuing along this line of discourse.

Amber choked down her dinner as fast as she could and quickly ran upstairs to lie next to her Grandma again; she knew she would be safe there.

ΔΔΔ

The two sisters walked to the Professor's flat in complete silence; one sister felt overwhelmed with excitement, the other bewildered beyond belief. Mavis clutched the key Raj had given her with such force that her palms were seeping droplets of sweat onto the pavement below. As soon as they arrived Mavis dashed up the stairs, three at time leaving Bunny behind. She raced to her husband's bedroom, flung the wardrobe door open with anticipation and heaved the wooden floorboards up. She thrust the key into the mysterious black safe and it made a loud click.

Moments later Bunny arrived; panting, she leaned against the bedroom door frame trying to catch her breath, her thin hair, greasy with perspiration and her heavy chest heaving from the unusual exertion!

"What's in it?" Bunny asked fretfully.

"All the answers." Mavis replied with tears in her eyes.

She carefully took out the contents of the safe and placed them on the wooden floor.

Bunny peered down at all the Professor's specimens and commented that they look like a bunch of random leaves and twigs from Hyde Park. Bunny opened a jar and nearly dropped it, the stench was so shocking.

"Mavis tell me why some poo in a jar will explain where your nut-job of a husband is?"

But Mavis hardly heard what Bunny said, she was too busy letting her fingers touch the delicate leaves and stones that she knew to be oldest that any human had ever touched.

"What is this?" Mavis asked curiously, holding up a video camera.

Bunny happily put the jar full of poo on the floor and showed Mavis how the camera worked. The sisters sat down on the edge of the Professor's bed and Bunny pressed play.

ΔΔΔ

Raj raced to Serendipity's house as soon as the two sisters had eventually left the science lab. The story behind the Professor's disappearance had taken Raj so long to tell that it was nearly six o'clock by the time he reached Pencombe Mews and he banged on the door as if his life depended on it.

Maggie Magnum rushed to the door in a panic and to her surprise saw an excited Raj grasping for breath.

"Raj dear, whatever is the matter?" Maggie Magnum asked.

"Is," Raj gasped, "Is Serendipity here?"

"Of course, in the den."

Raj rushed passed Mrs Magnum and raced down to the den.

293

Maggie looked after the frantic boy and wondered what on earth could put him in such a state. She put it down to raging hormones and carried on chopping vegetables for her next exotic concoction.

Raj burst into the den and found his best friend attempting to play pool. Raj grabbed the cue and spluttered that Mavis Inchenstein had woken up from her coma, that he had told her everything and to ensure she did not think him crazy, he had given her the key.

"Holy moly!" Serendipity finally said, her mouth left open with astonishment.

"I know. What on earth do we do?" Raj asked, relieved he had shared the burden with someone else.

"This is the worse timing in the world!"

"I know!"

"Do you think..." Serendipity hesitated.

"Yes I think we have to." Raj confirmed reading his friend's mind, "We have to find him!"

ΔΔΔ

The sisters watched the Professor's fascinating recording over and over again until eventually the battery died out. Neither of them had said a word during the film and now that it was over, neither of them knew what to say. Bunny contemplated that this could all be one big joke and the Professor had used special effects of some sort to achieve his footage, but then there was Raj's testimony and apparently all the dirt and soil in the safe were species that were millions of years old. Could it be true?

Mavis knew it was true. Everything Raj had told her was familiar to her in some abstract way, and that would only be possible if Boris had already told her the same stories. She just knew her husband, the one and only Boris Inchenstein was with a T-Rex in the Late Cretaceous period and she envied him mightily. They finally agreed after much debate, that the best course of action would be to meet the other children and discuss viable options. Mavis knew the option she wanted to take but she did not want to endanger the lives of these innocent children. She had to find a way to be with Boris even if it killed her.

ΔΔΔ

"Oh gee!"

"Blimey!"

Amber and Arthur said in unison as their friends told them the dramatic news.

"Raj, this is a joke, a really fantastic joke mind you, fair play to you," and Arthur slapped Raj in a brotherly fashion on the back, "But a joke all the same, right?" he questioned hesitantly.

Raj and Serendipity shook their heads. It was no joke.

Amber was going to tell her friends about her Grandma's death, but she was so distracted with this great news that it did not feel like the right time. She would tell them later she said to herself and turned to the dilemma at hand. The children discussed feverishly the awakening of Mavis Inchenstein and what should be done, ignoring Mrs Bromelow who told them several times to keep it down. They asked Raj to repeat again and again what had happened in the science lab and the four friends tried their best to come up with some sort of solution.

Suddenly the classroom diminished into a silence so prominent that the children could hear their own hearts' beating: Bunny Bristlepott had entered the room.

Miss Bristlepott walked steadily to the front of the classroom and murmured something into Mrs Bromelow's ear. Mrs Bromelow was watched intently by year six as they wondered who Bunny was after and if the Head Mistress would sacrifice or protect them. Mrs

Bromelow nodded, and the class knew the game was up and that someone was in big, big trouble. As Bunny walked solemnly through the desks to her prey, the pupils of year six kept their eyes glued to their desks and hoped to high heaven that the looming shadow would not stop beside them.

Raj gulped hard as he felt Bunny's curls accidently brush his ear, "May I have a word with you and your friends in my office please Raj?" Bunny asked this question in an extremely polite manner, (which was completely out of character) but she spoke so softly that the rest of the class still trembled with fear as they watched Raj, Serendipity, Amber and Arthur leave the classroom. The four children and their teacher walked down the long corridor until they reached Bunny's tiny office. The young pupils walked cautiously into the dreaded office and Bunny closed the door. Amber looked around the office and wondered what all the fuss was about; her classmates often talked about Bunny Bristlepott's office being similar to that of a dungeon / torture chamber. The small office was lined with shelves; neatly organised books sat on each shelf starting with the thicker books and ending with the skinny ones; in the middle of the room there was a large wooden desk with a bright blue office chair behind it. Amber could not see any torture-like instruments, the only ominous objects were a wooden ruler and stapler on the desk, but she hoped that they were purely used for stationary purposes! On the blue office chair sat a small blond woman; the children did not need to ask who it was; it had to be Mavis Inchenstein. Mavis was so excited to meet the four children who had shared so many adventures with her beloved husband. Mavis, not familiar at all with children thought it best to talk to them as adults so broke the silence and addressed them eagerly and sincerely, "I am so pleased to meet you all. I really am, so very very pleased!" Mavis beamed at them and the children understood straight away that she was a good sort and that they should try and help her.

"Raj already kindly explained what had happened, but I would be ever so grateful if you could tell me it all again?" Mavis smiled encouragingly at the pupils.

The children looked at each other and then nervously at Bunny Bristlepott who had taken position next to the door. Bunny attempted to smile at the students and as her smile formed, she realised how good it felt and decided from then on, she would smile all the time! Arthur turned around and saw Bunny grinning by the door and immediately started in shock; he had never noticed what gleaming white teeth Bunny had, and now there they were, all 18 of them, staring at him for the first time. Arthur flicked his hair uncomfortably and wondered if anyone else had noticed the unusual Cheshire smile on Bunny's face. No one else had; they were all too busy talking about their magnificent adventure with Tony and the Professor. They started from the beginning and once they got going, there was no stopping them. The sisters were transfixed and listened to every word the children said. When it came to the part of the story when the Professor had decided to stay with Tony, Serendipity hesitated; she could see how absorbed Mavis was and she did not want to upset her, she seemed like such a nice lady.

"It's OK." Mavis said sagely, "Please tell me everything."

Serendipity, confident it was the right thing to do, told Mavis and Bunny what happened next.

As soon as Serendipity had finished Amber interjected, "We tried to persuade him to come back."

"Yes we all did!" Arthur concurred, still with one eye watching the glistening teeth.

"He said we would not understand." Raj continued sorrowfully, "He said he could not live in the real world anymore, he said one day we would understand." Raj then looked sadly down at his shoes. "It was such a terrible mistake."

Mavis jumped up from the chair and held Raj's hands in hers, "Listen to me." Mavis said this with such authority that even Bunny dismantled her new-found smile and turned her attention to her sister. "None of you could have changed his mind. Boris is as stubborn as a wild boar (Bunny nodded in agreement) when he wants to be and if he wanted to stay with the dinosaurs then that was his decision. No-one could have changed what happened." Mavis looked firmly at all four of the children until she felt convinced they understood.

"But what do we do now?" Raj asked concerned "He would be so desperate to see you if he knew you woke up."

"Raj's right, he would never forgive himself." Serendipity agreed.

"He talked about you all the time." Arthur added.

"We need to save him from the monsters!" Amber said frantically.

"She means dinosaurs." Arthur whispered to Mavis who looked slightly taken aback by Amber's nervous outburst.

"I need to think." Mavis answered, "I need to think what the best thing to do is."

Mavis thanked the children and told them she would be in touch very soon. While Bunny (still smiling) took the children back to class, Mavis sat back on the chair, clasped her head in her hands and thought about everything the children had told her. She started documenting all the important information, references to dinosaurs, temperature, types of trees, terrain etc. anything to give a clear picture as to what she would be facing if she decided to go back and search for her husband.

Bunny, having dropped the children safely back to Mrs Bromelow, waltzed down the corridor to see her sister. All of these revelations concerning her nutty brother-in-law, odd as they were, at least gave some clarity to the situation and had stopped her sister's manic depression. Bunny thought about everything that had been revealed to her and how completely outrageous it all seemed, but the proof was clearly evident and perhaps, just perhaps it was all true... Bunny opened the door to her office and gasped in fright as she saw the state of her dear sister.

"Mavis, whatever is the matter now?" The same feeling of dread that Bunny had been feeling for the last month started to creep menacingly up her ankles again.

Mavis' blond hair, usually a collection of tight neat curls had been pulled so frantically in each direction that she looked as if she had been pulled violently through a gooseberry bush! Her skin was as white as ash and her pupils had grown so large that her familiar brown eyes had transformed into eerie black abysses.

"Mavis, you are scaring me, what on earth just happened in the ten minutes that I left you!" Bunny rushed towards her sister and clasped her shoulders anxiously.

Mavis did not know how to explain it; in the ten minutes while Bunny left the room Mavis had worked out the exact time period that the children and Professor had visited. She knew before from what Raj had told her that it was the Late Cretaceous period but now, after analysing all the information given she realised that the Professor was in imminent danger.

Bunny looked down alarmed at the erratic scribbles on her desk in black marker and cried, "Mavis, don't make me use the Lord's name in vain! Tell me what you have discovered?"

Mavis explained, the best she could that the time period that the Professor was in, was right at the end of the dinosaur era, so close in fact that the end could be at any moment!

"How did it end?" Bunny asked solemnly.

"With an enormous meteorite that crashed down and killed every living dinosaur within a 2000-mile radios!"

Bunny gasped and stumbled back until she fell against the wooden door and clutched it desperately for support.

"We have to save him Bunny!" Mavis wept and ran to her sister.

Bunny, having recovered from the initial shock, stroked her sister's hair and said, "We will find him Mavis my love, even if it is the last thing we do, we will find the old fool and bring him back in one safe and happy piece!"

Mavis suddenly broke away from Bunny's arms and said "But we have to go now? It might already be too late?"

"OK OK, keep your head. We will go very soon." Bunny said reassuringly wondering how on earth this was all going to be possible without someone getting hurt in the process.

  Once the sisters felt a little calmer after Mavis' discovery, Bunny decided it was best to tell the children what they knew; if time was of the essence, as Mavis insisted that it was, then they had to act swiftly. Bunny hurried down the corridor, her large bosoms wobbling conspicuously as she disturbed Mrs Bromelow's class again. On arrival Bunny swept into the classroom so quickly that some of the children cried out in surprise.

"Who could she want now?" Alison whispered nervously.

Bunny raced up to the Head Mistress' desk and thumped her palms down on the solid wood, she leaned over towards a startled Mrs Bromelow and explained that she did not feel that the four children in question really understood the consequences of not completing their religious studies' homework, and she thought it was imperative that she have another little chat with the naughty pupils. Bunny Bristlepott's ferocious brown eyes bore down on Mrs Bromelow until the young Head Mistress agreed that another chat was indeed much deserved.

Bunny, continued with the same speed as before and rushed over to Raj and the others, "You need to come with me. Now!"

Raj and his friends jumped up obediently and followed quickly behind their teacher. As soon as they got further down the corridor

Raj asked Bunny, "What is going on Miss Bristlepott, what happened?"

"No time to explain here!" Bunny replied in a shrill tone waving both her arms in the air in a frantic gesture.

The four children felt Bunny's panic and hurried after her down the corridor to her office. Once they had all arrived safely inside Bunny's small office, Bunny shut the door firmly and lent against the rigid wood, trying with great difficulty to normalise her breath.

"Can someone please tell us what is going on?" Serendipity asked.

Mavis lifted her head from the desk and the children gasped in shock; her skin had become white and pasty, the only colour on her face being the red blotches circling her large black eyes. Arthur glanced at Bunny hoping to catch a glimpse of her shiny white teeth, but alas no, Bunny's normal melancholy expression had formed firmly on her visage. The children knew that some thing awful must have happened.

"Now children," Bunny spoke at last, "We don't want to alarm you but we are terribly concerned about the Professor." She paused and wiped her sweaty brow, "In fact we believe he is in danger!"

"What do you mean?" Raj asked nervously "You do realise he is with Tony, a giant T-Rex?"

"Yes please don't worry," Serendipity added, "Tony is very brave and very strong. If anyone can protect the Professor it would be Tony!"

The children nodded in agreement trying to ease the tension and persuade Mavis and Bunny that the Professor was not in that much danger really.

"You don't understand," Mavis cried, "Tony is in danger too! They are all going to die unless we save them!" Mavis flung her head back down on the desk and sobbed uncontrollably.

"Miss Bristlepott you need to tell us exactly what is going on!" Serendipity said assertively.

Bunny, slightly taken aback by being addressed in such a direct way from a pupil, took a deep breath and began to explain everything, "You are quite right, we brought you here because we wanted to tell you what Mavis has discovered."

Mavis continued to moan loudly on the desk in the middle of the room.

"Apparently the end is coming!" Bunny hesitated, she did not want to upset the children too suddenly.

"The end of what?" Amber asked nervously

Bunny did not need to say anymore, because Raj answered for her, "The end of the dinosaurs. They are talking about the mass extinction."

"Oh boy that sounds awful!" Amber said, "What does it all mean?"

Mavis lifted her dishevelled head off the desk and finally pulled herself together enough to explain to the children the gravity of the situation her husband was in.

"I don't know how much you all know but I am going to start at the beginning." She paused and wiped the tears from her eyes, "The beginning of the end."

The children instinctively sat down on the floor ready to listen to every word the Professor's wife was about to tell them. Bunny too, was intrigued; natural history was not her specialisation and she was very keen to understand how such a humongous species could become, non-existent.

"You might have heard of the K-T boundary?" Mavis asked enquiringly.

All the students and Bunny shook their heads – they had no idea what Mavis was talking about!

"OK, let me break it down. Around 65million years ago something dramatic happened; something so dramatic that it wiped a whole species out. And not mind you a weak and feeble species, but a species that had dominated the world longer than any other, even to this day! The dinosaurs had been ruling the planet for 180 million years! To give you some perspective, our species known as the modern human has only been around for 200,000 years. That is a difference of 179.80 million years!" Mavis looked down enthusiastically at the children sitting on the floor.

"Basically what I am trying to say is that dinosaurs were kings of the world! So, the fact that they were wiped out, killed forever means that it happened so quickly they did not have enough time to adapt and survive!"

Bunny began to understand now why her sister was so frantic; if whatever killed the dinosaurs did so in such an immediate matter then they really did have to get their skates on and save Boris before it was too late.

"What killed the monsters Mavis?" Amber asked cautiously, afraid of the answer.

"There have been many different theories over the years and I am sure since my coma there have been many more but I always believed in one."

"Which one?" Serendipity asked nervously.

"The one where a meteorite the size of Mount Everest came crashing down to the earth killing practically every living thing in its path!"

"Oh gee!" Amber said alarmed "What's a meteorite? Sounds terrifying!"

Raj informed his friend that a meteorite was a rock that came from space and can enter the earth's atmosphere causing large craters the size of football stadiums when they landed.

"And there is proof of this, clear proof. As I mentioned before there is something called the K-T boundary and this refers to a layer in the rocks' history, a layer that is 65million years old and inside this old layer is a substance that can only be found in outer space or deep down in the Earth's crust; Iridium."

No one had heard of Iridium before apart from Mavis.

"The fact that huge amounts of Iridium (30 times more than average) was found in the earth's rocks, all at the same period in time, all over the world – well it can only mean one thing; that a meteorite hit the earth, so big that its impact effected every continent on the planet. And what confirms this theory for me is that there are no more dinosaur remains found since this level of Iridium in the rocks."

"What has this got to do with the Professor?" Serendipity asked.

Mavis sighed deeply. "Well I am afraid that the meteorite is on its way and Boris will not have long before it comes crashing down." Mavis wiped another tear from her eye. "You see it all depends where it hits, nobody knows, but if it hit anywhere near modern day America, where the Professor is, then he will be killed."

She paused, "Killed immediately."

Raj's throat was completely dry and his tummy churned with nerves. He had read something in one of his dinosaur books, but he was too upset to speak and to tell Mavis what he had learnt.

"But even if the meteorite were to hit far away from America, say Africa or Australia it would not be long before the consequences of such an impact were to take place and start killing species all over the planet."

Mavis continued. "You see if you were a dinosaur 65million years ago and you survived the initial impact of the meteorite hitting then you really did not have that long to live; after it hit the ground it would have sent tidal waves crashing against all the continents which in due course made all the volcanoes around the world erupt violently."

The children and Bunny looked terrified as they thought about the Professor's fate.

"And if the hot lava bursting from the volcanoes did not kill you by burning you to smithereens then the acid rain certainly would!"

"Blimely!" Arthur murmured under his breath.

"What is acid rain Mrs Inchenstein?" Amber asked innocently.

"Acid rain is something I hope we never see!" Mavis replied sternly. "Let me explain, when the meteorite hit the Earth, it would have fallen with such force that it would have vaporised immediately, sending up a huge cloud of dust, gasses and water vapour into the atmosphere. The dust would gradually spread and cause a global winter of darkness lasting up to three whole months!"

"Yikes!"

"Yikes indeed!" Mavis concurred, "Imagine clouds so thick and black that the powerful sun's rays could not light up the sky, everything would be completely black, pitch black, you could not even see your own hands!"

The children and Bunny struggled to imagine what that would have felt like.

Mavis continued, "There would be so much heat in the atmosphere caused by the meteorite, leading to chemical reactions that produced acid gases such as nitrous oxide that would eventually be washed out as acid rain."

"What happened when the rain fell?" Serendipity asked.

"Nothing good I am afraid!" Mavis sighed depressively. "The acid rain would kill all the vegetation, poison the drinking water which would lead to the dinosaurs' food chain being wiped out. If they had no food and water..."

"They would all die." Serendipity concluded gravely.

Silence befell the small office and the four friends and Bunny contemplated everything Mavis had just told them. If Mavis was right, then the Professor's future seemed a dismal one indeed.

Serendipity glanced at Raj and noticed him nervously pushing his glasses up his nose. She knew by now that he did this when he was uncomfortable but there was something strange about the way he was acting, "Raj, what's the matter?" Serendipity asked him.

"Acid rain, erupting volcanoes, a meteorite the size of Mount Everest. Do you really have to ask him?" Arthur replied.

"No there is something else." Serendipity said firmly, "Raj, what is going on?"

Suddenly, everyone turned to look at Raj; Mavis peered over the desk and observed that the child did look rather uneasy.

Raj tried to swallow but his throat was so dry that it made him cough. He tried to speak but the words came out again as a loud croaky cough. Arthur thought it his duty to help so wacked Raj on the back with such force that Raj bit his tongue by accident and he cried out in pain.

"Boys stop horsing around!" Bunny interposed, her previous disposition that all pupils found terrifying back in play, "Raj if you have something to say then just spit it out!"

"I know where the meteorite hit." Raj whispered.

Mavis dragged herself over the desk, much to the surprise of the children and threw herself on the floor next to Raj.

"Tell me." she demanded.

Raj, attempted for the fifth time to clear his throat and then muttered softly, afraid to look the Professor's wife in the eyes, "Yucatan Peninsula."

24

The Evangelist's Drama

Bunny crawled over to her sister and took her in her arms. Raj had revealed to the party that the meteorite that had killed off the dinosaurs had in fact landed in Mexico. Mexico as they all knew was uncomfortably close to the United States which was where Professor Inchenstein was assumed to be. If the meteorite hit Mexico before Mavis could go back and find her husband, he was sure to perish!

"Well it is obvious what we need to do!" Amber said assertively.

All eyes were on Amber.

"We need to go back there and save the Professor from those gigantic monsters and space rocks and acid rain and whatever else is going on back there!" Amber huffed.

Arthur admired Amber so much at this moment; he knew how afraid she always was especially when they were with the dinosaurs, and the fact that she was so determined to do the right thing, showed how brave she really was.

"I agree. We have got to go back and find him!" Arthur said.

"Yep I am in!" Serendipity said loudly.

Raj, finally finding his voice jumped up and said, "What are we waiting for?"

The sisters looked at each other and smiled; Bunny knew that her sister would not stop until she saved Boris and Bunny would do anything to make her sister happy, if that meant a trip to the Late Cretaceous period to find the old boy, then so be it! The six new companions discussed the best way to prepare for such a trip and when would be the best time to go. Mavis suggested the following Saturday as that would give them two full days to prepare and then the children would not be missed if they went on the weekend. Everyone agreed that Saturday seemed like a good day to save the Professor until Amber said softly, "I am so sorry but I can't go on Saturday." She looked uncomfortably at the floor, "It's my Grandma Rose's funeral."

Serendipity, Raj and Arthur stopped dead in their tracks.

"Why didn't you tell us?" Serendipity asked.

"I was going to but then what with everything going on with Mavis and Miss Bristlepoitt and the space rocks... Gee I did not have the time!"

Arthur took Amber's hand and squeezed it tightly.

"Well then we go on Sunday." Serendipity said looking at Mavis for approval.

"Absolutely!" Mavis replied. "Sunday it is."

The children walked back to Mrs Bromelow's class and left the two sisters in the little office planning the Professor's rescue.

ΔΔΔ

Saturday morning was quick to arrive, and Amber prepared herself for Grandma Rose's funeral. She stared at herself in the small bathroom mirror and realised that black was not her colour; it made her hair look an unnaturally bright orange, it made her skin seem so white it had an almost transparent air making all her freckles look like disorganised red ants lost in the snow. She rubbed the old gold locket that her Grandma had once worn, and she prayed; she prayed that her Grandma was happy and she prayed that they would get to the Professor before the space rocks did. Amber kissed the locket and tasted the old metal on her lips, a taste she found stale yet comforting at the same time. It was time to go and she rushed down the stairs ready to leave for the funeral. Grandma Rose's funeral was to take place in the Evangelist church in Islington. Grandma Rose, however, was a Catholic and had requested a Catholic burial, but Mr Bradshaw insisted that it was his duty to bury the old dear himself and his conscience could only do his duty if it was done the Evangelist way (for in his mind there really was no othe!)

Amber sat solemnly with her mother in the first pew and her eyes stared, fixated at the open coffin; the shiny ebony soon became blurred as the tears swelled in her sad blue eyes. She tried with all her might not to let them out because she was petrified her father would see and scold her in front of everyone, but the tears had to go somewhere, and they refused to go back in, so she rubbed them on her sleeve aggressively trying to get rid of them all before her father noticed. Once they had all disappeared Amber turned to look at the congregation of people behind them; a mixture of family friends she barely knew and then she saw them, sparkling in the soft light, Serendipity's braces and her heart suddenly felt lighter. Mr Bradshaw recommended Serendipity and her rock-star family should sit at the back. Amber noticed that next to Maggie Magnum sat Raj, then Arthur, then Mavis' blond hair full of composed tight curls and then to her surprise she saw Bunny Bristlepott. Amber turned her attention back to the smooth ebony at the front of the church and she felt a kind of contentment; she had friends, really good, fantastic friends who cared for her, and even though her Grandma had died, she was not alone anymore. After the ceremony the congregation crammed into the

Bradshaw's small unwelcoming home. Mrs Bradshaw did her best to add a bit of colour to the place so she positioned white lilies in a grey vase in the centre of the dining table. The grey vase was placed on an extra-large white doily which Mrs Bradshaw thought was rather fetching and bound to be the topic of much chatter and receive many compliments. The mourning friends gathered next to the dining table and quietly ate the cucumber sandwiches and sausage rolls whilst subtly admiring the tasteful centrepiece. Mavis and Bunny huddled the children in a corner and began to explain the plan for tomorrow's excursion. Everyone was packed and ready to go, the plan was to meet first thing at the school, so they had as much time as possible to find the Professor. The friends' quiet discussion was suddenly broken by Mr Bradshaw's bald head peering into the group and asking what was going on?

The children, well aware of Mr Bradshaw and his temper looked straight to the floor, however this obvious aversion was not enough to dissuade Mr Bradshaw from prying further.

"Curious to know, that's all, what my daughter has been talking about so intensely?" Mr Bradshaw stared at Amber's head, waiting for the moment when she would have to lift it and their eyes would at last meet.

Bunny, noticing the tension, decided it was best to intervene.

"Preacher Bradshaw, yes?" She questioned enthusiastically.

Mr Bradshaw nodded, not letting his gaze falter from the orange hair opposite him.

"Oh I am a huge fan of your work," Bunny continued.

Compliments on his work were always welcome, and Mr Bradshaw's eyes left his daughter momentarily and landed on Bunny instead.

"Let me introduce myself," Bunny continued graciously, "I am Pembridge Hall's religious teacher and I have been following your work ever since you arrived in London."

"Really! That's awesome!" Mr Bradshaw responded and he ushered Bunny away from the others and into a quieter spot to discuss his work and the Lord's word.

Amber was extremely grateful to Bunny Bristlepott; an interrogation from her father was the last thing her nerves could handle! The afternoon shortly came to an end and one by one the guests left the grey living room and the Bradshaw household was left quiet and calm as it normally was. Amber's friends, Bunny and Mavis all convened to see each other at Pembridge Hall's gates at 8am and agreed an early night was the best thing for all of them.

ΔΔΔ

At the crack of dawn Mr Bradshaw sat up in his bed and a grin the size of a German sausage formed on his pasty face; today he was going to take his family back to Texas where they belonged! He placed his cracked heels on the wooden floor and in a sharp shrill he screamed, "Dorothy where are the God damn eggs?"

Dorothy sat bolt upright in bed, so quickly it was as if she had been electrocuted. "She peered over her husband's side of the bed and to her dismay she saw no boiled eggs on the floor. She looked up at her husband with a look of twisted terror on her face.

"Blast it Dorothy not today of all days!"

"But I am sure I boiled them, just how you like them." Dorothy said quivering.

"Well they sure as hell are not on the floor where they should be! Damn it women today is a travelling day!"

"I, I, I, I." Dorothy stammered, "I am so sorry Brad, what with the funeral and packing I was so tired."

Mr Bradshaw held his hand in the air to stop his wife from speaking. Dorothy became silent. Mr Bradshaw reluctantly stepped out of his bed and walked towards the bathroom imagining the delightful squelch of egg shells and runny yoke beneath his bare skin. Once the bathroom door had closed Dorothy let her head fall back to the soft pillow and she racked her brains trying to work out what had happened to the eggs. She remembered putting Amber to bed after a long, exhausting day and as she came back into the sitting room her husband told her the news; he had bought 3 tickets to Houston, Texas and they would be on the next flight. Amber's mum had to pack everything that night! By the time she had finished all the packing it was 3am and she was completely wiped out, but even though she was so very tired she still remembered boiling the eggs for her husband's feet. Dorothy hurried out of bed and went down into the kitchen, worried that she was going mad. She saw on the hob a small pan and she looked inside; there they were, all six of them, enough to cover the steps needed for her husband to reach the bathroom.

Dorothy had spent the last 12 years boiling eggs for her husband to tread on each morning and she never forgot, never until this day! Mr Bradshaw always said it would be a terrible day the day he did not feel wondrous sharp shells breaking under his toes. However, he was not going to let it get to him, today he was going home, at long last, and even though the lack of broken eggs had disturbed his regime, he was not going to let it upset travelling day. Amber's alarm clock rang at 7am sharp and Amber jumped out of bed; she did not even want to snooze because today was a very important day! Amber got dressed and pulled her giant rucksack that was completely bursting full of necessary equipment for her journey out of the wardrobe. As she did she noticed that there was nothing in fact in her wardrobe! She looked in her drawers and the same thing happened – they were all empty. Amber's heart flipped in her chest, something was going on and she had a very bad feeling!

ΔΔΔ

Arthur, Serendipity, Raj, Mavis and Bunny were all waiting at Pembridge Hall's grand gates for Amber.

"She is twenty minutes late!" Serendipity said concerned.

"Do you think something is wrong?" Bunny asked.

"I will go and check on her!" Arthur suggested, "She does not live far I will be back with her in no time!"

The others agreed, and Arthur ran as fast as he could, blond hair blowing in front of his face as he sped through the London streets to find out what had happened to his friend.

Panting and sweating, Arthur finally arrived outside the Bradshaw home and knocked on the grey door. He hoped that Amber or her mum would open the door – anyone but Mr Bradshaw, but after several knocks, no one came to the door, the house looked deserted. Puzzled, Arthur looked through the window to try and see if his friend was inside but the reflection on the glass was too strong and he could see nothing helpful. Just as Arthur was beginning to panic he heard the door open and he hoped he would see his friend's orange head.

"That is strange!" Arthur murmured, "I swear I heard the door open!" as he stared at the closed door in front of him.

"Arthur?" an old women's voice shouted.

Arthur turned searching for the strange voice that said his name.

"Over here."

Arthur walked back a few steps and realised that the neighbour's door had opened and an old lady who looked about 100 years old, was standing outside with a walking stick.

"Are you Arthur?" The ancient voice said.

"Yes. Who are you?"

"I was a friend of Amber's Grandmother, Rose." The old lady wiped her eyes with a tissue as she thought about her friend's recent death.

Arthur stared at her confused, not knowing what to say to the old women and still no clue as to where his friend was. Time was running out and he had to get back to Pembridge Hall.

"I have a message for you from Amber."

Arthur's ears pricked up. "What is it?"

"They all left in such a hurry!" The neighbour explained, "Imagine, it was around 7.30am and I hear this frantic banging at the door. I thought there must be a fire so in my night dress I hurry to open it and Ito my surprise I see Rose's little granddaughter, all crying and panicky."

Arthur's stomach turned.

"She said very clearly to 'Tell Arthur they should all go without her.'" She stared at the young boy, "That was the message, that you should go without her, whatever that means!"

"But, where did they go?"

"She did not tell me her father was shouting something about missing the flight..."

"Did they have suitcases with them?" Arthur asked, dreading what else the old women would reveal.

"Why yes now you come to mention it, they had a lot of bags and they were rushing to get in a taxi!"

Before Rose's friend had finished her sentence, Arthur had already jumped down the steps and was racing back to school. "What are we going to do?" Raj asked.

"Are you sure they were going to the airport?" Serendipity confirmed.

"I really don't know for sure but they were getting in a taxi with suitcases and Amber's dad was shouting about a plane so I guess the airport is likely." Arthur looked so sad that Bunny went up to him and tapped him on the shoulder affectionately.

"There, there, maybe they have gone on a surprise holiday?" Bunny suggested.

"He has taken Amber back to Texas." Serendipity said, tears filling in her eyes. "We will never see her again!" she said barely audible as she sobbed into her hands.

The sisters looked at each other concerned, they did not want to hurry the children while they were so upset, but time really was running out for the Professor.

"Children, I know Amber going back so suddenly is a shock, but I am sure you will see her again so please don't be so sad." Mavis said trying to calm everyone.

"Yes, Mavis is right you will see Amber again, but she did say for us to go without her, so we really must get shifting!" Bunny added.

"Amber would want us to save the Professor," Serendipity said.

"From the monsters!" Arthur added humourously. He had become so close to Amber these last months that the thought of never seeing her again was crushing.

Bunny and Mavis led the children to the science lab and they all squeezed into the cupboard. There was no window in the cupboard so when Bunny closed the door it was pitch black, Bunny could not even lift her hand to her face they were so crammed in.

"Right what happens now?" Bunny asked the darkness.

A few minutes passed, and Mavis started to fidget nervously, "Aren't we supposed to fall down in some whirlwind of some sorts?"

"Serendipity, why aren't you rubbing the claw, what is the matter?" Raj asked.

Serendipity's forehead was covered with little beads of sweat and her hands were so slippery she could hardly clasp the magic claw. None of the others could see, but she had actually been rubbing the claw frantically since they arrived in the cupboard, but to her surprise nothing was happening.

"It's, it's not working." She mumbled confused.

"Whatever do you mean?" Raj asked.

"For pity sake can someone open this wretched cupboard I can hardly breath, I feel like a squashed sardine!" Bunny cried.

Arthur opened the door and they all tumbled out and stared at each other in dismay. Mavis started to pace up and down the science lab and Bunny tried her best to keep everyone calm.

"Now Serendipity, are you sure it is the same claw?"

"Of course it is!"

"OK don't panic, nobody panic! We need to think, there must be something different that is stopping the magic from working. Think everyone, what is different this time than the last times? What is missing?" Bunny scratched her head and thought over all the stories about the kids' adventures, trying to work out what went wrong.

"Not what but who?" Arthur said.

Everyone stared at Arthur and Mavis stopped her pacing for a brief moment, "Amber is missing. Every time we travelled she came with us."

"Oh wow!" Serendipity exclaimed, "You are right!"

"Well that is inconvenient!" Raj commented, "Considering the fact that she is probably half way across the Atlantic by now!"

Mavis slid to the floor in a swoon.

The children and Bunny rushed to Mavis trying to revive her. Panic befell the science lab; how would they save the Professor now? Bunny had a crazy idea; she knew it was a long shot but if it was the only way to save the Professor, then she had to try it. Mavis finally opened her eyes and hoped to see exotic dinosaurs, but reality soon kicked in as she felt the cold tiles under her body and her stomach lurched with anxiety. What if she never saw her husband again?

Bunny, waiting for her sister to regain her faculties shocked the party with her solution.

"Well then looks like we are going to Texas!" she declared, and her eyes sparkled so brightly the children barely recognised her.

"Are you for real?"

"Yes Arthur, I am! It is the only way, now let's get going!" Bunny leapt to the science lab door and opened it dramatically, "Follow me!" she cried as she raced down the corridor.

ΔΔΔ

Before too long, the sisters and three children huddled into a black London taxi, and hurtled towards Heathrow. Bunny kept pressing the red talking button and shouting, "Quick as you can sir, don't be shy!" much to the annoyance of the cockney taxi driver who was already trying to dodge the London traffic best he could. The driver had done a frantic tour of Notting Hill, going to four different houses so everyone could grab their passports before they headed to the airport. He was convinced he had picked up a bunch of loonies! As soon as they arrived at Heathrow, Bunny rushed to the customer service desk and asked when the next flight to Houston was. The information given made Bunny sweat even more, "Goodness me!" She turned to her worried party,

"They are boarding the plane in twenty minutes! We must hurry!"

Bunny dashed towards the BA departure's desk, dodging suitcases and bewildered travellers as she flew by! She thrust her way to the front of the queue, ignoring the polite disgruntles behind her.

"It is of the utmost importance that I and my friends here are on the next flight to Houston!"

The BA attendant, a young girl from Essex looked at the dishevelled women in front of her and contemplated calling security.

"Do you need water or somtink?" the attendant asked in a strong accent.

Bunny shook her head decisively.

"Medication?"

Bunny shook her head more vigorously.

"Tickets! I need 5 tickets!" Bunny cried.

"Please," Bunny said more gently this time and cleaned the steam from her glasses and tried to focus on the girl's badge, "Please Chantal, help me to get on the flight."

Chantal, still contemplating whether Bunny had lost her marbles or not replied.

"But it's boarding in like, fifteen minutes." She tapped her acrylic neon nails on her desk nonchalantly.

"Yes, yes, I am aware, hence the need for speed and co-operation!" Bunny forced a smile that made Chantal feel uncomfortable.

"I donnow if the system will let me."

"Try it!" Bunny ordered.

Chantal sighed and looked up the flight details. "Ow many are ye?"

"I beg your pardon?" Bunny replied confused.

"Ow many of ye is travelling?"

"Oh of course! We are five." Bunny replied relieved that some progress was being made.

"Ow much luggage you got to check in?"

"None."

Chantal raised her pencil drawn eyebrows at Bunny, now convinced that she was dealing with a nut-job.

"You is going to America with no luggage?"

"None!" Bunny glared the glare that always got a student to do as she commanded and she prayed that it would work on young Chantal.

"It will cost ya like three grand."

"Excellent."

Moments later Chantal processed their tickets and handed Bunny back her credit card.

"Gate 19, boarding now so if I was you I would like, get a move on."

"Good advice Chantal I shall go as fast as my legs will carry me!" And with that, Bunny sprinted best she could and hurried through security with Mavis and the children close behind her.

They could hear the tannoy calling for passengers on flight BA9587 to Houston Texas to go to Gate 19. The last call made the sisters and children run faster than they ever imagined they could. Drenched in perspiration, they finally arrived at gate 19 and Bunny collapsed on a chair, unable to move or do anything more. Arthur was the first to see Amber walking through the glass corridor about to board the flight and he started screaming her name as loud as he could. The passengers, on their way to Texas suddenly turned to look at the new arrivals with immense curiosity. Serendipity stood on a chair and was waving frantically in the air trying to get Amber's attention. The children and Mavis (Bunny was still recovering) were screaming and shouting so much that the entire gate came to a standstill. Amber turned around to see what everyone was looking at and to her surprise saw her friends acting very strangely indeed. She attempted to turn and go towards them to see what was going on but as she did she felt a tight grip on her arm.

"Where do you think you are going child?" Mr Bradshaw hissed at his daughter.

"Bunny do something!" Serendipity cried, "He won't let her see us, he is forcing her on the flight!"

Bunny searched deep and hard to find some remaining energy and eventually managed to heave herself off the chair and force her way to the front of the queue.

"This is a matter of life and death!" The children heard Bunny say to a flight attendant at the gate.

"Wot is going on?" A familiar voice was heard.

"Oh, thank goodness! Here is our friend Chantal, she knows that I am a women of integrity!"

Chantal's colleagues looked at her bizarrely, "Do you know this woman?" one of them asked Chantal.

Chantal shrugged and confirmed she had sold them the tickets, "I wouldn't say that makes us BFFs though."

"I am not familiar with the term 'BFF', but I am sure if we spent a bit of time together we would get along splendidly! Now please call for the Bradshaw family to get off the plane, it is a matter of life and death." Bunny's forced smile transformed into a natural glare.

The children finally heard the tannoy request for the Bradshaw family to get off the plane.

"Some kind of emergency init."

Chantal put the microphone down and blew a large pink bubble out of her mouth.

By this time everyone else had boarded the plane and the gate was empty apart from Chantal and the five desperate friends. Minutes later Mavis sighed with relief as she saw Amber and her parents walking down the glass corridor back towards the gate.

Mr Bradshaw was livid.

"Whatever possessed you to get me and my family off the plane?" he hollered at Chantal.

"Calm down, clam down." Chantal said in her heavy Essex accent, "It's a matter of life and death so I ad to get yous lot off the plane." Chantal replied, starting to get annoyed.

"Preposterous!" Mr Bradshaw spat back at Chantal.

Chantal, taken aback, threatened to call security if Mr Bradshaw continued to shout at her.

"Call them you bimbo and get these impostors taken away!" Mr Bradshaw pointed at Amber's friends with such disdain that Mavis slowly moved behind Bunny for protection.

"What's going on?" Amber whispered.

"It does not work without you?" Serendipity shouted trying to be heard over Mr Bradshaw's ranting.

"Amber you need to come with us if we are going to save the Professor!" Arthur screamed.

Amber hesitated, she looked at her father, still screaming at Chantal and demanding an explanation from Bunny who was running out of excuses. She looked at her friends' desperate faces and then at Mavis, who was close to tears. Amber knew what the right thing to do was and she walked towards Serendipity. Bunny also quickly turned around and headed back towards the group.

"Come back here child!" Mr Bradshaw screamed at his daughter, he was beside himself with rage.

Amber froze and instinctively turned to look at her father. She had never disobeyed him before, but her friends needed her, and she was fed up of being scared all the time.

"Sorry daddy but I have to go."

"In all my years!" he roared, "Get back here NOW!" He screamed.

Amber turned and ran towards her friends as fast as she could, but Mr Bradshaw bounded after her screaming so loudly that Chantal pressed the panic button not sure what on earth was going on.

"Rub the claw!" Amber screamed as she leapt in the air towards Serendipity.

But her father was so close behind her, he reached out to grab the bottom of her skirt, Serendipity rubbed the claw and Chantal screamed...

Forty minutes later, Flight BA9587 finally took off and Gate 19 was left quiet and abandoned, all that could be heard were the click-clack of Dorothy Bradshaw's knitting needles as she waited patiently for her husband and daughter to reappear.

25

Mr Bradshaw seeks the truth

Mr Bradshaw thought that he must be having a terrible nightmare; the last thing he remembered he was boarding the flight that was finally going to take him home, back to his precious Texas and away from the dreary rotten-weathered London that he had been despising for so many months. But suddenly, he was called off the flight and now he was falling down a black pit that felt like the journey to hell. He could not possibly be going to hell, a preacher of such stature would not be forgotten by the Lord, so he assumed he had nodded off on the plane and this was some frightful hallucination that he would soon wake up from. Moments later he did not wake up as such but felt his backside thunder to the ground with a hefty thud. Light streamed down so brightly on his face that he wondered if this might be a message from the Lord and that he should try and focus so as to remember every minute detail. A few meters away, Mr Bradshaw's daughter on the other hand knew exactly what had happened and she prayed that her father would not be too worried when she disappeared right in front of his eyes.

Arthur was feeling rather lucky; every other time he landed with a bang on the hard ground which left him covered in bruises, but this time he felt something soft and squidgy below his body.

"Err hem!" Bunny Bristlepott said disapprovingly as she glanced down at Arthur's blond head lying on her bosom.

The other children giggled out loud when Arthur's faced turned an embarrassed pink, "Sorry Miss Bristlepott." he mumbled as he lifted his head. Arthur hastily moved away from his soft-landing pad and did not feel so lucky after all!

Mavis was the first to stand on her feet and tilted her head back, gazing in awe at the wondrous pine trees that soared above her like ancient giants. She smelt the fresh warm air and even though it made no sense whatsoever she believed that she could smell Boris. Mavis closed her eyes and tried to gulp down the imaginary smell that only her memory could bring to life. "I will find you my love" she whispered to herself. For Mr Bradshaw the bright light was finally subsiding, and his vision became focused; he observed the rocks on the ground, the large and unusual trees that were surrounding him and the luscious vegetation that seemed to creep towards him. Could this be Heaven? The Garden of Eden perhaps? he pondered.

The confused preacher wiped his sweaty forehead and cleared his throat ready to address the Holy Spirit whom he felt was sure to appear. He waited and waited but no apparition became visible.

"Lord, I have arrived!" He said loudly in a very assertive voice (for Mr Bradshaw was always assured about everything).

Amber stopped deadly still when she heard her father's voice. "Surely it cannot be!" she gasped.

"Did anyone else hear that?" Raj asked as he pushed his glasses up his nose.

"Are we under attack already?" Bunny questioned groping for a rock to use as a weapon.

"Speak to me, oh mighty one, I am your humble servant!"

Arthur swung round towards the forest "You must be kidding me?"

The children and sisters walked towards the trees that surrounded the voice that they all feared. Serendipity held Amber's hand tightly as they followed the distant calls addressing the Lord above.

"Daddy?" Amber said softly as she approached the familiar silhouette belonging to her father.

Mr Bradshaw spun around in a frenzy. He blinked slowly, then blinked again. Staring in a startled manner at his daughter, he was, for once at a loss for words.

Amber did not know what else to say. How could she explain to someone like her father where he was and why? All she could muster was a stilted, "Hi."

"Hello." her father said in return, the same confusion in his eyes.

Then silence.

The rest of the crew stood quietly behind the trees at the edge of the forest, watching intently as Amber addressed her father. Bunny was ready to step in if things took an unexpected turn, although Bunny had no idea what to expect so she stood in an animated stance ready to leap out at any moment.

Amber took a step further then hesitated under her father's steady gaze.

Eventually after what seemed a lifetime to the friends hidden behind the prickly bushes Mr Bradshaw spoke, "Is this a dream?"

"No daddy." Amber replied softly.

"Then what is going on?" Mr Bradshaw said sternly. He was used to being in control, he always had control over every situation, especially his daughter, and the fact that at this exact moment, he neither knew where he was or how he got there made him feel uneasy, a feeling that he had never felt before.

Amber opened her mouth idle; no words could explain what happened and where they were.

"Speak child!" her father commanded. He assumed this must be some rotten prank and he was determined to get to the bottom of it.

"Allow me to intervene." Bunny said loudly as she gracefully appeared from beyond the wilderness.

Mr Bradshaw stumbled backwards at the sight of Bunny.

"Don't be scared Daddy, this is Miss Bristlepott, you met at Grandma Rose's funeral, remember?"

"What in the Lord's name is going on?!!!" Mr Bradshaw's own vulnerability was becoming more and more present to him. This complete lack of control made his face twitch erratically.

"Of course, your father remembers me. Pembridge Hall's religious teacher." Bunny almost bowed with pride but managed to refrain.

A sudden look of understanding appeared in Mr Bradshaw's eyes, yes, he recognised this woman but what did it all mean?

"We are on a journey and you happened to have accidently high-jacked a ride, so to speak."

Bunny began to explain.

Mr Bradshaw had to arch his neck in order to look directly at Bunny's face that was almost two feet above his own. He detested being so small and looking up (even if it was only physically) to so many other human beings.

"Let me explain further, your child and her friends," Bunny

beckoned towards the silent bushes encouraging them to come to life, "have stumbled upon a magical dinosaur claw that miraculously transports them to the dinosaur era."

"Ludicrous!" Mr Bradshaw spat the words at Bunny and his daughter.

Bunny, unfazed continued to talk in a calm but firm voice, "I agree, it is hard to believe, but the proof is in the pudding – we are here, in the Late Cret... where are we exactly?" Bunny turned to address her sister.

"Late Cretaceous period." Mavis interjected as she edged out from the bushes.

"Millions of years ago, apparently!" Bunny said excitedly.

Needless to say, Mr Bradshaw did not like being taken for a fool, and taken for a fool was exactly what he thought was happening. He walked directly towards Amber and grabbed her hand briskly.

"Now you come with me and you take me home or I'll."

"Or you'll what exactly?" Bunny said fiercely as she gripped hold of Mr Bradshaw's bony shoulder, preventing him from taking another step.

Mr Bradshaw had never been touched in such an aggressive manner and he was taken aback with such surprise that he let go of Amber and turned to face Miss Bristlepott's heaving bosoms that were unfortunately directly in his line of sight.

"We are here on a very important mission and I am not going to let you, or anyone stop us from achieving our objective. DO you understand me?" Bunny glared down at the bald sweaty head and twisted her mouth in such a way that Mr Bradshaw felt more comfortable staring straight ahead.

Amber's father realised that even he was no match for Bunny and changed his approach, for he could be an incredibly charming man if need be, "OK clearly we have got off on the wrong foot."

"Clearly!" Bunny huffed.

"So, tell me what the mission is so that I can understand?" Mr Bradshaw said smoothly, edging towards his daughter so that she was within arm's reach.

"I would be glad to, but do you mind if we walk and talk as we are under extreme time pressure and every second counts?" Bunny held out her hand to the agitated preacher.

Mr Bradshaw, realising his options were limited, placed his hand inside Bunny's and let her lead him towards the others and they all began to explain what had happened and why they were there. While the children chattered excitedly, trying to convince Amber's father that what they were saying was the truth, Mavis started to navigate and instructed her team that they should head west. Why she thought west was best, she could not explain, but this is what her gut told her, so everyone followed suit and continued to explain to Mr Bradshaw why it was so very important to find Professor Inchenstein before the meteorite hit.

"What meteorite?" Mr Bradshaw said as he walked hurriedly alongside the others.

"Space rocks daddy"

Mr Bradshaw muttered confused outbursts of "Preposterous!" "Absurd!" "Madness!" "Insane!" whenever there was a moments silence.

"This is all witch craft and trickery!" He huffed finally and stood still with his arms crossed while the others walked off in the distance.

It took a few seconds for the group to realise that someone was missing and eventually they all halted (apart from Mavis who continued to head west).

"Why have you stopped Preacher Bradshaw?" Bunny shouted

impatiently.

"I am not taking part in this ludicrous fantasy for one more minute." He swept the sweat from his eyelids in a nervous manner and shouted, "You are all a bunch of devil worshippers and this is some kind of test that I will not falter."

Mortified, Bunny stormed as fast as she could towards Amber's father. Never in all her life had she been called a devil worshipper before. Bunny was so livid that she wanted to box Mr Bradshaw's ear. Mr Bradshaw sensing the raw anger in Bunny's face stumbled backwards and once in control of his own feet he leapt in the opposite direction and ran back towards the safety of the forest.

"Oh gee!" Amber said burying her head in her hands.

"I had no idea Log Head could run so fast." Arthur said under his breath as they all watched Bunny dart and dive determined to catch Amber's father.

"This is a disaster!" Serendipity said.

Raj hurried after Mrs Inchenstein who was a hundred or so meters ahead and completely unaware of the drama that was bubbling due east behind her.

"We could always leave him here." Arthur suggested sheepishly.

Horrified Serendipity wacked Arthur on his arm, "He is her father for God's sake!" she hissed.

"I know but he is awful!"

"What's that?" Amber asked between sobs.

"Nothing." Serendipity threw Arthur a glare covered in daggers, "Arthur is just horsing around as usual!"

"What should we do go back and find them?" Arthur suggested rubbing his arm sulkily where Serendipity had hit it.

"We must never go back, only forward!" Mavis said loudly, "Why the hold-up?"

The children explained to Mavis what had happened and to the children's surprise Mavis began cursing and huffing and throwing her arms dramatically in the air.

"Why are adults so weird?" Arthur asked Raj as they watched Mavis throw a tantrum a few meters away.

"Beats me." Raj replied shrugging his shoulders.

Serendipity felt like the situation was becoming more and more hopeless; Amber was crying, Miss Bristlepott and Mr Bradshaw had vanished into the forest and Mavis looked like a toddler having a fit. Not knowing what else to do she fumbled inside her rucksack and pulled out a glass bottle sealed with a pipette lid.

"What is that?" Raj enquired and cleaned his glasses, so he could look closer, "Rescue Remedy?"

"My mum gave it to me in case of emergencies." Serendipity explained.

"How does it rescue you?" Arthur asked.

"No idea but you are supposed to squirt it on the tongue, here Amber, open your mouth and try this!" Serendipity said squirting the liquid inside Amber's mouth.

The boys laughed out loud as they watched Amber make the most repelling face she could fathom, "Yikes! What was that?" She spat out into the dry heat, "Oh gosh it tastes like rat pee, err yuk!"

"How do you feel now?" Serendipity asked.

"Apart from feeling like I have rat pee in my mouth, OK I guess. Why? Why are you all looking at me?"

The boys and Serendipity noticed straight away that Amber

became suddenly calmer and that she had stopped crying.

"Wow it worked!" Raj said intrigued.

"The rat pee worked!" Arthur said grinning.

"Well let's see if it will rescue Mavis!" Serendipity said and cautiously approached the Professor's erratic wife who was still cursing and hitting into the wind.

It took more than one squirt but eventually Mavis stopped her futile yells and came back to the children. They found some rocks in the shade and sat down quietly, keeping their eyes on the forest, waiting for Bunny and Mr Bradshaw to reappear.

26

The Batmobile

Mavis sat on the hot rocks and impatiently ripped the leaves off a dying branch that was scattered on the floor. Every second lost in her mind was a failure; Boris was soon to perish if she did not find him. Mavis was always the best at finding hidden fossils; she found the ominous Spinosaurus didn't she? But that took months and she did not have months, no one knew for sure how much time she had but it was clear to her that it was borrowed time to say the least! Luckily for Mavis, she did not have to wait too long before she saw her sister again. There was a distinct rustling heard on the outskirts of the forest and Arthur, hearing it first beckoned to the rest of the group to look in that direction. "What is going on?" Amber asked fearfully.

In a matter of seconds, it was as if the trees parted by some sudden and uncontrollable force and out spun Bunny, quickly followed by a haggard Mr Bradshaw.

The children wanted to feel relieved, but the wild look in Bunny's eyes and the trembling fear that absorbed the Preacher's expression as they sprinted towards the rocks, made the children spring to their feet preparing for a new danger. As Bunny came closer she waved her hands like a crazed baboon trying to communicate to her sister and pupils.

"Do you have some of the rat pea left?" Raj mumbled to Serendipity.

"You will need a barrel of it to rescue Log Head and the Preacher!" Arthur said humorously however, nobody laughed.

Bunny's arms now moved in a slicing action as if she was holding a film clacker and was trying to get the action rolling.

"What is she doing?" Amber asked puzzled. She tilted her head to try and understand what these gestures all meant.

Mavis pushed her way in front of the children and saw her sister sprinting towards them and flinging her arms in air. "She is trying to tell us something." Mavis observed.

Bunny then took her arms from the sky and curved her fingers as if she were a red eagle about to swoop down on an unsuspecting beaver.

"Oh my God!" Mavis exclaimed.

"What is it?" Serendipity cried.

"She has seen a dinosaur!" Mavis said and ran out to meet Bunny in the open plain. Mr Bradshaw threw himself down on the floor by his daughter's feet and clung onto her ankles like a scare child who had just been chased by a starved lion. Amber, who had never seen her father other than composed and self-assured looked down at the quivering man at her feet in total disbelief.

"Get the rat pea!" Arthur hissed at Serendipity.

Serendipity nervously tried to squirt it in Mr Bradshaw's mouth, but he refused to open it, so Serendipity accidently squirted it in his eye causing him to roll around and scream out with a new-found energy about human weakness and the mercy of the Lord.

"Tell me what you saw?" Mavis kept on saying over and over again.

But neither Bunny nor the Preacher could find any words to speak let alone describe a dinosaur that had scared the living daylights out of them.

"Dear Lord, I must have aged ten years, I must have aged ten years." Was all anyone could decipher from Bunny's mumblings.

The children and Mavis continued to fire questions at the quivering witnesses, determined to find out what they had seen.

"What did it look like?"

"Was it a T-Rex?" Mavis asking hopefully.

"Aged ten years!"

"Was it standing on its hind legs?"

"Did it have small arms?"

"Possibly twenty!" Bunny said and clasped her chest in shock.

"Or did it have horns on its head?"

"It was the devil that was what it was!" Mr Bradshaw said at last, finally unravelling himself from the safety of his daughter's ankles.

"Get out your dinosaur book, Raj. Maybe that will help." Serendipity suggested.

"Ginormous it was towering above us like the Eiffel Tower, only covered in scales and spots!" Bunny revealed, slowly gaining her composure.

"Did it see you?"

"It? They!" Bunny took a deep breath, "Monstrous looking creatures and so many of the vile beasts!"

"Here take a look, was it this one?" Raj asked pointing to a picture of a Tyrannosaurus.

"Oh, golly no! It was not like that, but it was large and had a funny mouth?"

"Did it have sharp teeth?" Mavis asked, stroking Bunny's sweat drenched hair comfortingly.

"Could not say, had its funny mouth shut. Just stared at me." Bunny crossed herself, "He stared me straight in the eye. Oh, ten years!" And she started to sob into Mavis's lap.

Mr Bradshaw, now sitting up, grabbed the book from Raj and stared mesmerised by the photographic illustrations of what could only be the most hideous, devil inspired monsters ever imagined.

"What are they?" he asked innocently.

"They are dinosaurs daddy." Amber said softly and stroked his hand.

Mr Bradshaw placed his hand on top of his daughter's and Amber felt a warmth swirl around her veins that she had never felt before. For the first time, her father was listening to her.

"They lived on Earth, millions of years ago." Amber continued cautiously.

"But how is this all possible?"

"I know, it is hard to believe but it's true daddy."

Mr Bradshaw took a deep breath and continued to flick through Raj's dinosaur book, trying to engage with what was on the pages. Could all this really have existed? Did he really just see a heard of dinosaurs? he thought to himself.

Mavis was busy squirting what remained of Serendipity's Rescue Remedy down her sister's throat until eventually, Bunny relaxed.

"Praise to the Lord! That is the one we saw." Mr Bradshaw pointed excitedly towards a frightful looking creature depicted in brown and beige on the page.

"Oh, that's OK then." Raj said relieved.

"How do you figure that young man?" Mr Bradshaw said aggressively staring at what he thought to be a very impertinent child.

"All I mean sir, is that he is an herbivore, not a hunter, so he does not want to eat us."

"Which one is it Raj?" Mavis asked enthusiastically.

"He pointed to an Edmontosaurus."

Bunny took a nervous peek towards the book and gasped out loud, "Oh that is the one we saw for sure! Monstrous looking fellow. Evil eyes like the devils!"

"I will be back in just a moment." And before anyone could investigate further, Mavis sprinted off towards the forest to the exact same spot where her sister and Amber's father had appeared from.

"She is mad!" Bunny whispered.

Mr Bradshaw stood up and almost ran after Mavis then thought twice about the danger at hand and sat on a hot rock despairingly.

"Guys don't panic, if Raj said they won't eat us then Mavis is safe. We rode on the heads of dinosaurs bigger than this one?" Arthur said trying to reassure the adults.

"You did what?" Mr Bradshaw stared fiercely at Arthur.

Arthur glanced at Amber who shook her head briefly.

"Why does it have such a funny mouth?" Serendipity asked Raj, trying to change the subject, "It looks almost like a duck's beak!"

"Well yes funnily enough this type of dinosaur is referred to as a duck-billed dinosaur, it is part of the hadrosaurids and they lived alongside Tyrannosaurus."

"That is great news!" Serendipity said enthusiastically.

"In fact T-Rexes often ate Edmontosaurus so if we hang around them then maybe they will attract a T-Rex!" Raj suggested.

"Tony!" Serendipity said hopefully.

"We can only hope." Bunny added softly. This conversation flew way over Mr Bradshaw's head; it felt like another language. It was like another world had just exploded right in front of his very eyes. Amber tried her best to explain things and she showed him the Tyrannosaurus in Raj's book.

"So let me get this straight," he paused looking at the kids. "Your science teacher is hanging out with one of these," he pointed to the picture of the Terrible Lizard who was illustrated with a leg belonging to a Triceratops in his mouth. "And you suggest we hang around here waiting for him to come to us?"

Raj wanted to nod but his neck was stiff with intimidation and refused to move in any direction.

"I think that is the general idea." Bunny said causally.

"Blind madness! That is what it is!" Mr Bradshaw said in response and flung his arms up in despair. "But daddy we need to save the Professor from the space rocks." Amber said quietly.

"Oh yes, the meteorite that is about to crash down and kill us all! How could I forget!" He said sarcastically. He turned to face Bunny, "Miss Bristlepott, do you think it was good judgement to bring four innocent children on this quest to save what sounds to me like a loony man who has chosen to live here? Do you think it is right to have put the life of my child at risk to save this deranged man?"

Bunny sighed deeply and met the gaze of her interrogator, front on, "No. No Mr Bradshaw it is not good judgement, but desperate judgement that has led us to be here."

"You see Daddy, Mavis has been in a coma for 25 years and

when she woke-up Professor Inchenstein had already left to be with the dinosaurs, he has no idea she is awake."

Mr Bradshaw tapped his daughter fondly on her head, another piece of affection that Amber felt so grateful for and wished would never end.

"Yes, all very romantic I am sure, but this is not some Hollywood movie, these are the lives of children that you have chosen to endanger!" Mr Bradshaw straightened his back on the rock he was sitting on to face Bunny directly.

"You are right of course, but Mavis was so desperate, I was worried she would do something sinister if we did not at least try and find him."

There were indeed moments when Bunny was so worried that Mavis would do something drastic like take her own life that she removed all the medication and sharp utensils in the house in case Mavis was tempted. Bunny ran her hand through her soggy curls and explained, "To be honest I did not really believe any of it until we were falling down the dark space that brought us here."

"If she is so desperate to find her husband then why did she dash off into the forest?"

"I imagine she is looking for clues. That is what she does, she used to hunt old bones. My sister had a natural flair for it, she was one of the best fossil hunters of all time." Bunny said proudly.

"Now she needs to hunt her husband."

 The children, Bunny and Mr Bradshaw sat around on the rocks and waited for Mavis to appear from the depths of the forest. Raj slowly began to answer Mr Bradshaw's questions about the dinosaurs he saw in the book with more and more confidence until it was Raj who was taking charge and telling Mr Bradshaw so many interesting facts, that the Preacher had to ask Raj to slow down so he could process all this new information.

"Look this one here is one of Arthur's favourites, it's a Triceratops and has three horns that are one-meter long."

Mr Bradshaw looked overwhelmed.

"It looks scary!"

"Yes, but that is for its defence, they are actually really docile, all they want to do is graze and drink and soak up the sun." Raj continued, thinking back to the time when he sat on the back of his dear Boudicca. "Look!" Serendipity cried suddenly, "Its Mavis, she is headed this way!"

"Oh, thank the heavens she is safe!" Bunny said and crossed herself several times in gratitude.

Mavis arrived at the scattered rocks and beamed down at her fellow hunters.

"It was flabbersatic!" Mavis cried out loud.

Bunny, smiling cautiously beckoned her sister to sit down on a neighbouring rock.

"No Bunny I am too agitated to sit! I just saw seven dinosaurs! Ahhhhhh!" Mavis started jumping up and down so erratically that even Mr Bradshaw let out a chuckle at the odd sight.

"Hang all the elements! Now I understand!" Mavis said breathlessly.

"Understand what dear?"

"Why Boris wanted to stay. I mean this is the most remarkable place in the whole wide world. Just look at the life here, look around you at the wondrous trees, the glorious air not to mention the beauty of these magnificent and intelligent dinosaurs!" Mavis flung herself down on the floor and stared up at the clear blue sky. "It is really the only possible place to be."

The children smiled at each other during Mavis's outburst because they were all thinking the same thing; the only other person they knew who talked in this manner was the Professor. They had to get them back together, no matter what.

After a few moments of silence, Bunny laid her hand on her sisters and asked, "Mavis dear, what is the plan, shall we make haste due west as before?"

Mavis propped up her blond, curly head with her other hand and replied casually, "No need, a T-Rex will come to us in no time, all we have to do is follow the Edmontosaurus' over there, if they move we move.

"Obscene!"

"It is actually a good plan." Raj said, avoiding Mr Bradshaw's fierce glare.

"Well if we are going to track them, should we not be in the forest, close to them." Arthur suggested.

"But we are close!" Mavis said springing up and pointing to the forest's edge about ten meters away. Bunny cleaned her glasses for the hundredth time since they had arrived and stared at the forest. After minutes of staring at the barks of trees and tangled undergrowth she saw them, she gasped and stepped backwards. "They are everywhere!" she whispered in horror.

Mavis was clapping with delight, "I know such an efficient camouflage! You have been a stone's throw away from them all this time and never knew it!"

Mr Bradshaw slowly moved behind his daughter and placed his hands on her shoulders. "It's OK daddy, they won't hurt us; they eat leaves, not humans." Amber said as she placed her hand on her father's

"Gee whizz I am not waiting to find out!"

Mr Bradshaw was just about to leap over the rocks in the direction of the desert when he felt a sturdy grasp on his elbow, "Sit down, Preacher Bradshaw." Bunny's shadow loomed over the scared preacher, "If Mavis says we stay, then we stay."

Mr Bradshaw did not fancy being chased again by Bunny, he had no more fight left in him so submitted and sat down on a bumpy rock whilst contemplating the best way to escape this preposterous situation.

Bunny poured everyone a glass of water and the adventurers chatted and ate sandwiches whilst waiting for a T-Rex they hoped would be Tony to turn up. The rocks they were sitting on were not the most comfortable of seats, but it would do, and shade from a neighbouring bush kept them cool enough under the merciless sun.

"Mrs Inchenstein," Raj said quietly.

"Yes?"

"The likelihood of the T-Rex that happens to hunt this herd of Edmontasaurus' is pretty, well, unlikely to be Tony…" Raj said.

Mavis sat up and moved next to Raj, "I understand more and more why my husband was so fond of you!" she beamed.

Raj blushed uncomfortably.

"Look I know the chances are slim, but a T-Rex will come, and we don't know if they hunt in packs or alone. We have to collect more data in order to analyse the behaviour. If one does come then, maybe we can follow it and see where that leads."

Raj began to protest but Mavis cut him short, "It is better than wondering aimlessly around the desert, believe me this is the best way to make progress, we just have to wait and follow the herd." Raj thought back to the last time they followed the herd per say and that led them into a mud-pit. "I can't believe you were going to go back to Texas and not say goodbye!" Arthur said quietly to Amber, flicking his hair out of his face and staring at her blue eyes in the raw sunlight. It was as if he was seeing her for the first time and he simply could not imagine never seeing her again.

"I did not have the chance! I was literately pulled out of bed and into the taxi!" Amber said awkwardly, "It was not my fault…"

"Hey, I know, I don't want to upset you." Arthur pushed the arid soil around with a twig. He still kept his eyes fixed on Amber, "It's just, I donno, I guess what I am trying to say is,"

"AHHHHHHHHHHHHHHHHHHHHHHHHHHHHHHHH!" Mr Bradshaw screamed as he was suddenly raised two meters into the sky.

"Heavens on earth!" Bunny cried as she witnessed the rock, which the Preacher had been resting on, lurch upwards and take Amber's father with it.

"Wowsers!" Arthur screamed and grabbed hold of Amber's hand, just in time to hold her back from following her father.

"Daddy!" Amber sobbed. She tried again to follow her father, but Arthur wrapped his arms around her and held her firmly.

"What on earth is going on?" Bunny asked for the umpteenth time.

"Oh golly, he had been sitting on the tail of an Euoplocephalus!" Mavis said, completely stunned. "How extraordinary that we did not notice!"

"Hold on Mr Bradshaw." Bunny bellowed holding her hands to her mouth trying to imitate a gramophone effect.

"I am trying!" Mr Bradshaw screamed as he wrapped his legs around the club tail and tried with all his power to grip onto the bumpy rock that turned out to belong to an Euoplocephalus.

"Nobody panic, I can handle this!" Mavis shouted. She moved cautiously next to the 6-meter-long dinosaur who was lunging forward at a very slow pace.

"It looks awfully, well awful looking!" Bunny commented as she watched the dinosaur with horror.

"He is actually alright," Raj began to explain, "I mean I see why you think he is terrifying to look at, but he is actually just really well equipped in self-defence. Kind of like an ancient Batmobile!"

"Awesome!" Arthur murmured to himself, not wanting to upset Amber who still struggled every few seconds to break free.

"What are you talking about Raj?" Serendipity asked.

"Well look at his back, he is covered in plates of bones, they are like armoured tiles all over his body to protect him." He beckoned the others to walk along the side of the dinosaur but at a safe distance, "Look, even his eyelids are protected!"

"Great so he is well protected!" Amber said annoyed with Raj's enthusiasm, "How is this protection going to help my dad?" And she tried again to go closer to the Batmobile, but Arthur's grip was as tight as steel.

"It means that no one will attack him unless they are stupid or desperate…." Raj's mind trailed off to one of the conversations that he had had with the Professor about the Euoplocephalus and how no dinosaur would dare to attack it because its tail (the same tail that Mr Bradshaw was clinging onto) is a whopping 20 kilos and one blow from it could cause a T-Rex to be thrown to the floor, never to rise again.

"So, what you are saying mate, is actually very reassuring." Arthur said loudly so Amber would listen. "Well yes of sorts," Raj pushed his glasses up his nose, "I mean the only way to eat him would be to flip him."

Amber gasped, "What do you mean flip him?"

Arthur glared at Raj and tightened his grip on Amber.

"He would have to be flipped over because his tummy is his soft spot." Raj's voice trailed off to a murmur as he felt Arthur's eyes burrowing into him.

"Children, I really think we need to stop talking about flipping and soft tummies and try and work out what to do next!" Bunny said assertively in her teacher's voice.

The children fell silent and continued to walk next the Euoplocephalus into the heart of the desert trying to think of a solution.

"Can you not jump down Preacher?" Bunny suggested.

"I am not letting go!" Mr Bradshaw screamed, his cheek pressed so tightly on the dinosaur's tail that dents were slowly forming in his skin.

Mavis, who had previously been up ahead of the group returned and said quietly to her sister, "This is all very inconvenient, he is leading us away from the herd of Edmontosaurus and the chance of spotting a T-Rex!" Mavis folded her arms.

"Inconvenient as this is, we can hardly leave him up there!" Bunny said and then glared softly as she saw that Mavis thought that it was not such a bad idea.

"OK, OK, but he is such a pain in the…"

Bunny glared some more.

"OK fine, let me think." Mavis started racking her brains, searching for a plan.

She beckoned Bunny and they went to talk to the children.

"Right so here is what we do," Mavis began, "We follow the Euoplocephalus until he gets tired and sits down again and then your dad can jump off."

"Is that it? We just wait? Just follow?" Amber said disappointedly.

"Do you have a better idea?" Mavis asked.

"Daddy can you hold on until the dinosaur gets tired and lies down again?"

"Do I have a choice?" Mr Bradshaw grunted with anger.

"No, you don't so hang on or jump off!" Bunny shouted firmly.

Mr Bradshaw cursed under his breath and reluctantly held on. There was nothing else he could do. Unfortunately for Mr Bradshaw the ancient Batmobile showed no sign of fatigue three hours later. With each heavy step, the dinosaur sent mountains of sand and dust into the air which caked the preacher and children in a thin layer of crusty dirt. The adventurers were no longer protected from the raging hot sun as there was not a tree in sight; the luscious forest where they had originally landed was now miles behind them and all that lay ahead were empty plains and random rocks jutting out from the thirsty soil.

"This is unbearable!" Bunny sighed to herself.

"We have been walking for hours!" Serendipity moaned, dragging her feet as she trailed behind the others.

"Daddy?" Amber coughed "Please takes some water?" and she attempted for the hundredth time to offer her father some bottled water, but he refused to lift his head from the security of the dinosaur's tail.

Mavis thought Mr Bradshaw was behaving like a complete wuss; he was only two meters high and if he had any balls in him he would have jumped off three hours ago and not made everyone traipse into the wilderness away from the Edmontosaurus. She started thinking of another way to get him down, maybe if she used some rope and made a lasso and literately yanked him down that might work...Her mind wondered to more drastic measures

347

but before any valid solution could unfold the Euoplocephalus halted suddenly and stayed eerily still.

Raj crashed into the back of Bunny by accident and Arthur grabbed hold of Amber's hand before she had time to approach the Batmobile. Mr Bradshaw prayed that the monster he was riding would finally lie down again; he was sure that the beast had stopped so he opened one eye and observed his surroundings. Mini tornadoes spun around the arid land like abandoned spin tops. Mr Bradshaw opened the other eye and slowly, ever so slowly lifted his head.

Mavis approached the tail and reached up her hand to the preacher. "This might be our only chance now you have got to just jump! I promise I will catch you!" Mavis shouted but most of the sentence was swept away in the wind.

Mr Bradshaw's throat was so dry he could not even swallow let alone talk. He closed his eyes and prayed, but he could not focus, his mind was spinning like the mini tornadoes he had just seen and every now and again he heard the word jump, jump, jump attack him again and again. After a few more disturbed moments, he surrendered to his fate. The preacher was just about to leap to the ground when the tail started to swing violently from side to side.

"Holy crickets!" Arthur cried.

It was with all Mr Bradshaw's strength that he managed to throw himself back down onto the club tail and he wrapped his legs around it in desperation, clinging for his life as he was swept from left to right, right to left. The movements were getting faster and faster and Mr Bradshaw was certain that his end had arrived and began to pray. He prayed for the souls of his followers in Texas, he prayed for his wife and he prayed for his only daughter, Amber.

Bunny instinctively huddled the children away from the vicious tail and lead them to the safety of a nearby rock.

"Help him! Please!" Amber sobbed, her tears splitting the dirt on her face into little streams.

"What's it doing Mavis?" Bunny whispered shuddering in dread, "This is not going to end well I fear."

The monstrous wind was getting stronger and stronger, so Mavis shielded her eyes searching for the danger that had made the Euoplocephalus prepare for a fight. Her blond curls fought across her face making it harder and harder for her to see anything and then, in the distance she saw it. Mavis froze.

Bunny and the children kept on shouting and talking but they soon became silent when the threatening shadow coming towards them from the horizon became visible.

27

The Grey Ape

"I have got a lovely bunch of coconuts didilideedee,

There they are all standing in a row,

Bum, bum, bum,

Pink ones, green ones, some as big as your head!"

Tony snorted in time to the Professor's tune or, so it seemed to the Professor, so he carried on at a higher octave with extra passion. As he sung, he swung merrily in his self-made hammock which was precariously hung between Tony's two front claws. The Professor was very proud of his new abode and it was actually very comfortable for an old cotton sheet. Each end was tied to Tony's front arms and the T-rex did not show any annoyance with his new accessory. Professor Inchenstein had been living with Tony in the Late Cretaceous period for six months and it had been the six most exciting months of his life! He had learnt more Boy Scout skills than his old teacher Geeves could have ever imagined! He could successfully catch fish with a self-made wooden rod with a chopping knife tied to the end; he was able to rustle up a fire under two minutes from twigs and dried bracken, and the skill he felt had developed the most was his culinary prowess. Indeed, the Professor rustled up a Cimolestes and Alphadon stew with fried ants on the side – the meal was so delicious that he named it Crunchy Ancient Rat Hotpot! Of course, life in the ancient land was not always hunky-dory and smooth sailing! The Professor nearly got crushed by a falling

Alamosaurus's tail when Tony decided he wanted to eat it and swiftly attacked the poor creature until he came thundering down to his doom and was eaten alive! Another disastrous moment was when they could not find any water for three whole days! Each watering hole they arrived at had dried up and Tony was becoming almost delirious; on the third day Boris had to slap Tony around the face (several times) to force the seven-tonne lizard to get up and when that did not work, the Professor resorted to poking twigs up the dinosaur's nostrils which eventually had the desired effect! At the end of the third day they finally stumbled upon a pathetic looking watering hole that was more like an enormous puddle, but it did the job and Tony and the Professor lapped up the remaining water until the puddle was almost empty. Even though there had been these near-death experiences and some, the excitement and discoveries that the Professor experienced compensated for all the grave hopping he had endured! He reassured himself that this was the best way to spend the rest of his life, even if it meant that it would be cut short at a moment's notice! The Professor kept a diary and he scribbled in it as much as he could whilst being swung from side to side in his sheet. He documented the species that he came across in great detail, he often wrote about what had happened that day, about Tony's behaviour which Doctor Dino thought to be fascinating. The Professor observed how Tony was a bit of a loner; ever since his mother had died he did not socialise much with the other dinosaurs or T-Rexes, if they did on the rare occasion come across another T-Rex, Tony was always wise enough to keep his distance and not engage in any direct combat. If Tony was planning to hunt and pounce on an unsuspecting prey, then he always gave the Professor enough time to step out of his hammock and watch from the safety of the side-lines. Boris observed how similar Tony's hunting technique was to a leopard. Tony would loom closely but remain hidden, and creep closer and closer until he was only a few metres away. Then in one aggressive leap he would bash the target so hard with the side of his head that he usually stunned them immediately giving him the perfect opportunity to crush their bewildered necks with his dagger shaped teeth! A very skilled hunter his Tony was indeed, the Professor thought proudly. The Professor had no idea what day it was, for what did it matter out here? No one pestered him to mark papers or teach; he was the freest he had ever felt in his entire life. Evidently, he missed his Mavis immensely and so he dedicated his diary to her which made him feel like he spoke to her on a daily basis and every entry began, Dear Mavis. On this extremely sweltering day, (the exact day being unknown to the Professor) Doctor Dino sang happily and swung in time to Tony's footsteps. Every time his stomach rumbled he sung louder, trying to bury his noisy complaining tummy. The Professor tried not to think when the last time he ate had been, and what was worse was that there were no more fried beetles in his snack jar to nibble on! Even though Doctor Dino had adapted considerably well to living with a T-Rex he did find it hard to cope with the binge eating that Tony was so fond of doing. For example, Tony would kill a Triceratops and practically eat all of it over a day or two, once Tony was full he would move on and then not stop to eat for sometimes two whole days! The Professor tried to stock pile as much as he could on these eating occasions but sometimes he would find himself with no snacks to munch on and unfortunately this was one of those days. Suddenly the Professor's singing was interrupted by an almighty noise that sounded like the Earth's crust was about to cave in! It took Doctor Dino a moment to calm his heart rate as he realised that it was in fact Tony's belly rumbling (not the Earth's crust) and he hoped this was a signal that they would soon be on the hunt for their next meal. The heat was unforgivable on this particular unknown day and the wind blew the Professor's hammock with such colossal force that at one stage Boris did a full 360-degree spin. The Professor also noticed a change of pace in Tony and wondered what was going on; he lifted his sweat drenched mop and cautiously peeked over the sheet. He could barely see a thing the wind was pushing everything in its path around in such a ruthless manner. The Professor kept on searching across the plain for what he hoped would soon be his dinner and then he was flung back in the hammock with such force that he hit his head on his saucepan and felt slightly dizzy. Tony's pace had turned into a charge, something that he rarely did, and the Professor was dying to see what was for supper! He attempted again to poke his head above the safety of the sheet.

ΔΔΔ

Amber saw her father being thrown from side to side by the most disgusting monster she had ever seen in her entire life, and all of a sudden, she felt terribly guilty; guilty that she had chosen rescuing the Professor over staying with her father. It was her fault he was about to die, and she wept uncontrollably. Arthur did not know what to do apart from hold onto her as tightly as he could in order to protect her from the same fate as her father. When Amber saw the danger that was approaching she screamed even louder for her father, but it was no use, her cries were kidnaped by the wind. Mavis and Bunny grabbed hold of the children and hurled them against the wind to the other side of the rock; it was not safe to run; the wind was too ferocious, and the attacking dinosaur could target them next. Mavis thought it best to stay as still as possible. Amber could not bear to watch and buried her head in Arthur's chest.

"We must do something!" Bunny shouted at Mavis through the wind.

"It's too dangerous! It's just a matter of time before…"

Mavis looked away from the preacher as she thought about the moment when it would soon be over.

"It could be Tony!" Serendipity shouted as loudly as she could, "Maybe I can stop him from attacking?" She said timidly.

Mavis clasped Serendipity's shoulders and cried, "There is no way you are going out there! Even if it is Tony he is charging at us. Look!" And she pointed to the ferocious T-Rex that was gaining speed with every stride and only moments away from the Batmobile. "He will trample you in the process. There is nothing we can do!" Mavis said resolutely. While the children and sisters were cowering behind an isolated rock awaiting the doomed fate of the preacher, the Professor was being jerked around in every direction; he felt as if he was on the most terrifying roller coaster at Alton Towers. Donk! Again, the saucepan struck him on the head, so he grasped it close to him preventing it from hitting him again at its leisure. He yelled to Tony hoping he would slow down and listen, but of course he didn't and carried on charging. The Professor managed to get into a foetal position ready to absorb the impact as best he could and waited fearfully. To the Professor's surprise the impact shock never arrived and instead he felt Tony slow down and continue to run at a slower pace until eventually he stopped and then began pacing erratically. Doctor Dino did not care about the danger anymore, he had to know what was going on and thrust his head out of the hammock and let out an astonished shriek of surprise.

"Hang all the elements!" The Professor cursed under his breath. What on earth is going on? Why are we attacking an Euoplocephalus and what is that unusual creature on its tail? He wondered frantically.

He struck Tony on the claw with his saucepan as hard as he could fathom (this was usually the signal that he needed to get down) but Tony did not listen, he was too busy pacing around his prey, working out the best way to attack.

The Professor stuck his head out once again and tried to find an escape plan before Tony would have a chance to attack.

"You are a stupid fool!" He hollered at Tony, "You are going to get us both killed! No dinosaur attacks a Euoplocephalus and I know you are not that hungry you are just being greedy now off you go, turn around, be a good boy and listen to Boris!"

But no matter how many times Boris struck Tony on the claw with his saucepan or tried to verbally reason with him, he kept on lunging forward attempting to catch the Batmobile off guard. With every move Tony made, the Euoplocephalus turned his tail to the predator and thrust it so violently that Tony often stumbled backwards trying to avoid his legs being smashed to smithereens.

"I am far too old for this!" Boris mumbled and tied a rope around his waist ready to escape if things escalated.

Tony was so close to the tail now, no matter which way he turned the Euoplocephalus was too quick and kept the tail swinging and protecting him as best he could. It was clear there would soon be a winner and a loser. The Professor looked out again and to his complete surprise he noticed that the animal clasping the swinging tale looked somewhat similar to himself. Could this be the first man? Boris thought excitedly. It must be an early species that has never been documented… It looks rather distorted and peculiar, maybe it is half human, half reptile! Well whatever it is, it is my duty to save this wretched animal from imminent doom so at least I can study it!

Doctor Dino tightened his rope and decided it was time for extreme action. He tied the other end securely around Tony 's front arm and then heaved himself out of the hammock and slowly threaded himself down the rope until he was in reach of the peculiar half reptile half human.

"Take my hand!" Doctor Dino cried.

Mr Bradshaw did not move.

The Professor, concerned that the animal reptile might actually be dead, decided to kick it hard on its backside.

"Oh, dear Lord!" Amber's father screamed as he was sure that he was about to be eaten.

"What did you say?" Doctor Dino shouted, somewhat stunned with the level of English which came out from the human lizard he was trying to save.

"Grab my hand, I am trying to save you!" The Professor screamed.

Mr Bradshaw looked up and saw to his complete disbelief a swinging ape on a rope that seemed to be speaking to him in a backward language. The ape had grey fur and an overgrown mane, deep set wrinkles and extremely lean build, almost alien like. Mr Bradshaw ducked quickly as the ape came swinging back towards him, trying to pull him off the tail. The preacher clung on even tighter.

None of the children had worked out yet that the attacker was in fact Tony and their beloved teacher. There was too much dust blowing in the air for them to see what was going on and Mavis would not let any of them move in case they were spotted by the T-Rex. Bunny felt dread thundering around her entire body, how could she ever live with herself knowing that she was responsible for the death of a child's father? She turned towards the dinosaurs and saw the gigantic predator skate around the swinging tail trying frantically to attack. Amber's father was doing incredibly well to keep holding on, but Bunny imagined it was only a matter of seconds before he let go and be gobbled up. She had to do something. Bunny thrust her arm in her handbag searching for an appropriate weapon, her hands felt something cold and metal and she tightened her fingers around the cylinder shape. There was no time to think, her dread turned to adrenalin and she shot off towards the danger.

"Take care of the children!" Bunny shouted in Mavis' ear as she ran out onto the plain.

Bunny ran up to the head of the Euoplocephalus, said a prayer and reached up as far as she could and sprayed her musk scent with all her might into the dinosaur's right eye.

The Euoplocephalus was not used to this kind of attack and shut his eyes for protection but some of the musk had already got through and the dinosaur suddenly froze in a panic.

Doctor Dino knew this was his chance; he grabbed hold of the human lizard and yanked him off the tail. Mr Bradshaw loosened his grip, he had no more fight left and let himself be hurled off the tail and landed with a thud. The Professor wriggled himself out of the rope and grabbed the creature at his feet and dragged him away from the dinosaurs to safety.

Tony also took advantage of this sudden stillness from his prey and smashed his head under the belly of the Euoplocephalus flipping him over. It landed like a helpless beetle, wriggling with desperation, his soft tummy finally exposed.

Tony let out an almighty roar of victory which made Amber faint in Arthur's arms! Tony then opened his mouth and started ripping flesh from the upside down Batmobile. Blood splatted on the rock where the children were hiding making the children feel sick. It was an absolutely gruesome sight. The Euoplocephalus kept moving his legs and screeching for help, but there was no point, his insides were being shredded out of him and he was doomed. Mr Bradshaw buried his head in his arms, fearful that the grey ape would try and eat him.

Doctor Dino knew how to handle peculiar creatures and he gently held its hand, which to the Professor's disbelief was uncannily similar to his own and shook it.

Mr Bradshaw felt the dry skin in his and looked up and saw a pair of bright blue eyes smiling down at him.

"What are you?" He asked, his voice gruff with dryness and fear.

"I am man." Doctor Dino replied. "What are you?"

"I am man" the preacher replied.

Both grey ape and human reptile stared at each other for a few profound moments trying to make sense of each other. "Is it over?" Amber asked Arthur as she came around. Tears were streaming from her eyes and she could not see a thing, she just hoped it was quick and her father had felt no pain.

"I am not sure." Arthur replied. Cautiously he stood up, bringing Amber to her feet.

Arthur peered over the side of the rock and gasped with shock as he saw the T-Rex ripping and gulping down tonnes of red flesh at a time. He quickly turned back to Amber, "Don't look. Please just stay here, let me find out what has happened."

Amber stood sobbing leaned against the large rock beside her for support as she wept uncontrollably. Serendipity hugged Amber and the two girls stood waiting for the boys and Mavis to investigate what had happened to the preacher. Mavis grabbed hold of Arthur and Raj, and together they slowly approached the repugnant scene in search of Amber's father.

"Do you think he made it?" Raj whispered to Arthur.

Arthur shrugged unconvincingly.

Mavis was searching frantically for any sign of life and then out of the corner of her eye she saw something move. "Quick follow me boys!" and she sped into the wind.

When Mavis realised that it was Mr Bradshaw she ran up to him and hugged him, crying with relief. Arthur and Raj joined in and the boys cried with emotion. Mr Bradshaw was quite taken aback by such physical contact (something he was not too familiar with) and patted Arthur awkwardly on the head. When Mavis finally released her grasp and asked what had happened, Mr Bradshaw pointed towards the grey ape that had saved him.

Mavis turned her head and let out a scream of surprise. "What is it?" she whispered to the preacher.

"Am I dreaming?" The Professor choked.

It was Raj that recognised him first, despite the Professor's ape-like appearance, he was still wearing a spotty bow tie that was tied in an untidy knot and popping out from underneath the Professor's overgrow beard.

"Professor!" he shouted with happiness and rushed into his arms. He held him so tightly, it felt so good to be with him again that he never wanted to let go. Arthur managed to pull him aside to make room for Mavis. Professor Inchenstein just stared at Mavis, his eyes as wide as saucers. "Is it really you?" he reached out his hand to touch her.

Mavis, ignoring the fact that her husband resembled a bedraggled baboon touched his out-stretched hand.

"My Boris!" Mavis sobbed.

Doctor Dino had no words. The raw emotion that he was feeling could not be expressed by the simplicity of the English Language. He pulled Mavis close to him and cupped her face in his wrinkly hands. Their eyes met and for the first time in twenty-five years the plate of metal that encased the Professor's heart disintegrated to dust. He could breathe once again. The Professor held his Mavis in his arms and they sobbed with overwhelming joy.

"Daddy!!" Amber yelled. "Daddy you are alive!" Amber rushed towards her father, ignoring the giant monsters covered in blood to her right and raced into his arms.

Mr Bradshaw was again touched by such warm, human contact and he hugged his daughter back and thought to himself how he should do this more often!

Serendipity, Raj and Arthur watched the happy scene in front of them with a mixture of joy and relief. All was well once more, the Professor was back with Mavis and Amber's father was alive.

Serendipity stared, mesmerized at her Tony eating ferociously the dead Euoplocephalus and she could hardly contain here excitement. Even though Tony was now 12 meters high and his head was the size of a Land Rover, she still wanted to kiss him and stroke his scaly belly.

Arthur looked around and suddenly realised someone was missing. "Where's Log Head?"

Raj pushed his glasses up his nose and squinted into the wind, trying to look for Bunny, she must be somewhere he thought. "No idea, where could she be?"

Serendipity tugged at Mavis' sleeve to let her know that Bunny was nowhere to be seen. In an instant Mavis broke away from her husband and raced towards the dying Euoplocephalus.

Boris darted after her and they called and called and searched and searched but there was no trace of Bunny.

"Do you think Tony ate her?" Arthur said quietly to Raj.

Raj was frantically analysing the situation; Log Head would not have run away and if she did, then she would have returned by now. Tony was too focused on the overturned Euoplocephalus so why would he eat her? The only place she could be.... Raj gulped hard and shouted "She is under the Euoplocephalus! She must be underneath the dinosaur!"

The party stared at the six-meter-long dinosaur, his stomach ripped open, broken ribs jutting into the air and blood absolutely everywhere. Mavis fell to her knees. Boris held her in his arms and everyone became silent with shock. Serendipity had an idea and crept away towards Tony. Tony still had his head buried inside the stomach of the dead dinosaur and it took a moment before he pulled it out of the half-eaten belly flinging up some intestines in the air and swallowing them whole as if it were a string of tagliatelle. Tony spotted Serendipity and he turned his head towards her and snorted. Serendipity hesitated, blood and guts were dripping down from his mouth and his white, bone-piercing teeth were now stained a vibrant red. Tony looked terrifying. Serendipity took a step forward and Tony bowed his head. Serendipity ran and flung herself at the giant, scaly head.

No one had noticed that Serendipity had disappeared, they were all too upset about Bunny but suddenly, the dead Batmobile started to move.

"Goodness me!" Mr Bradshaw shouted.

"Look! It's Tony!" Raj cried.

To everyone's amazement, (especially Mr Bradshaw's) Tony placed one of the Euoplocephalus' hind legs in his mouth and started to drag him backwards.

"How did he know what to do?" Amber asked confused.

Raj turned around and noticed Serendipity's absence, "It was Serendipity." Raj said under his breath with amazement.

Mavis leapt forward searching for her sister in the flattened sand. Boris was one step behind her, but he feared the worse, who could possibly survive being crushed by a two tonne Ankylosaur?

ΔΔΔ

Mavis was frantically pushing the sand around where the dinosaur had been lying. The children, Boris and Mr Bradshaw helped, digging best they could with their hands. Digging and hoping.

Minutes later Arthur yelled, "I found something!"

Mavis rushed to Arthur and pushed the sand away and eventually her hand felt something other than sand. She clenched the large plastic button between her fingers then traced her way up the jacket until she reached her sister's face. Mavis yanked Bunny's head out of the sand and brushed away all the sand and dust so that her sister's face became visible. Boris leapt to her side, grabbed Bunny's wrist from the sand and felt for a pulse.

Everyone watched in silence.

"I feel it!" The Professor choked, "It is faint, but it is there."

"Oh, thank goodness." Amber sighed.

Raj handed Mavis a bottle of water as requested and Mavis gently cleaned Bunny's face and dabbed her dry lips. Mavis hung her head low over her sister's and her blond curls fell limply with despair.

It was such an immense shock for everyone to think that Bunny might not make it. Bunny was the one who took them to Heathrow and found Amber in time, Bunny was the one who kept Mr Bradshaw from running away and in the end, it was Bunny who saved the preacher from imminent death. The four children stared down at the frail teacher, crushed in the sand and were overcome by a deep guilt; they felt ashamed that they had ever called her Log Head and that they were so terrified of her at school. Bunny was brave, Bunny was a hero and now she lay dying in the sand and there was nothing anyone could do to save her.

The children's guilty silence was broken by a coughing coming from the ground.

"Oh Bunny! Bunny!" Mavis wept.

Bunny slowly opened her eyes and saw her sister's sad upside down, brown eyes staring at her.

"Did we save him?" Bunny whispered.

Mavis nodded, unable to speak.

Professor Inchenstein cautiously crawled up towards Bunny's head and choked down a cry of emotion when their eyes met.

"You look like you could do with a good scrub!" Bunny said wryly.

"Forgive my animal like appearance dear, dear Bunny." The Professor replied.

Bunny smiled, "We found him Mavis!"

Mavis' eyes brimmed with tears.

"Don't cry." Bunny said gently, "You can be together now at last!"

"Oh, Bunny I am so so sorry." Boris said sobbing "I should never have left! This is all my fault!" And the Professor started to sob so loudly, his whole body jerked up and down with emotion.

"Are you hurt" Mavis whispered.

"Not at all!" Bunny said somewhat cheerily, "I cannot feel a thing."

Mavis and Boris exchanged a worried glance and then looked back at Bunny.

"Bunny I am sorry I left the way I did – it is just I was scared that if I saw you then I would be too ashamed to leave."

"Boris you don't owe me anything."

"Oh, Bunny there are many things I wanted to say to you before I left, but I did not have the guts."

"What did you want to say?" Bunny said, her voice barely audible.

"There was one lesson I did at school with the kids and I think I went a bit too far..."

"Only one?" A flash of mischief darted across Bunny's eyes

"It was my wretched Wall of Hullabaloo!" The Professor sighed "I did not mean for the kids to disrespect you and your beliefs!"

"Boris, I have been miserable for such a long time that it made me – I am sad to say, strict and somewhat rigid." Bunny's breath became coarse, so she continued slowly, "You see I turned to my faith when the accident happened to Mavis because it was the only thing that really gave me any comfort. I believed that if I prayed and prayed and did not lose my faith, no matter how hard it was sometimes, then Mavis would eventually wake up."

Mavis wiped the tears that were pouring continuously from her eyes.

363

"I know Bunny and that is why I did not want you to think that I did not respect your decision to turn to religion for support" Boris choked. "I just want you to know that I never meant for you to be hurt by my teachings."

"Boris, please I know you are a little eccentric, but I should not have taken my own view so seriously. We are here to teach the children, to give them knowledge and to let them decide the truth, not ram our own ideas down their throats and I believe we are both guilty of that."

Bunny closed her eyes and Mavis gasped in fear. Boris squeezed his wife's hand and they stared fixated at Bunny's face, hoping that her eyes would open again.

Bunny was still breathing. Just.

"Bunny don't leave me now. Not after everything we have been through?" Mavis cried, "I feel so guilty, since I woke up I have been terrible company, focusing only on Boris' disappearance and not ever thinking about you."

Boris bowed his head in shame.

"I just thought that you and I would have all the time in the world and now..."

Bunny forced her eyes open, "Mavis, listen to me, I have lived a good life. I have taught my religion and that is what I wanted to do! You have been asleep for 25 years and now you need to live. You need to be with your husband and you need to promise me that you will be happy." Bunny forced a smile, "For my sake be happy."

Bunny closed her eyes again but carried on breathing ever so softly, her chest barely moving.

The sad silence was broken by Raj shouting, "Look! Look at the sky! Oh my God! Professor, Mavis look at the sky!"

Everyone turned their eyes to the sky and watched a beam of light the size of Wales soar through the blue atmosphere.

"Oh gee, is that the space rock you guys have all been going on about?" Amber asked nervously.

"Nebulous' nether regions!" Doctor Dino whispered.

"Rub the claw!" Bunny said softly.

The Professor shouted at everyone to gather round.

"What about Tony? Can't we save him too?" Serendipity asked desperately.

"You need to say goodbye and let nature take its course." The Professor said gently to Serendipity. "Go quickly!"

Serendipity ran to Tony's side, but he was so busy crunching bones and ripping the flesh off the fresh carcass that she had to stroke his hind leg before he turned towards her. Tony bent his head down low and let Serendipity caress him. Serendipity sniffed quietly and said, "This is the last time I will see you."

Tony snorted.

"I don't know if you noticed the strange light in the sky just now – but it is not good news. Not good news for anyone."

Tony snorted again and then rubbed his snout on her tummy. Serendipity felt his scaly head against her cheek and she sobbed with all her strength as she said goodbye to her one and only Tony.

"Hurry!" Doctor Dino shouted. "Serendipity get over here NOW!"

Serendipity looked for the meteorite in the sky, but it had vanished. She clasped the claw in her hand and ran towards Bunny and her friends.

"Stay with me Bunny, stay with me, we will be home soon..." Mavis whispered in her sister's ear.

Mr Bradshaw began to pray.

Just as Serendipity reached her friends a massive light illuminated the skies as if a billion lightning bolts all crashed down at once.

28

The Palaeocene Epoch

Darkness, complete black darkness was all that could be seen when the adventurers opened their eyes. The Professor noticed straight away the difference in climate and how the hot sand that was once beneath him was now a cold, smooth concrete. The dusty, stale air that he breathed into his nostrils had a familiar comforting smell and he knew that they had all arrived safely in his beloved science cupboard. Arthur groped around trying to find the door knob and accidently tweaked Mr Bradshaw's nose in the process!

"Ah I am under attack!" Amber's father cried out.

"No, you're not, it was me!" Arthur said awkwardly.

Finally, Arthur clasped the cold metal handle in his hand and opened the cupboard door.

The group fell out into the science lab and sprawled onto the cold tiles Mavis leapt up and stared around looking for her sister.

"Bunny!" she cried in an awful hollow rasp.

She darted back in the cupboard and let out a wail that gave the children goose bumps. Boris groped in the dark cupboard and grabbed hold of Mavis and he held her tightly while she sobbed into his chest. The children and Mr Bradshaw stared into the cupboard not sure what to do. Raj edged his way to the door frame and peaked inside, moments later he reappeared and shook his head sadly. There was no sign of Bunny anywhere.

ΔΔΔ

The pupils of Pembridge Hall had reached the end of the summer term and the children gathered in the playground to say goodbye to one another. Most of the students chatted excitedly about their upcoming holidays on the French Rivera or other exotic locations, apart from four friends; who stood huddled, away from the rest of their class in the far corner of the playground. Arthur was showing off his skills on his new state of the art fidget spinner to Raj, while the girls talked away excitedly.

"Promise me you will write?" Amber said, raising her voice and addressing Arthur and Raj too.

"Write?" Arthur shouted over his shoulder, "Amber you are such a dinosaur!" he teased. "Next you will tell me to send my letters to you with a pigeon."

Amber blushed and smiled.

"Well how else are we going to stay in touch? We don't have a computer and my father does not like it when the telephone is in use in case one of his parish members might try and reach him..."

"I was thinking about this problem, so I bought you this!" Serendipity placed a white box in Amber's arms.

Arthur quickly stopped whizzing his fidget spinner and rushed over to see what Serendipity had given Amber.

"Oh gee, I said no presents guys!" Amber said as she stared confused at the white box in her hands.

"Oh wicked!" Arthur said and grabbed it out of Amber's hands and opened it.

"Em, thanks, but what is it?" Amber asked.

"You got her an iPad?" Raj said stunned.

Now it was Serendipity's turn to blush.

"Oh Serendipity, you should not have spent so much money on this ipid, I don't have a clue how to use it!"

"It's an iPad!" Arthur teased again laughing.

"Pid, pad, pod! Whatever it is I don't know what to do with it!"

"You will learn." Serendipity said softly. "I have already downloaded all the apps you will need and look here you have Skype, FaceTime and WhatsApp so we can video chat!"

Amber could feel the tears starting to swell, "I am going to miss you guys so much." She sniffed hard, "You are the only friends I ever really had."

Arthur watched her crying and held her hand, he whispered in her ear making sure the others could not overhear, "Friends for life remember?"

"I remember." Amber said wiping her eyes and smiling at her new screen while Serendipity tried to show her how it all worked.

"Oi Love Birds!" Rocky shouted from the other side of the playground.

"Just ignore him." Serendipity murmured as they all watched Rocky and his gang head towards them.

Raj pushed his glasses up his nose and shifted nervously from side to side.

"What have we here?" Rocky said provokingly.

Arthur clenched his fidget spinner in his fist. Rocky walked straight to Amber and grabbed the iPad out of her hands.

"Hey give it back!" Serendipity said and tried to get the iPad back from Rocky, but he held it above his head and being the tallest in the class, he knew no-one could take it from him.

"Rocky why are you such a jerk all the time?" Arthur asked.

The gang stopped pushing Raj around and became silent. No one ever spoke to Rocky like that. Rocky threw the iPad to the floor and the screen smashed. Serendipity quickly picked it up and grabbed Amber's hand, dragging her out of the way.

"What did you say?" Rocky said, rubbing his fist in his palm.

"You heard me!" Arthur said bravely.

The group of five boys closed in on Arthur. Raj picked himself up and went to stand next to Arthur.

"What have we here? Your little girlfriend is going to fight with you!" Rocky said meanly, laughing at Raj.

"It's quite clear that all you need is a big cuddle!" Raj said loudly, his voice trembling as he spoke.

Arthur and one of the other boys snorted with laughter. Rocky looked confused.

Raj felt more confident and spoke firmly this time, "It's true. Rocky you are so horrible to everyone, I actually feel sorry for you."

"You feel sorry for me?" Rocky spat at Raj.

"Yes, I do actually. If someone loved you then you would not be so mean all the time."

Rocky went red in the face.

"All you need is a big cuddle and you might feel better about yourself." Raj concluded.

"Watch it Paki!"

"Don't call him that. His name is Raj and he is Indian not Pakistani. Not that you are clever enough to know the difference." Arthur said defiantly.

The gang of boys looked puzzled, no one had ever stood up to Rocky before and they were impressed that Raj had the guts to do this and be smart enough to make Rocky look like a complete idiot.

"Let's get out of here." Richard said and walked away followed by the other boys.

"Oi!" Rocky shouted. "I am not finished with them!"

"Well I am finished with you." Arthur said, "For good!"

Arthur grabbed Amber's hand and the four friends walked away leaving Rocky bewildered and alone in the playground.

"Why are you crying?" Arthur turned to Amber.

"He broke my ipid!" Amber snivelled.

"Don't worry we can get it fixed within an hour. Flo is always breaking his screens and fixing them!" Serendipity said smiling.

Amber smiled at her friends. "I am going to miss you all so much!"

After many hugs and more tears from the girls, Amber eventually went home. Her flight was leaving that night, so she rushed home to finish packing. Serendipity promised to bring the iPad repaired to her house before Amber departed for the airport. Amber left her friends and walked down the tree-lined streets of Notting Hill; she tried to record everything she saw in her mind so that she would never forget, never forget how happy she was in London. Slowly the playground emptied out and only a few stragglers remained in the school grounds.

"Oh, why do we all look so glum? Should you not be happy to leave school for two months? That is the normal reaction you know!" Professor Inchenstein hollered down at the three friends.

"Amber's gone" Raj replied.

The smile fell sharply from the Professor's face. "Ah I see, well at least you all had a chance to say goodbye this time."

A big tear fell down Serendipity's rosy cheek, "Oh my little possum, you will see her again." Doctor Dino took a yellow silk hanky from his pocket and wiped her tears away.

"Come on Raj lad, say goodbye we don't want to keep Mavis waiting! She has cooked her special spicy meatballs for dinner!"

Raj grabbed his bag and said goodbye to his friends, "Call me when you are back from your holidays!" he shouted over his shoulder as the Professor led him away.

"Talking about holidays..." the Professor smiled mischievously at Raj through his bushy eyebrows. "Mavis and I thought we would all go on a little camping trip to Scotland."

"But I have never been to Scotland!" Raj said excitedly. As a matter of fact, Raj had never been anywhere, let alone visit another country and Scotland was kind of another country.

"I know dear boy. That is the point!"

The Professor patted Raj fondly on the head as they walked home together.

"Spicy meatballs here we come!"

THE END

THANK YOU

Writing a book in your spare time is not easy to do at all, especially when you have two kids, a full time job and a husband! I would like to thank my family for their continuous support, especially my sister Verity who always humoured me when I wanted to talk about the dinosaurs and my book's plot.

I would really appreciate it if you could write a review for my book on Amazon to help spread awareness.

Printed in Great Britain
by Amazon